The Hunters' Feast
Conversations Around
The Camp Fire

by

Captain Mayne Reid

Double 9
BOOKS

The Hunters' Feast
Conversations Around The Camp Fire
by Captain Mayne Reid

ISBN: 978-93-61158-66-7

Published by

DOUBLE 9 BOOKS
2/13-B, Ansari Road
Daryaganj, New Delhi – 110002
info@double9books.com
www.double9books.com
Tel. 011-40042856

ABOUT THE AUTHOR

Thomas Mayne Reid, an Irish-American novelist, participated in the Mexican–American War. His numerous books on American life discuss colonial policy in the American colonies, the horrors of slave labor, and the lifestyles of American Indians. "Captain" Reid created adventure stories similar to those of Frederick Marryat and Robert Louis Stevenson. They were primarily situated in the American West, Mexico, South Africa, the Himalayas, and Jamaica. He admired Lord Byron. Dion Boucicault turned his anti-slavery novel Quadroon (1856) into a drama called The Octoroon (1859), which was staged in New York. Reid was born in Ballyroney, a hamlet near Katesbridge in County Down, Northern Ireland, as the son of Rev. Thomas Mayne Reid Sr., a senior clerk of the General Assembly of the Presbyterian Church in Ireland, and his wife. Reid's father intended him to become a Presbyterian pastor, so he enrolled at the Royal Belfast Academical Institution in September 1834. He stayed for four years, but lacked the ambition to finish his studies and graduate. He returned to Ballyroney to teach at a school.

CONTENTS

Chapter One
A Hunting Party

On the western bank of the Mississippi, twelve miles below the *embouchure* of the Missouri, stands the large town of Saint Louis, poetically known as the "Mound City." Although there are many other large towns throughout the Mississippi Valley, Saint Louis is the true metropolis of the "far west"—of that semi-civilised, ever-changing belt of territory known as the "Frontier."

Saint Louis is one of those American cities in the history of which there is something of peculiar interest. It is one of the oldest of North-American settlements, having been a French trading port at an early period.

Though not so successful as their rivals the English, there was a degree of picturesqueness about French colonisation, that, in the present day, strongly claims the attention of the American poet, novelist, and historian. Their dealings with the Indian aborigines—the facile manner in which they glided into the habits of the latter—meeting them more than half-way between civilisation and savage life—the handsome nomenclature which they have scattered freely, and which still holds over the trans-Mississippian territories—the introduction of a new race (the half blood—peculiarly French)—the heroic and adventurous character of their earliest pioneers, De Salle Marquette, Father Hennepin, etcetera—their romantic explorations and melancholy fate—all these circumstances have rendered extremely interesting the early history of the French in America. Even the Quixotism of some of their attempts at colonisation cannot fail to interest us, as at Gallipolis on the Ohio, a colony composed of expatriated people of the French court;—perruquiers, coachbuilders, tailors, *modistes*, and the like. Here, in the face of hostile Indians, before an acre of ground was cleared, before the slightest provision was made for their future subsistence, the first house erected was a large log structure, to serve as the *salon du Lal*!

Besides its French origin, Saint Louis possesses many other points of interest. It has long been the *entrepôt* and *depôt* of commerce with the wild tribes of prairie-land. There the trader is supplied with his stock for the Indian market—his red and green blanket—his beads and trinkets—his rifles, and powder, and lead; and there, in return, he disposes of the spoils of the prairie collected in many a far and perilous wandering. There the emigrant rests on the way to his wilderness home; and the hunter equips himself before starting forth on some new expedition.

To the traveller, Saint Louis is a place of peculiar interest. He will hear around him the language of every nation in the civilised world. He will behold faces of every hue and variety of expression. He will meet with men of every possible calling.

All this is peculiarly true in the latter part of the summer season. Then the motley population of New Orleans fly from the annual scourge of the yellow fever, and seek safety in the cities that lie farther north. Of these, Saint Louis is a favourite "city of refuge,"—the Creole element of its population being related to that kindred race in the South, and keeping up with it this annual correspondence.

In one of these streams of migration I had found my way to Saint Louis, in the autumn of 18—. The place was at the time filled with loungers, who seemed to have nothing else to do but kill time. Every hotel had its quota, and in every verandah and at the corners of the streets you might see small knots of well-dressed gentlemen trying to entertain each other, and laugh away the hours. Most of them were the annual birds of passage from New Orleans, who had fled from "yellow Jack," and were sojourning here till the cold frosty winds of November should drive that intruder from the "crescent city;" but there were many other *flaneurs* as well. There were travellers from Europe:—men of wealth and rank who had left behind them the luxuries of civilised society to rough it for a season in the wild West—painters in search of the picturesque—naturalists whose love of their favourite study had drawn them from their comfortable closets to search for knowledge under circumstances of extremest difficulty—and sportsmen, who, tired of chasing small game, were on their way to the great plains to take part in the noble sport of hunting the buffalo. I was myself one of the last-named fraternity.

There is no country in the world so addicted to the *table d'hôte* as America, and that very custom soon makes idle people acquainted with each other. I was not very long in the place before I was upon terms of intimacy with a large number of these loungers, and I found several, like myself, desirous of making a hunting expedition to the prairies. This chimed in with my plans to a nicety, and I at once set about getting up the expedition. I found five others who were willing to join me.

After several *conversaziones*, with much discussion, we succeeded at length in "fixing" our plan. Each was to "equip" according to his own fancy, though it was necessary for each to provide himself with a riding horse or mule. After that, a general fund was to be "raised," to be appropriated to the purchase of a waggon and team, with tents, stores, and cooking utensils. A couple of professional hunters were to be engaged; men who knew the ground to be traversed, and who were to act as guides to the expedition.

About a week was consumed in making the necessary preparations, and at the end of that time, under the sunrise of a lovely morning, a small cavalcade was seen to issue from the back suburbs of Saint Louis, and, climbing the undulating slopes in its rear, head for the far-stretching wilderness of the prairies. It was our hunting expedition.

The cavalcade consisted of eight mounted men, and a waggon with its full team of six tough mules. These last were under the *manège* of "Jake"—a free negro, with a shining black face, a thick full mop, and a set of the best "ivories," which were almost always uncovered in a smile.

Peeping from under the tilt of the waggon might be seen another face strongly contrasting with that of Jake. This had been originally of a reddish hue, but sun-tan, and a thick sprinkling of freckles, had changed the red to golden-yellow. A shock of fiery hair surmounted this visage, which was partially concealed under a badly-battered hat. Though the face of the black expressed good-humour, it might have been called sad when brought into comparison with that of the little red man, which peeped out beside it. Upon the latter, there was an expression irresistibly comic—the expression of an actor in broad farce. One eye was continually on the wink, while the other looked knowing enough for both. A short clay-pipe, stuck jauntily between the lips, added to the comical expression of the face, which was that of Mike Lanty from Limerick. No one ever mistook the nationality of Michael.

Who were the eight cavaliers that accompanied the waggon? Six of them were gentlemen by birth and education. At least half that number were scholars. The other two laid no claim either to gentleness or scholarship— they were rude trappers—the hunters and guides of the expedition.

A word about each one of the eight, for there was not one of them without his peculiarity. First, there was an Englishman—a genuine type of his countrymen—full six feet high, well proportioned, with broad chest and shoulders, and massive limbs. Hair of a light brown, complexion florid, moustache and whiskers full and hay-coloured, but suiting well the complexion and features. The last were regular, and if not handsome, at least good humoured and noble in their expression. The owner was in reality a nobleman—a true nobleman—one of that class who, while travelling through the "States," have the good sense to carry their umbrella along, and leave their title behind them. To us he was known as Mr Thompson, and, after some time, when we had all become familiar with each other, as plain "Thompson." It was only long after, and by accident, that I became acquainted with his rank and title; some of our companions do not know it to this day, but that is of no consequence. I mention the circumstance here to aid me in illustrating the character of our travelling companion, who was "close" and modest almost to a fault.

His costume was characteristic. A "tweed" shooting jacket, of course, with eight pockets—a vest of the same material with four—tweed browsers, and a tweed cap. In the waggon was *the hat-box*; of strong yellow leather, with straps and padlock. This was supposed to contain the dress hat; and some of the party were merry about it. But no—Mr Thompson was a more experienced traveller than his companions thought him at first. The contents of the hat-case were sundry brushes—including one for the teeth—combs, razors, and pieces of soap. The hat had been left at Saint Louis.

But the umbrella had *not*. It was then under Thompson's arm, with its full proportions of whalebone and gingham. Under that umbrella he had hunted tigers in the jungles of India—under that umbrella he had chased the lion upon the plains of Africa—under that umbrella he had pursued the ostrich and the vicuña over the pampas of South America; and now under that same hemisphere of blue gingham he was about to carry terror and destruction among the wild buffaloes of the prairies.

Besides the umbrella—strictly a weapon of defence—Mr Thompson carried another, a heavy double-barrelled gun, marked "Bishop, of Bond Street," no bad weapon with a loading of buck-shot, and with this both barrels were habitually loaded.

So much for Mr Thompson, who may pass for Number 1 of the hunting party. He was mounted on a strong bay cob, with tail cut short, and English saddle, both of which objects—the short tail and the saddle—were curiosities to all of the party except Mr Thompson and myself.

Number 2 was as unlike Number 1 as two animals of the same species could possibly be. He was a Kentuckian, full six inches taller than Thompson, or indeed than any of the party. His features were marked, prominent and irregular, and this irregularity was increased by a "cheekful" of half-chewed tobacco. His complexion was dark, almost olive, and the face quite naked, without either moustache or whisker; but long straight hair, black as an Indian's, hung down to his shoulders. In fact, there was a good deal of the Indian look about him, except in his figure. That was somewhat slouched, with arms and limbs of over-length, loosely hung about it. Both, however, though not modelled after the Apollo, were evidently full of muscle and tough strength, and looked as though their owner could return the hug of a bear with interest. There was a gravity in his look, but that was not from any gravity of spirits; it was his swarth complexion that gave him this appearance, aided, no doubt, by several lines of "ambeer" proceeding from the corners of his mouth in the direction of the chin. So far from being grave, this dark Kentuckian was as gay and buoyant as any of the party. Indeed, a light and boyish spirit is a characteristic of the Kentuckian as well as of all the natives of the Mississippi Valley — at least such has been my observation.

Our Kentuckian was costumed just as he would have been upon a cool morning riding about the "woodland" of his own plantation, for a "planter" he was. He wore a "Jeans" frock, and over that a long-tailed overcoat of the best green blanket, with side pockets and flaps. His jeans pantaloons were stuck into a pair of heavy horse-leather pegged boots, sometimes known as "nigger" boots; but over these were "wrappers" of green baize, fastened with a string above the knees. His hat was a "broad-brimmed felt," costly enough, but somewhat crushed by being sat upon and slept in. He bestrode a tall raw-boned stood that possessed many of the characteristics of the rider; and in the same proportion that the latter overtopped his companions, so did the steed out-size all the other horses of the cavalcade. Over the shoulders of the Kentuckian were suspended, by several straps, pouch, horn, and haversack, and resting upon his toe was the butt of a heavy rifle, the muzzle of which reached to a level with his shoulder.

He was a rich Kentucky planter, and known in his native state as a great deer-hunter. Some business or pleasure had brought him to Saint Louis. It was hinted that Kentucky was becoming too thickly settled for him — deer becoming scarce, and bear hardly to be found — and that his visit to Saint Louis had something to do with seeking a new "location" where these animals were still to be met with in greater plenty. The idea of buffalo-hunting was just to his liking. The expedition would carry him through the frontier country, where he might afterwards choose his "location" — at all events the sport would repay him, and he was one of the most enthusiastic in regard to it.

He that looms up on the retrospect of my memory as Number 3 was as unlike the Kentuckian, as the latter was to Thompson. He was a disciple of Esculapius — not thin and pale, as these usually are, but fat, red, and jolly. I think he was originally a "Yankee," though his long residence in the Western States had rubbed the Yankee out of him to a great extent. At all events he had few of their characteristics about him. He was neither staid, sober, nor, what is usually alleged as a trait of the true bred Yankee, "stingy." On the contrary, our doctor was full of talk and joviality — generous to a fault. A fault, indeed; for, although many years in practice in various parts of the United States, and having earned large sums of money, at the date of our expedition we found him in Saint Louis almost without a dollar, and with no great stock of patients. The truth must be told; the doctor was of a restless disposition, and liked his glass too well. He was a singer too, a fine amateur singer, with a voice equal to Mario's. That may partly account for his failure in securing a fortune. He was a favourite with all—ladies included—and so fond of good company, that he preferred the edge of the jovial board to the bed-side of a patient.

Not from any fondness for buffalo-hunting, but rather through an attachment to some of the company, had the doctor volunteered. Indeed, he was solicited by all to make one of us—partly on account of his excellent society, and partly that his professional services might be called into requisition before our return.

The doctor still preserved his professional costume of black—somewhat russet by long wear—but this was modified by a close-fitting fur cap, and wrappers of brown cloth, which he wore around his short thick legs. He was not over-well mounted—a very spare little horse was all he had, as his funds would not stretch to a better. It was quite a quiet one, however, and carried the doctor and his "medical saddle-bags" steadily enough, though not without a good deal of spurring and whipping. The doctor's name was "Jopper"—Dr John Jopper.

A very elegant youth, with fine features, rolling black eyes, and luxuriant curled hair, was one of us. The hands were well formed and delicate; the complexion silky, and of nearly an olive tint; but the purplish-red broke through upon his cheeks, giving the earnest of health, as well as adding to the picturesque beauty of his face. The form was perfect, and full of manly expression, and the pretty sky-blue plaited pantaloons and close-fitting jacket of the same material, sat gracefully on his well-turned limbs and arms. These garments were of "cottonade," that beautiful and durable fabric peculiar to Louisiana, and so well suited to the southern climate. A costly Panama hat cast its shadow over the wavy curls and pictured cheek of this youth, and a cloak of fine broad cloth, with velvet facings, hung loosely from his shoulders. A slight moustache and imperial lent a manlier expression to his chiselled features.

This young fellow was a Creole of Louisiana—a student of one of the Jesuit Colleges of that State—and although very unlike what would be expected from such a dashing personage, he was an ardent, even passionate, lover of nature. Though still young, he was the most accomplished botanist in his State, and had already published several discoveries in the *Flora* of the South.

Of course the expedition was to him a delightful anticipation. It would afford the finest opportunity for prosecuting his favourite study in a new field; one as yet almost unvisited by the scientific traveller. The young Creole was known as Jules Besançon.

He was not the only naturalist of the party. Another was with us; one who had already acquired a world-wide fame; whose name was as familiar to the *savans* of Europe as to his own countrymen. He was already an old man, almost venerable in his aspect, but his tread was firm, and his arm still strong enough to steady his long, heavy, double-barrelled rifle. An ample coat of dark blue covered his body; his limbs were enveloped in long buttoned leggings of drab cloth, and a cap of sable surmounted his high, broad forehead. Under this his blueish grey eye glanced with a calm but clear intelligence, and a single look from it satisfied you that you were in the presence of a superior mind. Were I to give the name of this person, this would readily be acknowledged. For certain reasons I cannot do this. Suffice it to say, he was one of the most distinguished of modern zoologists, and to his love for the study we were indebted for his companionship upon our hunting expedition. He was known to us as Mr A— the "hunter-naturalist." There was no jealousy between him and the young Besançon. On the contrary, a similarity of tastes soon brought about a mutual friendship, and the Creole was observed to treat the other with marked deference and regard.

I may set myself down as Number 6 of the party. Let a short description of me suffice. I was then but a young fellow, educated somewhat better than common; fond of wild sports; not indifferent to a knowledge of nature; fond almost to folly of a good horse, and possessing one of the very best; not ill-looking in the face, and of middle stature; costumed in a light hunting-shirt of embroidered buckskin, with fringed cape and skirt; leggings of scarlet cloth, and cloth forage-cap, covering a flock of dark hair. Powder-flask and pouch of tasty patterns; belt around the waist, with hunting-knife and pistols—revolvers. A light rifle in one hand, and in the other a bridle-rein, which guided a steed of coal blackness; one that would have been celebrated in song by a troubadour of the olden time. A deep Spanish saddle of stamped leather; holsters with bearskin covers in front; a scarlet blanket, folded and strapped on the croup; lazo and haversack hanging from the "horn"—*voilà tout!*

There are two characters still undescribed. Characters of no mean importance were they—the "guides." They were called respectively, Isaac Bradley and Mark Redwood. A brace of trappers they were, but as different from each other in personal appearance as two men could well be. Redwood was a man of large dimensions, and apparently as strong as a buffalo, while his *confrère* was a thin, wiry, sinewy mortal, with a tough, weasel-like look and gait. The expression of Redwood's countenance was open and manly, his eyes were grey, his hair light-coloured, and huge brown whiskers covered his cheeks. Bradley, on the other hand, was dark—his eyes small, black, and piercing—his face as hairless as an Indian's, and bronzed almost to the Indian hue, with the black hair of his head closely cropped around it.

Both these men were dressed in leather from head to foot, yet they were very differently dressed. Redwood wore the usual buckskin hunting-shirt, leggings, and moccasins, but all of full proportions and well cut, while his large 'coon-skin cap, with the plume-like tail, had an imposing appearance. Bradley's garments, on the contrary, were tight-fitting and "skimped." His hunting-shirt was without cape, and adhered so closely to his body that it appeared only an outer skin of the man himself. His leggings were pinched and tight. Shirt, leggings, and moccasins were evidently of the oldest kind, and as dirty as a cobbler's apron. A close-fitting otter cap, with a Mackinaw blanket, completed the wardrobe of Isaac Bradley. He was equipped with a pouch of greasy leather hanging by an old black strap, a small buffalo-horn suspended by a thong, and a belt of buffalo-leather, in which was stuck a strong blade, with its handle of buckhorn. His rifle was of the "tallest" kind—being full six feet in height—in fact, taller than he was, and at least four fifths of the weapon consisted of barrel. The straight narrow stock was a piece of manufacture that had proceeded from the hands of the trapper himself.

Redwood's rifle was also a long one, but of more modern build and fashion, and his equipments—pouch, powder-horn and belt—were of a more tasty design and finish.

Such were our guides, Redwood and Bradley. They were no imaginary characters these. Mark Redwood was a celebrated "mountain-man" at that time, and Isaac Bradley will be recognised by many when I give him the name and title by which he was then known,—viz. "Old Ike, the wolf-killer."

Redwood rode a strong horse of the half-hunter breed, while the "wolf-killer" was mounted upon one of the scraggiest looking quadrupeds it would be possible to imagine—an old mare "mustang."

Chapter Two
The Camp and Camp-Fire

Our route was west by south. The nearest point with which we expected to fall in with the buffalo was two hundred miles distant. We might travel three hundred without seeing one, and even much farther at the present day; but a report had reached Saint Louis that the buffalo had been seen that year upon the Osage River, west of the Ozark Hills, and towards that point we steered our course. We expected in about twenty days to fall in with the game. Fancy a cavalcade of hunters making a journey of twenty days to get upon the field! The reader will, no doubt, say we were in earnest.

At the time of which I am writing, a single day's journey from Saint Louis carried the traveller clear of civilised life. There were settlements beyond; but these were sparse and isolated—a few small towns or plantations upon the main watercourses—and the whole country between them was an uninhabited wilderness. We had no hope of being sheltered by a roof until our return to the mound city itself, but we had provided ourselves with a couple of tents, part of the freight of our waggon.

There are but few parts of the American wilderness where the traveller can depend upon wild game for a subsistence. Even the skilled hunter when stationary is sometimes put to his wits' end for "daily bread." Upon the "route" no great opportunity is found of killing game, which always requires time to approach it with caution. Although we passed through what appeared to be excellent cover for various species of wild animals, we reached our first camp without having ruffled either hair or feathers. In fact, neither bird nor quadruped had been seen, although almost every one of the party had been on the look out for game during most of the journey.

This was rather discouraging, and we reasoned that if such was to be our luck until we got into the buffalo-range we should have a very dull time of it. We were well provisioned, however, and we regretted the absence of game only on account of the sport. A large bag of biscuit, and one of flour, several pieces of "hung bacon," some dry ox-tongues, a stock of green coffee, sugar, and salt, were the principal and necessary stores. There were "luxuries," too, which each had provided according to his fancy, though not much of these, as every one of the party had had some time or other in his life a little experience in the way of "roughing it." Most of the loading of the waggon consisted of provender for our horses and mules.

We made full thirty miles on the first day. Our road was a good one. We passed over easy undulations, most of them covered with "black-jack." This is a species of dwarf oak, so called from the very dark colour of its wrinkled bark. It is almost worthless as a timber, being too small for most purposes. It is ornamental, however, forming copse-like groves upon the swells of the prairie, while its dark green foliage contrasts pleasantly with the lighter green of the grasses beneath its shade. The young botanist, Besançon, had least cause to complain. His time had been sufficiently pleasant during the day. New foliage fell under his observation—new flowers opened their corollas to his delighted gaze. He was aided in making his collections by the hunter-naturalist, who of course was tolerably well versed in this kindred science.

We encamped by the edge of a small creek of clear water. Our camp was laid out in due form, and everything arranged in the order we designed habitually to follow.

Every man unsaddled his own horse. There are no servants in prairie-land. Even Lanty's services extended not beyond the *cuisine*, and for this department he had had his training as the cook of a New Orleans trading ship. Jake had enough to do with his mules; and to have asked one of our hunter-guides to perform the task of unsaddling your horse, would have been a hazardous experiment. Menial service to a free trapper! There are no servants in prairie-land.

Our horses and mules were picketed on a piece of open ground, each having his "trail-rope," which allowed a circuit of several yards. The two tents were pitched side by side, facing the stream, and the waggon drawn up some twenty feet in the rear. In the triangle between the waggon and the tents was kindled a large fire, upon each side of which two stakes, forked at the top, were driven into the ground. A long sapling resting in the forks traversed the blaze from side to side. This was Lanty's "crane,"—the fire was his kitchen.

Let me sketch the camp more minutely, for our first camp was a type of all the others in its general features. Sometimes indeed the tents did not front the same way, when these openings were set to "oblige the wind," but they were always placed side by side in front of the waggon. They were small tents of the old-fashioned conical kind, requiring only one pole each. They were of sufficient size for our purpose, as there were only three of us to each—the guides, with Jake and Lanty, finding their lodgment under the tilt of the waggon. With their graceful shape, and snowy-white colour against the dark green foliage of the trees, they formed an agreeable contrast; and a *coup d'oeil* of the camp would have been no mean picture to the eye of an artist. The human figures may be arranged in the following manner.

Supper is getting ready, and Lanty is decidedly at this time the most important personage on the ground. He is stooping over the fire, with a small but long-handled frying-pan, in which he is parching the coffee. It is already browned, and Lanty stirs it about with an iron spoon. The crane carries the large coffee-kettle of sheet iron, full of water upon the boil; and a second frying-pan, larger than the first, is filled with sliced ham, ready to be placed upon the hot cinders.

Our English friend Thompson is seated upon a log, with the hat-box before him. It is open, and he has drawn out from it his stock of combs and brushes. He has already made his ablutions, and is now giving the finish to his toilet, by putting his hair, whiskers, moustache, teeth, and even his nails, in order. Your Englishman is the most comfortable traveller in the world.

The Kentuckian is differently engaged. He is upon his feet; in one hand gleams a knife with ivory handle and long shining blade. It is a "bowie," of that kind known as an "Arkansas toothpick." In the other hand you see an object about eight inches in length, of the form of a parallelogram, and of a dark brown colour. It is a "plug" of real "James's River tobacco." With his knife the Kentuckian cuts off a piece—a "chunk," as he terms it—which is immediately transferred to his mouth, and chewed to a pulp. This is his occupation for the moment.

The doctor, what of him? Doctor Jopper may be seen close to the water's edge. In his hand is a pewter flask, of the kind known as a "pocket pistol." That pistol is loaded with brandy, and Dr Jopper is just in the act of drawing part of the charge, which, with a slight admixture of cool creek water, is carried aloft and poured into a very droughty vessel. The effect, however, is instantly apparent in the lively twinkle of the doctor's round and prominent eyes.

Besançon is seated near the tent, and the old naturalist beside him. The former is busy with the new plants he has collected. A large portfolio-looking book rests upon his knees, and between its leaves he is depositing his stores in a scientific manner. His companion, who understands the business well, is kindly assisting him. Their conversation is interesting, but every one else is too busy with his affairs to listen to it just now.

The guides are lounging about the waggon. Old Ike fixes a new flint in his rifle, and Redwood, of a more mirthful disposition, is occasionally cracking a joke with Mike or the "darkey."

Jake is still busy with his mules, and I with my favourite steed, whose feet I have washed in the stream, and anointed with a little spare grease. I shall not always have the opportunity of being so kind to him, but he will need it the less, as his hoofs become more hardened by the journey.

Around the camp are strewed our saddles, bridles, blankets, weapons, and utensils. These will all be collected and stowed under cover before we go to rest. Such is a picture of our camp before supper.

When that meal is cooked, the scene somewhat changes.

The atmosphere, even at that season, was cool enough, and this, with Mike's announcement that the coffee was ready, brought all the party—guides as well—around the blazing pile of logs. Each found his own platter, knife, and cup; and, helping himself from the general stock, set to eating on his own account. Of course there were no fragments, as a strict regard to economy was one of the laws of our camp.

Notwithstanding the fatigue, always incidental to a first day's march, we enjoyed this *al fresco* supper exceedingly. The novelty had much to do with our enjoyment of it, and also the fine appetites which we had acquired since our luncheon at noon halt.

When supper was over, smoking followed, for there was not one of the party who was not an inveterate burner of the "noxious weed." Some chose cigars, of which we had brought a good stock, but several were pipe-smokers. The zoologist carried a meerschaum; the guides smoked out of Indian calumets of the celebrated steatite, or red claystone. Mike had his dark-looking "dudeen," and Jake his pipe of corn "cob" and cane-joint shank.

Our English friend Thompson had a store of the finest Havannahs, which he smoked with the grace peculiar to the English cigar smoker; holding his cigar impaled upon the point of his knife-blade. Kentucky also smoked cigars, but his was half buried within his mouth, slanted obliquely towards the right cheek. Besançon preferred the paper cigarette, which he made extempore, as he required them, out of a stock of loose tobacco. This is Creole fashion—now also the *mode de Paris*.

A song from the doctor enlivened the conversation, and certainly so melodious a human voice had never echoed near the spot. One and all agreed that the grand opera had missed a capital "first tenor" in not securing the services of our companion.

The fatigue of our long ride caused us to creep into our tents at an early hour, and rolling ourselves in our blankets we went to sleep. Of course everything had been carefully gathered in lest rain might fall in the night. The trail-ropes of our animals were looked to: we did not fear their being stolen, but horses on their first few days' journey are easily "stampeded," and will sometimes stray home again. This would have been a great misfortune, but most of us were old travellers, and every caution was observed in securing against such a result. There was no guard kept, though we knew the time would come when that would be a necessary duty.

Chapter Three
Besançon's adventure in the swamps

The prairie traveller never sleeps after daybreak. He is usually astir before that time. He has many "*chores*" to perform, unknown to the ordinary traveller who rests in the roadside inn. He has to pack up his tent and bed, cook his own breakfast, and saddle his horse. All this requires time, therefore an early start is necessary.

We were on our feet before the sun had shown his disc above the black-jacks. Lanty had the start of us, and had freshened up his fire. Already the coffee-kettle was bubbling audibly, and the great frying-pan perfumed the camp with an incense more agreeable than the odours of Araby.

The raw air of the morning had brought everybody around the fire. Thompson was pruning and cleansing his nails; the Kentuckian was cutting a fresh "chunk" from his plug of "James's River;" the doctor had just returned from the stream, where he had refreshed himself by a "nip" from his pewter flask; Besançon was packing up his portfolios; the zoologist was lighting his long pipe, and the "Captain" was looking to his favourite horse, while inhaling the fragrance of an "Havannah." The guides stood with their blankets hanging from their shoulders silent and thoughtful.

In half an hour breakfast was over, the tents and utensils were restored to the waggon, the horses were brought in and saddled, the mules "hitched up," and the expedition once more on its way.

This day we made not quite so good a journey. The roads were heavier, the country more thickly timbered, and the ground more hilly. We had several small streams to ford, and this retarded our progress. Twenty miles was the extent of our journey.

We encamped again without any of us having killed or seen game. Although we had beaten the bushes on both sides of our course, nothing bigger than the red-bird (scarlet tanager, *Pyranga rubra*), a screaming jay, or an occasional flight of finches, gratified our sight.

We reached our camp somewhat disappointed. Even old Ike and Redwood came into camp without game, alleging also that they had not met with the sign of a living quadruped.

Our second camp was also on the bank of a small stream. Shortly after our arrival on the ground, Thompson started out afoot, taking with him his gun. He had noticed a tract of marsh at no great distance off. He thought it promised well for snipe.

He had not been long gone, when two reports echoed back, and then shortly after another and another. He had found something to empty his gun at.

Presently we saw him returning with a brace and a half of birds that looked very much like large snipe. So he thought them, but that question was set at rest by the zoologist, who pronounced them at once to be the American "Curlew" of Wilson (*Numenius longirostris*). Curlew or snipe, they were soon divested of the feathery coat, and placed in Lanty's frying-pan. Excellent eating they proved, having only the fault that there was not enough of them.

These birds formed the topic of our after-supper conversation, and then it generalised to the different species of wading birds of America, and at length that singular creature, the "ibis," became the theme. This came round by Besançon remarking that a species of ibis was brought by the Indians to the markets of New Orleans, and sold there under the name of "Spanish Curlew." This was the white ibis (*Tantalus albas*), which the zoologist stated was found in plenty along the whole southern coast of the United States. There were two other species, he said, natives of the warm parts of North America, the "wood-ibis" (*Tantalus loculator*), which more nearly resembles the sacred ibis of Egypt, and the beautiful "sacred ibis" (*Tantalus ruber*), which last is rarer than the others.

Our venerable companion, who had the ornithology of America, if I may use the expression, at his fingers' ends, imparted many curious details of the habits of these rare birds. All listened with interest to his statements—even the hunter-guides, for with all their apparent rudeness of demeanour, there was a dash of the naturalist in these fellows.

When the zoologist became silent, the young Creole took up the conversation. Talking of the ibis, he said, reminded him of an adventure he had met with while in pursuit of these birds among the swamps of his native state. He would relate it to us. Of course we were rejoiced at the proposal. We were just the audience for an "adventure," and after rolling a fresh cigarette, the botanist began his narration.

"During one of my college vacations I made a botanical excursion to the south-western part of Louisiana. Before leaving home I had promised a dear friend to bring him the skins of such rare birds as were known to frequent the swampy region I was about to traverse, but he was especially desirous

I should obtain for him some specimens of the red ibis, which he intended to have 'mounted.' I gave my word that no opportunity should be lost of obtaining these birds, and I was very anxious to make good my promise.

"The southern part of the State of Louisiana is one vast labyrinth of swamps, bayous, and lagoons. The bayous are sluggish streams that glide sleepily along, sometimes running one way, and sometimes the very opposite, according to the season of the year. Many of them are outlets of the Mississippi, which begins to shed off its waters more than 300 miles from its mouth. These bayous are deep, sometimes narrow, sometimes wide, with islets in their midst. They and their contiguous swamps are the great habitat of the alligator and the fresh-water shark—the gar. Numerous species of water and wading fowl fly over them, and plunge through their dark tide. Here you may see the red flamingo, the egret, the trumpeter-swan, the blue heron, the wild goose, the crane, the snake-bird, the pelican, and the ibis; you may likewise see the osprey, and the white-headed eagle robbing him of his prey. Both swamps and bayous produce abundantly fish, reptile, and insect, and are, consequently, the favourite resort of hundreds of birds which prey upon these creatures. In some places, their waters form a complete net-work over the country, which you may traverse with a small boat in almost any direction; indeed, this is the means by which many settlements communicate with each other. As you approach southward towards the Gulf, you get clear of the timber; and within some fifty miles of the sea, there is not a tree to be seen.

"In the first day or two that I was out, I had succeeded in getting all the specimens I wanted, with the exception of the ibis. This shy creature avoided me; in fact I had only seen one or two in my excursions, and these at a great distance. I still, however, had hopes of finding them before my return to my friend.

"About the third or fourth day I set out from a small settlement on the edge of one of the larger bayous. I had no other company than my gun. I was even unattended by a dog, as my favourite spaniel had the day before been bitten by an alligator while swimming across the bayou, and I was compelled to leave him at the settlement. Of course the object of my excursion was a search after new flora, but I had become by this time very desirous of getting the rare ibis, and I was determined half to neglect my botanising for that purpose. I went of course in a boat, a light skiff, such as is commonly used by the inhabitants of these parts.

"Occasionally using the paddles, I allowed myself to float some four or live miles down the main bayou; but as the birds I was in search of did not appear, I struck into a 'branch,' and sculled myself up-stream. This carried me through a solitary region, with marshes stretching as far as the eye could see, covered with tall reeds. There was no habitation, nor aught that betokened the presence of man. It was just possible that I was the first human being who had ever found a motive for propelling a boat through the dark waters of this solitary stream.

"As I advanced, I fell in with game; and I succeeded in bagging several, both of the great wood-ibis and the white species. I also shot a fine white-headed eagle (*Falco leucocephalus*), which came soaring over my boat, unconscious of danger. But the bird which I most wanted seemed that which could not be obtained. I wanted the scarlet ibis.

"I think I had rowed some three miles up-stream, and was about to take in my oars and leave my boat to float back again, when I perceived that, a little farther up, the bayou widened. Curiosity prompted me to continue; and after pulling a few hundred strokes, I found myself at the end of an oblong lake, a mile or so in length. It was deep, dark, marshy around the shores, and full of alligators. I saw their ugly forms and long serrated backs, as they floated about in all parts of it, hungrily hunting for fish and eating one another; but all this was nothing new, for I had witnessed similar scenes during the whole of my excursion. What drew my attention most, was a small islet near the middle of the lake, upon one end of which stood a row of upright forms of a bright scarlet colour. These red creatures were the very objects I was in search of. They might be flamingoes: I could not tell at that distance. So much the better, if I could only succeed in getting a shot at them; but these creatures are even more wary than the ibis; and as the islet was low, and altogether without cover, it was not likely they would allow me to come within range: nevertheless, I was determined to make the attempt. I rowed up the lake, occasionally turning my head to see if the game had taken the alarm. The sun was hot and dazzling; and as the bright scarlet was magnified by refraction, I fancied for a long time they were flamingoes. This fancy was dissipated as I drew near. The outlines of the bills, like the blade of a sabre, convinced me they were the ibis; besides, I now saw that they were less than three feet in height, while the flamingoes stand five. There were a dozen of them in all. These were balancing themselves, as is their usual habit, on one leg, apparently asleep, or *buried in deep thought*. They were on the upper extremity of the islet, while I was approaching it from below. It was not above sixty yards across; and could I only reach the point nearest me, I knew my gun would throw shot to kill at that distance. I feared the stroke of the sculls would start them, and I pulled slowly and cautiously. Perhaps the great heat—for it was as hot a day as I can remember—had rendered them torpid or lazy. Whether or not, they sat still until the cut-water of my skiff touched the bank of the islet. I drew my gun up cautiously, took aim, and fired both barrels almost simultaneously. When the smoke cleared out of my eyes, I saw that all the birds had flown off except one, that lay stretched out by the edge of the water.

"Gun in hand, I leaped out of the boat, and ran across the islet to bag my game. This occupied but a few minutes; and I was turning to go back to the skiff, when, to my consternation, I saw it out upon the lake, and rapidly floating downward!

"In my haste I had left it unfastened, and the bayou current had carried it off. It was still but a hundred yards distant, but it might as well have been a hundred miles, for at that time I could not swim a stroke.

"My first impulse was to rush down to the lake, and after the boat. This impulse was checked on arriving at the water's edge, which I saw at a glance was fathoms in depth. Quick reflection told me that the boat was gone—irrecoverably gone!

"I did not at first comprehend the full peril of my situation; nor will you, gentlemen. I was on an islet, in a lake, only half a mile from its shores—alone, it is true, and without a boat; but what of that? Many a man had been so before, with not an idea of danger.

"These were first thoughts, natural enough; but they rapidly gave place to others of a far different character. When I gazed after my boat, now beyond recovery—when I looked around, and saw that the lake lay in the middle of an interminable swamp, the shores of which, even could I have reached them, did not seem to promise me footing—when I reflected that, being unable to swim, I could *not* reach them—that upon the islet there was neither tree, nor log, nor bush; not a stick out of which I might make a raft—I say, when I reflected upon all these things, there arose in my mind a feeling of well-defined and absolute horror.

"It is true I was only in a lake, a mile or so in width; but so far as the peril and helplessness of my situation were concerned, I might as well have been upon a rock in the middle of the Atlantic. I knew that there was no settlement within miles—miles of pathless swamp. I knew that no one could either see or hear me—no one was at all likely to come near the lake; indeed, I felt satisfied that my faithless boat was the first keel that had ever cut its waters. The very tameness of the birds wheeling round my head was evidence of this. I felt satisfied, too, that without some one to help me, I should never go out from that lake: I must die on the islet, or drown in attempting to leave it!

"These reflections rolled rapidly over my startled soul. The facts were clear, the hypothesis definite, the sequence certain; there was no ambiguity, no supposititious hinge upon which I could hang a hope; no, not one. I could not even expect that I should be missed and sought for; there was no one to search for me. The simple *habitans* of the village I had left knew me not—I was a stranger among them: they only knew me as a stranger, and fancied me a strange individual; one who made lonely excursions, and brought home hunches of weeds, with birds, insects, and reptiles, which they had never before seen, although gathered at their own doors. My absence, besides, would be nothing new to them, even though it lasted for days: I had often been absent before, a week at a time. There was no hope of my being missed.

"I have said that these reflections came and passed quickly. In less than a minute, my affrighted soul was in full possession of them, and almost yielded itself to despair. I shouted, but rather involuntarily than with any hope that I should be heard; I shouted loudly and fiercely: my answer—the echoes of my own voice, the shriek of the osprey, and the maniac laugh of the white-headed eagle.

"I ceased to shout, threw my gun to the earth, and tottered down beside it. I can imagine the feelings of a man shut up in a gloomy prison—they are not pleasant. I have been lost upon the wild prairie—the land sea— without bush, break, or star to guide me—that was worse. There you look around; you see nothing; you hear nothing: you are alone with God, and you tremble in his presence; your senses swim; your brain reels; you are afraid of yourself; you are afraid of your own mind. Deserted by everything else, you dread lest it, too, may forsake you. There is horror in this—it is very horrible—it is hard to bear; but I have borne it all, and would bear it again twenty times over rather than endure once more the first hour I spent on that lonely islet in that lonely lake. Your prison may be dark and silent, but you feel that you are not utterly alone; beings like yourself are near, though they be your jailers. Lost on the prairie, you are alone; but you are free. In the islet, I felt that I was alone; that I was not free: in the islet I experienced the feelings of the prairie and the prison combined.

"I lay in a state of stupor—almost unconscious; how long I know not, but many hours I am certain; I knew this by the sun—it was going down when I awoke, if I may so term the recovery of my stricken senses. I was aroused by a strange circumstance: I was surrounded by dark objects of hideous shape and hue—reptiles they were. They had been before my eyes for some time, but I had not seen them. I had only a sort of dreamy consciousness of their presence; but I heard them at length: my ear was in better tune, and the strange noises they uttered reached my intellect. It sounded like the blowing of great bellows, with now and then a note harsher and louder, like the roaring of a bull. This startled me, and I looked up and bent my eyes upon the objects: they were forms of the *crocodilidae*, the giant lizards—they were alligators.

"Huge ones they were, many of them; and many were they in number—a hundred at least were crawling over the islet, before, behind, and on all sides around me. Their long gaunt jaws and channelled snouts projected forward so as almost to touch my body; and their eyes, usually leaden, seemed now to glare.

"Impelled by this new danger, I sprang to my feet, when, recognising the upright form of man, the reptiles scuttled off, and plunging hurriedly into the lake; hid their hideous bodies under the water.

"The incident in some measure revived me. I saw that I was not alone; there was company even in the crocodiles. I gradually became more myself; and began to reflect with some degree of coolness on the circumstances that surrounded me. My eyes wandered over the islet; every inch of it came under my glance; every object upon it was scrutinised—the moulted feathers of wildfowl, the pieces of mud, the fresh-water mussels (*unios*) strewed upon its beach—all were examined. Still the barren answer—no means of escape.

"The islet was but the head of a sand-bar, formed by the eddy, perhaps gathered together within the year. It was bare of herbage, with the exception of a few tufts of grass. There was neither tree nor bush upon it: not a stick. A raft indeed! There was not wood enough to make a raft that would have floated a frog. The idea of a raft was but briefly entertained; such a thought had certainly crossed my mind, but a single glance round the islet dispelled it before it had taken shape.

"I paced my prison from end to end; from side to side I walked it over. I tried the water's depth; on all sides I sounded it, wading recklessly in; everywhere it deepened rapidly as I advanced. Three lengths of myself from the islet's edge, and I was up to the neck. The huge reptiles swam around, snorting and blowing; they were bolder in this element. I could not have waded safely ashore, even had the water been shallow. To swim it—no—even though I swam like a duck, they would have closed upon and quartered me before I could have made a dozen strokes. Horrified by their demonstrations, I hurried back upon dry ground, and paced the islet with dripping garments.

"I continued walking until night, which gathered around me dark and dismal. With night came new voices—the hideous voices of the nocturnal swamp; the qua-qua of the night-heron, the screech of the swamp-owl, the cry of the bittern, the cl-l-uk of the great water-toad, the tinkling of the bell-frog, and the chirp of the savanna-cricket—all fell upon my ear. Sounds still harsher and more, hideous were heard around me—the plashing of the alligator, and the roaring of his voice; these reminded me that I must not go to sleep. To sleep! I durst not have slept for a single instant. Even when I lay for a few minutes motionless, the dark reptiles came crawling round me—so close that I could have put forth my hand and touched them.

"At intervals, I sprang to my feet, shouted, swept my gun around, and chased them back to the water, into which they betook themselves with a sullen plunge, but with little semblance of fear. At each fresh demonstration on my part they showed less alarm, until I could no longer drive them either with shouts or threatening gestures. They only retreated a few feet, forming an irregular circle round me.

"Thus hemmed in, I became frightened in turn. I loaded my gun and fired; I killed none. They are impervious to a bullet, except in the eye, or under the forearm. It was too dark to aim at these parts; and my shots glanced harmlessly from the pyramidal scales of their bodies. The loud report, however, and the blaze frightened them, and they fled, to return again after a long interval. I was asleep when they returned; I had gone to sleep in spite of my efforts to keep awake. I was startled by the touch of something cold; and half-stilled by the strong musky odour that filled the air. I threw out my arms; my fingers rested upon an object slippery and clammy: it was one of these monsters—one of gigantic size. He had crawled close alongside me, and was preparing to make his attack; as I saw that he was bent in the form of a bow, and I knew that these creatures assume that attitude when about to strike their victim. I was just in time to spring aside, and avoid the stroke of his powerful tail, that the next moment swept the ground where I had lain. Again I fired, and he with the rest once more retreated to the lake.

"All thoughts of going to sleep were at an end. Not that I felt wakeful; on the contrary, wearied with my day's exertion—for I had had a long pull under a hot tropical sun—I could have lain down upon the earth, in the mud, anywhere, and slept in an instant. Nothing but the dread certainty of my peril kept me awake. Once again before morning, I was compelled to battle with the hideous reptiles, and chase them away with a shot from my gun.

"Morning came at length, but with it no change in my perilous position. The light only showed me my island prison, but revealed no way of escape from it. Indeed, the change could not be called for the better, for the fervid rays of an almost vertical sun poured down upon me until my skin blistered. I was already speckled by the bites of a thousand swamp-flies and mosquitoes, that all night long had preyed upon me. There was not a cloud in the heavens to shade me; and the sunbeams smote the surface of the dead bayou with a double intensity.

"Towards evening, I began to hunger; no wonder at that: I had not eaten since leaving the village settlement. To assuage thirst, I drank the water of the lake, turbid and slimy as it was. I drank it in large quantities, for it was hot, and only moistened my palate without quenching the craving of my appetite. Of water there was enough; I had more to fear from want of food.

"What could I eat? The ibis. But how to cook it? There was nothing wherewith to make a fire—not a stick. No matter for that. Cooking is a modern invention, a luxury for pampered palates. I divested the ibis of its brilliant plumage, and ate it raw. I spoiled my specimen, but at the time there was little thought of that: there was not much of the naturalist left in me. I anathematised the hour I had ever promised to procure the bird. I wished my friend up to his neck in a swamp.

"The ibis did not weigh above three pounds, bones and all. It served me for a second meal, a breakfast; but at this *déjeuner sans fourchette* I picked the bones.

"What next? starve? No—not yet. In the battles I had had with the alligators during the second night, one of them had received a shot that proved mortal. The hideous carcass of the reptile lay dead upon the beach. I need not starve; I could eat that. Such were my reflections. I must hunger, though, before I could bring myself to touch the musky morsel.

"Two more days' fasting conquered my squeamishness. I drew out my knife, cut a steak from the alligator's tail, and ate it—not the one I had first killed, but a second; the other was now putrid, rapidly decomposing under the hot sun: its odour filled the islet.

"The stench had grown intolerable. There was not a breath of air stirring, otherwise I might have shunned it by keeping to windward. The whole atmosphere of the islet, as well as a large circle around it, was impregnated with the fearful effluvium. I could bear it no longer. With the aid of my gun, I pushed the half-decomposed carcass into the lake; perhaps the current might carry it away. It did: I had the gratification to see it float off.

"This circumstance led me into a train of reflections. Why did the body of the alligator float? It was swollen—inflated with gases. Ha!

"An idea shot suddenly through my mind—one of those brilliant ideas, the children of necessity. I thought of the floating alligator, of its intestines—what if I inflated them? Yes, yes! buoys and bladders, floats and life-preservers! that was the thought. I would open the alligators, make a buoy of their intestines, and that would bear me from the islet!

"I did not lose a moment's time; I was full of energy: hope had given me new life. My gun was loaded—a huge crocodile that swam near the shore received the shot in his eye. I dragged him on the beach; with my knife I laid open his entrails. Few they were, but enough for my purpose. A plume-quill from the wing of the ibis served me for a blow-pipe. I saw the bladder-like skin expand, until I was surrounded by objects like great sausages. Those were tied together, and fastened to my body, and then, with a plunge, I entered the waters of the lake, and floated downward. I had tied on my life-preservers in such a way that I sat in the water in an upright position, holding my gun with both hands. This I intended to have, used as a club in case I should be attacked by the alligators; but I had chosen the hot hour of noon, when these creatures lie in a half-torpid state, and to my joy I was not molested.

"Half an hour's drifting with the current carried me to the end of the lake, and I found myself at the *debouchure* of the bayou. Here, to my great delight, I saw my boat in the swamp, where it had been caught and held fast by the sedge. A few minutes more, and I had swung myself over the gunwale, and was sculling with eager strokes down the smooth waters of the bayou.

"Of course my adventure was ended, and I reached the settlement in safety, but without the object of my excursion. I was enabled, however, to procure it some days after, and had the gratification of being able to keep my promise to my friend."

Besançon's adventure had interested all of us; the old hunter-naturalist seemed delighted with it. No doubt it revived within him the memories of many a perilous incident in his own life.

It was evident that in the circle of the camp-fire there was more than one pair of lips ready to narrate some similar adventure, but the hour was late, and all agreed it would be better to go to rest. On to-morrow night, some other would take their turn; and, in fact, a regular agreement was entered into that each one of the party who had at any period of his life been the hero or participator in any hunting adventure should narrate the same for the entertainment of the others. This would bring out a regular "round of stories by the camp-fire," and would enable us to kill the many long evenings we had to pass before coming up with the buffalo. The conditions were, that the stories should exclusively relate to birds or animals—in fact, any hunted game belonging to the *fauna* of the American Continent: furthermore, that each should contribute his *quota* of information about whatever animal should chance to be the subject of the narration— about its habits, its geographical range; in short, its general natural history, as well as the various modes of hunting it, practised in different places by different people. This, it was alleged, would render our camp conversation instructive as well as entertaining.

The idea originated with the old hunter-naturalist, who very wisely reasoned that among so many gentlemen of large hunting experience he might collect new facts for his favourite science—for to just such men, and not to the closet-dreamer, is natural history indebted for its most interesting chapters. Of course every one of us, guides and all, warmly applauded the proposal, for there was no one among us averse to receiving a little knowledge of so entertaining a character. No doubt to the naturalist himself we should be indebted for most part of it; and his mode of communicating was so pleasant, that even the rude trappers listened to him with wonder and attention. They saw that he was no "greenhorn" either in woodcraft or prairie knowledge, and that was a sufficient claim to their consideration.

There is no character less esteemed by the regular "mountain-man" than a "greenhorn,"—that is, one who is new to the ways of their wilderness life.

With the design of an early start, we once more crept into our several quarters, and went to sleep.

Chapter Four
The Passenger-Pigeons

After an early breakfast we lit our pipes and cigars, and took to the road. The sun was very bright, and in less than two hours after starting we were sweltering under a heat almost tropical. It was one of those autumn days peculiar to America, where even a high latitude seems to be no protection against the sun, and his beams fall upon one with as much fervour as they would under the line itself. The first part of our journey was through open woods of black-jack, whose stunted forms afforded no shade, but only shut off the breeze which might otherwise have fanned us.

While fording a shallow stream, the doctor's scraggy, ill-tempered horse took a fit of kicking quite frantical. For some time it seemed likely that either the doctor himself, or his saddle-bags, would be deposited in the bottom of the creek, but after a severe spell of whipping and kicking on the part of the rider, the animal moved on again. What had set it dancing? That was the question. It had the disposition to be "frisky," but usually appeared to be lacking in strength. The buzz of a horse-fly sounding in our ears explained all. It was one of those large insects—the "horse-bug,"—peculiar to the Mississippi country, and usually found near watercourses. They are more terrible to horses than a fierce dog would be. I have known horses gallop away from them as if pursued by a beast of prey.

There is a belief among western people that these insects are propagated by the horses themselves; that is, that the eggs of the female are deposited upon the grass, so that the horses may swallow them; that incubation goes on within the stomach of the animal, and that the chrysalis is afterwards voided. I have met with others who believed in a still stranger theory; that the insect itself actually sought, and found, a passage into the stomach of the horse, some said by passing down his throat, others by boring a hole through his abdomen; and that in such cases the horse usually sickened, and was in danger of dying!

After the doctor's mustang had returned to proper behaviour, these odd theories became the subject of discussion. The Kentuckian believed in them—the Englishman doubted them—the hunter-naturalist could not endorse them—and Besançon ignored them entirely.

Shortly after the incident we entered the bottom lands of a considerable stream. These were heavily-timbered, and the shadow of the great forest trees afforded us a pleasant relief from the hot sun. Our guides told us we had several miles of such woods to pass through, and we were glad of the information. We noticed that most of the trees were beech, and their smooth straight trunks rose like columns around us.

The beech (*Fagus sylvatica*) is one of the most beautiful of American forest trees. Unlike most of the others, its bark is smooth, without fissures, and often of a silvery hue. Large beech-trees standing by the path, or near a cross road, are often seen covered with names, initials, and dates. Even the Indian often takes advantage of the bark of a beech-tree to signalise his presence to his friends, or commemorate some savage exploit. Indeed, the beautiful column-like trunk seems to invite the knife, and many a souvenir is carved upon it by the loitering wayfarer. It does not, however, invite the axe of the settler. On the contrary, the beechen woods often remain untouched, while others fall around them—partly because these trees are not usually the indices of the richest soil, but more from the fact that clearing a piece of beech forest is no easy matter. The green logs do not burn so readily as those of the oak, the elm, the maple, or poplar, and hence the necessity of "rolling" them off the ground to be cleared—a serious thing where labour is scarce and dear.

We were riding silently along, when all at once our ears were assailed by a strange noise. It resembled the clapping of a thousand pairs of hands, followed by a whistling sound, as if a strong wind had set suddenly in among the trees. We all knew well enough what it meant, and the simultaneous cry of "pigeons," was followed by half a dozen simultaneous cracks from the guns of the party, and several bluish birds fell to the ground. We had stumbled upon a feeding-place of the passenger-pigeon (*Columba migratoria*).

Our route was immediately abandoned, and in a few minutes we were in the thick of the flock, cracking away at them both with shot-gun and rifle. It was not so easy, however, to bring them down in any considerable numbers. In following them up we soon strayed from each other, until our party was completely scattered, and nearly two hours elapsed before we got back to the road. Our game-bag, however, made a fine show, and about forty brace were deposited in the waggon. With the anticipation of roast pigeon and "pot-pie," we rode on more cheerily to our night-camp. All along the route the pigeons were seen, and occasionally large flocks whirled over our heads under the canopy of the trees. Satiated with the sport, and not caring to waste our ammunition, we did not heed them farther.

In order to give Lanty due time for the duties of the *cuisine*, we halted a little earlier than usual. Our day's march had been a short one, but the excitement and sport of the pigeon-hunt repaid us for the loss of time. Our dinner-supper—for it was a combination of both—was the dish known in America as "pot-pie," in which the principal ingredients were the pigeons, some soft flour paste, with a few slices of bacon to give it a flavour. Properly speaking, the "pot-pie" is not a pie, but a stew. Ours was excellent, and as our appetites wore in a similar condition, a goodly quantity was used up in appeasing them.

Of course the conversation of the evening was the "wild pigeon of America," and the following facts regarding its natural history—although many of them are by no means new—may prove interesting to the reader, as they did to those who listened to the relation of them around our camp-fire.

The "passenger" is less in size than the house pigeon. In the air it looks not unlike the kite, wanting the forked or "swallow" tail. That of the pigeon is cuneiform. Its colour is best described by calling it a nearly uniform slate. In the male the colours are deeper, and the neck-feathers present the same changeable hues of green, gold, and purple-crimson, generally observed in birds of this species. It is only in the woods, and when freshly caught or killed, that these brilliant tints can be seen to perfection. They fade in captivity, and immediately after the bird has been shot. They seem to form part of its life and liberty, and disappear when it is robbed of either. I have often thrust the wild pigeon, freshly killed, into my game-bag, glittering like an opal. I have drawn it forth a few hours after of a dull leaden hue, and altogether unlike the same bird.

As with all birds of this tribe, the female is inferior to the male, both in size and plumage. The eye is less vivid. In the male it is of the most brilliant fiery orange, inclosed in a well-defined circle of red. The eye is in truth its finest feature, and never fails to strike the beholder with admiration.

The most singular fact in the natural history of the "passenger," is their countless numbers. Audubon saw a flock that contained "one billion one hundred and sixteen millions of birds!" Wilson counted, or rather computed, another flock of "two thousand two hundred and thirty millions!" These numbers seem incredible. I have no doubt of their truth. I have no doubt that they are *under* rather than *over* the numbers actually seen by both these naturalists, for both made most liberal allowances in their calculations.

Where do these immense flocks come from?

The wild pigeons breed in all parts of America. Their breeding-places are found as far north as the Hudson's Bay, and they have been seen in the southern forests of Louisiana and Texas. The nests are built upon high trees, and resemble immense rookeries. In Kentucky, one of their breeding-places was forty miles in length, by several in breadth! One hundred nests will often be found upon a single tree, and in each nest there is but one "squab." The eggs are pure white, like those of the common kind, and, like them, they breed several times during the year, but principally when food is plenty. They establish themselves in great "roosts," sometimes for years together, to which each night they return from their distant excursions—hundreds of miles, perhaps; for this is but a short fly for travellers who can pass over a mile in a single minute, and some of whom have even strayed across the Atlantic to England! They, however, as I myself have observed, remain in the same woods where they have been feeding for several days together. I have also noticed that they prefer roosting in the low underwood, even when tall trees are close at hand. If near water, or hanging over a stream, the place is still more to their liking; and in the morning they may be seen alighting on the bank to drink, before taking to their daily occupation.

The great "roosts" and breeding-places are favourite resorts for numerous birds of prey. The small vultures (*Cathartes aura* and *Atratus*), or, as they are called in the west, "turkey buzzard," and "carrion crow," do not confine themselves to carrion alone. They are fond of live "squabs," which they drag out of their nests at pleasure. Numerous hawks and kites prey upon them; and even the great white-headed eagle (*Falco leucocephalus*) may be seen soaring above, and occasionally swooping down for a dainty morsel. On the ground beneath move enemies of a different kind, both biped and quadruped. Fowlers with their guns and long poles; farmers with waggons to carry off the dead birds; and even droves of hogs to devour them. Trees fall under the axe, and huge branches break down by the weight of the birds themselves, killing numbers in their descent. Torches are used—for it is usually a night scene, after the return of the birds from feeding,—pots of burning sulphur, and other engines of destruction. A noisy scene it is. The clapping of a million pair of wings, like the roaring of thunder; the shots; the shouts; men hoarsely calling to each other; women and children screaming their delight; the barking of dogs; the neighing of horses; the "crashes" of breaking branches; and the "chuck" of the woodman's axe, all mingled together.

When the men—saturated with slaughter, and white with ordure—have retired beyond the borders of the roost to rest themselves for the night, their ground is occupied by the prowling wolf and the fox; the racoon and the cougar; the lynx and the great black bear.

With so many enemies, one would think that the "passengers" would soon be exterminated. Not so. They are too prolific for that. Indeed, were it not for these enemies, they themselves would perish for want of food.

Fancy what it takes to feed them! The flock seen by Wilson would require eighteen million bushels of grain every day!—and it, most likely, was only one of many such that at the time were traversing the vast continent of America. Upon what do they feed? it will be asked. Upon the fruits of the great forest—upon the acorns, the nuts of the beech, upon buck-wheat, and Indian corn; upon many species of berries, such as the huckleberry (*whortleberry*), the hackberry (*Celtis crassifolia*), and the fruit of the holly. In the northern regions, where these are scarce, the berries of the juniper tree (*Juniperus communis*) form the principal food. On the other hand, among the southern plantations, they devour greedily the rice, as well as the nuts of the chestnut-tree and several species of oaks. But their staple food is the beech-nut, or "mast," as it is called. Of this the pigeons are fond, and fortunately it exists in great plenty. In the forests of Western America there are vast tracts covered almost entirely with the beech-tree.

As already stated, these beechen forests of America remain almost intact, and so long as they shower down their millions of bushels of "mast," so long will the passenger-pigeons flutter in countless numbers amidst their branches.

Their migration is semi-annual; but unlike most other migratory birds, it is far from being regular. Their flight is, in fact, not a periodical migration, but a sort of nomadic existence—food being the object which keeps them in motion and directs their course. The scarcity in one part determines their movement to another. When there is more than the usual fall of snow in the northern regions, vast flocks make their appearance in the middle States, as in Ohio and Kentucky. This may in some measure account for the overcrowded "roosts" which have been occasionally seen, but which are by no means common. You may live in the west for many years without witnessing a scene such as those described by Wilson and Audubon, though once or twice every year you may see pigeons enough to astonish you.

It must not be imagined that the wild pigeons of America are so "tame" as they have been sometimes represented. That is their character only while young at the breeding-places, or at the great roosts when confused by crowding upon each other, and mystified by torch-light.

Far different are they when wandering through the open woods in search of food. It is then both difficult to approach and hard to kill them. Odd birds you may easily reach; you may see them perched upon the branches on all sides of you, and within shot-range; but the *thick* of the flock, somehow or other, always keeps from one to two hundred yards off. The sportsman cannot bring himself to fire at single birds. No. There is a tree near at hand literally black with pigeons. Its branches creak under the weight. What a fine havoc he will make if he can but get near enough! But that is the difficulty; there is no cover, and he must approach as he best can without it. He continues to advance; the birds sit silent, watching his movements. He treads lightly and with caution; he inwardly anathematises the dead leaves and twigs that make a loud rustling under his feet. The birds appear restless; several stretch out their necks as if to spring off.

At length he deems himself fairly within range, and raises his gun to take aim; but this is a signal for the shy game, and before he can draw trigger they are off to another tree!

Some stragglers still remain; and at them he levels his piece and fires. The shot is a random one; for our sportsman, having failed to "cover" the flock, has become irritated and careless, and in all such cases the pigeons fly off with the loss of a few feathers.

The gun is reloaded, and our amateur hunter, seeing the thick flock upon another tree, again endeavours to approach it, but with like success.

Chapter Five
Hunt with a Howitzer

When the conversation about the haunts and habits of these birds began to flag, some one called for a "pigeon story." Who could tell a pigeon story? To our surprise the doctor volunteered one, and all gathered around to listen.

"Yes, gentlemen," began the doctor, "I have a pigeon adventure, which occurred to me some years ago. I was then living in Cincinnati, following my respectable calling, when I had the good fortune to set a broken leg for one Colonel P—, a wealthy planter, who lived upon the bank of the river some sixty miles from the city. I made a handsome set of if, and won the colonel's friendship for ever. Shortly after, I was invited to his house, to be present at a great pigeon-hunt which was to come off in the fall. The colonel's plantation stood among beech woods, and he had therefore an annual visitation of the pigeons, and could tell almost to a day when they would appear. The hunt he had arranged for the gratification of his numerous friends.

"As you all know, gentlemen, sixty miles in our western travel is a mere bagatelle; and tired of pills and prescriptions, I flung myself into a boat, and in a few hours arrived at the colonel's stately home. A word or two about this stately home and its proprietor.

"Colonel P— was a splendid specimen of the backwoods' gentleman—you will admit there *are* gentlemen in the backwoods." (Here the doctor glanced good-humouredly, first at our English friend Thompson, and then at the Kentuckian, both of whom answered him with a laugh.) "His house was the type of a backwoods mansion; a wooden structure, both walls and roof. No matter. It has distributed as much hospitality in its time as many a marble palace; that was one of its backwoods' characteristics. It stood, and I hope still stands, upon the north bank of the Ohio—that beautiful stream—'*La belle rivière*,' as the French colonists, and before their time the Indians, used to call it. It was in the midst of the woods, though around it were a thousand acres of 'clearing,' where you might distinguish fields of golden wheat, and groves of shining maize plants waving aloft their yellow-flower tassels. You might note, too, the broad green leaf of the Nicotian 'weed,' or the bursting pod of the snow-white cotton. In the garden you might observe the sweet potato, the common one, the refreshing tomato, the huge water-melon, cantelopes, and musk melons, with many other delicious vegetables. You could see pods of red and green pepper growing upon trailing plants; and beside them several species of peas and beans—all valuable for the colonel's *cuisine*. There was an orchard, too, of several acres in extent. It was filled with fruit-trees, the finest peaches in the world, and the finest apples—the Newton pippins. Besides, there were luscious pears and plums, and upon the espaliers, vines bearing bushels of sweet grapes. If Colonel P— lived in the woods, it cannot be said that he was surrounded by a desert.

"There were several substantial log-houses near the main building or mansion. They were the stable—and good horses there were in that stable; the cow-house, for milk cattle; the barn, to hold the wheat and maize-corn; the smoke-house, for curing bacon; a large building for the dry tobacco; a cotton-gin, with its shed of clap-boards; bins for the husk fodder, and several smaller structures. In one corner you saw a low-walled erection that reminded you of a kennel, and the rich music that from time to time issued from its apertures would convince you that it *was* a kennel. If you had peeped into it, you would have seen a dozen of as fine stag-hounds as ever lifted a trail. The colonel was somewhat partial to these pets, for he was a 'mighty hunter.' You might see a number of young colts in an adjoining lot; a pet deer, a buffalo-calf, that had been brought from the far prairies, pea-fowl, guinea-hens, turkeys, geese, ducks, and the usual proportion of common fowls. Rail-fences zigzagged off in all directions towards the edge of the woods. Huge trees, dead and divested of their leaves, stood up in the cleared fields. Turkey buzzards and carrion, crows might be seen perched upon their grey naked limbs; upon their summit you might observe the great rough-legged falcon; and above all, cutting sharply against the blue sky, the fork-tailed kite sailing gently about."

Here the doctor's auditory interrupted him with a murmur of applause. The doctor was in fine spirits, and in a poetical mood. He continued.

"Such, gentlemen, was the sort of place I had come to visit; and I saw at a glance that I could spend a few days there pleasantly enough—even without the additional attractions of a pigeon-hunt.

"On my arrival I found the party assembled. It consisted of a score and a half of ladies and gentlemen, nearly all young people. The pigeons had not yet made their appearance, but were looked for every hour. The woods had assumed the gorgeous tints of autumn, that loveliest of seasons in the 'far west.' Already the ripe nuts and berries were scattered profusely over the earth offering their annual banquet to God's wild creatures. The 'mast' of the beech-tree, of which the wild pigeon is so fond, was showering down among the dead leaves. It was the very season at which the birds were accustomed to visit the beechen woods that girdled the colonel's plantation. They would no doubt soon appear. With this expectation everything was made ready; each of the gentlemen was provided with a fowling-piece, or rifle if he preferred it; and even some of the ladies insisted upon being armed.

"To render the sport more exciting, our host had established certain regulations. They were as follows:—The gentlemen were divided into two parties, of equal numbers. These were to go in opposite directions, the ladies upon the first day of the hunt accompanying whichever they chose. Upon all succeeding days, however, the case would be different. The ladies were to accompany that party which upon the day previous had bagged the greatest number of birds. The victorious gentlemen, moreover, were endowed with other privileges, which lasted throughout the evening; such as the choice of partners for the dinner-table and the dance.

"I need not tell you, gentlemen, that in these conditions existed powerful motives for exertion. The colonel's guests were the *élite* of western society. Most of the gentlemen were young men or bachelors; and among the ladies there were *belles*; three or four of them rich and beautiful. On my arrival I could perceive signs of incipient flirtations. Attachments had already arisen; and by many it would have been esteemed anything but pleasant to be separated in the manner prescribed. A strong *esprit du corps* was thus established; and, by the time the pigeons arrived, both parties had determined to do their utmost. In fact, I have never known so strong a feeling of rivalry to exist between two parties of amateur sportsmen.

"The pigeons at length arrived. It was a bright sunny morning, and yet the atmosphere was darkened, as the vast flock, a mile in breadth by several in length, passed across the canopy. The sound of their wings resembled a strong wind whistling among tree-tops, or through the rigging of a ship. We saw that they hovered over the woods, and settled among the tall beeches.

"The beginning of the hunt was announced, and we set forth, each party taking the direction allotted to it. With each went a number of ladies, and even some of these were armed with light fowling-pieces, determined that the party of their choice should be the victorious one. After a short ride, we found ourselves fairly 'in the woods,' and in the presence of the birds, and then the cracking commenced.

"In our party we had eight guns, exclusive of the small fowling-pieces (two of those), with which a brace of our heroines were armed, and which, truth compels me to confess, were less dangerous to the pigeons than to ourselves. Some of our guns were double-barrelled shot-guns, others were rifles. You will wonder at rifles being used in such a sport, and yet it is a fact that the gentlemen who carried rifles managed to do more execution than those who were armed with the other species. This arose from the circumstance that they were contented to aim at single birds, and, being good shots, they were almost sure to bring these down. The woods were filled with straggling pigeons. Odd birds were always within rifle range; and thus, instead of wasting their time in endeavouring to approach the great flocks, our riflemen did nothing but load and fire. In this way they soon counted their game by dozens.

"Early in the evening, the pigeons, having filled their crops with the mast, disappeared. They flew off to some distant 'roost.' This of course concluded our sport for the day. We got together and counted our numbers. We had 640 birds. We returned home full of hope; we felt certain that we had won for that day. Our antagonists had arrived before us. They showed us 736 dead pigeons. We were beaten.

"I really cannot explain the chagrin which this defeat occasioned to most of our party. They felt humiliated in the eyes of the ladies, whose company they were to lose on the morrow. To some there was extreme bitterness in the idea; for, as I have already stated, attachments had sprung up, and jealous thoughts were naturally their concomitants. It was quite tantalising, as we parted next morning, to see the galaxy of lovely women ride off with our antagonists, while we sought the woods in the opposite direction, dispirited and in silence.

"We went, however, determined to do our best, and win the ladies for the morrow. A council was held, and each imparted his advice and encouragement; and then we all set to work with shot-gun and rifle.

"On this day an incident occurred that aided our 'count' materially. As you know, gentlemen, the wild pigeons, while feeding, sometimes cover the ground so thickly that they crowd upon each other. They all advance in the same direction, those behind continually rising up and fluttering to the front, so that the surface presents a series of undulations like sea-waves. Frequently the birds alight upon each other's backs, for want of room upon the ground, and a confused mass of winged creatures is seen rolling through the woods. At such times, if the sportsman can only 'head' the flock, he is sure of a good shot. Almost every pellet tells, and dozens may be brought down at a single discharge.

"In my progress through the woods, I had got separated from my companions, when I observed an immense flock approaching me after the manner described. I saw from their plumage that they were young birds, and therefore not likely to be easily alarmed. I drew my horse (I was mounted) behind a tree, and awaited their approach. This I did more from curiosity than any other motive, as, unfortunately I carried a rifle, and could only have killed one or two at the best. The crowd came 'swirling' forward, and when they were within some ten or fifteen paces distant, I fired into their midst. To my surprise, the flock did not take flight, but continued to advance as before, until they were almost among the horse's feet. I could stand it no longer. I drove the spurs deeply, and galloped into their midst, striking right and left as they fluttered up round me. Of course they were soon off; but of those that had been trodden upon by my horse, and others I had knocked down, I counted no less than twenty-seven! Proud of my exploit, I gathered the birds into my bag, and rode in search of my companions.

"Our party on this day numbered over 800 head killed; but, to our surprise and chagrin, our antagonists had beaten us by more than a hundred!

"The gentlemen of 'ours' were wretched. The belles were monopolised by our antagonists; we were scouted, and debarred every privilege.

"It was not to be endured; something must be done. What was to be done? counselled we. If fair means will not answer, we must try the opposite. It was evident that our antagonists were better shots than we.

"The colonel, too, was one of them, and he was sure to kill every time he pulled trigger. The odds were against us; some plan must be devised; some *ruse* must be adopted, and the idea of one had been passing through my mind during the whole of that day. It was this:—I had noticed, what has been just remarked, that, although the pigeons will not allow the sportsman to come within range of a fowling-piece, yet at a distance of little over a hundred yards they neither fear man nor beast. At that distance they sit unconcerned, thousands of them upon a single tree. It struck me that a gun large enough to throw shot among them would be certain of killing hundreds at each discharge; but where was such a gun to be had? As I reflected thus, 'mountain howitzers' came into my mind. I remembered the small mountain howitzers I had seen at Covington. One of these loaded with shot would be the very weapon. I knew there was a battery of them at the Barracks. I knew that a friend of mine commanded the battery. By steamer, should one pass, it was but a few hours to Covington. I proposed sending for a 'mountain howitzer.'

"I need hardly say that my proposal was hailed with a universal welcome on the part of my companions; and without dropping a hint to the other party, it was at once resolved that the design should be carried into execution. It was carried into execution. An 'up-river' boat chanced to pass in the nick of time. A messenger was forthwith, despatched to Covington, and before twelve o'clock upon the following day another boat on her down trip brought the howitzer, and we had it secretly landed and conveyed to a place in the woods previously agreed upon. My friend, Captain C—, had sent a 'live corporal' along with it, and we had no difficulty in its management.

"As I had anticipated, it answered our purpose as though it had been made for it. Every shot brought down a shower of dead birds, and after one discharge alone the number obtained was 123! At night our 'game-bag' counted over three thousand birds! We were sure of the ladies for the morrow.

"Before returning home to our certain triumph, however, there were some considerations. To-morrow we should have the ladies in our company; some of the fair creatures would be as good as sure to 'split' upon the howitzer. What was to be done to prevent this?

"We eight had sworn to be staunch to each other. We had taken every precaution; we had only used our 'great gun' when far off, so that its report might not reach the ears of our antagonists; but how about to-morrow? Could we trust our fair companions with a secret? Decidedly not. This was the unanimous conclusion. A new idea now came to our aid. We saw that we might dispense with the howitzer, and still manage to out-count our opponents. We would make a depository of birds in a safe place. There was a squatter's house near by: that would do. So we took the squatter into our council, and left some 1500 birds in his charge, the remainder being deemed sufficient for that day. From the 1500 thus left, we might each day take a few hundred to make up our game-bag just enough to out-number the other party. We did not send home the corporal and his howitzer. We might require him again; so we quartered him upon the squatter.

"On returning home, we found that our opponents had also made a 'big day's work of it;' but they were beaten by hundreds. The ladies were ours!

"And we kept them until the end of the hunt, to the no little mortification of the gentlemen in the 'minority:' to their surprise, as well; for most of them being crack-shots, and several of us not at all so, they could not comprehend why they were every day beaten so outrageously. We had hundreds to spare, and barrels of the birds were cured for winter use.

"Another thing quite puzzled our opponents, as well as many good people in the neighbourhood. That was the loud reports that had been heard in the woods. Some argued they were thunder, while others declared they must have proceeded from an earthquake. This last seemed the more probable, as the events I am narrating occurred but a few years after the great earthquake in the Mississippi Valley, and people's minds were prepared for such a thing.

"I need not tell you how the knowing ones enjoyed the laugh for several days, and it was not until the colonel's *reunion* was about to break up, that our secret was let out, to the no small chagrin of our opponents, but to the infinite amusement of our host himself, who, although one of the defeated party, often narrates to his friends the story of the 'Hunt with a Howitzer.'"

Chapter Six
Killing a Cougar

Although we had made a five miles' march from the place where we had halted to shoot the pigeons, our night-camp was still within the boundaries of the flock. During the night we could hear them at intervals at no great distance off. A branch occasionally cracked, and then a fluttering of wings told of thousands dislodged or frightened by its fall. Sometimes the fluttering commenced without any apparent cause. No doubt the great-horned owl (*Strix virginiana*), the wild cat (*felis rufa*), and the raccoon, were busy among them, and the silent attacks of these were causing the repeated alarms.

Before going to rest, a torch-hunt was proposed by way of variety, but no material for making good torches could be found, and the idea was abandoned. Torches should be made of dry pine-knots, and carried in some shallow vessel. The common frying-pan, with a long handle, is best for the purpose. Link-torches, unless of the best pitch-pine (*Pinus resinosa*), do not burn with sufficient brightness to stultify the pigeons. They will flutter off before the hunter can get his long pole within reach, whereas with a very brilliant light, he may approach almost near enough to lay his hands upon them. As there were no pitch-pine-trees in the neighbourhood, nor any good torch-wood, we were forced to give up the idea of a night-hunt.

During the night strange noises were heard by several who chanced to be awake. Some said they resembled the howling of dogs, while others compared them to the screaming of angry cats. One party said they were produced by wolves; another, that the wild cats (lynxes) made them. But there was one that differed from all the rest. It was a sort of prolonged hiss, that all except Ike believed to be the snort of the black bear, lice, however, declared that it was not the bear, but the "sniff," as he termed it, of the "painter" (cougar). This was probable enough, considering the nature of the place. The cougar is well-known to frequent the great roosts of the passenger-pigeon, and is fond of the flesh of these birds.

In the morning our camp was still surrounded by the pigeons, sweeping about among the tree-trunks, and gathering the mast as they went. A few shots were fired, not from any inclination to continue the sport of killing them, but to lay in a fresh stock for the day's dinner. The surplus from yesterday's feast was thrown away, and left by the deserted camp—a banquet for the preying creatures that would soon visit the spot.

We moved on, still surrounded by masses upon the wing. A singular incident occurred as we were passing through a sort of avenue in the forest. It was a narrow aisle, on both sides walled in by the thick foliage of the beeches. We were fairly within this hall-like passage, when it suddenly darkened at the opposite end. We saw that a cloud of pigeons had entered it, flying towards us. They were around our heads before they had noticed us. Seeing our party, they suddenly attempted to diverge from their course, but there was no other open to them, except to rise upward in a vertical direction. This they did on the instant—the clatter of their wings producing a noise like the continued roar of thunder. Some had approached so near, that the men on horseback, striking with their guns, knocked several to the ground; and the Kentuckian, stretching upward his long arm, actually caught one of them on the wing. In an instant they were out of sight; but at that instant two great birds appeared before us at the opening of the forest, which were at once recognised as a brace of white-headed eagles (*Falco leucocephalus*). This accounted for the rash flight of the pigeons; for the eagles had evidently been in pursuit of them, and had driven them to seek shelter under the trees. We were desirous of emptying our guns at the great birds of prey, and there was a simultaneous spurring of horses and cocking of guns: to no purpose, however. The eagles were on the alert. They had already espied us; and, uttering their maniac screams, they wheeled suddenly, and disappeared over the tree-tops.

We had hardly recovered from this pleasant little bit of excitement, when the guide Ike, who rode in the advance, was seen suddenly to jerk up, exclaiming—

"Painter, by God! I know'd I heard a painter."

"Where? where?" was hurriedly uttered by several voices, while all pressed forward to the guide.

"Yander!" replied Ike, pointing to a thicket of young beeches. "He's tuk to the brush: ride round, fellers. Mark, boy, round! quick, damn you!"

There was a scramble of horsemen, with excited, anxious looks and gestures. Every one had his gun cocked and ready, and in a few seconds the small copse of beeches, with their golden-yellow leaves, was inclosed by a ring of hunters. Had the cougar got away, or was he still within the thicket? Several large trees grew out of its midst. Had he taken to one? The eyes of the party were turned upwards. The fierce creature was nowhere visible.

It was impossible to see into every part of the jungle from the outside, as we sat in our saddles. The game might be crouching among the grass and brambles. What was to be done? We had no dogs. How was the cougar to be started? It would be no small peril to penetrate the thicket afoot. Who was to do it?

The question was answered by Redwood, who was now seen dismounting from his horse.

"Keep your eyes about you," cried he. "I'll make the varmint show if he's thur. Look sharp, then!"

We saw Redwood enter fearlessly, leaving his horse hitched over a branch. We heard him no longer, as he proceeded with that stealthy silence known only to the Indian fighter. We listened, and waited in profound suspense. Not even the crackling of a branch broke the stillness. Full five minutes we waited, and then the sharp crack of a rifle near the centre of the copsewood relieved, us. The next moment was heard Redwood's voice crying aloud—

"Look out thur? By God! I've missed him."

Before we had time to change our attitudes another rifle cracked, and another voice was heard, crying in answer to Redwood—

"But, by God! I hain't."

"He's hyur," continued the voice; "dead as mutton. Come this a way, an' yu'll see the beauty."

Ike's voice was recognised, and we all galloped to the spot where it proceeded from. At his feet lay the body of the panther quite dead. There was a red spot running blood between the ribs, where Ike's bullet had penetrated. In trying to escape from the thicket, the cougar had halted a moment, in a crouching attitude, directly before Ike's face, and that moment was enough to give the trapper time to glance through his sights, and send the fatal bullet.

Of course the guide received the congratulations of all, and though he pretended not to regard the thing in the light of a feat, he knew well that killing a "painter" was no everyday adventure.

The skin of the animal was stripped off in a trice, and carried to the waggon. Such a trophy is rarely left in the woods.

The hunter-naturalist performed some farther operations upon the body for the purpose of examining the contents of the stomach. These consisted entirely of the half-digested remains of passenger-pigeons, an enormous quantity of which the beast had devoured during the previous night—having captured them no doubt upon the trees.

This adventure formed a pleasant theme for conversation during the rest of our journey, and of course the cougar was the subject. His habits and history were fully discussed, and the information elicited is given below.

Chapter Seven
The Cougar

The cougar (*Felis concolor*) is the only indigenous long-tailed cat in America north of the parallel of 30 degrees. The "wild cats" so called, are lynxes with short tails; and of these there are three distinct species. But there is only one true representative of the genus Felis, and that is the animal in question.

This has received many trivial appellations. Among Anglo-American hunters, it is called the panther—in their *patois*, "painter." In most parts of South America, as well as in Mexico, it receives the grandiloquent title of "lion" (*leon*), and in the Peruvian countries is called the "puma," or "poma." The absence of stripes, such as those of the tiger—or spots, as upon the leopard—or rosettes, as upon the jaguar, have suggested the name of the naturalists, *concolor*. *Discolor* was formerly in use; but the other has been generally adopted.

There are few wild animals so regular in their colour as the cougar: very little variety has been observed among different specimens. Some naturalists speak of spotted cougars—that is, having spots that may be seen in a certain light. Upon young cubs, such markings do appear; but they are no longer visible on the full-grown animal. The cougar of mature age is of a tawny red colour, almost uniform over the whole body, though somewhat paler about the face and the parts underneath. This colour is not exactly the tawny of the lion; it is more of a reddish hue—nearer to what is termed calf-colour.

The cougar is far from being a well-shaped creature: it appears disproportioned. Its back is long and hollow; and its tail does not taper so gracefully as in some other animals of the cat kind. Its legs are short and stout; and although far from clumsy in appearance, it does not possess the graceful *tournure* of body so characteristic of some of its congeners. Though considered the representative of the lion in the New World, its resemblance to the royal beast is but slight; its colour seems to be the only title it has to such an honour. For the rest, it is much more akin to the tigers, jaguars, and true panthers. Cougars are rarely more than six feet in length, including the tail, which is usually about a third of that measurement.

The range of the animal is very extensive. It is known from Paraguay to the Great Lakes of North America. In no part of either continent is it to be seen every day, because it is for the most part not only nocturnal in its activity, but one of those fierce creatures that, fortunately, do not exist in large numbers. Like others of the genus, it is solitary in its habits, and at the approach of civilisation betakes itself to the remoter parts of the forest. Hence the cougar, although found in all of the United States, is a rare animal everywhere, and seen only at long intervals in the mountain-valleys, or in other difficult places of the forest. The appearance of a cougar is sufficient to throw any neighbourhood into an excitement similar to that which would be produced by the chase of a mad dog.

It is a splendid tree-climber. It can mount a tree with the agility of a cat; and although so large an animal, it climbs by means of its claws—not by hugging, after the manner of the bears and opossums. While climbing a tree, its claws can be heard crackling along the bark as it mounts upward. It sometimes lies "squatted" along a horizontal branch, a lower one, for the purpose of springing upon deer, or such other animals as it wishes to prey upon. The ledge of a cliff is also a favourite haunt, and such are known among the hunters as "panther-ledges." It selects such a position in the neighbourhood of some watering-place, or, if possible, one of the salt or soda springs (licks) so numerous in America. Here it is more certain that its vigil will not be a protracted one. Its prey—elk, deer, antelope, or buffalo— soon appears beneath, unconscious of the dangerous enemy that cowers over them. When fairly within reach, the cougar springs, and pouncing down upon the shoulders of the victim, buries its claws in the flesh. The terrified animal starts forward, leaps from side to side, dashes into the papaw thickets, or breasts the dense cane-brake, in hopes of brushing off its relentless rider. All in vain! Closely clasping its neck, the cougar clings on, tearing its victim in the throat, and drinking its blood throughout the wild gallop. Faint and feeble, the ruminant at length totters and falls, and the fierce destroyer squats itself along the body, and finishes its red repast. If the cougar can overcome several animals at a time, it will kill them all, although but the twentieth part may be required to satiate its hunger. Unlike the lion in this, even in repletion it will kill. With it, destruction of life seems to be an instinct.

There is a very small animal, and apparently a very helpless one, with which the cougar occasionally quarrels, but often with ill success—this is the Canada porcupine. Whether the cougar ever succeeds in killing one of these creatures is not known, but that it attacks them is beyond question, and its own death is often the result. The quills of the Canada porcupine are slightly barbed at their extremities; and when stuck into the flesh of a living animal, this arrangement causes them to penetrate mechanically deeper and deeper as the animal moves. That the porcupine can itself discharge them to some distance, is not true, but it is true that it can cause them to be easily *detached*; and this it does when rashly seized by any of the predatory animals. The result is, that these remarkable spines become fast in the tongue, jaws, and lips of the cougar, or any other creature which may make an attack on that seemingly unprotected little animal. The fisher (*Mustela Canadensis*) is said to be the only animal that can kill the porcupine with impunity. It fights the latter by first throwing it upon its back, and then springing upon its upturned belly, where the spines are almost entirely wanting.

The cougar is called a cowardly animal: some naturalists even assert that it will not venture to attack man. This is, to say the least, a singular declaration, after the numerous well-attested instances in which men have been attacked, and even killed by cougars. There are many such in the history of early settlement in America. To say that cougars are cowardly now when found in the United States—to say they are shy of man, and will not attack him, may be true enough. Strange, if the experience of 200 years' hunting, and by such hunters too, did not bring them to that. We may safely believe, that if the lions of Africa were placed in the same circumstances, a very similar shyness and dread of the upright biped would soon exhibit itself. What all these creatures—bears, cougars, lynxes, wolves, and even alligators—are now, is no criterion of their past. Authentic history proves that their courage, at least so far as regards man, has changed altogether since they first heard the sharp detonation of the deadly rifle. Even contemporaneous history demonstrates this. In many parts of South America, both jaguar and cougar attack man, and numerous are the deadly encounters there. In Peru, on the eastern declivity of the Andes, large settlements and even villages have been abandoned solely on account of the perilous proximity of those fierce animals.

In the United States, the cougar is hunted by dog and gun. He will run from the hounds, because he knows they are backed by the unerring rifle of the hunter; but should one of the yelping pack approach too near, a single blow of the cougar's paw is sufficient to stretch him out. When closely pushed, the cougar takes to a tree, and, halting in one of its forks, humps his back, bristles his hair, looks downward with gleaming eyes, and utters a sound somewhat like the purring of a cat, though far louder. The crack of the hunter's rifle usually puts an end to these demonstrations, and the cougar drops to the ground either dead or wounded. If only the latter, a desperate fight ensues between him and the dogs, with several of whom he usually leaves a mark that distinguishes them for the rest of their lives.

The scream of the cougar is a common phrase. It is not very certain that the creature is addicted to the habit of screaming, although noises of this kind heard in the nocturnal forest have been attributed to him. Hunters, however, have certainly never heard him, and they believe that the scream talked about proceeds from one of the numerous species of owls that inhabit the deep forests of America. At short intervals, the cougar does make himself heard in a note which somewhat resembles a deep-drawn sigh, or as if one were to utter with an extremely guttural expression the syllables "Co-oa," or "Cougar." Is it from this that he derives his trivial name?

Chapter Eight
Old Ike's Adventure

Now a panther story was the natural winding-up of this day, and it had been already hinted that old Ike had "rubbed out" several of these creatures in his time, and no doubt could tell more than one "painter" story.

"Wal, strengers," began he, "it's true thet this hyur ain't the fust painter I've comed acrosst. About fifteen yeern ago I moved to Loozyanny, an' thur I met a painter, an' a queer story it are."

"Let us have it by all means," said several of the party, drawing closer up and seating themselves to listen attentively. We all knew that a story from Ike could not be otherwise than "queer," and our curiosity was on the *qui vive*.

"Wal then," continued he, "they have floods dowd thur in Loozyanny, sich as, I guess, you've never seen the like o' in England." Here Ike addressed himself specially to our English comrade. "England ain't big enough to hev sich floods. One o' 'm ud kiver yur hul country, I hev heern said. I won't say that ar's true, as I ain't acquainted with yur jography. I know, howsomdever, they're mighty big freshets thur, as I hev sailed a skift more 'n a hundred mile acrosst one o' 'm, whur thur wan't nothin' to be seen but cypress tops peep in out o' the water. The floods, as ye know, come every year, but them ar big ones only oncest in a while.

"Wal, as I've said about fifteen yeern ago, I located in the Red River bottom, about fifty mile or tharabout below Nacketosh, whur I built me a shanty. I hed left my wife an' two young critters in Mississippi state, intendin' to go back for 'em in the spring; so, ye see, I wur all alone by meself, exceptin' my ole mar, a Collins's axe, an' of coorse my rifle.

"I hed finished the shanty all but the chinkin' an' the buildin' o' a chimbly, when what shed come on but one o' 'm tarnation floods. It wur at night when it begun to make its appearance. I wur asleep on the floor o' the shanty, an' the first warnin' I hed o' it wur the feel o' the water soakin' through my ole blanket. I hed been a-dreamin', an' thort it wur rainin', an' then agin I thort that I wur bein' drownded in the Mississippi; but I wan't many seconds awake, till I guessed what it wur in raality; so I jumped to my feet like a started buck, an' groped my way to the door.

"A sight that wur when I got thur. I hed chirred a piece o' ground around the shanty—a kupple o' acres or better—I hed left the stumps a good three feet high: thur wan't a stump to be seen. My clearin', stumps an' all, wur under water; an' I could see it shinin' among the trees all round the shanty.

"Of coorse, my fust thoughts wur about my rifle; an I turned back into the shanty, an' laid my claws upon that quick enough.

"I next went in search o' my ole mar. She wan't hard to find; for if ever a critter made a noise, she did. She wur tied to a tree close by the shanty, an' the way she wur a-squealin' wur a caution to cats. I found her up to the belly in water, pitchin' an' flounderin' all round the tree. She hed nothin' on but the rope that she wur hitched by. Both saddle an' bridle hed been washed away: so I made the rope into a sort o' halter, an' mounted her bare-backed.

"Jest then I begun to think whur I wur agoin'. The hul country appeared to be under water: an' the nearest neighbour I hed lived acrosst the paraary ten miles off. I knew that his shanty sot on high ground, but how wur I to get thur? It wur night; I mout lose my way, an' ride chuck into the river.

"When I thort o' ibis, I concluded it mout be better to stay by my own shanty till mornin'. I could hitch the mar inside to keep her from bein' floated away; an' for meself, I could climb on the roof.

"While I wur thinkin' on this, I noticed that the water wur a-deepenin', an' it jest kim into my head, that it ud soon be deep enough to drownd my ole mar. For meself I wan't frightened. I mout a clomb a tree, an' stayed thur till the flood fell; but I shed a lost the mar, an' that critter wur too valleyble to think o' such a sacryfize; so I made up my mind to chance crossin' the paraary. Thur wan't no time to be wasted—ne'er a minnit; so I gin the mar a kick or two in the ribs an' started.

"I found the path out to the edge of the paraary easy enough. I hed blazed it when I fust come to the place; an', as the night wur not a very dark one, I could see the blazes as I passed atween the trees. My mar knew the track as well as meself, an' swaltered through at a sharp rate, for she knew too thur wan't no time to be wasted. In five minnites we kim out on the edge o' the pairairy, an' jest as I expected, the hul thing wur kivered with water, an' lookin' like a big pond, I could see it shinin' clur acrosst to the other side o' the openin'.

"As luck ud hev it, I could jest git a glimp o' the trees on the fur side o' the paraary. Thur wur a big clump o' cypress, that I could see plain enough; I knew this wur clost to my neighbour's shanty; so I gin my critter the switch, an' struck right for it.

"As I left the timmer, the mar wur up to her hips. Of coorse, I expected a good grist o' heavy wadin'; but I hed no idee that the water wur a-gwine to git much higher; thur's whur I made my mistake.

"I hedn't got more'n a kupple o' miles out when I diskivered that the thing wur a-risin' rapidly, for I seed the mar wur a-gettin' deeper an' deeper.

"'Twan't no use turnin' back now. I ud lose the mar to a dead sartinty, if I didn't make the high ground; so I spoke to the critter to do her best, an' kep on. The poor beast didn't need any whippin'—she knew as well's I did meself thur wur danger, an' she wur a-doin' her darndest, an' no mistake. Still the water riz, an' kep a-risin', until it come clur up to her shoulder.

"I begun to git skeart in airnest. We wan't more 'n half acrosst, an' I seed if it riz much more we ud hav to swim for it. I wan't far astray about that. The minnit arter it seemed to deepen suddintly, as if thur wur a hollow in the parairy: I heerd the mar give a loud gouf, an' then go down, till I wur up to the waist. She riz agin the next minnit, but I could tell from the smooth ridin' that she wur off o' the bottom. She wur swimmin', an' no mistake.

"At fust I thort o' headin' her back to the shanty; an' I drew her round with that intent; but turn her which way I would, I found she could no longer touch bottom.

"I guess, strengers, I wur in a quandairy about then. I 'gun to think that both my own an' my mar's time wur come in airnest, for I hed no idee that the critter could iver swim to the other side, 'specially with me on her back, an' purticklarly as at that time these hyur ribs had a sight more griskin upon 'em than they hev now.

"Wal, I wur about reckinin' up. I hed got to thinkin' o' Mary an' the childer, and the old shanty in the Mississippi, an' a heap o' things that I hed left unsettled, an' that now come into my mind to trouble me. The mar wur still plungin' ahead; but I seed she wur sinkin' deeper an' deeper an' fast loosin' her strength, an' I knew she couldn't hold out much longer.

"I thort at this time that if I got off o' her back, an' tuk hold o' the tail, she mout manage a leetle hotter. So I slipped backwards over her hips, an' grupped the long hair. It did do some good, for she swum higher; but we got mighty slow through the water, an' I hed but leetle behopes we should reach land.

"I wur towed in this way about a quarter o' a mile, when I spied somethin' floatin' on the water a leetle ahead. It hed growed considerably darker; but thur wur still light enough to show me that the thing wur a log.

"An idee now entered my brain-pan, that I mout save meself by takin' to the log. The mar ud then have a better chance for herself; an' maybe, when eased o' draggin' my carcass, that wur a-keepin' her back, she mout make footin' somewhur. So I waited till she got a leetle closter; an' then, lettin' go o' her tail, I clasped the log, an' crawled on to it.

"The mar swum on, appeerintly 'ithout missin' me. I seed her disappear through the darkness; but I didn't as much as say good-bye to her, for I wur afeard that my voice mout bring her back agin', an' she mout strike the log with her hoofs, an' whammel it about. So I lay quiet, an' let her hev her own way.

"I wan't long on the log till I seed it wur a-driftin', for thur wur a current in the water that set tol'uble sharp acrosst the parairy. I hed crawled up at one eend, an' got stride-legs; but as the log dipped considerable, I wur still over the hams in the water.

"I thort I mout be more comfortable towards the middle, an' wur about to pull the thing more under me, when all at once I seed thur wur somethin' clumped up on t'other eend o' the log.

"'Twan't very clur at the time, for it had been a-growin' cloudier ever since I left the shanty, but 'twur clur enough to show me that the thing wur a varmint: what sort, I couldn't tell. It mout be a bar, an' it mout not; but I had my suspects it wur eyther a bar or a painter.

"I wan't left long in doubt about the thing's gender. The log kep makin' circles as it drifted, an' when the varmint kim round into a different light, I caught a glimp o' its eyes. I knew them eyes to be no bar's eyes: they wur painter's eyes, an' no mistake.

"I reckin, strengers, I felt very queery jest about then. I didn't try to go any nearer the middle o' the log; but instead of that, I wriggled back until I wur right plum on the eend of it, an' could git no further.

"Thur I sot for a good long spell 'ithout movin' hand or foot. I dasen't make a motion, as I wur afeard it mout tempt the varmint to attackt me.

"I hed no weepun but my knife; I hed let go o' my rifle when I slid from the mar's back, an' it hed gone to the bottom long since. I wan't in any condition to stand a tussle with the painter nohow; so I 'wur determined to let him alone as long's he ud me.

"Wal, we drifted on for a good hour, I guess, 'ithout eyther o' us stirrin'. We sot face to face; an' now an' then the current ud set the log in a sort o' up-an'-down motion, an' then the painter an' I kep bowin' to each other like a pair o' bob-sawyers. I could see all the while that the varmint's eyes wur fixed upon mine, an' I never tuk mine from hisn; I know'd 'twur the only way to keep him still.

"I wur jest prospectin' what ud be the eendin' o' the business, when I seed we wur a-gettin' closter to the timmer: 'twan't more 'n two miles off, but 'twur all under water 'ceptin' the tops o' the trees. I wur thinkin' that when the log shed float in among the branches, I mout slip off, an' git my claws upon a tree, 'ithout sayin anythin' to my travellin' companion.

"Jest at that minnit somethin' appeared dead ahead o' the log. It wur like a island; but what could hev brought a island thur? Then I recollects that I hed seed a piece o' high ground about that part o' the parairy—a sort o' mound that hed been made by Injuns, I s'pose. This, then, that looked like a island, wur the top o' that mound, sure enough.

"The log wur a-driftin' in sich a way that I seed it must pass within twenty yards o' the mound. I determined then, as soon as we shed git alongside, to put out for it, an' leave the painter to continue his voyage 'ithout me.

"When I fust sighted the island I seed somethin' that; hed tuk for bushes. But thur wan't no bushes on the mound—that I knowd.

"Howsomdever, when we got a leetle closter, I diskivered that the bushes wur beests. They wur deer; for I spied a pair o' buck's horns atween me an' the sky. But thur wur a somethin' still bigger than a deer. It mout be a hoss, or it mout be an Opelousa ox, but I thort it wur a hoss.

"I wur right about that, for a horse it wur, sure enough, or rayther I shed say, a *mar*, an' that mar no other than my ole crittur!

"Arter partin' company, she hed turned with the current; an', as good luck ud hev it, hed swum in a beeline for the island, an' thur she stood lookin' as slick as if she hed been greased.

"The log hed by this got nigh enough, as I kalklated; an', with as little rumpus as possible, I slipped over the eend an' lot go my hold o' it. I wan't right spread in the water, afore I heerd a plump, an' lookin' round a bit, I seed the painter hed left the log too, an' tuk to the water.

"At fust, I thort he wur arter me; an' I drawed my knife with one hand, while I swum with the other. But the painter didn't mean fight that time. He made but poor swimmin' himself, an' appeared glad enough to get upon dry groun' 'ithout molestin' me; so we swum on side by side, an' not a word passed atween us.

"I didn't want to make a race o' it; so I let him pass me, rayther than that he should fall behind, an' get among my legs.

"Of coorse, he landed fust; an' I could hear by the stompin' o' hoofs, that his suddint appearance hed kicked up a jolly stampede among the critters upon the island. I could see both deer and mar dancing all over the groun', as if Old Nick himself hed got among 'em.

"None o' 'em, howsomdever, thort o' takin' to the water. They hed all hed enough o' that, I guess.

"I kep a leetle round, so as not to land near the painter; an' then, touchin' bottom, I climbed quietly up on the mound. I hed hardly drawed my drippin' carcass out o' the water, when I heerd a loud squeal, which I knew to be the whigher o' my ole mar; an' jest at that minnit the critter kim runnin' up, an' rubbed her nose agin my shoulder. I tuk the halter in my hand, an' sidling round a leetle, I jumped upon her back, for I still wur in fear o' the painter; an' the mar's back appeared to me the safest place about, an' that wan't very safe, eyther.

"I now looked all round to see what new company I hed got into. The day wur jest breakin', an' I could distinguish a leetle better every minnit. The top o' the mound which, wur above water wan't over half an acre in size, an' it wur as clur o' timmer as any other part o' the parairy, so that I could see every inch o' it, an' everythin' on it as big as a tumble-bug.

"I reckin, strengers, that you'll hardly believe me when I tell you the concatenation o' varmints that wur then an' thur caucused together. I could hardly believe my own eyes when I seed sich a gatherin', an' I thort I hed got aboard o' Noah's Ark. Thur wur—listen, strengers—fust my ole mar an' meself, an' I wished both o' us anywhur else, I reckin—then thur wur the painter, yur old acquaintance—then thur wur four deer, a buck an' three does. Then kim a catamount; an' arter him a black bar, a'most as big as a buffalo. Then thur wur a 'coon an' a 'possum, an' a kupple o' grey wolves, an' a swamp rabbit, an', darn the thing! a stinkin' skunk. Perhaps the last wan't the most dangerous varmint on the groun', but it sartintly wur the most disagreeableest o' the hul lot, for it smelt only as a cussed polecat kin smell.

"I've said, strengers, that I wur mightily tuk by surprise when I fust seed this curious clanjamfrey o' critters; but I kin tell you I wur still more dumbfounded when I seed thur behaveyur to one another, knowin' thur different naturs as I did. Thur wur the painter lyin' clost up to the deer—its nat'ral prey; an' thur wur the wolves too; an' thur wur the catamount standin' within three feet o' the 'possum an' the swamp rabbit; an' thur wur the bar an' the cunnin' old 'coon; an' thur they all wur, no more mindin' one another than if they hed spent all thur days together in the same penn.

"'Twur the oddest sight I ever seed, an' it remembered me o' bit o' Scripter my ole mother hed often read from a book called the Bible, or some sich name—about a lion that wur so tame he used to squat down beside a lamb, 'ithout layin' a claw upon the innocent critter.

"Wal, stranger, as I'm sayin', the hul party behaved in this very way. They all appeared down in the mouth, an' badly skeart about the water; but for all that, I hed my fears that the painter or the bar—I wan't afeard o' any o' the others—mout git over thur fright afore the flood fell; an' thurfore I kept as quiet as any one o' them during the hul time I wur in thur company, an' stayin' all the time clost by the mar. But neyther bar nor painter showed any savage sign the hul o' the next day, nor the night that follered it.

"Strengers, it ud tire you wur I to tell you all the movements that tuk place among these critters durin' that long day an' night. Ne'er a one o' 'em laid tooth or claw on the other. I wur hungry enough meself, and ud a liked to hev taken a steak from the buttocks o' one o' the deer, but I dasen't do it. I wur afeard to break the peace, which mout a led to a general shindy.

"When day broke, next mornin' arter, I seed that the flood wur afallin'; and as soon as it wur shallow enough, I led my mar quietly into the water, an' climbin' upon her back, tuk a silent leave o' my companions. The water still tuk my mar up to the flanks, so that I knew none o' the varmint could follow 'ithout swimmin', an' ne'er a one seemed inclined to try a swim.

"I struck direct for my neighbour's shanty, which I could see about three mile off, an', in a hour or so, I wur at his door. Thur I didn't stay long, but borrowin' an extra gun which he happened to hev, an' takin' him along with his own rifle, I waded my mar back to the island. We found the game not exactly as I hed left it. The fall o' the flood hed given the painter, the cat, an' the wolves courage. The swamp rabbit an' the 'possum wur clean gone—all but bits o' thur wool—an' one o' the does wur better 'n half devoured.

"My neighbour tuk one side, an' I the other, an' ridin' clost up, we surrounded the island.

"I plugged the painter at the fust shot, an' he did the same for the bar. We next layed out the wolves, an' arter that cooney, an' then we tuk our time about the deer—these last and the bar bein' the only valley'ble things on the island. The skunk we kilt last, as we didn't want the thing to stink us off the place while we wur a-skinnin' the deer.

"Arter killin' the skunk, we mounted an' left, of coorse loaded with our bar-meat an' venison.

"I got my rifle arter all. When the flood went down, I found it near the middle of the parairy, half buried in the sludge.

"I saw I hed built my shanty in the wrong place; but I soon looked out a better location, an' put up another. I hed all ready in the spring, when I went back to Massissippi, an' brought out Mary and the two young uns."

The singular adventure of old Ike illustrates a point in natural history that, as soon as the trapper had ended, became the subject of conversation. It was that singular trait in the character of predatory animals, as the cougar, when under circumstances of danger. On such occasions fear seems to influence them so much as to completely subdue their ferocity, and they will not molest other animals sharing the common danger, even when the latter are their natural and habitual prey. Nearly every one of us had observed this at some time or other; and the old naturalist, as well as the hunter-guides, related many incidents confirming the strange fact. Humboldt speaks of an instance observed by him on the Orinoco, where the fierce jaguar and some other creatures were seen quietly and peacefully floating together on the same log—all more or less frightened at their situation!

Ike's story had very much interested the doctor, who rewarded him with a "nip" from the pewter flask; and, indeed, on this occasion the flask was passed round, as the day had been one of unusual interest. The killing of a cougar is a rare adventure, even in the wildest haunts of the backwoods' country.

Chapter Nine
The Musquash

Our next day's march was unenlivened by any particular incident. We had left behind us the heavy timber, and again travelled through the "oak openings." Not an animal was started during the whole day, and the only one seen was a muskrat that took to the water of a small creek and escaped. This occurred at the spot where we had halted for our night-camp, and after the tents were pitched, several of the party went "rat-hunting." The burrow of a family of these curious little animals was discovered in the bank, and an attempt was made to dig them out, but without success. The family proved to be "not at home."

The incident, however, brought the muskrat on the *tapis*.

The "muskrat" of the States is the musquash of the fur-traders (*Fiber sibethicus*). He is called muskrat, from his resemblance to the common rat, combined with the musky odour which he emits from glands situated near the anus. Musquash is said to be an Indian appellative—a strange coincidence, as the word, "musk" is of Arabic origin, and "musquash" would seem a compound of the French *musque,* as the early Canadian fur-traders were French, or of French descent, and fixed the nomenclature of most of the fur-bearing animals of that region. Naturalists have used the name of "Musk Beaver" on account of the many points of resemblance which this animal bears to the true beaver (*Castor fiber*). Indeed, they seem to be of the same genus, and so Linnaeus classed them; but later systematists have separated them, for the purpose, I should fancy, not of simplifying science, but of creating the impression that they themselves were very profound observers.

The teeth—those great friends of the closet naturalist, which help him to whole pages of speculation—have enabled him to separate the beaver from the musquash, although the whole history and habits of these creatures prove them to be congeners, as much as a mastiff is the congener of a greyhound—indeed, far more. So like are they in a general sense, that the Indians call them "cousins."

In form the muskrat differs but little from the beaver. It is a thick, rounded, and flat-looking animal, with blunt nose, short ears almost buried in the fur, stiff whiskers like a cat, short legs and neck, small dark eyes, and sharply-clawed feet. The hinder ones are longest, and are half-webbed. Those of the beaver are full-webbed.

There is a curious fact in connection with the tails of these two animals. Both are almost naked of hair, and covered with "scales," and both are flat. The tail of the beaver, and the uses it makes of this appendage, are things known to every one. Every one has read of its trowel-shape and use, its great breadth, thickness, and weight, and its resemblance to a cricket-bat. The tail of the muskrat is also naked, covered with scales, and compressed or flattened; but instead of being horizontally so, as with the beaver, it is the reverse; and the thin edges are in a vertical plane. The tail of the former, moreover, is not of the trowel-shape, but tapers like that of the common rat. Indeed, its resemblance to the house-rat is so great as to render it a somewhat disagreeable object to look upon.

Tail and all, the muskrat is about twenty inches in length; and its body is about half as big as that of a beaver. It possesses a strange power of contracting its body, so as to make it appear about half its natural size, and to enable it to pass through a chink that animals of much smaller dimensions could not enter.

Its colour is reddish-brown above, and light-ash underneath. There are eccentricities, however, in this respect. Specimens have been found quite black, as also mixed and pure white. The fur is a soft, thick down, resembling that of the beaver, but not quite so fine. There are long rigid hairs, red-coloured, that overtop the fur; and these are also sparely scattered over the tail.

The habits of the muskrat are singular—perhaps not less so than those of his "cousin" the beaver, when you strip the history of the latter of its many exaggerations. Indeed the former animal, in the domesticated state, exhibits much greater intelligence than the latter.

Like the beaver, it is a water animal, and is only found where water exists; never among the dry hills. Its "range" extends over the whole continent of North America, wherever "grass grows and water runs." It is most probable it is an inhabitant of the Southern Continent, but the natural history of that country is still but half told.

Unlike the beaver, the race of the muskrat is not likely soon to become extinct. The beaver is now found in America, only in the remotest parts of the uninhabited wilderness. Although formerly an inhabitant of the Atlantic States, his presence there is now unknown; or, if occasionally met with, it is no longer in the beaver dam, with its cluster of social domes, but only as a solitary creature, a "terrier beaver," ill-featured, shaggy in coat, and stunted in growth.

The muskrat, on the contrary, still frequents the settlements. There is hardly a creek, pond, or watercourse, without one or more families having an abode upon its banks. Part of the year the muskrat is a social animal; at other seasons it is solitary. The male differs but little from the female, though he is somewhat larger, and better furred.

In early spring commences the season of his loves. His musky odour is then strongest, and quite perceptible in the neighbourhood of his haunt. He takes a wife, to whom he is for ever after faithful; and it is believed the connection continues to exist during life. After the "honeymoon" a burrow is made in the bank of a stream or pond; usually in some solitary and secure spot by the roots of a tree, and always in such a situation that the rising of the water cannot reach the nest which is constructed within. The entrance to this burrow is frequently under water, so that it is difficult to discover it. The nest within is a bed of moss or soft grasses. In this the female brings forth five or six "cubs," which she nourishes with great care, training them to her own habits. The male takes no part in their education; but during this period absents himself, and wanders about alone. In autumn the cubs are nearly full-grown, and able to "take care of themselves." The "old father" now joins the family party, and all together proceed to the erection of winter quarters. They forsake the "home of their nativity," and build a very different sort of a habitation. The favourite site for their new house, is a swamp not likely to freeze to the bottom, and if with a stream running through it, all the better. By the side of this stream, or often on a little islet in the midst, they construct a dome-shaped pile, hollow within, and very much like the house of the beaver. The materials used are grass and mud, the latter being obtained at the bottom of the swamp or stream. The entrance to this house is subterranean, and consists of one or more galleries debouching under the water. In situations where there is danger of inundation, the floor of the interior is raised higher, and frequently terraces are made to admit of a dry seat, in case the ground-floor should get flooded. Of course there is free egress and ingress at all times, to permit the animal to go after its food, which consists of plants that grow in the water close at hand.

The house being completed, and the cold weather having set in, the whole family, parents and all, enter it, and remain there during the winter, going out only at intervals for necessary purposes. In spring they desert this habitation and never return to it.

Of course they are warm enough during winter while thus housed, even in the very coldest weather. The heat of their own bodies would make them so, lying as they do, huddled together, and sometimes on top of one another, but the mud walls of their habitations are a foot or more in thickness, and neither frost nor rain can penetrate within.

Now, a curious fact has been observed in connection with the houses of these creatures. It shows how nature has adapted them to the circumstances in which they may be placed. By philosophers it is termed "instinct"; but in our opinion it is the same sort of instinct which enables Mr Hobbs to pick a "Chubb" lock. It is this:—

In southern climates—in Louisiana, for instance—the swamps and rivers do not freeze over in winter. There the muskrat does not construct such houses as that described, but is contented all the year with his burrow in the banks. He can go forth freely and seek his food at all seasons.

In the north it is different. There for months the rivers are frozen over with thick ice. The muskrat could only come out under the ice, or above it. If the latter, the entrance of his burrow would betray him, and men with their traps, and dogs, or other enemies, would easily get at him. Even if he had also a water entrance, by which he might escape upon the invasion of his burrow, he would drown for want of air. Although an amphibious animal, like the beaver and otter, he cannot live altogether under water, and must rise at intervals to take breath. The running stream in winter does not perhaps furnish him with his favourite food—the roots and stems of water-plants. These the swamp affords to his satisfaction; besides, it gives him security from the attacks of men and preying animals, as the wolverine and fisher. Moreover, his house in the swamp cannot be easily approached by the hunter—man—except when the ice becomes very thick and strong. Then, indeed, is the season of peril for the muskrat, but even then he has loopholes of escape. How cunningly this creature adapts itself to its geographical situation! In the extreme north—in the hyperborean regions of the Hudson's Bay Company—lakes, rivers, and even springs freeze up in winter. The shallow marshes become solid ice, congealed to their very bottoms. How is the muskrat to get under water there? Thus, then, he manages the matter:—

Upon deep lakes, as soon as the ice becomes strong enough to bear his weight, he makes a hole in it, and over this he constructs his dome-shaped habitation, bringing the materials up through the hole, from the bottom of the lake. The house thus formed sits prominently upon the ice. Its entrance is in the floor—the hole which has already been made—and thus is kept open during the whole season of frost, by the care and watchfulness of the inmates, and by their passing constantly out and in to seek their food—the water-plants of the lake.

This peculiar construction of the muskrat's dwelling, with its water-passage, would afford all the means of escape from its ordinary enemies—the beasts of prey—and, perhaps, against these alone nature has instructed it to provide. But with all its cunning it is, of course, outwitted by the superior ingenuity of its enemy—man.

The food of the muskrat is varied. It loves the roots of several species of *nymphae*, but its favourite is *calamus* root (*calamus* or *acorus aromaticus*). It is known to eat shell-fish, and heaps of the shells of fresh-water muscles (*unios*) are often found near its retreat. Some assert that it eats fish, but the same assertion is made with regard to the beaver. This point is by no means clearly made out; and the closet naturalists deny it, founding their opposing theory, as usual, upon the teeth. For my part, I have but little faith in the "teeth," since I have known horses, hogs, and cattle greedily devour both fish, flesh, and fowl.

The muskrat is easily tamed, and becomes familiar and docile. It is very intelligent, and will fondly caress the hand of its master. Indians and Canadian settlers often have them in their houses as pets; but there is so much of the rat in their appearance, and they emit such a disagreeable odour in the spring, as to prevent them from becoming general favourites. They are difficult to cage up, and will eat their way out of a deal box in a single night. Their flesh, although somewhat musky, is eaten by the Indians and white hunters, but these gentry eat almost everything that "lives, breathes, and moves." Many Canadians, however, are fond of the flesh.

It is not for its flesh that the muskrat is so eagerly hunted. Its fur is the important consideration. This is almost equal to the fur of the beaver in the manufacture of hats, and sells for a price that pays the Indians and white trappers for the hardships they undergo in obtaining it. It is, moreover, used in the making of boas and muffs, as it somewhat resembles the fur of the pine marten or American sable (*Mustela martes*), and on account of its cheapness is sometimes passed off for the latter. It is one of the regular articles of the Hudson's Bay Company's commerce, and thousands of muskrat skins are annually obtained. Indeed, were it not that the animal is prolific and difficult to capture, its species would soon suffer extermination.

The mode of taking it differs from that practised in trapping the beaver. It is often caught in traps set for the latter, but such a "catch" is regarded in the light of a misfortune, as until it is taken out the trap is rendered useless for its real object. As an amusement it is sometimes hunted by dogs, as the otter is, and dug out of its burrow; but the labour of laying open its deep cave is ill repaid by the sport. The amateur sportsman frequently gets a shot at the muskrat while passing along the bank near its haunts, and almost as frequently misses his aim. The creature is too quick for him, and dives almost without making a bubble. Of course once in the pool it is seen no more.

Many tribes of Indians hunt the muskrat both for its flesh and skin. They have peculiar modes of capturing it, of one of which the hunter-naturalist gave an account. A winter which he had spent at a fort in the neighbourhood of a settlement of Ojibways gave him an opportunity of witnessing this sport in perfection.

Chapter Ten
A Rat-Hunt

"Chingawa," began he, "a Chippeway or Ojibway Indian, better-known at the fort as 'Old Foxey,' was a noted hunter of his tribe. I had grown to be a favourite with him. My well-known passion for the chase was a sort of masonic link between us; and our friendship was farther augmented by the present of an old knife for which I had no farther use. The knife was not worth twopence of sterling money, but it made 'Old Foxey' my best friend; and all his 'hunter-craft'—the gatherings of about sixty winters—became mine.

"I had not yet been inducted into the mystery of 'rat-catching,' but the season for that 'noble' sport at length arrived, and the Indian hunter invited me to join him in a muskrat hunt.

"Taking our 'traps' on our shoulders, we set out for the place where the game was to be found. This was a chain of small lakes or ponds that ran through a marshy valley, some ten or twelve miles distant from the fort.

"The traps, or implements, consisted of an ice-chisel with a handle some five feet in length, a small pickaxe, an iron-pointed spear barbed only on one side, with a long straight shaft, and a light pole about a dozen feet in length, quite straight and supple.

"We had provided ourselves with a small stock of eatables as well as materials for kindling a fire—but no Indian is ever without these. We had also carried our blankets along with us, as we designed to make a night of it by the lakes.

"After trudging for several hours through the silent winter forests, and crossing both lakes and rivers upon the ice, we reached the great marsh. Of course, this, as well as the lakes, was frozen over with thick ice; we could have traversed it with a loaded waggon and horses without danger of breaking through.

"We soon came to some dome-shaped heaps rising above the level of the ice. They were of mud, bound together with grass and flags, and were hardened by the frost. Within each of these rounded heaps, Old Foxey knew there was at least half a dozen muskrats—perhaps three times that number—lying snug and warm and huddled together.

"Since there appeared no hole or entrance, the question was how to get at the animals inside. Simply by digging until the inside should be laid open, thought I. This of itself would be no slight labour. The roof and sides, as my companion informed me, were three feet in thickness; and the tough mud was frozen to the hardness and consistency of a fire-brick. But after getting through this shell, where should we find the inmates? Why, most likely, we should not find them at all after all this labour. So said my companion, telling me at the same time that there were subterranean, or rather subaqueous, passages, by which the muskrats would be certain to make off under the ice long before he had penetrated near them.

"I was quite puzzled to know how we should proceed. Not so Old Foxey. He well knew what he was about, and pitching his traps down by one of the 'houses,' commenced operations.

"The one he had selected stood out in the lake, some distance from its edge. It was built entirely upon the ice; and, as the hunter well knew, there was a hole in its floor by which the animals could get into the water at will. How then was he to prevent them from escaping by the hole, while we removed the covering or roof? This was what puzzled me, and I watched his movements with interest.

"Instead of digging into the house, he commenced cutting a hole in the ice with his ice-chisel about two feet from the edge of the mud. That being accomplished, he cut another, and another, until four holes were pierced forming the corners of a square, and embracing the house of the muskrat within.

"Leaving this house, he then proceeded to pierce a similar set of holes around another that also stood out on the open lake. After that he went to a third one, and this and then a fourth were prepared in a similar manner.

"He now returned to the first, this time taking care to tread lightly upon the ice and make as little stir as possible. Having arrived there, he took out from his bag a square net made of twisted deer-thongs, and not much, bigger than a blanket. This in a most ingenious manner he passed under the ice, until its four corners appeared opposite the four holes; where, drawing them through, he made all last and 'taut' by a line stretching from one corner to the other.

"His manner of passing the net under the ice I have pronounced ingenious. It was accomplished by reeving a line from hole to hole by means of the long slender pole already mentioned. The pole, inserted through one of the holes, conducted the line, and was itself conducted by means of two forked sticks that guided it, and pushed it along to the other holes. The line being attached to the comers of the net made it an easy matter to draw the latter into its position.

"All the details of this curious operation were performed with a noiseless adroitness which showed 'Old Foxey' was no novice at 'rat-catching.'

"The net being now quite taut along the lower surface of the ice, must of course completely cover the hole in the 'floor.' It followed, therefore, that if the muskrats were 'at home,' they were now 'in the trap.'

"My companion assured me that they would be found inside. The reason why he had not used the net on first cutting the holes, was to give any member of the family that had been frightened out, a chance of returning; and this he knew they would certainly do, as these creatures cannot remain very long under the water.

"He soon satisfied me of the truth of his statement. In a few minutes, by means of the ice-chisel and pickaxe, we had pierced the crust of the dome; and there, apparently half asleep,—because dazzled and blinded by the sudden influx of light—were no less than eight full-grown musquashes!

"Almost before I could count them, Old Foxey had transfixed the whole party, one after the other, with his long spear.

"We now proceeded to another of the houses, at which the holes had been cut. There my companion went through a similar series of operations; and was rewarded by a capture of six more 'rats.'

"In the third of the houses only three were found.

"On opening a fourth, a singular scene met our eyes. There was but, one muskrat alive, and that one seemed to be nearly famished to death. Its body was wasted to mere 'skin and bone;' and the animal had evidently been a long time without food. Beside it lay the naked skeletons of several small animals that I at once saw were those of the muskrat. A glance at the bottom of the nest explained all. The hole, which in the other houses had passed through the ice, and which we found quite open, in this one was frozen up. The animals had neglected keeping it open, until the ice had got too thick for them to break through; and then, impelled by the cravings of hunger, they had preyed upon each other, until only one, the strongest, survived!

"I found upon counting the skeletons that no less than eleven had tenanted this ice-bound prison.

"The Indian assured me that in seasons of very severe frost such an occurrence is not rare. At such times the ice forms so rapidly, that the animals—perhaps not having occasion to go out for some hours—find themselves frozen in; and are compelled to perish of hunger, or devour one another!

"It was now near night—for we had not reached the lake until late in the day—and my companion proposed that we should leave farther operations until the following morning. Of course I assented to the proposal, and we betook ourselves to some pine-trees that grew on a high bank near the shore, where we had determined to pass the night.

"There we kindled a roaring fire of pine-knots; but we had grown very hungry, and I soon found that of the provisions I had brought, and upon which I had already dined, there remained but a scanty fragment for supper. This did not trouble my companion, who skinned several of the 'rats,' gave them a slight warming over the fire, and then ate them up with as much *goût* as if they had been partridges. I was hungry, but not hungry enough for that; so I sat watching him with some astonishment, and not without a slight feeling of disgust.

"It was a beautiful moonlight night, one of the clearest I ever remember. There was a little snow upon the ground, just enough to cover it; and up against the white sides of the hills could be traced the pyramidal outlines of the pines, with their regular gradations of dark needle-clothed branches. They rose on all sides around the lake, looking like ships with furled sails and yards square-set.

"I was in a reverie of admiration, when I was suddenly aroused by a confused noise, that resembled the howling and baying of hounds. I turned an inquiring look upon my companion.

"'Wolves!' he replied, unconcernedly, chawing away at his 'roast rat.'

"The howling sounded nearer and nearer; and then there was a rattling among dead trees, and the quickly-repeated 'crunch, crunch,' as of the hoofs of some animal breaking through frozen snow. The next moment a deer dashed past in full run, and took to the ice. It was a large buck, of the 'Caribou' or reindeer species (*Cervus tarandus*), and I could see that he was smoking with heat, and almost run down.

"He had hardly passed the spot when the howl again broke out in a continued strain, and a string of forms appeared from out the bushes. They were about a dozen in all; and they were going at full speed like a pack of hounds on the view. Their long muzzles, erect ears, and huge gaunt bodies, were outlined plainly against the snowy ground. I saw that they were wolves. They were white wolves, and of the largest species.

"I had suddenly sprung to my feet, not with the intention of saving the deer, but of assisting in its capture; and for this purpose I seized the spear, and ran out. I heard my companion, as I thought, shouting some caution after me; but I was too intent upon the chase to pay any attention to what he said. I had at the moment a distinct perception of hunger, and an indistinct idea of roast venison for supper.

"As I got down to the shore, I saw that the wolves had overtaken the deer, and dragged it down upon the ice. The poor creature made but poor running on the slippery track, sprawling at every bound; while the sharp claws of its pursuers enabled them to gallop over the ice like cats. The deer had, no doubt, mistaken the ice for water, which these creatures very often do, and thus become an easy prey to wolves, dogs, and hunters.

"I ran on, thinking that I would soon scatter the wolves, and rob them of their prey. In a few moments I was in their midst, brandishing my spear; but to my surprise, as well as terror, I saw that, instead of relinquishing the deer, several of them still held on it, while the rest surrounded me with open jaws, and eyes glancing like coals of fire.

"I shouted and fought desperately, thrusting the spear first at one and then at another; but the wolves only became more bold and fierce, incensed by the wounds I was inflicting.

"For several minutes I continued this unexpected conflict. I was growing quite exhausted; and a sense of terrible dread coming over me, had almost paralysed me, when the tall, dark form of the Indian, hurrying over the ice, gave me new courage; and I plied the spear with all my remaining strength, until several of my assailants lay pierced upon the ice. The others, now seeing the proximity of my companion with his huge ice-chisel, and frighted, moreover, by his wild Indian yells, turned tail and scampered off.

"Three of them, however, had uttered their last howl, and the deer was found close by—already half devoured!

"There was enough left, however, to make a good supper for both myself and my companion; who, although, he had already picked the bones of three muskrats, made a fresh attack upon the venison, eating of it as though he had not tasted food for a fortnight."

Chapter Eleven
Musquitoes and their Antidote

Our next day's journey brought us again into heavy timber—another creek bottom. The soil was rich and loamy, and the road we travelled was moist, and in some places very heavy for our waggon. Several times the latter got stalled in the mud, and then the whole party were obliged to dismount, and put their shoulders to the wheel. Our progress was marked by some noise and confusion, and the constant din made by Jake talking to his team, his loud sonorous "woha!" as they were obliged to halt, and the lively "gee-up—gee-up" as they moved on again—frighted any game long before we could come up with it. Of course we were compelled to keep by the waggon until we had made the passage of the miry flat.

We were dreadfully annoyed by the mosquitoes, particularly the doctor, of whose blood they seemed to be especially fond! This is a curious fact in relation to the mosquitoes—of two persons sleeping in the same apartment, one will sometimes be bitten or rather punctured, and half bled to death, while the other remains untouched! Is it the quality of the blood or the thickness of the skin that guides to this preference?

This point was discussed amongst us—the doctor taking the view that it was always a sign of good blood when one was more than usually subject to the attack of mosquitoes. He was himself an apt illustration of the fact. This statement of course produced a general laugh, and some remarks at the doctor's expense, on the part of the opponents of his theory. Strange to say, old Ike was fiercely assailed by the little blood-suckers. This seemed to be an argument against the doctor's theory, for in the tough skinny carcass of the old trapper, the blood could neither have been very plenteous nor delicate.

Most of us smoked as we rode along, hoping by that means to drive off the ferocious swarm, but although tobacco smoke is disagreeable to the mosquitoes, they cannot be wholly got rid of by a pipe or cigar. Could one keep a constant *nimbus* of the smoke around his face it might be effective, but not otherwise. A sufficient quantity of tobacco smoke will kill mosquitoes outright, as I have more than once proved by a thorough fumigation of my sleeping apartment.

These insects are not peculiar, as sometimes supposed, to the inter-tropical regions of America. They are found in great numbers even to the shores of the Arctic Sea, and as fierce and bloodthirsty as anywhere else—of course only in the summer season, when, as before remarked, the thermometer in these Northern latitudes mounts to a high figure. Their haunts are the banks of rivers, and particularly those of a stagnant and muddy character.

There is another singular fact in regard to them. Upon the banks of some of the South-American rivers, life is almost unendurable on account of this pest—the *"plaga de mosquitos,"* as the Spaniards term it—while upon other streams in the very same latitude musquitoes are unknown. These streams are what are termed *"rios negros,"* or black-water rivers—a peculiar class of rivers, to which many tributaries of the Amazon and Orinoco belong.

Our English comrade, who had travelled all over South America, gave us this information as we rode along. He stated, that he had often considered it a great relief, a sort of escape from purgatory, while on his travels he parted from one of the yellow or white water streams, to enter one of the *"rios negros."* Many Indian tribes settled upon the banks of the latter solely to get clear of the *"plaga de mosquitos."* The Indians who reside in the mosquito districts habitually paint their bodies, and smear themselves with oil, as a protection against their bites; and it is a common thing among the natives, when speaking of any place, to inquire into the "character" of its mosquitoes!

On some tributaries of the Amazon the mosquitoes are really a life torment, and the wretched creatures who inhabit such places frequently bury their bodies in the sand in order to get sleep! Even the pigments with which they anoint themselves are pierced by the poisoned bills of their tormentors.

Besançon and the Kentuckian both denied that any species of ointment would serve as a protection against mosquitoes. The doctor joined them in their denial. They asserted that they had tried everything that could be thought of—camphor, ether, hartshorn, spirits of turpentine, etcetera.

Some of us were of a different opinion, and Ike settled the point soon after in favour of the dissentients by a practical illustration. The old trapper, as before stated, was a victim to the fiercest attacks, as was manifested by the slapping which he repeatedly administered to his cheeks, and an almost constant muttering of bitter imprecations. He knew a remedy he said in a "sartint weed," if he could only "lay his claws upon it." We noticed that from time to time as he rode along his eyes swept the ground in every direction. At length a joyous exclamation told that he had discovered the "weed."

"Thur's the darned thing at last," muttered he, as he flung himself to the ground, and commenced gathering the stalks of a small herb that grew plentifully about. It was an annual, with leaves very much of the size and shape of young garden box-wood, but of a much brighter green. Of course we all knew well enough what it was, for there is not a village "common" in the Western United States that is not covered with it. It was the well-known "penny-royal" (*Hedcoma pulegioides*), not the English herb of that name, which is a species of *mentha*.

Redwood also leaped from his horse, and set to plucking the "weed." He too, from experience, knew its virtues.

We all drew bridle, watching the guides. Both operated in a similar manner. Having collected a handful of the tenderest tops, they rubbed them violently between their palms—rough and good for such service—and then passed the latter over the exposed skin of their necks and laces. Ike took two small bunches of the stalks, crushed them under his heel, and then stuck them beneath his cap, so that the ends hung down over his cheeks. This being done, he and his comrade mounted their horses and rode on.

Some of us—the hunter-naturalist, the Englishman, and myself— dismounted and imitated Ike—of course under a volley of laughter and "pooh-poohs" from Besançon, the Kentuckian, and the doctor; but we had not ridden two hundred paces until the joke changed sides. From that moment not a mosquito approached us, while our three friends were bitten as badly as ever.

In the end they were convinced, and the torment of the mosquitoes proving stronger than the fear of our ridicule, all three sprang out of their saddles, and made a rush at the next bed of penny-royal that came in sight.

Whether it is the highly aromatic odour of the penny-royal that keeps off these insects, or whether the juice when touched by them burns the delicate nerves of their feet I am unable to say. Certain it is they will not alight upon the skin which has been plentifully anointed with it. I have tried the same experiment often since that time with a similar result, and in fact have never since travelled through a mosquito country without a provision of the "essence of penny-royal." This is better than the herb itself, and can be obtained from any apothecary. A single drop or two spilled in the palm of the hand is sufficient to rub over all the parts exposed, and will often ensure sleep, where otherwise such a thing would be impossible. I have often lain with my face so smeared, and listened to the sharp hum of the mosquito as it approached, fancying that the next moment I should feel its tiny touch, as it settled down upon my cheek, or brow. As soon, however, as it came within the influence of the penny-royal I could hear it suddenly tack round and wing its way off again, until its disagreeable "music" was no longer heard.

The only drawback in the use of the penny-royal lies in the burning sensation which the fluid produces upon the skin; and this in a climate where the thermometer is pointing to 90 degrees is no slight disqualification of the remedy. The use of it is sometimes little better than "Hobbson's choice."

The application of it on the occasion mentioned restored the spirits of our party, which had been somewhat kept under by the continuous attacks of the mosquitoes, and a lively little incident that occurred soon after, viz. the hunt and capture of a raccoon, made us all quite merry.

Cooney, though a night prowler, is sometimes abroad during the day, but especially in situations where the timber is high, and the woods dark and gloomy. On the march we had come so suddenly upon this one, that he had not time to strike out for his own tree, where he would soon have hidden from us in its deep cavity. He had been too busy with his own affairs—the nest of a wild turkey upon the ground, under some brush and leaves, the broken eggs in which told of the delicious meal he had made. Taken by surprise—for the guides had ridden nearly on top of him—he galloped up the nearest tree, which fortunately contained neither fork nor cavity in which he could shelter himself; and a well-directed shot from Redwood's rifle brought him with a heavy "thump" back to the ground again.

We were all stirred up a little by this incident; in fact, the unusual absence of game rendered ever so trifling an occurrence an "event" with us. No one, however, was so pleased as the black waggoner Jake, whose eyes fairly danced in his head at the sight of a "coon." The "coon" to Jake was well-known game—natural and legitimate—and Jake preferred "roast coon" to fried bacon at any time. Jake knew that none of us would care to eat of his coonship. He was therefore sure of his supper; and the "varmint" was carefully deposited in the corner of the waggon.

Jake did not have it all to himself. The trappers liked fresh meat too, even "coon-meat;" and of course claimed their share. None of the rest of the party had any relish for such a fox-like carcass.

After supper, cooney was honoured with a description, and for many of the facts of his history we are indebted to Jake himself.

Chapter Twelve
The 'Coon, and his Habits

Foremost of all the wild creatures of America in point of being generally known is the raccoon (*Procyon lotor*). None has a wider geographical distribution, as its "range" embraces the entire Continent, from the Polar Sea to Terra del Fuego. Some naturalists have denied that it is found in South America. This denial is founded on the fact, that neither Ulloa nor Molina have spoken of it. But how many other animals have these crude naturalists omitted to describe? We may safely assert that the raccoon exists in South America, as well in the tropical forests of Guyana as in the colder regions of the Table Land—everywhere that there exists tree-timber. In most parts where the Spanish language is spoken, it is known as the "*zorro negro*," or black fox. Indeed, there are two species in South America, the common one (*Procyon lotor*), and the crab-eater (*Procyon cancrivorus*).

In North America it is one of the most common of wild animals. In all parts you may meet with it. In the hot lowlands of Louisiana—in the tropical "chapparals" of Mexico—in the snowy regions of Canada—and in the vernal valleys of California. Unlike the deer, the wild cat, and the wolverine, it is never mistaken for any other animal, nor is any animal taken for it. It is as well-known in America as the red fox is in England, and with a somewhat similar reputation.

Although there is a variety in colour and size, there is no ambiguity about species or genus. Wherever the English language is spoken, it has but one name, the "raccoon." In America, every man, woman and child knows the "sly ole 'coon."

This animal has been placed by naturalists in the family *Ursidae*, genus *Procyon*. Linnaeus made it a *bear*, and classed it with *Ursus*. It has, in our opinion, but little in common with the bear, and far more resembles the fox. Hence the Spanish name of "*zorro negro*" (black fox).

A writer quaintly describes it thus:—"The limbs of a bear, the body of a badger, the head of a fox, the nose of a dog, the tail of a cat, and sharp claws, by which it climbs trees like a monkey." We cannot admit the similarity of its tail to that of a cat. The tail of the raccoon is full and bushy, which is not true of the cat's tail. There is only a similarity in the annulated or banded appearance noticed in the tails of some cats, which in that of the raccoon is a marked characteristic.

The raccoon, to speak in round terms, is about the size of an English fox, but somewhat thicker and "bunchier" in the body. Its legs are short in proportion, and as it is *plantigrade* in the hind-feet, it stands and runs low, and cat-like. The muzzle is extremely pointed and slender, adapted to its habit of prying into every chink and corner, in search of spiders, beetles, and other creatures.

The general colour of the raccoon is dark brown (nearly black) on the upper part of the body, mixed with iron-grey. Underneath it is of a lighter hue. There is, here and there, a little fawn colour intermixed. A broad black band runs across the eyes and unites under the throat. This band is surrounded and sharply defined with a margin of greyish-white, which gives a unique expression to the "countenance" of the "'coon."

One of the chief beauties of this animal is its tail, which is characteristic in its markings. It exhibits twelve annulations or ring-bands, six black and six greyish-white, in regular alternation. The tip is black, and the tail itself is very full or "bushy." When the 'coon-skin is made into a cap—which it often is among hunters and frontiers-men—the tail is left to hang as a drooping plume; and such a head-dress is far from ungraceful. In some "settlements" the 'coon-skin cap is quite the fashion among the young "backwoodsmen."

The raccoon is an animal of an extremely amorous disposition; but there is a fact connected with the sex of this creature which is curious: the female is larger than the male. Not only larger, but in every respect a finer-looking animal. The hair, long on both, is more full and glossy upon the female, its tints deeper and more beautiful. This is contrary to the general order of nature. By those unacquainted with this fact, the female is mistaken for the male, and *vice versa*, as in the case of hawks and eagles.

The fur of the raccoon has long been an article of commerce, as it is used in making beaver hats; but as these have given place in most countries to the silk article, the 'coon-skin now commands but a small price.

The raccoon is a tree-climber of the first quality. It climbs with its sharp-curved claws, not by hugging, as is the case with the bear tribe. Its lair, or place of retreat, is in a tree—some hollow, with its entrance high up. Such trees are common in the great primeval forests of America. In this tree-cave it has its nest, where the female brings forth three, four, five, or six "cubs" at a birth. This takes place in early spring—usually the first week in April.

The raccoon is a creature of the woods. On the prairies and in treeless regions it is not known. It prefers heavy "timber," where there are huge logs and hollow trees in plenty. It requires the neighbourhood of water, and in connection with this may be mentioned a curious habit it has, that of plunging all its food into the water before devouring it. It will be remembered that the otter has a similar habit. It is from this peculiarity that the raccoon derives its specific name of *Lotor* (washer). It does not always moisten its morsel thus, but pretty generally. It is fond, moreover, of frequent ablutions, and no animal is more clean and tidy in its habits.

The raccoon is almost omnivorous. It eats poultry or wild fowls. It devours frogs, lizards, lame, and insects without distinction. It is fond of sweets, and is very destructive to the sugar-cane and Indian corn of the planter. When the ear of the maize is young, or, as it is termed, "in the milk," it is very sweet. Then the raccoon loves to prey upon it. Whole troops at night visit the corn-fields and commit extensive havoc. These mischievous habits make the creature many enemies, and in fact it has but few friends. It kills hares, rabbits, and squirrels when it can catch them, and will rob a bird's nest in the most ruthless manner. It is particularly fond of shell-fish; and the *unios*, with which many of the fresh-water lakes and rivers of America abound, form part of its food. These it opens as adroitly with its claws as an oyster-man could with his knife. It is partial to the "soft-shell" crabs and small tortoises common in the American waters.

Jake told us of a trick which the 'coon puts in practice for catching the small turtles of the creek. We were not inclined to give credence to the story, but Jake almost swore to it. It is certainly curious if true, but it smacks very much of Buffon. It may be remarked, however, that the knowledge which the plantation negroes have of the habits of the raccoon surpasses that of any mere naturalist. Jake boldly declares that the 'coon fishes for turtles! that it squats upon the bank of the stream, allowing its bushy tail to hang over into the water; that the turtles swimming about in search of food or amusement, spies the hairy appendage and lays hold of it; and that the 'coon, feeling the nibble, suddenly draws the testaceous swimmer upon dry land, and then "cleans out de shell" at his leisure!

The 'coon is often domesticated in America. It is harmless as a dog or cat except when crossed by children, when it will snarl, snap, and bite like the most crabbed cur. It is troublesome, however, where poultry is kept, and this prevents its being much of a favourite. Indeed, it is not one, for it is hunted everywhere, and killed—wherever this can be done—on sight.

There is a curious connection between the negro and the raccoon. It is not a tie of sympathy, but a kind of antagonism. The 'coon, as already observed, is the negro's legitimate game. 'Coon-hunting is peculiarly a negro sport. The negro is the 'coon's mortal enemy. He kills the 'coon when and wherever he can, and cats it too. He loves its "meat," which is pork-tasted, and in young 'coons palatable enough, but in old ones rather rank. This, however, our "darkie" friend does not much mind, particularly if his master be a "stingy old boss," and keeps him on rice instead of meat rations. The negro, moreover, makes an odd "bit" (twelve and a half cents) by the skin, which he disposes of to the neighbouring "storekeeper."

The 'coon-hunt is a "nocturnal" sport, and therefore does not interfere with the negro's regular labour. By right the night belongs to him, and he may then dispose of his time as he pleases, which he often does in this very way.

The negro is not, allowed to carry fire-arms, and for this reason the squirrel may perch upon a high limb, jerk its tail about and defy him; the hare may run swiftly away, and the wild turkey may tantalise him with its incessant "gobbling." But the 'coon can be killed without fire-arms. The 'coon can be overtaken and "treed." The negro is not denied the use of an axe, and no man knows better how to handle it than he. The 'coon, therefore, is his natural game, and much sport does he have in its pursuit. Nearly the same may be said of the opossum (*Didelphis Virginiana*); but the "'possum" is more rare, and it is not our intention now to describe that very curious creature. From both 'coon and 'possum does the poor negro derive infinite sport—many a sweet excitement that cheers his long winter nights, and chequers with brighter spots the dull and darksome monotony of his slave-life. I have often thought what a pity it would be if the 'coon and the opossum should be extirpated before slavery itself became extinct. I had often shared in this peculiar sport of the negro, and joined in a real 'coon-chase, but the most exciting of all was the first in which I had been engaged, and I proffered my comrades an account of it.

Chapter Thirteen
A 'Coon-Chase

"My 'coon-chase took place in Tennessee, where I was sojourning for some time upon a plantation. It was the first affair of the kind I had been present at, and I was somewhat curious as to the mode of carrying it on. My companion and inductor was a certain 'Uncle Abe,' a gentleman very much after the style and complexion of our own Jake here.

"I need not tell you, gentlemen, that throughout the Western States every neighbourhood has its noted 'coon-hunter. He is usually a wary old 'nigger,' who knows all the tricks and dodges of the 'coon. He either owns a dog himself, or has trained one of his master's, in that peculiar line. It is of little importance what breed the dog may be. I have known curs that were excellent ''coon-dogs.' All that is wanted is, that he have a good nose, and that he be a good runner, and of sufficient bulk to be able to bully a 'coon when taken. This a very small dog cannot do, as the 'coon frequently makes a desperate fight before yielding. Mastiffs, terriers, and half-bred pointers make the best ''coon-dogs.'

"Uncle Abe was the mighty hunter, the Nimrod of the neighbourhood in which I happened to be; and Uncle Abe's dog—a stout terrier—was esteemed the 'smartest 'coon-dog' in a circle of twenty miles. In going out with Uncle Abe, therefore, I had full confidence that I should see sport.

"On one side of the plantation was a heavily-timbered 'bottom', through which meandered a small stream, called, of course, a 'creek.' This bottom was a favourite *habitat* of the 'coons, as there were large trees growing near the water, many of which were hollow either in their trunks or some of their huge limbs. Moreover, there were vast trellises of vines extending from tree to tree; some of them, as the fox and muscadine (*Vitis Labrusca*), yielding sweet grapes, of which the raccoons are very fond.

"To this bottom, then, we directed our course, Abe acting as guide, and holding his dog, Pompo, in the leash Abe carried no other weapon than an axe, while I had armed myself with a double-barrel. Pompo knew as well as either of us the errand on which we were bent, as appeared from his flashing eyes and the impatient leaps which he now and then made to get free.

"We had to cross a large corn-field, a full half-mile in breadth, before we reached the woods. Between this and the timber was a zigzag fence—the common 'rail' fence of the American farmer. For some distance beyond the fence the timber was small, but farther on was the creek 'bottom,' where the 'coons were more likely to make their dwelling-place.

"We did not, however, proceed direct to the bottom. Abe knew better than that. The young corn was just then 'in the milk,' and the 'coon-hunter expected to find his game nearer the field. It was settled, therefore, that we should follow the line of the fence, in hopes that the dog would strike a fresh trail, leading either to or from the corn-field.

"It was now night—two hours after sundown. The 'coon-chase, I have already said, is a nocturnal sport. The raccoon does range by day, but rarely, and only in dark and solitary woods. He often basks by day upon high limbs, or the broken tops, of trees. I have shot several of his tribe while asleep, or sunning themselves in such situations. Perhaps before they knew their great enemy man, they were less nocturnal in their activity. We had a fine moonlight; but so far as a view of the chase was concerned, that would benefit us but little. During the hunt there is not much to be seen of either dog or 'coon, as it is always a scramble through trees and underwood. The dog trusts altogether to his nose, and the hunter to his ears; for the latter has no other guide save the yelp or bark of his canine assistant. Nevertheless, moonlight, or a clear night, is indispensable; without one or the other, it would be impossible to follow through the woods. A view of a 'coon-chase is a luxury enjoyed only by the bats and owls.

"Pompo was now let loose in the corn; while Abe and I walked quietly along the fence, keeping on different sides. Abe remained in the field for the purpose of handing over the dog, as the fence was high—a regular 'ten rail, with stalks and riders.' A 'coon could easily cross it, but not a dog, without help.

"We had not gone more than a hundred yards, when a quick sharp yelp from Pompo announced that he had come suddenly upon something in the corn-field.

"'A varmint!' cried Abe; and the next moment appeared the dog, running up full tilt among the maize plants and up to the fence. I could see some dark object before him, that passed over the rails with a sudden spring, and bounded into the timbers.

"'A varmint, massa!' repeated Abe, as he lifted the dog over, and followed himself.

"I knew that in Abe's vocabulary—for that night at least—a 'varmint' meant a 'coon; and as we dashed through the brushwood, following the dog, I felt all the excitement of a 'coon-chase.

"It was not a long one—I should think of about five minutes' duration; at the end of which time the yelp of the dog which had hitherto guided us, changed into a regular and continuous harking. On hearing this, Abe quietly announced—

"'The varmint am treed.'

"Our only thought now was to get to the tree as speedily as possible, but another thought entered our minds as we advanced; that was, what sort of a tree had the 'coon taken shelter in?

"This was an important question, and its answer involved the success or failure of our hunt. If a very large tree, we might whistle for the 'coon. Abe knew this well, and as we passed on, expressed his doubts about the result.

"The bark of Pompo sounded some hundred yards off, in the very heaviest of the bottom timber. It was not likely, therefore, that the 'coon had taken to a small tree, while there were large ones near at hand. Our only hope was that he had climbed one that was not 'hollow.' In that case we might still have a chance with the double-barrel and buck-shot. Abe had but little hope.

"'He hab reach him own tree, massa; an' that am sartin to be a big un wi' a hole near um top. Wagh! 'twar dat ar fence. But for de dratted fence ole Pomp nebber let um reach um own tree. Wagh!'

"From this I learned that one point in the character of a good 'coon-dog was speed. The 'coon runs well for a few hundred yards. He rarely strays farther from his lair. If he can beat his pursuer for this distance he is safe, as his retreat is always in a hollow tree of great size. There is no way of getting at him there, except by felling the tree, and this the most zealous 'coon-hunter would not think of attempting. The labour of cutting down such a tree would be worth a dozen 'coons. A swift dog, therefore, will overtake the raccoon, and force him to the nearest tree—often a small one, where he is either shaken off or the tree cut down. Sometimes the hunter climbs after and forces him to leap out, so as to fall into the very jaws of the watchful dog below.

"In Abe's opinion Pompo would have 'treed' his 'coon before reaching, the bottom, had not the fence interfered, but now—

"'Told ye so, massa!' muttered he, interrupting my thoughts. 'Look dar! dar's de tree—trunk thick as a haystack. Wagh!'

"I looked in the direction indicated by my companion. I saw Pompo standing by the root of a very large tree, looking upward, shaking his tail, and barking at intervals. Before I had time to make any farther observations Abe's voice again sounded in my ears.

"'Gollies! it am a buttonwood! Why, Pomp, ole fellur, you hab made a mistake—de varmint ain't dar, 'Cooney nebber trees upon buttonwood—nebber—you oughter know better'n dat, ole fool!'

"Abe's speech drew my attention to the tree. I saw that it was the American sycamore (*Platanus Occidentalis*), familiarly known by the trivial name, 'buttonwood,' from the use to which its wood is sometimes put. But why should the 'coon not 'tree' upon it, as well as any other? I put the question to my companion.

"'Cause, massa, its bark am slickery. De varmint nebber takes to 'im. He likes de oak, an' de poplum, an' de scaly-bark. Gosh! but he am dar!' continued Abe, raising his voice, and looking outward—'Look yonder, massa! He had climb by de great vine. Dat's right, Pomp! you am right after all, and dis nigga's a fool. Hee—up, ole dog! hee—up!'

"Following the direction in which Abe pointed, my eyes rested on a huge parasite of the lliana kind, that, rising out of the ground at some distance, slanted upward and joined the sycamore near its top. This had no doubt been the ladder by which the 'coon had climbed.

"This discovery, however, did not mend the matter as far as we were concerned. The 'coon had got into the buttonwood, fifty feet from the ground, where the tree had been broken off by the lightning or the wind, and where the mouth of a large cavity was distinctly visible by the light of the moon. The trunk was one of the largest, and it would have been sheer folly (so we concluded) to have attempted felling it.

"We left the spot without farther ado, and took our way back to the corn-field.

"The dog had now been silent for some time, and we were in hopes that another 'varmint' might have stolen into the corn.

"Our hopes were not doomed to disappointment. Pompo had scarcely entered the field when a second 'coon was sprung, which, like the other, ran directly for the fence and the woods.

"Pomp followed as fast as he could be flung over; and this 'coon was also 'treed' in a few minutes.

"From the direction of the barking, we calculated that it must be near where the other had escaped us; but our astonishment equalled our chagrin, when upon arriving at the spot, we found that both the 'varmints' had taken to the same tree!

"With some rather emphatic ejaculations we returned to the corn-field, and after a short while a third 'coon was raised, which, like the others, made of course for the timber.

"Pomp ran upon his trail with an angry yelping, that soon changed into the well-known signal that he had treed the game.

"We ran after through brush and brake, and soon came up with the dog. If our astonishment was great before, it was now beyond bounds. The identical buttonwood with its great parasite was before us, the dog barking at its foot! The third 'coon had taken shelter in its capacious cavity.

"'Wagh! massa!' ejaculated Abe, in a voice of terror, 'its de same varmint. It ain't no 'coon, it's de debil! For de lub o' God, massa, let's get away from here!'

"Of course I followed his advice, as to get at the 'coons was out of the question.

"We returned once more to the corn-field, but we found that we had at last cleared it of 'coons. It was still early, however, and I was determined not to give up the hunt until I had assisted in killing a 'coon. By Abe's advice, therefore, we struck into the woods with the intention of making a circuit where the trees were small. Some 'coon might be prowling there in search of birds' nests. So thought Abe.

"He was right in his conjecture. A fourth was started, and off went Pompo after him. In a few minutes the quick constant bark echoed back. This time we were sure, from the direction, in a new tree.

"It proved to be so, and such a small one that, on coming up, we saw the animal squatted upon the branches, not twenty feet from the ground.

"We were now sure of him, as we thought; and I had raised my gun to fire; when all at once, as if guessing my intent, the 'coon sprang into another tree, and then ran down to the ground and off again, with Pompo veiling in his track.

"Of course we expected that the dog would speedily tree him again, which after a few minutes he did, but this time in the heavy timber.

"We hastened forward, guided by the barking. To the extreme of my astonishment, and I fancy to the very extreme of Abe's terror, we again found ourselves at the foot of the buttonwood.

"Abe's wool stood on end. Superstition was the butt-end of his religion; and he not only protested, but I am satisfied that he believed, that all the four 'coons were one and the same individual, and that individual 'de debil.'

"Great 'coon-hunter as he was, he would now have gone home, if I had let him. But I had no thoughts of giving up the matter in that easy way. I was roused by the repeated disappointment. A new resolve had entered my mind. I was determined to get the 'coons out of the buttonwood, cost what it might. The tree must come down, if it should take us till morning to fell it.

"With this determination I caught hold of Abe's axe, and struck the first blow. To my surprise and delight the tree sounded hollow. I repeated the stroke. The sharp axe went crashing inwards. The tree was hollow to the ground; on the side where I had commenced chopping, it was but a shell.

"A few more blows, and I had made a hole large enough to put a head through. Felling such a tree would be no great job after all, and I saw that it would hardly occupy an hour. The tree must come down.

"Abe seeing me so resolute, had somewhat recovered his courage and his senses, and now laid hold of the axe. Abe was a 'first hand' at 'chopping,' and the hole soon gaped wider.

"'If de hole run clar up, massa,' said he, resting for a moment, 'we can smoke out de varmint—wid de punk and de grass here we can smoke out de debil himself. S'pose we try 'im, massa?'

"'Good!' cried I, catching at Abe's suggestion; and in a few minutes we had made a fire in the hole, and covered it with leaves, grass, and weeds.

"The smoke soon did its work. We saw it ooze out above at the entrance of the 'coon hole—at first in a slight filmy stream, and then in thick volumes. We heard a scraping and rattling within the hollow trunk, and a moment after a dark object sprang out upon the lliana, and ran a short way downward. Another followed, and another, and another, until a string of no less than six raccoons squatted along the parasite threatening to run downward!

"The scene that followed was indescribable. I had seized my gun, and both barrels were emptied in a 'squirrel's jump.' Two of the 'coons came to the ground, badly wounded. Pompo tackled another, that had run down the lliana, and was attempting to get off; while Abe with his axe clove the skull of a fourth, that had tried to escape in a similar manner.

"The other two ran back into the 'funnel,' but only to come out again just in time to receive a shot each from the reloaded gun, which brought both of them tumbling from the tree. We succeeded in bagging the whole family; and thus finished what Abe declared to be the greatest ''coon-chase on de record.'

"As it was by this time far in the night, we gathered up our game, and took the 'back track to hum.'"

Chapter Fourteen
Wild Hogs of the Woods

Next day while threading our way through a patch of oak forest—the ground covered thickly with fallen leaves—we were startled by a peculiar noise in front of us. It was a kind of bellows-like snort, exactly like that made by the domestic swine when suddenly affrighted.

Some of the party cried out "bear," and of course this announcement threw us all into a high state of excitement. Even the buffalo itself would be but secondary game, when a bear was upon the ground.

The "snuff" of the bear has a very considerable resemblance to that of terrified hogs, and even our guides were deceived. They thought it might be "bar" we had heard.

It proved we were all wrong. No wonder we fancied the noise resembled that made by hogs. The animal that uttered it was nothing else than a wild boar.

"What!" you will exclaim, "a wild boar in the forests of Missouri? Oh! a peccary I suppose."

No, not a peccary; for these creatures do not range so far north as the latitude of Missouri—not a wild boar, neither, if you restrict the meaning of the phrase to the true indigenous animal of that kind. For all that, it was a wild boar, or rather a boar *ran wild*. Wild enough and savage too it appeared, although we had only a glimpse of its shaggy form as it dashed into the thicket with a loud grunt. Half a dozen shots followed it. No doubt it was tickled with some of the "leaden hail" from the double-barrelled guns, but it contrived to escape, leaving us only the incident as a subject for conversation.

Throughout the backwoods there are large numbers of half-wild hogs, but they are usually the denizens of woods that are inclosed by a rail-fence, and therefore private property. One part of the year they are tamer, when a scarcity of food renders it necessary for them to approach the owner's house, and eat the corn placed for them in a well-known spot. At this season they answer to a call somewhat similar to the "milk oh!" of the London dairyman, but loud enough to be heard a mile or more through the woods. A traveller passing through the backwoods' settlements will often hear this singular call sounding afar off in the stillness of the evening.

These hogs pick up most of their subsistence in the forest. The "mast" of the beech-tree, the nut of the hickory, the fruit of the Chinquapin oak, the acorn, and many other seeds and berries, furnish them with food. Many roots besides, and grasses, contribute to sustain them, and they make an occasional meal off a snake whenever they can get hold of one. Indeed it may be safely asserted, that no other cause has contributed so much to the destruction of these reptiles, as the introduction of the domestic hog into the forests of America. Wherever a tract of woods has been used as the "run" of a drove of hogs, serpents of every kind become exceedingly scarce, and you may hunt through such a tract for weeks without seeing one. The hog seems to have the strongest antipathy to the snake tribe; without the least fear of them. When one of the latter is discovered by a hog, and no crevice in the rocks, or hollow log, offers it a shelter, its destruction is inevitable. The hog rushes to the spot, and, bounding forward, crushes the reptile under his hoof's. Should the first attempt not succeed, and the serpent glide away, the hog nimbly follows, and repeats his efforts until the victim lies helpless. The victor then goes to work with his powerful jaws, and quietly devours the prey.

The fondness of the hog for this species of food proves that in a state of nature it is partially a carnivorous animal. The peccary, which is the true representative of the wild hog in America—has the very same habit, and is well-known to be one of the most fatal enemies of the serpent tribe to be found among American animals.

The hog shows no fear of the snake. His thick hide seems to protect him. The "skin" of the rattle-snake or the "hiss" of the deadly "moccasin," are alike unheeded by him. He kills them as easily as he does the innocent "chicken snake" or the black constrictor. The latter often escapes from its dreaded enemy by taking to a bush or tree; but the rattle-snake and the moccasin are not tree-climbers, and either hide themselves in the herbage and dead leaves, or retreat to their holes.

It is not true that the hog eats the body of the snake he has killed, leaving the head untouched, and thus avoiding the poisoned fangs. He devours the whole of the creature, head and all. The venom of the snake, like the "curari" poison of the South-American Indians, is only effective when coming in contact with the blood. Taken internally its effects are innoxious—indeed there are those who believe it to be beneficial, and the curari is often swallowed as a medicine.

Most of this information about the half-wild hogs of the backwoods was given by our Kentucky comrade, who himself was the proprietor of many hundreds of them. An annual hog-hunt was part of the routine of his life. It was undertaken not merely for the sport of the thing—though that was by no means to be despised—and the season of the hog-hunting is looked forward to with pleasant anticipation by the domestics of the plantation, as well as a few select friends or neighbours who are invited to participate in it.

When the time arrives, the proprietor, with his pack of hounds, and accompanied by a party mounted and armed with rifles, enters the large tract of woodland—perhaps miles in extent, and in many places covered with cane-brakes, and almost impenetrable thickets of undergrowth. To such places the hogs fly for shelter, but the dogs can penetrate wherever hogs can go; and of course the latter are soon driven out, and forced into the more open ground, where the mounted men are waiting to receive them with a volley of bullets. Sometimes a keen pursuit follows, and the dogs in full cry are carried across the country, over huge logs, and through thickets and ravines, followed by the horsemen—just as if an old fox was the game pursued.

A large waggon with drivers and attendants follows the chase, and in this the killed are deposited, to be "hauled" home when the hunt is over.

This, however, often continues for several days, until all, or at least all the larger hogs, are collected and brought home, and then the sport terminates. The produce of the hunt sometimes amounts to hundreds— according to the wealth of the proprietor. Of course a scene of slaughtering and bacon-curing follows. A part of the bacon furnishes the "smoke-house" for home consumption during the winter; while the larger part finds its way to the great pork-market of Cincinnati.

The Kentuckian related to us a curious incident illustrating the instinct of the swinish quadruped; but which to his mind, as well as to ours, seemed more like a proof of a rational principle possessed by the animal. The incident he had himself been witness to, and in his own woodlands. He related it thus:—

"I had strayed into the woods in search of a wild turkey with nothing but my shot-gun, and having tramped about a good bit, I sat down upon a log to rest myself. I had not been seated live minutes when I heard a rustling among the dead leaves in front of me. I thought it might be deer, and raised my gun; but I was greatly disappointed on seeing some half dozen of my own hogs make their appearance, rooting as they went along.

"I paid no more heed to them at the time; but a few minutes after, my attention was again drawn to them, by seeing them make a sudden rush across a piece of open ground, as if they were in pursuit of something.

"Sure enough they were. Just before their snouts, I espied the long shining body of a black snake doing its best to get out of their way. In this it succeeded, for the next moment I saw it twisting itself up a pawpaw sapling, until it had reached the top branches, where it remained looking down at its pursuers.

"The snake may have fancied itself secure at the moment, and so thought I, at least so far as the hogs were concerned. I had made up my mind to be its destroyer myself, and was just about to sprinkle it with shot, when a movement on the part of one of the hogs caused me to hold back and remain quiet. I need not tell you I was considerably astonished to see the foremost of these animals seize the sapling in its jaws and jerk it about in a determined manner, as if with the intention of shaking off the snake! Of course it did not succeed in this, for the latter was wound around the branches, and it would have been as easy to have shaken off the bark.

"As you all know, gentlemen, the pawpaw—not the pawpaw (*Carica papaya*), but a small tree of the *anonas* or custard apple tribe, common in the woods of western America—is one of the softest and most brittle of our trees, and the hog seemed to have discovered this, for he suddenly changed his tactics, and instead of shaking at the sapling, commenced grinding it between his powerful jaws. The others assisted him, and the tree fell in a few seconds. As soon as the top branches touched the ground, the whole drove dashed forward at the snake; and in less than the time I take in telling it, the creature was crushed and devoured."

After hearing the singular tale, our conversation now returned to the hog we had just "jumped." All agreed that it must be some stray from the plantations that had wandered thus far from the haunts of men, for there was no settlement within twenty miles of where we then were.

Our trapper guides stated that wild hogs are frequently found in remote parts, and that many of them are not "strays," but have been "littered" and brought up in the forest. These are as shy and difficult to approach as deer, or any other hunted animals. They are generally of a small breed, and it is supposed that they are identical with the species found throughout Mexico, and introduced by the Spaniards.

Chapter Fifteen
Treed by Peccaries

Talking of these Spanish hogs naturally led us to the subject of the peccary—for this creature is an inhabitant only of those parts of North America which have been hitherto in possession of the Spanish race. Of the peccary (*dicotyles*), there are two distinct species known—the "collared," and the "white-lipped." In form and habits they are very similar to each other. In size and colour they differ. The "white-lipped" is the larger. Its colour is dark brown, nearly black, while that of the collared peccary is a uniform iron-grey, with the exception of the band or collar upon its shoulders.

The distinctive markings are, on the former species a greyish-white patch along the jaws, and on the other a yellowish-white belt, embracing the neck and shoulders, as a collar does a horse. These markings have given to each its specific name. They are farther distinguished, by the forehead of the white-lipped peccary being more hollowed or concave than that of its congener.

In most other respects these creatures are alike. Both feed upon roots, fruits, frogs, toads, lizards, and snakes. Both make their lair in hollow logs, or in caves among the rocks, and both are gregarious in their habits. In this last habit, however, they exhibit some difference. The white-lipped species associate in troops to the number of hundreds, and even as many as a thousand have been seen together; whereas the others do not live in such large droves, but are oftener met with in pairs. Yet this difference of habit may arise from the fact that in the places where both have been observed, the latter have not been so plentiful as the white-lipped species. As many as a hundred of the collared peccary have been observed in one "gang," and no doubt had there been more of them in the neighbourhood, the flock would have been still larger.

The white-lipped species does not extend to the northern half of the American Continent. Its *habitat* is in the great tropical forests of Guyana and Brazil, and it is found much farther south, being common in Paraguay. It is there known as the "vaquira," whence our word "peccary." The other species is also found in South America, and is distinguished as the "vaquira de collar" (collared peccary). Of course, they both have trivial Indian names, differing in different parts of the country. The former is called in Paraguay "Tagnicati," while the latter is the "Taytetou."

Neither species is so numerous as they were in former times. They have been thinned off by hunting—not for the value either of their flesh or their skins, not for the mere sport either, but on account of their destructive habits. In the neighbourhood of settlements they make frequent forays into the maize and mandioc fields, and they will lay waste a plantation of sugar-cane in a single night. For this reason it is that a war of extermination has long been waged against them by the planters and their dependents.

As already stated, it is believed that the white-lipped species is not found in North America. Probably it does exist in the forests of Southern Mexico. The natural history of these countries is yet to be thoroughly investigated. The Mexicans have unfortunately employed all their time in making revolutions. But a new period has arrived. The Panama railroad, the Nicaragua canal, and the route of Tehuantepec, will soon be open, when among the foremost who traverse these hitherto unfrequented regions, will be found troops of naturalists, of the Audubon school, who will explore every nook and corner of Central America. Indeed, already some progress has been made in this respect. The two species of peccaries, although so much alike never associate together, and do not seem to have any knowledge of a relationship existing between them. Indeed, what is very singular, they are never found in the same tract of woods. A district frequented by the one is always without the other.

The Collared Peccary is the species found in North America; and of it we more particularly speak. It is met with when you approach the more southern latitudes westward of the Mississippi River. In that great wing of the continent, to the eastward of this river, and now occupied by the United States, no such animal exists, nor is there any proof that it was ever known to exist there in its wild state. In the territory of Texas, it is a common animal, and its range extends westward to the Pacific, and south throughout the remainder of the Continent.

As you proceed westwards, the line of its range rises considerably; and in New Mexico it is met with as high as the 38rd parallel. This is just following the isothermal line, and proves that the peccary cannot endure the rigours of a severe winter climate. It is a production of the tropics and the countries adjacent.

Some naturalists assert that it is a forest-dwelling animal, and is never seen in open countries. Others, as Buffon, state that it makes its *habitat* in the mountains, never the low countries and plains; while still others have declared that it is never found in the mountains!

None of these "theories" appears to be the correct one. It is well-known to frequent the forest-covered plains of Texas, and Emory (one of the most talented of modern observers) reports having met with a large drove of peccaries in the almost treeless mountains of New Mexico. The fact is, the peccary is a wide "ranger," and frequents either plains or mountains wherever he can find the roots or fruits which constitute his natural food. The haunts he likes best appear to be the dry hilly woods, where he finds several species of nuts to his taste—such as the chinquapin (*Castanea pumila*), the pecan (*Juglans olivaformis*), and the acorns of several species of oak, with which the half-prairie country of western Texas abounds.

Farther than to eat their fruit, the forest trees are of no use to the peccary. He is not a climber, as he is a hoofed animal. But in the absence of rocks, or crevices in the cliffs, he makes his lair in the bottoms of hollow trees, or in the great cavities so common in half-decayed logs. He prefers, however, a habitation among rocks, as experience has no doubt taught him that it is a safer retreat both from hunters and fire.

The peccary is easily distinguished from the other forest animals by his rounded, hog-like form, and long, sharp snout. Although pig-shaped, he is extremely active and light in his movements. The absence of a tail—for that member is represented only by a very small protuberance or "knob" — imparts a character of lightness to his body. His jaws are those of the hog, and a single pair of tusks, protruding near the angles of the mouth, gives him a fierce and dangerous aspect. These tusks are seen in the old males or "boars." The ears are short, and almost buried in the long harsh hairs or bristles that cover the whole body, but which are much longer on the back. These, when erected or thrown forward—as is the case when the peccary is incensed—have the appearance of a stiff mane rising all along the neck, shoulders, and spine. At such times, indeed, the rigid, bristling coat over the whole body gives somewhat of a porcupine appearance to the animal.

The peccary, as already stated, is gregarious. They wander in droves of twenty, or sometimes more. This, however, is only in the winter. In the season of love, and during the period of gestation, they are met with only in pairs—a male and female. They are very true to each other, and keep close together.

The female produces two young at a litter. These are of a reddish-brown colour, and at first not larger than young puppies; but they are soon able to follow the mother through the woods; and then the "family party" usually consists of four.

Later in the season, several of these families unite, and remain together, partly perhaps from having met by accident, and partly for mutual protection; for whenever one of their number is attacked, all the drove takes part against the assailant, whether he be hunter, cougar, or lynx. As they use both their teeth, tusks, and sharp fore-hoofs with rapidity and effect, they become a formidable and dangerous enemy.

The cougar is often killed and torn to pieces by a drove of peccaries, that he has been imprudent enough to attack. Indeed, this fierce creature will not often meddle with the peccaries when he sees them in large numbers. He attacks only single ones; but their "grunting," which can be heard to the distance of nearly a mile, summons the rest, and he is surrounded before he is aware of it, and seized by as many as can get around him.

The Texan hunter, if afoot, will not dare to disturb a drove of peccaries. Even when mounted, unless the woods be open, he will pass them by without rousing their resentment. But, for all this, the animal is hunted by the settlers, and hundreds are killed annually. Their ravages committed upon the corn-fields make them many enemies, who go after them with a desire for wholesale slaughter.

Hounds are employed to track the peccary and bring it to bay, when the hunters ride up and finish the chase by their unerring rifles.

A flock of peccaries, when pursued, will sometimes take shelter in a cave or cleft of the rocks, one of their number standing ready at the mouth. When this one is shot by the hunter, another will immediately rush out and take its place. This too being destroyed, will be replaced by a third, and so on until the whole drove has fallen.

Should the hounds attack the peccary while by themselves, and without the aid and encouragement of the hunter, they are sure to be "routed," and some of their number destroyed. Indeed, this little creature, of not more than two feet in length, is a match for the stoutest bull-dog! I have myself seen a peccary (a caged one, too)—that had killed no less than six dogs of bull and mastiff breed—all of them considered fighting dogs of first-rate reputation.

The Kentuckian had a peccary adventure which had occurred to him while on an excursion to the new settlements of Texas. "It was my first introduction to these animals," began he, "and I am not likely soon to forget it. It gave me, among the frontier settlers of Texas, the reputation of a 'mighty hunter,' though how far I deserved that name you may judge for yourselves.

"I was for some weeks the guest of a farmer or 'planter,' who lived upon the Trinity Bottom. We had been out in the 'timber' several times, and had filled both bear, deer, and turkeys, but had not yet had the luck to fall in with the peccary, although we never went abroad without seeing their tracks, or some other indications of what my friend termed 'peccary sign.' The truth is, that these animals possess the sense of smell in the keenest degree; and they are usually hidden long before the hunter can see them or come near them. As we had gone without dogs, of course we were not likely to discover which of the nine hundred and ninety-nine hollow logs passed in a day, was the precise one in which the peccaries had taken shelter.

"I had grown very curious about these creatures. Bear I had often hunted—deer I had driven; and turkeys I had both trapped and shot. But I had never yet killed a peccary; in fact, had never seen one. I was therefore very desirous of adding the tusk of one of these wild boars to my trophies of the chase.

"My desire was gratified sooner than I expected, and to an extent I had never dreamt of; for in one morning—before tasting my breakfast—I caused no less than nineteen of these animals to utter their last squeak! But I shall give the details of this 'feat' as they happened.

"It was in the autumn season—the most beautiful season of the forest—when the frondage obtains its tints of gold, orange, and purple. I was abed in the house of my friend, but was awakened out of my sleep by the 'gobbling' of wild turkeys that sounded close to the place.

"Although there was not a window in my room, the yellow beams streaming in through the chinks of the log wall told me that it was after 'sun-up.'

"I arose, drew on my garments and hunting-habiliments, took my rifle, and stole out. I said nothing to any one, as there was no one—neither 'nigger' nor white man—to be seen stirring about the place. I wanted to steal a march upon my friend, and show him how smart I was by bagging a fat young 'gobbler' for breakfast.

"As soon as I had got round the house, I saw the turkeys—a large 'gang' of them. They were out in an old corn-field, feeding upon such of the seeds as had been dropped in the corn-gathering. They were too far off for my gun to reach them, and I entered among the corn-stalks to get near them.

"I soon perceived that they were feeding towards the woods, and that they were likely to enter them at a certain point. Could I only reach that point before them, reflected I, I should be sure of a fair shot. I had only to go back to the house and keep around the edge of the field, where there happened to be some 'cover.' In this way I should be sure to 'head' them—that is, could I but reach the woods in time.

"I lost not a moment in setting out; and, running most of the way, I reached the desired point.

"I was now about a mile from my friend's house—for the corn-field was a very large one—such as you may only see in the great plantations of the far western world. I saw that I had 'headed' the turkeys, with some time to spare; and choosing a convenient log, I sat down to await their coming. I placed myself in such a situation that I was completely hidden by the broad green leaves of some bushy trees that grew over the log.

"I had not been in that position over a minute I should think, when a slight rustling among the leaves attracted my attention. I looked, and saw issuing from under the rubbish the long body of a snake. As yet, I could not see its tail, which was hidden by the grass; but the form of the head and the peculiar chevron-like markings of the body, convinced me it was the 'Banded Rattle-snake.' It was slowly gliding out into some open ground, with the intention of crossing to a thicket upon the other side. I had disturbed it from the log, where it had no doubt been sunning itself; and it was now making away from me.

"My first thought was to follow the hideous reptile, and kill it; but reflecting that if I did so I should expose myself to the view of the turkeys, I concluded to remain where I was, and let it escape.

"I watched it slowly drawing itself along—for this species makes but slow progress—until it was near the middle of the glade, when I again turned my attention to the birds that had now advanced almost within range of my gun.

"I was just getting ready to fire, when a strange noise, like the grunt of a small pig, sounded in my ears from the glade, and again caused me to look in that direction. As I did so, my eyes fell upon a curious little animal just emerging from the bushes. Its long, sharp snout—its pig-like form—the absence of a tail—the high rump, and whitish band along the shoulders, were all marks of description which I remembered. The animal could be no other than a peccary.

"As I gazed upon it with curious eyes, another emerged from the bushes, and then another, and another, until a good-sized drove of them were in sight.

"The rattle-snake, on seeing the first one, had laid his head flat upon the ground; and evidently terrified, was endeavouring to conceal himself in the grass. But it was a smooth piece of turf, and he did not succeed. The peccary had already espied him; and upon the instant his hinder parts were raised to their full height, his mane became rigid, and the hair over his whole body stood erect, radiating on all sides outwards. The appearance of the creature was changed in an instant, and I could perceive that the air was becoming impregnated with a disagreeable odour, which the incensed animal emitted from its dorsal gland. Without stopping longer than a moment, he rushed forward, until he stood within three feet of the body of the snake.

"The latter, seeing he could no longer conceal himself, threw himself into a coil, and stood upon his defence. His eyes glared with a fiery lustre: the skir-r-r of his rattles could be heard almost incessantly; while with his upraised head he struck repeatedly in the direction of his enemy.

"These demonstrations brought the whole drove of peccaries to the spot, and in a moment a circle of them had formed around the reptile, that did not know which to strike at, but kept launching out its head recklessly in all directions. The peccaries stood with their backs highly arched and their feet drawn up together, like so many angry cats, threatening and uttering shrill grunts. Then one of them, I think the first that had appeared, rose suddenly into the air, and with his four hoofs held close together, came pounce down upon the coiled body of the snake. Another followed in a similar manner, and another, and another, until I could see the long carcase of the reptile unfolded, and writhing over the ground.

"After a short while it lay still, crushed beneath their feet. The whole squad then seized it in their teeth, and tearing it to pieces, devoured it almost instantaneously.

"From the moment the peccaries had appeared in sight, I had given up all thoughts about the turkeys. I had resolved to send my leaden messenger in quite a different direction. Turkeys I could have at almost any time; but it was not every day that peccaries appeared. So I 'slewed' myself round upon the log, raised my rifle cautiously, 'marked' the biggest 'boar' I could see in the drove, and fired.

"I heard the boar squeak (so did all of them), and saw him fall over, either killed or badly wounded. But I had little time to tell which, for the smoke had hardly cleared out of my eyes, when I perceived the whole gang of peccaries, instead of running away, as I had expected, coming full tilt towards me.

"In a moment I was surrounded by a dark mass of angry creatures, leaping wildly at my legs, uttering shrill grunts, and making their teeth crack like castanets.

"I ran for the highest part of the log, but this proved no security. The peccaries leaped upon it, and followed. I struck with the butt of my clubbed gun, and knocked them off; but again they surrounded me, leaping upward and snapping at my legs, until hardly a shred remained of my trousers.

"I saw that I was in extreme peril, and put forth all my energies. I swept my gun wildly around me; but where one of the fierce brutes was knocked over, another leaped into his place, as determined as he. Still I had no help for it, and I shouted at the top of my voice, all the while battling with desperation.

"I still kept upon the highest point of the log, as there they could not all come around me at once; and I saw that I could thus better defend myself. But even with this advantage, the assaults of the animals were so incessant, and my exertions in keeping them off so continuous, that I was in danger of falling into their jaws from very exhaustion.

"I was growing weak and wearied—I was beginning to despair for my life—when on winding my gun over my head in order to give force to my blows, I felt it strike against something behind me. It was the branch of a tree, that stretched over the spot where I was standing.

"A new thought came suddenly into my mind. Could I climb the tree? I knew that they could not, and in the tree I should be safe.

"I looked upward; the branch was within reach. I seized upon it and brought it nearer. I drew a long breath, and with all the strength that remained in my body sprang upward.

"I succeeded in getting upon the limb, and the next moment I had crawled along it, and sat close in by the trunk. I breathed freely—I was safe.

"It was some time before I thought of anything else than resting myself. I remained a full half-hour before I moved in my perch. Occasionally I looked down at my late tormentors. I saw that instead of going off, they were still there. They ran around the root of the tree, leaping up against its trunk, and tearing the bark with their teeth. They kept constantly uttering their shrill, disagreeable grunts; and the odour, resembling the smell of musk and garlic, which they emitted from their dorsal glands, almost stifled me. I saw that they showed no disposition to retire, but, on the contrary, were determined to make me stand siege.

"Now and then they passed out to where their dead comrade lay upon the grass, but this seemed only to bind their resolution the faster, for they always returned again, grunting as fiercely as ever.

"I had hopes that my friend would be up by this time, and would come to my rescue; but it was not likely neither, as he would not 'miss' me until I had remained long enough to make my absence seem strange. As it was, that would not be until after night, or perhaps far in the next day. It was no unusual thing for me to wander off with my gun, and be gone for a period of at least twenty hours.

"I sat for hours on my painful perch—now looking down at the spiteful creatures beneath—now bending my eyes across the great corn-field, in hopes of seeing some one. At times the idea crossed my mind, that even upon the morrow I might not be missed!

"I might perish with hunger, with thirst—I was suffering from both at the moment—or even if I kept alive, I might become so weak as not to be able to hold on to the tree. My seat was far from being an easy one. The tree was small—the branch was slender. It was already cutting into my thighs. I might, in my feebleness, be compelled to let it go, and then—.

"These reflections were terrible; and as they came across my mind, I shouted to the highest pitch of my voice, hoping I should be heard.

"Up to this time I had not thought of using my gun, although clinging to it instinctively. I had brought it with me into the tree. It now occurred to me to fire it, in hopes that my friend or some one might hear the report.

"I balanced myself on the branch as well as I could, and loaded it with powder. I was about to fire it off in the air, when it appeared to me that I might just as well reduce the number of my enemies. I therefore rammed down a ball, took aim at the forehead of one, and knocked him over.

"Another idea now arose in my mind, and that was, that I might serve the whole gang as I had done this one. His fall had not frightened them in the least; they only came nearer, throwing up their snouts and uttering their shrill notes—thus giving me a better chance of hitting them.

"I repeated the loading and firing. Another enemy the less.

"Hope began to return. I counted my bullets, and held my horn up to the sun. There were over twenty bullets, and powder sufficient. I counted the peccaries. Sixteen still lived, with three that I had done for.

"I again loaded and fired—loaded and fired—loaded and fired. I aimed so carefully each time, that out of all I missed only one shot.

"When the firing ceased, I dropped down from my perch in the midst of a scene that resembled a great slaughter-yard. Nineteen of the creatures lay dead around the tree, and the ground was saturated with their blood!

"The voice of my friend at this moment sounded in my ears, and turning, I beheld him standing, with hands uplifted and eyes as large as saucers.

"The 'feat' was soon reported through the settlement, and I was looked upon for the time as the greatest hunter in the 'Trinity Bottom.'"

Chapter Sixteen
A Duck-Shooting Adventure

During our next day's journey we again fell in with flocks of the wild pigeon, and our stock was renewed. We were very glad of this, as we were getting tired of the dry salt bacon, and another "pot-pie" from Lanty's *cuisine* was quite welcome. The subject of the pigeons was exhausted, and we talked no more about them. Ducks were upon the table in a double sense, for during the march we had fallen in with a brood of the beautiful little summer ducks (*Anas sponsa*), and had succeeded in shooting several of them. These little creatures, however, did not occupy our attention, but the far more celebrated species known as the "canvas-back" (*Anas vallisneria*).

Of the two dozen species of American wild-ducks, none has a wider celebrity than that known as the canvas-back; even the eider-duck is less thought of, as the Americans care little for beds of down. But the juicy, fine-flavoured flesh of the canvas-back is esteemed by all classes of people; and epicures prize it above that of all other winged creatures, with the exception, perhaps, of the reed-bird or rice-hunting, and the prairie-hen. These last enjoy a celebrity almost if not altogether equal. The prairie-hen, however, is the *bon morceau* of western epicures; while the canvas-back is only to be found in the great cities of the Atlantic. The reed-bird—in the West Indies called "ortolan"—is also found in the same markets with the canvas-back. The flesh of all three of these birds—although the birds themselves are of widely-different families—is really of the most delicious kind; it would be hard to say which of them is the greatest favourite.

The canvas-back is not a large duck, rarely exceeding three pounds in weight. Its colour is very similar to the pochard of Europe: its head is a uniform deep chestnut, its breast black; while the back and upper parts of the wings present a surface of bluish-grey, so lined and mottled as to resemble—though very slightly—the texture of canvas: hence the trivial name of the bird.

Like most of the water-birds of America, the canvas-back is migratory. It proceeds in spring to the cold countries of the Hudson's Bay territory, and returns southward in October, appearing in immense flocks along the

Atlantic shores. It does not spread over the fresh-water lakes of the United States, but confines itself to three or four well-known haunts, the principal of which is the great Chesapeake Bay. This preference for the Chesapeake Bay is easily accounted for, as here its favourite food is found in the greatest abundance. Hound the mouths of the rivers that run into this bay, there are extensive shoals of brackish water; these favour the growth of a certain plant of the genus *vallisneria*—a grass-like plant, standing several feet out of the water, with deep green leaves, and stems, and having a white and tender root. On this root, which is of such a character as to have given the plant, the trivial name of "wild celery," the canvas-back feeds exclusively; for wherever it is not to be found, neither does the bird make its appearance. Diving for it, and bringing it up in its bill, the canvas-back readily breaks off the long lanceolate leaves, which float off, either to be eaten by another species—the pochard—or to form immense banks of wrack, that are thrown up against the adjacent shores.

It is to the roots of the wild celery that the flesh of the canvas-back owes its esteemed flavour, causing it to be in such demand that very often a pair of these ducks will bring three dollars in the markets of New York and Philadelphia. When the finest turkey can be had for less than a third of that sum, some idea may be formed of the superior estimation in which the web-footed favourites are held.

Of course, shooting the canvas-back duck is extensively practised, not only as an amusement, but as a professional occupation. Various means are employed to slaughter these birds: decoys by means of dogs, duck boats armed with guns that resemble infernal-machines, and disguises of every possible kind. The birds themselves are extremely shy; and a shot at them is only obtained by great ingenuity, and after considerable dodging. They are excellent divers; and when only wounded, almost always make good their escape. Their shyness is overcome by their curiosity. A dog placed upon the shore, near where they happen to be, and trained to run backwards and forwards, will almost always seduce them within shot. Should the dog himself not succeed, a red rag wrapped around his body, or tied to his tail, will generally bring about the desired result. There are times, however, when the ducks have been much shot at, that even this decoy fails of success.

On account of the high price the canvas-backs bring in the market, they are pursued by the hunters with great assiduity, and are looked upon as a source of much profit. So important has this been considered, that in the international treaties between the States bordering upon the Chesapeake, there are several clauses or articles relating to them that limit the right of shooting to certain parties. An infringement of this right, some three or four years ago, led to serious collisions between the gunners of Philadelphia and

Baltimore. So far was the dispute carried, that schooners armed, and filled with armed men, cruised for some time on the waters of the Chesapeake, and all the initiatory steps of a little war were taken by both parties. The interference of the general government prevented what would have proved, had it been left to itself, a very sanguinary affair.

It so chanced that I had met with a rather singular adventure while duck-shooting on the Chesapeake Bay, and the story was related thus: "I was staying for some days at the house of a friend—a planter—who lived near the mouth of a small river that runs into the Chesapeake. I felt inclined to have a shot at the far-famed canvas-backs. I had often eaten of these birds, but had novel shot one, or even seen them in their natural *habitat*. I was, therefore, anxious to try my hand upon them, and I accordingly set out one morning for that purpose.

"My friend lived upon the bank of the river, some distance above tidewater. As the wild celery grows only in brackish water—that is, neither in the salt sea itself nor yet in the fresh-water rivers—I had to pass down the little stream a mile or more before I came to the proper place for finding the ducks. I went in a small skiff, with no other companion than an ill-favoured cur-dog, with which I had been furnished, and which was represented to me as one of the best 'duck-dogs' in the country.

"My friend having business elsewhere, unfortunately could not upon that day give me his company; but I knew something of the place, and being *au fait* in most of the dodges of duck-hunting, I fancied I was quite able to take care of myself.

"Floating and rowing by turns, I soon came in sight of the bay and the wild celery fields, and also of flocks of water-fowl of different species, among which I could recognise the pochards, the canvas-backs, and the common American widgeon.

"Seeking a convenient place near the mouth of the stream, I landed; and, tying the skiff to some weeds, proceeded in search of a cover. This was soon found—some bushes favoured me; and having taken my position, I set the dog to his work. The brute, however, took but little notice of my words and gestures of encouragement, I fancied that he had a wild and frightened look, but I attributed this to my being partially a stranger to him; and was in hopes that, as soon as we became better acquainted, he would work in a different manner.

"I was disappointed, however, as, do what I might, he would not go near the water, nor would he perform the trick of running to and fro which I had been assured by my friend he would be certain to do. On the contrary, he cowered among the bushes, near where I had stationed myself, and seemed unwilling to move out of them. Two or three times, when I dragged him forward, and motioned him toward the water, he rushed back again, and ran under the brushwood.

"I was exceedingly provoked with this conduct of the dog, the more so that a flock of canvas-backs, consisting of several thousands, was seated upon the water not more than half a mile from the shore. Had my dog done his duty, I have no doubt they might have been brought within range; and, calculating upon this, I had made sure of a noble shot. My expectations, however, were defeated by the waywardness of the dog, and I saw there was no hope of doing anything with him.

"Having arrived at this conclusion, after some hours spent to no purpose, I rose from my cover, and marched back to the skiff. I did not even motion the wretched cur to follow me; and I should have rowed off without him, risking the chances of my friend's displeasure, but it pleased the animal himself to trot after me without invitation, and, on arriving at the boat, to leap voluntarily into it.

"I was really so provoked with the brute, that I felt much inclined to pitch him out, again. My vexation, however, gradually left me; and I stood up in the skiff, turning over in my mind what course I should pursue next.

"I looked toward the flock of canvas-backs. It, was a tantalising sight. They sat upon the water as light as corks, and as close together as sportsman could desire for a shot. A well-aimed discharge could not have failed to kill a score of them at least.

"Was there no way of approaching them? This question I had put to myself for the twentieth time without being able to answer it to my satisfaction.

"An idea at length flitted across my brain. I had often approached common mallards by concealing my boat under branches or furze, and then floating down upon them, impelled either by the wind or the current of a stream. Might not this also succeed with the canvas-backs?

"I resolved upon making the experiment. The flock was in a position to enable me to do so. They were to the leeward of a sedge of the *vallisneria*. The wind would carry my skiff through this; and the green bushes with which I intended to disguise it would not be distinguished from the sedge, which was also green.

"The thing was feasible. I deemed it so. I set about cutting some leafy branches that grew near, and trying them along the gunwales of my little craft. In less than half an hour, I pushed her from the shore; and no one at a distance would have taken her for aught else than a floating raft of brushwood.

"I now pulled quietly out until I had got exactly to windward of the ducks, at about half a mile's distance from the edge of the flock. I then took in the paddles, and permitted the skiff to glide before the wind. I took the precaution to place myself in such a manner that I was completely hidden, while through the branches I commanded a view of the surface on any side I might wish to look.

"The bushes acted as a sail, and I was soon drifted down among the plants of the wild celery. I feared that this might stay my progress, as the breeze was light, and might not carry me through. But the sward, contrary to what is usual, was thin at the place where the skiff had entered, and I felt, to my satisfaction, that I was moving, though slowly, in the right direction.

"I remember that the heat annoyed me at the time. It was the month of November; but it was that peculiar season known as 'Indian summer', and the heat was excessive—not under 90 degrees, I am certain. The shrubbery that encircled me prevented a breath of air from reaching my body; and the rays of the noonday sun fell almost vertically in that southern latitude, scorching me as I lay along the bottom of the boat. Under other circumstances, I should not have liked to undergo such a roasting; but with the prospect of a splendid shot before me, I endured it as best I could.

"The skiff was nearly an hour in pushing its way through the field of *vallisneria*, and once or twice it remained for a considerable time motionless. A stronger breeze, however, would spring up, and then the sound of the reeds rubbing the sides of the boat would gratefully admonish me that I was moving ahead.

"I saw, at length, to my great gratification, that I was approaching the selvage of the sedge, and, moreover, that the flock itself was moving, as it were, to meet me! Many of the birds were diving and feeding in the direction of the skiff.

"I lay watching them with interest. I saw that the canvas-backs were accompanied by another species of a very different colour from themselves: this was the American widgeon. It was a curious sight to witness the constant warfare that was carried on between these two species of birds. The widgeon is but a poor diver, while the canvas-back is one of the very best. The widgeon, however, is equally fond of the roots of the wild celery with his congener; but he has no means of obtaining them except by robbing the latter. Being a smaller and less powerful bird, he is not able to do this openly; and it was curious to observe the means by which he effected his purpose. It was as follows: When the canvas-back descends, he must perforce remain some moments under water. It requires time to seize hold of the plant, and pluck it up by the roots. In consequence of this, he usually reaches the surface in a state of half-blindness, holding the luscious morsel in his bill. The widgeon has observed him going down; and, calculating to a nicety the spot where he will reappear, seats himself in readiness. The moment the other emerges, and before he can fully recover his sight or his senses, the active spoliator makes a dash, seizes the celery in his horny mandibles, and makes off with it as fast as his webbed feet can propel him. The canvas-back, although chagrined at being plundered in this impudent manner, knows that pursuit would be idle, and, setting the root down as lost, draws a fresh breath, and dives for another. I noticed in the flock a continual recurrence of such scenes.

"A third species of birds drew my attention. These were the pochards, or, as they are termed by the gunners of the Chesapeake, 'red-heads.' These creatures bear a very great resemblance to the canvas-backs, and can hardly be distinguished except by their bills: those of the former being concave along the upper surface, while the bills of the canvas-backs exhibit a nearly straight line.

"I saw that the pochards did not interfere with either of the other species, contenting themselves with feeding upon what neither of the others cared for—the green leaves of the *vallisneria*, which, after being stripped of their roots, were floating in quantities on the surface of the water. Yet these pochards are almost as much prized for the table as their cousins the canvas-backs; and, indeed, I have since learnt that they are often put off for the latter by the poulterers of New York and Philadelphia. Those who would buy a real canvas-back should know something of natural history. The form and colour of the bill would serve as a criterion to prevent their being deceived. In the pochard, the bill is of a bluish colour; that of the canvas-back is dark green; moreover, the eye of the pochard is yellow, while that of its congener is fiery red.

"I was gratified in perceiving that I had at last drifted within range of a thick clump of the ducks. Nothing now remained but to poke my gun noiselessly through the bushes, set the cocks of both barrels, take aim, and fire.

"It was my intention to follow the usual plan—that is, fire one barrel at the birds while sitting, and give them the second as they rose upon the wing. This intention was carried out the moment after; and I had the gratification of seeing some fifteen or twenty ducks strewed over the water, at my service. The rest of the flock rose into the heavens, and the clapping of their wings filled the air with a noise that resembled thunder.

"I say that there appeared to have been fifteen or twenty killed; how many I never knew: I never laid my hands upon a single bird of them. I became differently occupied, and with a matter that soon drove canvas-backs, and widgeons, and pochards as clean out of my head as if no such creatures had ever existed.

"While drifting through the sedge, my attention had several times been attracted by what appeared to be strange conduct on the part of my canine companion. He lay cowering in the bottom of the boat near the bow, and half covered by the bushes; but every now and then he would start to his feet, look wildly around, utter a strange whimpering, and then resume his crouching attitude. I noticed, moreover, that at intervals he trembled as if he was about to shake out his teeth. All this had caused me wonder—nothing more. I was too much occupied in watching the game, to speculate upon causes; I believed, if I formed any belief on the subject, that these manoeuvres were caused by fear; that the cur had never been to sea, and that he was now either sea-sick or sea-scared.

"This explanation had hitherto satisfied me, and I had thought no more upon the matter. I had scarcely delivered my second barrel, however, when my attention was anew attracted to the dog; and this time was so arrested, that in one half-second I thought of nothing else. The animal had arisen, and stood within three feet of me, whining hideously. His eyes glared upon me with a wild and unnatural expression, his tongue lolled out, and saliva fell copiously from his lips. *The dog was mad*!

"I saw that the dog was mad, as certainly as I saw the dog. I had seen mad dogs before, and knew the symptoms well. It was hydrophobia of the most dangerous character.

"Fear, quick and sudden, came over me. Fear is a tame word; horror I should call it; and the phrase would not be too strong to express my sensations at that moment. I knew myself to be in a situation of extreme peril, and I saw not the way out of it. Death—death painful and horrid—appeared to be nigh, appeared to confront me, glaring from out the eyes of the hideous brute.

"Instinct had caused me to put myself in an attitude of defence. My first instinct was a false one. I raised my gun, at the same moment manipulating the lock, with the design of cocking her. In the confusion of terror, I had even forgotten that both barrels were empty, that I had just scattered their contents in the sea.

"I thought of re-loading; but a movement of the dog towards me showed that that would be a dangerous experiment; and a third thought or instinct directed me to turn the piece in my hand, and defend myself, if necessary, with the butt. This instinct was instantly obeyed, and in a second's time I held the piece clubbed and ready to strike.

"I had retreated backward until I stood in the stern of the skiff. The dog had hitherto lain close up to the bow, but after the shots, he had sprung up and taken a position nearer the centre of the boat. In fact, he had been within biting distance of me before I had noticed his madness. The position into which I had thus half involuntarily thrown myself, offered me but a trifling security.

"Any one who has ever rowed an American skiff will remember that these little vessels are 'crank' to an extreme degree. Although boat-shaped above, they are without keels, and a rude step will turn them bottom upward in an instant. Even to stand upright in them, requires careful balancing; but to fight a mad dog in one without being bitten, would require the skill and adroitness of an acrobat. With all my caution, as I half stood, half crouched in the stern, the skiff rocked from side to side, and I was in danger of being pitched out. Should the dog spring at me, I knew that any violent exertion to fend him off would either cause me to be precipitated into the water, or would upset the boat—a still more dreadful alternative.

"These thoughts did not occupy half the time I have taken to describe them. Short, however, as that time was in actual duration, to me it seemed long enough, for the dog still held a threatening attitude, his forepaws resting upon one of the seats, while his eyes continued to glare upon me with a wild and uncertain expression.

"I remained for some moments in fearful suspense. I was half paralysed with terror, and uncertain what action it would be best to take. I feared that any movement would attract the fierce animal, and be the signal for him to spring upon me. I thought of jumping out of the skiff into the water. I could not wade in it. It was shallow enough—not over five feet in depth, but the bottom appeared to be of soft mud. I might sink another foot in the mud. No; I could not have waded. The idea was dismissed.

"To swim to the shore? I glanced sideways in that direction: it was nearly half a mile distant. I could never reach it, cumbered with my clothes. To have stripped these off, would have tempted the attack. Even could I have done so, might not the dog follow and seize me in the water? A horrible thought!

"I abandoned all hope of escape, at least that might arise from any active measures on my part. I could do nothing to save myself; my only hope lay in passively awaiting the result.

"Impressed with this idea, I remained motionless as a statue; I moved neither hand nor foot from the attitude I had first assumed; I scarcely permitted myself to breathe, so much did I dread attracting the farther attention of my terrible companion, and interrupting the neutrality that existed.

"For some minutes—they seemed hours—this state of affairs continued. The dog still stood up, with his forepaws raised upon the bench; the oars were among his feet. In this position he remained, gazing wildly, though it did not appear to me steadily, in my face. Several times I thought he was about to spring on me; and, although I carefully avoided making any movement, I instinctively grasped my gun with a firmer hold. To add to my embarrassment, I saw that I was fast drifting seaward! The wind was from the shore; it was impelling the boat with considerable velocity, in consequence of the mass of bushes acting as sails. Already it had cleared the sedge, and was floating out in open water. To my dismay, at less than a mile's distance, I descried a line of breakers!

"A side-glance was sufficient to convince me, that unless the skiff was checked, she would drift upon these in the space of ten minutes.

"A fearful alternative now presented itself: I must either drive the dog from the oars, or allow the skiff to be swamped among the breakers. The latter would be certain death, the former offered a chance for life; and, nerving myself with the palpable necessity for action, I instantly resolved to make the attack.

"Whether the dog had read my intention in my eyes; or observed my fingers taking a firmer clutch of my gun, I know not, but at this moment he seemed to evince sudden fear, and, dropping down from the seat, he ran backward to the bow, and cowered there as before.

"My first impulse was to get hold of the oars, for the roar of the breakers already filled my ears. A better idea suggested itself immediately after, and that was to load my gun. This was a delicate business, but I set about it with all the caution I could command.

"I kept my eyes fixed upon the animal, and *felt* the powder, the wadding, and the shot, into the muzzle. I succeeded in loading one barrel, and fixing the cap.

"As I had now something upon which I could rely, I proceeded with more confidence, and loaded the second barrel with greater care, the dog eyeing me all the while. Had madness not obscured his intelligence, he would no doubt have interrupted my manipulations; as it was, he remained still until both barrels were loaded, capped, and cocked.

"I had no time to spare; the breakers were nigh; their hoarse 'sough' warned me of their perilous proximity; a minute more, and the little skiff would be dancing among them like a shell, or sunk for ever.

"Not a moment was to be lost, and yet I had to proceed with caution. I dared not raise the gun to my shoulder—I dared not glance along the barrels: the manoeuvre might rouse the dangerous brute.

"I held the piece low, slanting along my thighs. I guided the barrels with my mind, and, feeling the direction to be true, I fired.

"I scarcely heard the report, on account of the roaring of the sea; but I saw the dog roll over, kicking violently. I saw a livid patch over his ribs, where the shot had entered in a clump. This would no doubt have proved sufficient; but to make sure, I raised the gun to my shoulder, took aim, and sent the contents of the second barrel through the ribs of the miserable brute. His kicking ended almost instantly, and he lay dead in the bottom of the boat.

"I dropped my gun and flew to the oars: it was a close 'shave;' the skiff was already in white water, and dancing like a feather; but with a few strokes I succeeded in backing her out, and then heading her away from the breakers, I pulled in a direct line for the shore.

"I thought not of my canvas-backs—they had floated by this time, I neither knew nor cared whither: the sharks might have them for me. My only care was to get away from the scene as quickly as possible, determined never again to go duck-shooting with a cur for my companion."

Chapter Seventeen
Hunting the Vicuña

During our next day's march the only incident that befel us was the breaking of our waggon-tongue, which delayed our journey. There was plenty of good hickory-wood near the place, and Jake, with a little help from Redwood and Ike and Lanty, soon spliced it again, making it stronger than ever. Of course it shortened our journey for the day, and we encamped at the end of a ten miles' march. Strange to say, on the whole ten miles we did not meet with a single animal to give us a little sport, or to form the subject of our camp talk.

We were not without a subject, however, as our English friend proposed giving us an account of the mode of hunting the vicuña, and the details of a week's hunting he had enjoyed upon the high table-lands of the Peruvian Andes. He also imparted to our camp-fire circle much information about the different species of that celebrated animal the llama or "camel-sheep" of Peru, which proved extremely interesting, not only to the old hunter-naturalist, but to the "mountain-men," to whom this species of game, as well as the mode of hunting it, was something new.

Thompson began his narrative as follows:—"When Pizarro and his Spaniards first climbed the Peruvian Andes, they were astonished at seeing a new and singular species of quadrupeds, the camel-sheep, so called from their resemblance to these two kinds of animals. They saw the 'llama' domesticated and trained to carrying burdens, and the 'alpaca,' a smaller species, reared on account of its valuable fleece.

"But there were still two other species of these odd animals only observed in a wild state, and in the more desolate and uninhabited parts of the Cordilleras. These were the 'guanaco' and 'vicuña.'

"Up to a very late period the guanaco was believed to be the llama in its wild state, and by some the llama run wild. This, however, is not the case. The four species, llama, alpaca, guanaco, and vicuña as quite distinct from each other, and although the guanaco can be tamed and taught to carry burdens, its labour is not of sufficient value to render this worth while. The alpaca is never used as a beast of burden. Its fleece is the consideration for which it is domesticated and reared, and its wool is much finer and more valuable than that of the llama.

"The guanaco is, perhaps, the least prized of the four, as its fleece is of indifferent quality, and its flesh is not esteemed. The vicuña, on the contrary, yields a wool which is eagerly sought after, and which in the Andes towns will sell for at least five times its weight in alpaca wool. Ponchos woven out of it are deemed the finest made, and command the fabulous price of 20 pounds or 30 pounds sterling. A rich proprietor in the cordilleras is often seen with such a poncho, and the quality of the garment, the length of time it will turn rain, etcetera, are favourite subjects of conversation with the wearers of them. Of course everybody in those parts possesses one, as everybody in England or the United States must have a great coat; but the ponchos of the poorer classes of Peruvians—the Indian labourers, shepherds, and miners—are usually manufactured out of the coarse wool of the llama. Only the 'ricos' can afford the beautiful fabric of the vicuña's fleece.

"The wool of the vicuña being so much in demand, it will be easily conceived that hunting the animal is a profitable pursuit; and so it is. In many parts of the Andes there are regular vicuña hunters, while, in other places, whole tribes of Peruvian Indians spend a part of every year in the chase of this animal and the guanaco. When we go farther south, in the direction of Patagonia, we find other tribes who subsist principally upon the guanaco, the vicuña, and the rhea or South-American ostrich.

"Hunting the vicuña is by no means an easy calling. The hunter must betake himself to the highest and coldest regions of the Andes—far from civilised life, and far from its comforts. He has to encamp in the open air, and sleep in a cave or a rude hut, built by his own hands. He has to endure a climate as severe as a Lapland winter, often in places where not a stick of wood can be procured, and where he is compelled to cook his meals with the dry ordure of wild cattle.

"If not successful in the chase he is brought to the verge of starvation, and must have recourse to roots and berries—a few species of which, such as the tuberous root 'maca,' are found growing in these elevated regions. He is exposed, moreover, to the perils of the precipice, the creaking 'soga' bridge, the slippery path, and the hoarse rushing torrent—and these among the rugged Cordilleras of the Andes are no mean dangers. A life of toil, exposure, and peril is that of the vicuña hunter.

"During my travels in Peru I had resolved to enjoy the sport of hunting the vicuña. For this purpose I set out from one of the towns of the Lower Sierra, and climbed up the high region known as the 'Puna,' or sometimes as the 'Despoblado' (the uninhabited region).

"I reached at length the edge of a plain to which I had mounted by many a weary path—up many a dark ravine. I was twelve or fourteen thousand feet above sea level, and although I had just parted from the land of the palm-tree and the orange, I was now in a region cold and sterile. Mountains were before and around me—some bleak and dark, others shining under a robe of snow, and still others of that greyish hue as if snow had freshly fallen upon them, but not enough to cover their stony surface. The plain before me was several miles in circumference. It was only part of a system of similar levels separated from each other by spurs of the mountains. By crossing a ridge another comes in view, a deep cleft leads you into a third, and so on.

"These table plains are too cold for the agriculturist. Only the cereal barley will grow there, and some of those hardy roots—the natives of an arctic zone. But they are covered with a sward of grass—the 'ycha' grass, the favourite food of the llamas—and this renders them serviceable to man. Herds of half-wild cattle may be seen, tended by their wilder-looking shepherds. Flocks of alpacas, female llamas with their young, and long-tailed Peruvian sheep, stray over them, and to some extent relieve their cheerless aspect. The giant vulture—the condor, wheels above all, or perches on the jutting rock. Here and there, in some sheltered nook, may be seen the dark mud hut of the 'vaquero' (cattle herd), or the man himself, with his troop of savage curs following at his heels, and this is all the sign of habitation or inhabitant to be met with for hundreds of miles. This bleak land, up among the mountain tops of the Andes, as I have already said, is called the 'Puna.'

"The Puna is the favourite haunt of the vicuña, and, of course, the home of the vicuña hunter. I had directions to find one of these hunters, and an introduction to him when found, and after spending the night at a shepherd's hut, I proceeded next morning in search of him—some ten miles farther into the mountains.

"I arrived at the house, or rather hovel, at an early hour. Notwithstanding, my host had been abroad, and was just returned with full hands, having a large bundle of dead animals in each. They were chinchillas and viscachas, which he had taken out of his snares set overnight. He said that most of them had been freshly caught, as their favourite time of coming out of their dens to feed is just before daybreak.

"These two kinds of animals, which in many respects resemble our rabbits, also resemble each other in habits. They make their nests in crevices of the rocks, to which they retreat, when pursued, as rabbits to their burrows. Of course, they are snared in a very similar manner—by setting the snares upon, their tracks, and at the entrances to their holes. One difference I noted.

The Peruvian hunter used snares made of twisted horse-hair, instead of the spring wire employed by our gamekeepers and poachers. The chinchilla is a much more beautiful creature than the viscacha, and is a better-known animal, its soft and beautifully-marbled fur being an article of fashionable wear in the cities of Europe.

"As I approached his hut, the hunter had just arrived with the night's produce of his snares, and was hanging them up to the side of the building, skinning them one by one. Not less than half a score of small, foxy-looking dogs were around him—true native dogs of the country.

"Of the disposition of these creatures I was soon made aware. No sooner had they espied me, than with angry yelps the whole pack ran forward to meet me, and came barking and grinning close around the feet of my horse. Several of them sprang upward at my legs, and would, no doubt, have bitten them, had I not suddenly raised my feet up to the withers, and for some time held them in that position. I have no hesitation in saying that had I been afoot, I should have been badly torn by the curs; nor do I hesitate to say, that of all the dogs in the known world, these Peruvian mountain dogs are the most vicious and spiteful. They will bite even the friends of their own masters, and very often their masters themselves have to use the stick to keep them in subjection. I believe the dogs found among many tribes of your North-American Indians have a very similar disposition, though by no means to compare in fierceness and savage nature with their cousins of the cold Puna.

"The masters of these dogs are generally Indians, and it is a strange fact, that they are much more spiteful towards the whites than Indians. It is difficult for a white man to get on friendly terms with them.

"After a good deal of kicking and cuffing, my host succeeded in making his kennel understand that I had not come there to be eaten up. I then alighted from my horse, and walked (I should say crawled) inside the hut.

"This was, as I have already stated, a mere hovel. A circular wall of mud and stone, about five feet high, supported a set of poles that served as rafters. These poles were the flower stalks of the great American aloe, or maguey-plant—the only thing resembling wood that grew near. Over these was laid a thick layer of Puna grass, which was tied with strong ropes of the same material, to keep it from flying off when the wind blew violently, which it there often does. A few blocks of stone in the middle of the floor constituted the fireplace, and the smoke got out the best way it could through a hole in the roof.

"The owner of this mansion was a true Indian, belonging to one of those tribes of the mountains that could not be said ever to have been conquered by the Spaniards. Living in remote districts, many of these people never submitted to the *repartimientos*, yet a sort of religious conquest was made of some of them by the missionaries, thus bringing them under the title of 'Indios mansos' (tame Indians), in contradistinction to the 'Indios bravos,' or savage tribes, who remain unconquered and independent to this day.

"As already stated, I had come by appointment to share the day's hunt. I was invited to partake of breakfast. My host, being a bachelor, was his own cook, and some parched maize and 'macas,' with a roasted chinchilla, furnished the repast.

"Fortunately, I carried with me a flask of Catalan brandy; and this, with a cup of water from the icy mountain spring, rendered our meal more palatable I was not without some dry tobacco, and a husk to roll it in, so that we enjoyed our cigar; but what our hunter enjoyed still more was a 'coceada,' for he was a regular chewer of 'coca.' He carried his pouch of chinchilla skin filled with the dried leaves of the coca plant, and around his neck was suspended the gourd bottle, filled with burnt lime and ashes of the root of the 'molle' tree.

"All things arranged, we started forth. It was to be a 'still' hunt, and we went afoot, leaving our horses safely tied by the hut. The Indian took with him only one of his dogs—a faithful and trusty one, on which, he could rely.

"We skirted the plain, and struck into a defile in the mountains. It led upwards, among rocky boulders. A cold stream gurgled in its bottom, now and then leaping over low falls, and churned into foam. At times the path was a giddy one, leading along narrow ledges, rendered more perilous by the frozen snow, that lay to the depth of several inches. Our object was to reach the level of a plain still higher, where my companion assured me we should be likely to happen upon a herd of vicuñas.

"As we climbed among the rocks, my eye was attracted by a moving object, higher up. On looking more attentively, several animals were seen, of large size, and reddish-brown colour. I took them at first for deer, as I was thinking of that animal. I saw my mistake in a moment. They were not deer, but creatures quite as nimble. They were bounding from rock to rock, and running along the narrow ledges with the agility of the chamois. These must be the vicuñas, thought I.

"'No,' said my companion; 'guanacos—nothing more.'

"I was anxious to have a shot at them.

"'Better leave them now,' suggested the hunter; 'the report would frighten the vicuñas, if they be in the plain—it is near. I know these guanacos.

I know where they will retreat to—a defile close by—we can have a chance at them on our return.'

"I forbore firing, though I certainly deemed the guanacos within shot, but the hunter was thinking of the more precious skin of the vicuñas, and we passed on. I saw the guanacos run for a dark-looking cleft between two mountain spurs.

"'We shall find them in there,' muttered my companion, 'that is their haunt.'

"Noble game are these guanacos—large fine animals—noble game as the red deer himself. They differ much from the vicuñas. They herd only in small numbers, from six to ten or a dozen: while as many as four times this number of vicuñas may be seen together. There are essential points of difference in the habits of the two species. The guanacos are dwellers among the rocks, and are most at home when bounding from cliff to cliff, and ledge to ledge. They make but a poor run upon the level grassy plain, and their singular contorted hoofs seem to be adapted for their favourite haunts. The vicuñas, on the contrary, prefer the smooth turf of the table plains, over which they dart with the swiftness of the deer. Both are of the same family of quadrupeds, but with this very essential difference—the one is a dweller of the level plain, the other of the rocky declivity; and nature has adapted each to its respective *habitat*."

Here the narrator was interrupted by the hunter-naturalist, who stated that he had observed this curious fact in relation to other animals of a very different genus, and belonging to the *fauna* of North America. "The animals I speak of," said he, "are indigenous to the region of the Rocky Mountains, and well-known to our trapper friends here. They are the big horn (*Ovis montana*) and the prong-horned antelope (*A. furcifer*). The big horn is usually denominated a sheep, though it possesses far more of the characteristics of the deer and antelope families. Like the chamois, it is a dweller among the rocky cliffs and declivities, and only there does it feel at home, and in the full enjoyment of its faculties for security. Place it upon a level plain, and you deprive it of confidence, and render its capture comparatively easy. At the base of these very cliffs on which the *Ovis montana* disports itself, roams the prong-horn, not very dissimilar either in form, colour, or habits; and yet this creature, trusting to its heels for safety, feels at home and secure only on the wide open plain where it can see the horizon around it! Such is the difference in the mode of life of two species of animals almost cogenerie, and I am not surprised to hear you state that a somewhat like difference exists between the guanaco and vicuña."

The hunter-naturalist was again silent, and the narrator continued.

"A few more strides up the mountain pass brought us to the edge of the plain, where we expected to see the vicuñas. We were not disappointed. A herd was feeding upon it, though at a good distance off. A beautiful sight they were, quite equalling in grace and stateliness the lordly deer. In fact, they might have passed for the latter to an unpractised eye, particularly at that season when deer are 'in the red.' Indeed the vicuña is more deer-like than any other animal except the antelope—much more so than its congeners the llama, alpaca, or guanaco. Its form is slender, and its gait light and agile, while the long tapering neck and head add to the resemblance. The colour, however, is peculiarly its own, and any one accustomed to seeing the vicuña can distinguish the orange-red of its silky coat at a glance, and at a great distance. So peculiar is it, that in Peru the *'Colour de vicuña'* (vicuña colour) has become a specific name.

"My companion at once pronounced the animals before us a herd of vicuñas. There were about twenty in all, and all except one were quietly feeding on the grassy plain. This one stood apart, his long neck raised high in air, and his head occasionally turning from side to side, as though he was keeping watch for the rest. Such was in fact the duty he was performing; he was the leader of the herd—the patriarch, husband and father of the flock. All the others were ewes or young ones. So affirmed my companion.

"The vicuña is polygamous—fights for his harem with desperate fierceness, watches over its number while they feed or sleep, chooses the ground for browsing and rest—defends them against enemies—heads them in the advance, and covers their retreat with his own 'person'—such is the domestic economy of the vicuña.

"'Now, señor,' said the hunter, eyeing the herd, 'if I could only kill him (he pointed to the leader) I would have no trouble with the rest. I should get every one of them.'

"'How?' I inquired.

"'Oh!—they would!—ha! The very thing I wished for!'

"'What?'

"'They are heading towards yonder rocks.' He pointed to a clump of rocky boulders that lay isolated near one side of the plain—'let us get there, comrade—*vamos*!'

"We stole cautiously round the edge of the mountain until the rocks lay between us and the game; and then crouched forward and took our position among them. We lay behind a jagged boulder, whose seamed outline looked as if it had been designed for loop-hole firing. It was just the cover we wanted.

"We peeped cautiously through the cracks of the rock. Already the vicuñas were near, almost within range of our pieces. I held in my hands a double-barrel, loaded in both barrels with large-sized buck-shot; my companion's weapon was a long Spanish rifle.

"I received his instructions in a whisper. I was not to shoot until he had fired. Both were to aim at the leader. About this he was particular, and I promised obedience.

"The unconscious herd drew near. The leader, with the long white silky hair hanging from his breast, was in the advance, and upon him the eyes of both of us were fixed. I could observe his glistening orbs, and his attitude of pride, as he turned at intervals to beckon his followers on.

"'I hope he has got the worms,' muttered my companion; 'if he has, he'll come to rub his hide upon the rocks.'

"Some such intention was no doubt guiding the vicuña, for at that moment it stretched forth its neck, and trotted a few paces towards us. It suddenly halted. The wind was in our favour, else we should have been scented long ago. But we were suspected. The creature halted, threw up its head, struck the ground with its hoof, and uttered a strange cry, somewhat resembling the whistling of a deer. The echo of that cry was the ring of my companion's rifle, and I saw the vicuña leap up and fall dead upon the plain.

"I expected the others to break off in flight, and was about to fire at them though they were still at long range. My companion prevented me.

"'Hold!' he whispered, 'you'll have a better chance—see there!—now, if you like, Señor!'

"To my surprise, the herd, instead of attempting to escape, came trotting up to where the leader lay, and commenced running around at intervals, stooping over the body, and uttering plaintive cries.

"It was a touching sight, but the hunter is without pity for what he deems his lawful game. In an instant I had pulled both triggers, and both barrels had sent forth their united and deadly showers.

"Deadly indeed—when the smoke blew aside, nearly half of the herd were seen lying quiet or kicking on the plain.

"The rest remained as before! another ring of the long rifle, and another fell—another double detonation of the heavy deer-gun, and several came to the ground; and so continued the alternate fire of bullets and shot, until the whole herd were strewn dead and dying upon the ground!

"Our work was done—a great day's work for my companion, who would realise nearly a hundred dollars for the produce of his day's sport.

"This, however, he assured me was a very unusual piece of good luck. Often for days and even weeks, he would range the mountains without killing a single head—either vicuña or guanaco, and only twice before had he succeeded in thus making a *battue* of a whole herd. Once he had approached a flock of vicuñas disguised in the skin of a guanaco, and killed most of them before they thought of retreating.

"It was necessary for us to return to the hut for our horses in order to carry home the game, and this required several journeys to be made. To keep off the wolves and condors my companion made use of a very simple expedient, which I believe is often used in the North—among your prairie trappers here. Several bladders were taken from the vicuñas and inflated. They were then tied upon poles of maguey, and set upright over the carcasses, so as to dangle and dance about in the wind. Cunning as is the Andes wolf this 'scare' is sufficient to keep him off, as well as his ravenous associate, the condor.

"It was quite night when we reached the Indian hut with our last load. Both of us were wearied and hungry, but a fresh vicuña cutlet, washed down by the Catalan, and followed by a cigarette, made us forget our fatigues. My host was more than satisfied with his day's work, and promised me a guanaco hunt for the morrow."

Chapter Eighteen
A Chacu of Vicuñas

"Well, upon the morrow," continued the Englishman, "we had our guanaco hunt, and killed several of the herd we had seen on the previous day. There was nothing particular in regard to our mode of hunting — farther than to use all our cunning in getting within shot, and then letting fly at them.

"It is not so easy getting near the guanaco. He is among the shyest game I have ever hunted, and his position is usually so far above that of the hunter, that he commands at all times a view of the movements of the latter. The over-hanging rocks, however, help one a little, and by diligent creeping he is sometimes approached. It requires a dead shot to bring him down, for, if only wounded, he will scale the cliffs, and make off — perhaps to die in some inaccessible haunt.

"While sojourning with my hunter-friend, I heard of a singular method practised by the Indians, of capturing the vicuña in large numbers. This was called the 'chacu.'

"Of course I became very desirous of witnessing a 'chacu,' and the hunter promised to gratify me. It was now the season of the year for such expeditions, and one was to come off in a few days. It was the annual hunt got up by the tribe to which my host belonged; and, of course, he, as a practised and professional hunter, was to bear a distinguished part in the ceremony.

"The day before the expedition was to set out, we repaired to the village of the tribe — a collection of rude huts, straggling along the bottom of one of the deep clefts or valleys of the Cordilleras. This village lay several thousand feet below the level of the Puna plains, and was therefore in a much warmer climate. In fact, the sugar-cane and yucca plant (*Jatropha mainhot*) were both seen growing in the gardens of the villagers, and Indian corn flourished in the fields.

"The inhabitants were '*Indios mansos*' (civilised Indians). They attended part of the year to agriculture, although the greater part of it was spent in idleness, amusements, or hunting. They had been converted—that is nominally—to Christianity; and a church with its cross was a prominent feature of the village.

"The curé, or priest, was the only white man resident in the place, and he was white only by comparison. Though of pure Spanish blood, he would have passed for a 'coloured old gentleman' in any part of Europe or the States.

"My companion introduced me to the padre, and I was at once received upon terms of intimacy. To my surprise I learnt that he was to accompany the chacu—in fact to take a leading part in it. He seemed to be as much interested in the success of the hunt as any of them—more so, perhaps, and with good reason too. I afterwards learnt why. The produce of the annual hunt was part of the padre's income. By an established law, the skins of the vicuñas were the property of the church, and these, being worth on the spot at least a dollar a-piece, formed no despicable tithe. After hearing this I was at no loss to understand the padre's enthusiasm about the chacu. All the day before he had been bustling about among his parishioners, aiding them with his counsel, and assisting them in their preparations. I shared the padre's dwelling, the best in the village; his supper too—a stewed fowl, killed for the occasion, and rendered fiery hot with 'aji,' or capsicum. This was washed down with 'chica,' and afterwards the padre and I indulged in a cigarette and a chat.

"He was a genuine specimen of the South-American missionary priest; rather more scrupulous about getting his dues than about the moral welfare of his flock; fat, somewhat greasy, fond of a good dinner, a glass of 'Yea' brandy, and a cigarette. Nevertheless, his rule was patriarchal in a high degree, and he was a favourite with the simple people among whom he dwelt.

"Morning came, and the expedition set forth; not, however, until a grand mass had been celebrated in the church, and prayers offered up for the success of the hunt. The cavalcade then got under weigh, and commenced winding up the rugged path that led toward the 'Altos,' or Puna heights. We travelled in a different direction from that in which my companion and I had come.

"The expedition itself was a picturesque affair. There were horses, mules, and llamas, men, women, children, and dogs; in fact, almost every living thing in the village had turned out. A chacu is no common occasion— no one day affair. It was to be an affair of weeks. There were rude tents carried along; blankets and cooking utensils; and the presence of the women was as necessary as any part of the expedition. Their office would be to do the cooking, and keep the camp in order! as well as to assist in the hunt.

"Strung out in admirable confusion, we climbed up the mountain—a picturesque train—the men swinging along in their coloured ponchos of llama wool, and the women dressed in bright mantas of 'bayeta' (a coarse cloth, of native manufacture). I noticed several mules and llamas packed with loads of a curious character. Some carried large bundles of rags— others were loaded with coils of rope—while several were 'freighted' with short poles, tied in bunches. I had observed these cargoes being prepared before leaving the village, and could not divine the use of them. That would no doubt be explained when we had reached the scene of the chacu, and I forbore to trouble my companions with any interrogatories, as I had enough to do to guide my horse along the slippery path we were travelling.

"About a mile from the village there was a sudden halt. I inquired the cause.

"'The *huaro*,' was the reply.

"I knew the huaro to be the name of a peculiar kind of bridge, and I learnt that one was here to be crossed. I rode forward, and found myself in front of the huaro. A singular structure it was. I could scarcely believe in the practicability of our getting over it. The padre, however, assured me it was a good one, and we should all be on the other side in a couple of hours!

"I at first felt inclined to treat this piece of information as a joke: but it proved that the priest was in earnest. It was full two hours before we were all crossed with our bag and baggage.

"The huaro was nothing more than a thick, rope stretched across the chasm, and made fast at both ends. On this rope was a strong piece of wood, bent into the shape of the letter U, and fastened to a roller which rested upon the rope, and moved along it when pulled by a cord from either side. There were two cords, or ropes, attached to the roller, one leading to each side of the chasm, and their object was to drag the passenger across: of course, only one of us could be carried over at a time. No wonder we were so long in making the crossing, when there were over one hundred in all, with numerous articles of baggage.

"I shall never forget the sensations I experienced in making the passage of the huaro. I had felt giddy enough in going over the 'soga' bridges and 'barbacoas' common throughout Peru, but the passage of the huaro is really a gymnastic feat of no easy accomplishment. I was first tied, back downwards, with my back resting in the concavity of the bent wood; my legs were then crossed over the main rope—the bridge itself—with nothing to hold them there farther than my own muscular exertion. With my hands I clutched the vertical side of the wooden yoke, and was told to keep my head in as upright a position as possible. Without farther ado I felt myself jerked out until I hung in empty air over a chasm that opened at least two hundred feet beneath, and through the bottom of which a white torrent was foaming over black rocks! My ankles slipped along the rope, but the sensation was so strange, that I felt several times on the point of letting them drop off. In that case my situation would have been still more painful, as I should have depended mainly on my arms for support. Indeed, I held on tightly with both hands, as I fancied that the cord with which I had been tied to the yoke would every minute give way.

"After a good deal of jerking and hauling, I found myself on the opposite side, and once more on my feet!

"I was almost repaid for the fright I had gone through, by seeing the great fat padre pulled over. It was certainly a ludicrous sight, and I laughed the more, as I fancied the old fellow had taken occasion to laugh at me. He took it all in good part, however, telling me that it caused him no fear, as he had long been accustomed to those kind of bridges.

"This slow and laborious method of crossing streams is not uncommon in many parts of the Andes. It occurs in retired and thinly-populated districts, where there is no means for building bridges of regular construction. Of course, the traveller himself only can be got over by the huaro. His horse, mule, or llamas must swim the stream, and in many instances these are carried off by the rapid current, or dashed against the rocks, and killed.

"The whole *cavallada* of the expedition got safely over, and in a short while we were all *en route*, once more climbing up toward the 'altos.' I asked my companion why we could not have got over the stream at some other point, and thus have saved the time and labour. The answer was, that it would have cost us a twenty miles' journey to have reached a point no nearer our destination than the other end of the huaro rope! No wonder such pains had been taken to ferry the party across.

"We reached the heights late in the evening. The hunt would not begin until the next day.

"That evening was spent in putting up tents, and getting everything in order about the camp. The tent of the padre was conspicuous—it was the largest, and I was invited to share it with him. The horses and other animals were picketted or hoppled upon the plain, which was covered with a short brown grass.

"The air was chill—cold, in fact—we were nearly three miles above ocean level. The women and youths employed themselves in collecting *taquia* to make fires. There was plenty of this, for the plain where we had halted was a pasture of large flocks of llamas and horned cattle. It was not there we expected to fall in with the vicuñas. A string of 'altos,' still farther on were their favourite haunts. Our first camp was sufficiently convenient to begin the hunt. It would be moved farther on when the plains in its neighbourhood had been hunted, and the game should grow scarce.

"Morning arrived; but before daybreak, a large party had set off, taking with them the ropes, poles, and bundles of rags I have already noticed. The women and boys accompanied this party. Their destination was a large table plain, contiguous to that on which we had encamped.

"An hour afterwards the rest of the party set forth—most of them mounted one way or other. These were the real hunters, or 'drivers.' Along with them went the dogs—the whole canine population of the village. I should have preferred riding with this party, but the padre took me along with himself, promising to guide me to a spot where I should get the best view of the chacu. He and I rode forward alone.

"In half an hour we reached the plain where the first party had gone. They were all at work as we came up—scattered over the plain—and I now saw the use that was to be made of the ropes and rags. With them a pound, or 'corral,' was in process of construction. Part of it was already finished, and I perceived that it was to be of a circular shape. The poles, or stakes, were driven into the ground in a curving line at the distance of about a rod from each other. When thus driven, each stake stood four feet high, and from the top of one to the other, ropes were ranged and tied, thus making the inclosure complete. Along these ropes were knotted the rags and strips of cotton, so as to hang nearly to the ground, or flutter in the wind; and this slight semblance of a fence was continued over the plain in a circumference of nearly three miles in length. One side, for a distance of several hundred yards, was left unfinished, and this was the entrance to the corral. Of course, this was in the direction from which the drove was to come.

"As soon as the inclosure was ready, those engaged upon it withdrew in two parties to the opposite flanks, and then deployed off in diverging lines, so as to form a sort of funnel, at least two miles in width. In this position they remained to await the result of the drive, most of them squatting down to rest themselves.

"Meanwhile the drive was proceeding, although the hunters engaged in it were at a great distance—scarcely seen from our position. They, too, had gone out in two parties, taking opposite directions, and skirting the hills that surrounded the plain. Their circuit could not have been less than a dozen miles; and, as soon as fairly round, they deployed themselves into a long arc, with its concavity towards the rope corral. Then, facing inward, the forward movement commenced. Whatever animals chanced to be feeding between them and the inclosure were almost certain of being driven into it.

"The padre had led me to an elevated position among the rocks. It commanded a view of the rope circle; but we were a long while waiting before the drivers came in sight. At length we descried the line of mounted men far off upon the plain, and, on closely scrutinising the ground between them and us, we could distinguish several reddish forms gliding about: these were the vicuñas. There appeared to be several bands of them, as we saw some at different points. They were crossing and recrossing the line of the drive, evidently startled, and not knowing in what direction to run. Every now and then a herd, led by its old male, could be seen shooting in a straight line—then suddenly making a halt—and the next minute sweeping off in a contrary direction. Their beautiful orange-red flanks, glistening in the sun, enabled us to mark them at a great distance.

"The drivers came nearer and nearer, until we could distinguish the forms of the horsemen as they rose over the swells of the plain. We could now hear their shouts—the winding of their ox-horns, and even the yelping of their dogs. But what most gratified my companion was to see that several herds of vicuñas were bounding backwards and forwards in front of the advancing line.

"'*Mira*!' he cried exultingly, '*mira! Señor*, one, two, three, four—four herds, and large ones—ah! *Carrambo*! Jesus!' continued he, suddenly changing tone, '*carrambo! esos malditos guanacos*!' (those cursed guanacos). I looked as he was pointing. I noticed a small band of guanacos springing over the plain. I could easily distinguish them from the vicuñas by their being larger and less graceful in their motions, but more particularly by the duller hue of brownish red. But what was there in their presence to draw down the maledictions of the padre, which he continued to lavish upon them most unsparingly? I put the question.

"'Ah! Señor,' he answered with a sigh, 'these guanacos will spoil all— they will ruin the hunt. Caspita!'

"'How? in what manner, mio padre?' I asked in my innocence, thinking that a fine herd of guanacos would be inclosed along with their cousins, and that 'all were fish,' etcetera.

"'Ah!' exclaimed the padre, 'these guanacos are *hereticos*—reckless brutes, they pay no regard to the ropes—they will break through and let the others escape—*santissima virgen*! what is to be done?'

"Nothing could be done except leave things to take their course, for in a few minutes the horsemen were seen advancing, until their line closed upon the funnel formed by the others. The vicuñas, in several troops, now rushed wildly from side to side, turning sharply as they approached the figures of the men and women, and running in the opposite direction. There were some fifty or sixty in all, and at length they got together in a single but confused clump. The guanacos, eight or ten in number, became mixed up with them, and after several quarterings, the whole flock, led by one that thought it had discovered the way of escape, struck off into a gallop, and dashed into the inclosure.

"The hunters, who were afoot with the women, now rushed to the entrance, and in a short while new stakes were driven in, ropes tied upon them, rags attached, and the circle of the chacu was complete.

"The mounted hunters at the same time had galloped around the outside, and flinging themselves from their horses, took their stations, at intervals from each other. Each now prepared his 'holas,' ready to advance and commence the work of death, as soon as the corral should be fairly surrounded by the women and boys who acted as assistants.

"The hunters now advanced towards the centre, swinging their bolas, and shouting to one another to direct the attack. The frightened vicuñas rushed from side to side, everywhere headed by an Indian. Now they broke into confused masses and ran in different directions—now they united again and swept in graceful curves over the plain. Everywhere the bolas whizzed through the air, and soon the turf was strewed with forms sprawling and kicking. A strange picture was presented. Here a hunter stood with the leaden balls whirling around his head—there another rushed forward upon a vicuña hoppled and falling—a third bent over one that was already down, anon he brandished a bleeding knife, and then, releasing the thong from the limbs of his victim, again swung his bolas in the air, and rushed forward in the chase.

"An incident occurred near the beginning of the *mêlée*, which was very gratifying to my companion the padre, and at once restored the equanimity of his temper. The herd of guanacos succeeded in making their escape, and without compromising the success of the hunt. This, however, was brought about by a skilful manoeuvre on the part of my old friend the Puna hunter.

These animals had somehow or other got separated from the vicuñas, and dashed off to a distant part of the inclosure. Seeing this, the hunter sprang to his horse, and calling his pack of curs after him, leaped over the rope fence and dashed forward after the guanacos. He soon got directly in their rear, and signalling those who stood in front to separate and let the guanacos pass, he drove them out of the inclosure. They went head foremost against the ropes, breaking them free from the stakes; but the hunter, galloping up, guarded the opening until the ropes and rags were freshly adjusted.

"The poor vicuñas, nearly fifty in number, were all killed or captured. When pursued up to the 'sham-fence' they neither attempted to rush against it or leap over, but would wheel suddenly round, and run directly in the faces of their pursuers!

"The sport became even more interesting when all but a few were *hors de combat*. Then the odd ones that remained were each attacked by several hunters at once, and the rushing and doubling of the animals—the many headings and turnings—the shouts of the spectators—the whizzing of the bolas—sometimes two or three of these missiles hurled at a single victim— all combined to furnish a spectacle to me novel and exciting.

"About twenty minutes after the animals had entered the rope inclosure the last of them was seen to 'bite the dust,' and the chacu of that day was over. Then came the mutual congratulations of the hunters, and the joyous mingling of voices. The slain vicuñas were collected in a heap—the skins stripped off, and the flesh divided among the different families who took part in the chacu.

"The skins, as we have said, fell to the share of the 'church,' that is, to the church's representative—the padre, and this was certainly the lion's share of the day's product.

"The ropes were now unfastened and coiled—the rags once more bundled, and the stakes pulled up and collected—all to be used on the morrow in some other part of the Puna. The meat was packed on the horses and mules, and the hunting party, in a long string, proceeded to camp. Then followed a scene of feasting and merriment—such as did not fall to the lot of these poor people every day in the year.

"This chacu lasted ten days, during which time I remained in the company of my half-savage friends. The whole game killed amounted to five hundred and odd vicuñas, with a score or two guanacos, several tarush, or deer of the Andes (*Cervus antisensis*) and half a dozen black bears (*Ursus ornatus*). Of course only the vicuñas were taken in the chacu. The other animals were started incidentally, and killed by the hunters either with their bolas, or guns, with which a few of them were armed."

The "chacu" of the Andes Indians corresponds to the "surround" of the Indian hunters on the great plains of North America. In the latter case, however, buffaloes are usually the objects of pursuit, and no fence is attempted—the hunters trusting to their horses to keep the wild oxen inclosed. The "pound" is another mode of capturing wild animals practised by several tribes of Indians in the Hudson's Bay territory. In this case the game is the caribou or reindeer, but no rope fence would serve to impound these. A good substantial inclosure of branches and trees is necessary, and the construction of a "pound" is the work of time and labour. I know of no animal except the vicuña itself, that could be captured after the manner practised in the "chacu."

Chapter Nineteen
Squirrel-Shooting

We were now travelling among the spurs of the "Ozark hills," and our road was a more difficult one. The ravines were deeper, and as our course obliged us to cross the direction in which most of them ran, we were constantly climbing or descending the sides of steep ridges. There was no road except a faint Indian trail, used by the Kansas in their occasional excursions to the borders of the settlements. At times we were compelled to cut away the underwood, and ply the axe lustily upon some huge trunk that had fallen across the path and obstructed the passage of our waggon. This rendered our progress but slow.

During such halt most of the party strayed off into the woods in search of game. Squirrels were the only four-footed creatures found, and enough of these were shot to make a good-sized "pot-pie;" and it may be here remarked, that no sort of flesh is better for this purpose than that of the squirrel.

The species found in these woods was the large "cat-squirrel" (*Sciurus cinereus*), one of the noblest of its kind. Of course at that season, amid the plenitude of seeds, nuts, and berries, they were as plump as partridges. This species is usually in good condition, and its flesh the best flavoured of all. In the markets of New York they bring three times the price of the common grey squirrel.

As we rode along, the naturalist stated many facts in relation to the squirrel tribe, that were new to most of us. He said that in North America there were not less than twenty species of true squirrels, all of them dwellers in the trees, and by including the "ground" and "flying" squirrels (*tamias* and *pteromys*), the number of species might be more than forty. Of course there are still new species yet undescribed, inhabiting the half-explored regions of the western territory.

The best-known of the squirrels is the common "grey squirrel," as it is in most parts of the United States the most plentiful. Indeed it is asserted that some of the other species, as the "black squirrel" (*Sciurus niger*), disappear from districts where the grey squirrels become numerous—as the native rat gives place to the fierce "Norway."

The true fox squirrel (*Sciurus vulpinus*) differs essentially from the "cat," which is also known in many States by the name of fox squirrel. The former is larger, and altogether a more active animal, dashing up to the top of a pine-tree in a single run. The cat-squirrel, on the contrary, is slow and timid among the branches, and rarely mounts above the first fork, unless when forced higher by the near approach of its enemy. It prefers concealing itself behind the trunk, dodging round the tree as the hunter advances upon it. It has one peculiarity, however, in its mode of escape that often saves it, and disappoints its pursuer. Unless very hotly pursued by a dog, or other swift enemy, it will not be treed until it has reached the tree that contains its nest, and, of course, it drops securely into its hole, bidding defiance to whatever enemy—unless, indeed, that enemy chance to be the pine-martin, which is capable of following it even to the bottom of its dark tree-cave.

Now most of the other squirrels make a temporary retreat to the nearest large tree that offers. This is often without a hole where they can conceal themselves, and they are therefore exposed to the small shot or rifle-bullet from below.

It does not always follow, however, that they are brought down from their perch. In very heavy bottom timber the squirrel often escapes among the high twigs, even where there are no leaves to conceal it, nor any hole in the tree. Twenty shots, and from good marksmen too, have been fired at a single squirrel in such situations, without bringing it to the ground, or seriously wounding it! A party of hunters have often retired without getting such game, and yet the squirrel has been constantly changing place, and offering itself to be sighted in new positions and attitudes!

The craft of the squirrel on these occasions is remarkable. It stretches its body along the upper part of a branch, elongating it in such a manner, that the branch, not thicker than the body itself, forms almost a complete shield against the shot. The head, too, is laid close, and the tail no longer erect, but flattened along the branch, so as not to betray the whereabouts of the animal.

Squirrel-shooting is by no means poor sport. It is the most common kind practised in the United States, because the squirrel is the most common game. In that country it takes the place that snipe or partridge shooting holds in England. In my opinion it is a sport superior to either of these last, and the game, when killed, is not much less in value. Good fat squirrel can be cooked in a variety of ways, and many people prefer it to feathered game of any kind. It is true the squirrel has a rat-like physiognomy, but that is only in the eyes of strangers to him. A residence in the backwoods, and a short practice in the eating of squirrel pot-pie, soon removes any impression of that kind. A hare, as brought upon the table-cloth in England, is far more likely to produce *degoût*—from its very striking likeness to "puss," that is purring upon the hearth-rug.

In almost all parts of the United States, a day's squirrel-shooting may be had without the necessity of making a very long journey. There are still tracts of woodland left untouched, where these animals find a home. In the Western States a squirrel-hunt may be had simply by walking a couple of hundred yards from your house, and in some places you may shoot the creatures out of the very door.

To make a successful squirrel-hunt two persons at least are necessary. If only one goes out, the squirrel can avoid him simply by "dodging" round the trunk, or any large limb of the tree. When there are two, one remains stationary, while the other makes a circuit, and drives the game from the opposite side. It is still better when three or four persons make up the party, as then the squirrel is assailed on all sides, and can find no resting-place, without seeing a black tube levelled upon him, and ready to send forth its deadly missile.

Some hunt the squirrel with shot-guns. These are chiefly young hands. The old hunter prefers the rifle; and in the hands of practised marksmen this is the better weapon. The rifle-bullet, be it ever so small, kills the game at once; whereas a squirrel severely peppered with shot will often escape to the tree where its hole is, and drop in, often to die of its wounds. No creature can be more tenacious of life—not even a cat. When badly wounded it will cling to the twigs to its last breath, and even after death its claws sometimes retain their hold, and its dead body hangs suspended to the branch!

The height from which a squirrel will leap to the ground without sustaining injury, is one of those marvels witnessed by every squirrel-hunter. When a tree in which it has taken refuge is found not to afford sufficient shelter, and a neighbouring tree is not near enough for it to leap to, it then perceives the necessity of returning to the ground, to get to some other part of the woods. Some species, as the cat-squirrel, fearing to take the dreadful leap (often nearly a hundred feet), rush down by the trunk. Not so the more active squirrels, as the common grey kind. These run to the extremity of a branch, and spring boldly down in a diagonal direction. The hunter—if a stranger to the feat—would expect to see the creature crushed or crippled by the fall. No danger of that. Even the watchful dog that is waiting for such an event, and standing close to the spot, has not time to spring upon it, until it is off again like a flying bird, and, almost as quick as sight can follow, is seen ascending some other tree.

There is an explanation required about this precipitous leap. The squirrel is endowed with the capability of spreading out its body to a great extent, and this in the downward rush it takes care to do—thus breaking its fall by the resistance of the air. This alone accounts for its not killing itself.

Nearly all squirrels possess this power, but in different degrees. In the flying squirrels it is so strongly developed, as to enable them to make a flight resembling that of the birds themselves.

The squirrel-hunter is often accompanied by a dog—not that the dog ever by any chance catches one of these creatures. Of him the squirrel has but little fear, well knowing that he cannot climb a tree. The office of the dog is of a different kind. It is to "tree" the squirrel, and, by remaining at the root, point out the particular tree to his master.

The advantage of the dog is obvious. In fact, he is almost as necessary as the pointer to the sportsman. First, by ranging widely, he beats a greater breadth of the forest. Secondly, when a squirrel is seen by him, his swiftness enables him to hurry it up some tree *not its own*. This second advantage is of the greatest importance. When the game has time enough allowed it, it either makes to its own tree (with a hole in it of course), or selects one of the tallest near the spot. In the former case it is impossible, and in the latter difficult, to have a fair shot at it.

If there be no dog, and the hunter trusts to his own eyes, he is often unable to find the exact tree which the squirrel has climbed, and of course loses it.

A good squirrel-dog is a useful animal. The breed is not important. The best are usually half-bred pointers. They should have good sight as well as scent; should range widely, and run fast. When well trained they will not take after rabbits, or any other game. They will bark only when a squirrel is treed, and remain staunchly by the root of the tree. The barking is necessary, otherwise the hunter, often separated from them by the underwood, would not know when they had succeeded in "treeing."

The squirrel seems to have little fear of the dog, and rarely ascends to a great height. It is often seen only a few feet above him, jerking its tail about, and apparently mocking its savage enemy below.

The coming up of the hunter changes the scene. The squirrel then takes the alarm, and shooting up, conceals itself among the higher branches.

Taking it all in all, we know none of the smaller class of field sports that requires greater skill, and yields more real amusement, than hunting the squirrel.

Our Kentuckian comrade gave us an account of a grand squirrel-hunt got up by himself and some neighbours, which is not an uncommon sort of thing in the Western States. The hunters divided themselves into two parties of equal numbers, each taking its own direction through the woods. A large wager was laid upon the result, to be won by that party that could bring in the greatest number of squirrels. There were six guns on each side, and the numbers obtained at the end of a week—for the hunt lasted so long—were respectively 5000, and 4780! Of course the sport came off in a tract of country where squirrels were but little hunted, and were both tame and plenty.

Such hunts upon a grand scale are, as already stated, not uncommon in some parts of the United States. They have another object besides the sport— that of thinning off the squirrels for the protection of the planter's corn-field. So destructive are these little animals to the corn and other grains, that in some States there has been at times a bounty granted, for killing them. In early times such a law existed in Pennsylvania, and there is a registry that in one year the sum of 8000 pounds was paid out of the treasury of this bounty-money, which at threepence a head—the premium—would make 640,000, the number of the squirrels killed in that year!

The "migration of the squirrels" is still an unexplained fact. It is among the grey squirrels it takes place; hence the name given to that species, *Sciurus migratorius*. There is no regularity about these migrations, and their motive is not known. Immense bands of the squirrels are observed in a particular neighbourhood, proceeding through the woods or across tracts of open ground, all in one direction. Nothing stays their course. Narrow streams and broad rivers are crossed by them by swimming, and many are drowned in the attempt.

Under ordinary circumstances, these little creatures are as much afraid of water as cats, yet when moving along their track of migration they plunge boldly into a river, without calculating whether they will ever reach the other side. When found upon the opposite bank, they are often so tired with the effort, that one may overtake them with a stick; and thousands are killed in this way when a migration has been discovered.

It is stated that they roll pieces of dry wood, or bark, into the water, and, seating themselves on these, are wafted across, their tails supplying them with a sail: of course this account must be held as apocryphal.

But the question is, what motive impels them to undertake these long and perilous wanderings, from which it is thought they never return to their original place of abode? It cannot be the search of food, nor the desire to change from a colder to a warmer climate. The direction of the wanderings forbids us to receive either of these as the correct reason. No light has been yet thrown upon this curious habit. It would seem as if some strange instinct propelled them, but for what purpose, and to what end, no one can tell.

Chapter Twenty
Treeing a Bear

The doctor was the only one not taking part in the conversation. Even the rude guides listened. All that related to game interested them, even the scientific details given by the hunter-naturalist. The doctor had ridden on in front of us. Some one remarked that he wanted water to mix with the contents of his flask, and was therefore searching for a stream. Be this as it may, he was seen suddenly to jerk his spare horse about, and spur back to us, his countenance exhibiting symptoms of surprise and alarm.

"What is it, doctor?" inquired one.

"He has seen Indians," remarked another.

"A bear—a bear!" cried the doctor, panting for breath; "a grizzly bear! a terrible-looking creature I assure you."

"A bar! d'you say?" demanded Ike, shooting forward on his old mare.

"A bar!" cried Redwood, breaking through the bushes in pursuit.

"A bear!" shouted the others, all putting spurs to their horses, and galloping forward in a body.

"Where, doctor? Where?" cried several.

"Yonder," replied the doctor, "just by that great tree. I saw him go in there—a grizzly, I'm sure."

It was this idea that had put the doctor in such affright, and caused him to ride back so suddenly.

"Nonsense, doctor," said the naturalist, "we are yet far to the east of the range of the grizzly bear. It was a black bear you saw."

"As I live," replied the doctor, "it was not black, anything but that. I should know the black bear. It was a light brown colour—almost yellowish."

"Oh! that's no criterion. The black bear is found with many varieties of colour. I have seen them of the colour you describe. It must be one of them. The grizzly is not found so far to the eastward, although it is possible we may see them soon; but not in woods like these."

There was no time for farther explanation. We had come up to the spot where the bear had been seen; and although an unpractised eye could have detected no traces of the animal's presence, old Ike, Redwood, and the hunter-naturalist could follow its trail over the bed of fallen leaves, almost as fast as they could walk. Both the guides had dismounted, and with their bodies slightly bent, and leading their horses after them, commenced tracking the bear. From Ike's manner one would have fancied that he was guided by scent rather than by sight.

The trail led us from our path, and we had followed it some hundred yards into the woods. Most of us were of the opinion that the creature had never halted after seeing the doctor, but had run off to a great distance. If left to ourselves, we should have given over the chase.

The trappers, however, knew what they were about. They asserted that the bear had gone away slowly—that it had made frequent halts—that they discovered "sign" to lead them to the conclusion that the animal's haunt was in the neighbourhood—that its "nest" was near. We were, therefore, encouraged to proceed.

All of us rode after the trackers. Jake and Lanty had been left with the waggon, with directions to keep on their route. After a while we heard the waggon moving along directly in front of us. The road had angled as well as the bear's trail, and the two were again converging.

Just at that moment a loud shouting came from the direction of the waggon. It was Lanty's voice, and Jake's too.

"Och! be the Vargin mother! luck there! Awch, mother o' Moses, Jake, such a haste!"

"Golly, Massa Lanty, it am a bar!"

We all heard this at once. Of course we thought of the trail no longer, but made a rush in the direction of the voices, causing the branches to fly on every side.

"Whar's the bar?" cried Redwood, who was first up to the waggon, "whar did ye see't?"

"Yander he goes!" cried Lanty, pointing to a pile of heavy timber, beset with an undergrowth of cane, but standing almost isolated from the rest of the forest on account of the thin open woods that were around it.

We were too late to catch a glimpse of him, but perhaps he would halt in the undergrowth. If so we had a chance.

"Surround, boys, surround!" cried the Kentuckian, who understood bear-hunting as well as any of the party. "Quick, round and head him;"

and, at the same time, the speaker urged his great horse into a gallop. Several others rode off on the opposite side, and in a few seconds we had surrounded the cane-brake.

"Is he in it?" cried one.

"Do you track 'im thur, Mark?" cried Ike to his comrade from the opposite side.

"No," was the reply, "he hain't gone out this away."

"Nor hyur," responded Ike.

"Nor here," said the Kentuckian.

"Nor by here," added the hunter-naturalist.

"Belike, then, he's still in the timmor," said Redwood. "Now look out all of yees. Keep your eyes skinned; I'll hustle him out o' thar."

"Hold on, Mark, boy," cried Ike, "hold on thur. Damn the varmint! hyur's his track, paddled like a sheep pen. Wagh, his den's hyur—let me rout 'im."

"Very wal, then," replied the other, "go ahead, old fellow—I'll look to my side—thu'll no bar pass me 'ithout getting a pill in his guts. Out wi' 'im!" We all sat in our saddles silent and watchful. Ike had entered the cane, but not a rustle was heard. A snake could not have passed through it with less noise than did the old trapper.

It was full ten minutes before the slightest sound warned of what he was about. Then his voice reached us.

"This way, all of you! The bar's treed."

The announcement filled all of us with pleasant anticipations. The sport of killing a bear is no everyday amusement, and now that the animal was "treed" we were sure of him. Some dismounted and hitched their horses to the branches; others boldly dashed into the cane, hurrying to the spot, with the hope of having first shot.

Why was Ike's rifle not heard if he saw the bear treed? This puzzled some. It was explained when we got up. Ike's words were figurative. The bear had not taken shelter in a tree, but a hollow log, and, of course, Ike had not yet set eyes on him. But there was the log, a huge one, some ten or more feet in thickness, and there was the hole, with the well-beaten track leading into it. It was his den. He was there to a certainty.

How to get him out? That was the next question.

Several took their stations, guns in hand, commanding the entrance to the hollow. One went back upon the log, and pounded it with the butt of his gun. To no purpose. Bruin was not such a fool as to walk out and be peppered by bullets.

A long pole was next thrust up the hollow. Nothing could be felt. The den was beyond reach.

Smoking was next tried, but with like success. The bear gave no sign of being annoyed with it. The axes were now brought from the waggon. It would be a tough job—for the log (a sycamore) was sound enough except near the heart. There was no help for it, and Jake and Lanty went to work as if for a day's rail splitting.

Redwood and the Kentuckian, both good axemen, relieved them, and a deep notch soon began to make its appearance on each side of the log. The rest of us kept watch near the entrance, hoping the sound of the axe might drive out the game. We were disappointed in that hope, and for full two hours the chopping continued, until the patience and the arms of those that plied the axe were nearly tired out.

It is no trifling matter to lay open a tree ten feet in diameter. They had chosen the place for their work guided by the long pole. It could not be beyond the den, and if upon the near side, of it, the pole would then be long enough to reach the bear, and either destroy him with a knife-blade attached to it, or force him out. This was our plan, and therefore we were encouraged to proceed.

At length the axes broke through the wood and the dark interior lay open. They had cut in the right place, for the den of the bear was found directly under, but no bear! Poles were inserted at both openings, but no bear could be felt either way. The hollow ran up no farther, so after all there was no bear in the log.

There were some disappointed faces about—and some rather rough ejaculations were heard. I might say that Ike "cussed a few," and that would be no more than the truth. The old trapper seemed to be ashamed of being so taken in, particularly as he had somewhat exultingly announced that the "bar was treed."

"He must have got off before we surrounded," said one.

"Are you sure he came into the timber?" asked another—"that fool, Lanty, was so scared, he could hardly tell where the animal went."

"Be me soul! gintlemen, I saw him go in wid my own eyes, Oi swear—"

"Cussed queer!" spitefully remarked Redwood.

"Damn the bar!" ejaculated Ike, "whur kid the varmint a gone?"

Where was A—? All eyes were turned to look for the hunter-naturalist, as if he could clear up the mystery. He was nowhere to be seen. He had not been seen for some time!

At that moment, the clear sharp ring of a rifle echoed in our ears. There was a moment's silence, and the next moment a loud "thump" was heard, as of a heavy body falling from a great height to the ground. The noise startled even our tired horses, and some of them broke their ties and scampered off.

"This way, gentlemen!" said a quiet voice, "here's the bear!"

The voice was A—'s; and we all, without thinking of the horses, hurried up to the spot. Sure enough, there lay the great brute, a red stream oozing out of a bullet-hole in his ribs.

A— pointed to a tree—a huge oak that spread out above our heads.

"There he was, in yonder fork," said he. "We might have saved ourselves a good deal of trouble had we been more thoughtful. I suspected he was not in the log when the smoke failed to move him. The brute was too sagacious to hide there. It is not the first time I have known the hunter foiled by such a trick."

The eyes of Redwood were turned admiringly on the speaker, and even old Ike could not help acknowledging his superior hunter-craft.

"Mister," he muttered, "I guess you'd make a darned fust-rate mountain-man. He's a gone Injun when you look through sights."

All of us were examining the huge carcass of the bear—one of the largest size.

"Your sure it's no grizzly?" inquired the doctor.

"No, doctor," replied the naturalist, "the grizzly never climbs a tree."

Chapter Twenty One
The Black Bear of America

After some time spent in recovering the horses, we lifted the bear into Jake's waggon, and proceeded on our journey. It was near evening, however, and we soon after halted and formed camp. The bear was skinned in a trice,—Ike and Redwood performing this operation with the dexterity of a pair of butchers; of course "bear-meat" was the principal dish for supper; and although some may think this rather a savage feast, I envy those who are in the way of a bear-ham now.

Of course for that evening nothing was talked of but Bruin, and a good many anecdotes were related about the beast. With the exception of the doctor, Jake and Lanty, all of us had something to say upon that subject, for all the rest had more or less practice in bear-hunting.

The black or "American bear" (*Ursus Americanus*) is one of the best-known of his tribe. It is he that is oftenest seen in menageries and zoological gardens, for the reason, perhaps, that he is found in great plenty in a country of large commercial intercourse with other nations. Hence he is more frequently captured and exported to all parts.

Any one at a glance may distinguish him from the "brown bear" of Europe, as well as the other bears of the Eastern continent—not so much by his colour (for he is sometimes brown too), as by his form and the regularity and smoothness of his coat. He may be as easily distinguished, too, from his congeners of North America—of which there are three—the grizzly (*Ursus ferox*), the brown (*Ursus arctus*), and the "polar" (*Ursus maritimus*). The hair upon other large bears (the polar excepted) is what may be termed "tufty," and their forms are different, being generally more uncouth and "chunkier." The black bear is, in fact, nearer to the polar in shape, as well as in the arrangement of his fur,—than to any other of the tribe. He is much smaller, however, rarely exceeding two-thirds the weight of large specimens of the latter.

His colour is usually a deep black all over the body, with a patch of rich yellowish red upon the muzzle, where the hair is short and smooth. This ornamental patch is sometimes absent, and varieties of the black bear are seen of very different colours. Brown ones are common in some parts, and others of a cinnamon colour, and still others with white markings, but these last are rare. They are all of one species, however, the assertion of some naturalists to the contrary notwithstanding. The proof is, that the black varieties have been seen followed by coloured cubs, and *vice versa*.

The black bear is omnivorous—feeds upon flesh as well as fruit, nuts, and edible roots. Habitually his diet is not carnivorous, but he will eat at times either carrion or living flesh. We say living flesh, for on capturing prey he does not wait to kill it, as most carnivorous animals, but tears and destroys it while still screaming. He may be said to swallow some of his food alive!

Of honey he is especially fond, and robs the bee-hive whenever it is accessible to him. It is not safe from him even in the top of a tree, provided the entrance to it is large enough to admit his body; and when it is not, he often contrives to make it so by means of his sharp claws. He has but little fear of the stings of the angry bees. His shaggy coat and thick hide afford him ample protection against such puny weapons. It is supposed that he spends a good deal of his time ranging the forest in search of "bee trees."

Of course he is a tree-climber—climbs by the "hug," not by means of his claws, as do animals of the cat kind; and in getting to the ground again descends the trunk, stern-foremost, as a hod-carrier would come down a ladder. In this he again differs from the *felidae*.

The range of the black bear is extensive—in fact it may be said to be colimital with the forest, both in North and South America—though in the latter division of the continent, another species of large black bear exists, the *Ursus ornatas*. In the northern continent the American bear is found in all the wooded parts from the Atlantic to the Pacific, but not in the open and prairie districts. There the grizzly holds dominion, though both of them range together in the wooded valleys of the Rocky Mountains. The grizzly, on the other hand, is only met with west of the Mississippi, and affects the dry desert countries of the uninhabited West. The brown bear, supposed to be identical with the *Ursus arctus* of North Europe, is only met with in the wild and treeless track known as "Barren grounds," which stretch across nearly the whole northern part of the continent from the last timber to the shores of the Arctic Sea, and in this region the black bear is not found. The zone of the polar bear joins with that of the brown, and the range of the former extends perhaps to the pole itself.

At the time of the colonisation of America, the area of the present United States was the favourite home of the black bear. It was a country entirely covered with thick forests, and of course a suitable *habitat* for him.

Even to this day a considerable number of bears is to be found within the limits of the settlements. Scarcely a State in which some wild woodlands or mountain fastnesses do not afford shelter to a number of bears, and to kill one of them is a grand object of the hunter's ambition. Along the whole range of the Alleghanies black bears are yet found, and it will be long ere they are finally extirpated from such haunts. In the Western States they are still more common, where they inhabit the gloomy forests along the rivers, and creek bottoms, protected alike by the thick undergrowth and the swampy nature of the soil.

Their den is usually in a hollow tree—sometimes a prostrate log if the latter be large enough, and in such a position as is not likely to be observed by the passing hunter. A cave in the rocks is also their favourite lair, when the geological structure of the country offers them so secure a retreat. They are safer thus; for when a bear-tree or log has been discovered by either hunter or farmer the bear has not much chance of escape. The squirrel is safe enough, as his capture will not repay the trouble of felling the tree; but such noble game as a bear will repay whole hours of hard work with the axe.

The black bear lies torpid during several months of the winter. The time of his hibernation depends upon the latitude of the place and the coldness of the climate. As you approach the south this period becomes shorter and shorter, until in the tropical forests, where frost is unknown, the black bear ranges throughout the year.

The mode of hunting the black bear does not differ from that practised with the fox or wild cat. He is usually chased by dogs, and forced into his cave or a tree. If the former, he is shot down, or the tree, if hollow, is felled. Sometimes smoking brings him out. If he escapes to a cave, smoking is also tried; but if that will not succeed in dislodging him, he must be left alone, as no dogs will venture to attack him there.

The hunter often tracks and kills him in the woods with a bullet from his rifle. He will not turn upon man unless when wounded or brought to bay. Then his assault is to be dreaded. Should he grasp the hunter between his great forearms, the latter will stand a fair chance of being hugged to death. He does not attempt to use his teeth like the grizzly bear, but relies upon the muscular power of his arms. The nose appears to be his tenderest part, and his antagonist, if an old bear-hunter, and sufficiently cool, will use every effort to strike him there. A blow upon the snout has often caused the black bear to let go his hold, and retreat terrified!

The log trap is sometimes tried with success. This is constructed in such a way that the removal of the bait operates upon a trigger, and a large heavy log comes down on the animal removing it—either crushing it to death or holding it fast by pressure. A limb is sometimes only caught; but this proves sufficient.

The same kind of trap is used throughout the northern regions of America by the fur trappers—particularly the sable hunters and trappers of the white weasel (*Mustela erminea*). Of course that for the bear is constructed of the heaviest logs, and is of large dimensions.

Redwood related an adventure that had befallen him while trapping the black bear at an earlier period of his life. It had nearly cost him his life too, and a slight halt in his gait could still be observed, resulting from that very adventure.

We all collected around the blazing logs to listen to the trapper's story.

Chapter Twenty Two
The Trapper Trapped

"Well, then," began Redwood, "the thing I'm agoin' to tell you about, happened to me when I war a younker, long afore I ever thought I was a coming out hyar upon the parairas. I wan't quite growed at the time, though I was a good chunk for my age.

"It war up thar among the mountains in East Tennessee, whar this child war raised, upon the head waters of the Tennessee River.

"I war fond o' huntin' from the time that I war knee high to a duck, an' I can jest remember killin' a black bar afore I war twelve yeer old. As I growed up, the bar had become scacer in them parts, and it wan't every day you could scare up such a varmint, but now and then one ud turn up.

"Well, one day as I war poking about the crik bottom (for the shanty whar my ole mother lived war not on the Tennessee, but on a crik that runs into it), I diskivered bar sign. There war tracks o' the bar's paws in this mud, an' I follered them along the water edge for nearly a mile—then the trail turned into about as thickety a bottom as I ever seed anywhar. It would a baffled a cat to crawl through it.

"After the trail went out from the crik and towards the edge o' this thicket, I lost all hopes of follerin' it further, as the ground was hard, and covered with donicks, and I couldn't make the tracks out no how. I had my idea that the bar had tuk the thicket, so I went round the edge of it to see if I could find whar he had entered.

"For a long time I couldn't see a spot whar any critter as big as a bar could a-got in without makin' some sort o' a hole, and then I begun to think the bar had gone some other way, either across the crik or further down it.

"I war agoin' to turn back to the water, when I spied a big log lyin' half out o' the thicket, with one eend buried in the bushes. I noticed that the top of this log had a dirty look, as if some animal had tramped about on it; an' on goin' up and squintin' at it a little closter, I seed that that guess war the right one.

"I clomb the log, for it war a regular rouster, bigger than that 'n we had so much useless trouble with, and then I scrammelled along the top o' it in the direction of the brush. Thar I seed the very hole whar the bar had got into the thicket, and thar war a regular beaten-path runnin' through the brake as far as I could see.

"I jumped off o' the log, and squeezed myself through the bramble. It war a trail easy enough to find, but mighty hard to foller, I can tell ye. Thar war thistles, and cussed stingin' nettles, and briars as thick as my wrist, with claws upon them as sharp as fish-hooks. I pushed on, howsomever, feelin' quite sartin that sich a well-used track must lead to the bar's den, an' I war safe enough to find it. In coorse I reckoned that the critter had his nest in some holler tree, and I could go home for my axe, and come back the next morning—if smoking failed to git him out.

"Well, I poked on through the thicket a good three hundred yards, sometimes crouching, and sometimes creeping on my hands and knees. I war badly scratched, I tell you, and now and then I jest thought to myself, what would be the consyquince if the bar should meet me in that narrow passage. We'd a had a tough tussel, I reckon—but I met no bar.

"At last the brash grew thinner, and jest as I was in hopes I might stumble on the bar tree, what shed I see afore me but the face o' a rocky bluff, that riz a consid'able height over the crik bottom. I begun to fear that the varmint had a cave, and so, cuss him! he had—a great black gulley in the rocks was right close by, and thar was his den, and no mistake. I could easily tell it by the way the clay and stones had been pattered over by his paws.

"Of coorse, my tracking for that day war over, and I stood by the mouth of the cave not knowin' what to do. I didn't feel inclined to go in.

"After a while I bethought me that the bar mout come out, an' I laid myself squat down among the bushes facing the cave. I had my gun ready to give him a mouthful of lead, as soon as he should show his snout outside o' the hole.

"'Twar no go. I guess he had heard me when I first come up, and know'd I war thar. I laid still until 'twar so dark I thought I would never find my way back agin to the crik; but, after a good deal of scramblin' and creepin' I got out at last, and took my way home.

"It warn't likely I war agoin' to give that bar up. I war bound to fetch him out o' his boots if it cost me a week's hunting. So I returned the next morning to the place, and lay all day in front o' the cave. No bar appeared, an' I went back home a cussin'.

"Next day I come again, but this time I didn't intend to stay. I had fetched my axe with me wi' the intention of riggin' up a log trap near the mouth o' the cave. I had also fetched a jug o' molasses and some yeers o' green corn to bait the trap, for I know'd the bar war fond o' both.

"Well, I got upon the spot, an' makin' as leetle rumpus as possible, I went to work to build my trap. I found some logs on the ground jest the scantlin, and in less than an hour I hed the thing rigged an' the trigger set. 'Twan't no small lift to get up the big log, but I managed it wi' a lever I had made, though it took every pound o' strength in my body. If it come down on the bar I knew it would hold him.

"Well, I had all ready except layin' the bait; so I crawled in, and was fixin' the green yeers and the 'lasses, when, jest at that moment, what shed I hear behind me but the 'sniff' o' the bar!

"I turned suddenly to see. I had jest got my eye on the critter standin' right in the mouth o' his cave, when I feeled myself struck upon the buttocks, and flattened down to the airth like a pancake!

"At the first stroke I thought somebody had hit me a heavy blow from behind, and I wish it had been that. It war wusser than that. It war the log had hit me, and war now lying with all its weight right acrosst my two leg's. In my hurry to git round I had sprung the trigger, and down comed the infernal log on my hams.

"At fust I wan't scared, but I war badly hurt. I thought it would be all right as soon as I had crawled out, and I made an attempt to do so. It was then that I become scared in airnest; for I found that I couldn't crawl out. My legs were held in such a way that I couldn't move them, and the more I pulled the more I hurt them. They were in pain already with the heavy weight pressin' upon them, and I couldn't bear to move them. No more could I turn myself. I war flat on my face, and couldn't slew myself round any way, so as to get my hands at the log. I war fairly catched in my own trap!

"It war jest about then I began to feel scared. Thar wan't no settlement in the hul crik bottom but my mother's old shanty, an' that were two miles higher up. It war as unlikely a thing as could happen that anybody would be passing that way. And unless some one did I saw no chance of gettin' clar o' the scrape I war in. I could do nothin' for myself.

"I hollered as loud as I could, and that frightened the bar into his cave again. I hollered for an hour, but I could hear no reply, and then I war still a bit, and then I hollered again, an' kept this up pretty much for the hul o' that blessed day.

"Thar wan't any answer but the echo o' my own shoutin', and the whoopin' of the owls that flew about over my head, and appeared as if they war mockin' me.

"I had no behopes of any relief comin' from home. My ole mother had nobody but myself, and she wan't like to miss me, as I'd often stayed out a huntin' for three or four days at a time. The only chance I had, and I knew it too, war that some neighbour might be strayin' down the crik, and you may guess what sort o' chance that war, when I tell you thar wan't a neighbour livin' within less than five mile o' us. If no one come by I knew I must lay there till I died o' hunger and rotted, or the bar ate me up.

"Well, night come, and night went. 'Twar about the longest night this child remembers. I lay all through it, a sufferin' the pain, and listening to the screechin' owls. I could a screeched as loud as any of them if that would a done any good. I heerd now and then the snuffin' o' the bar, and I could see thar war two o' them. I could see thar big black bodies movin' about like shadows, and they appeared to be gettin' less afeerd o' me, as they come close at times, and risin' up on their hind-quarters stood in front o' me like a couple o' black devils.

"I begun to get afeerd they would attack me, and so I guess they would a-done, had not a circumstance happened that put them out o' the notion.

"It war jest grey day, when one o' them come so clost that I expected to be attacked by him. Now as luck would have it, my rifle happened to be lyin' on the ground within reach. I grabbed it without saying a word, and slewin' up one shoulder as high as I could, I was able to sight the bar jest behind the fore leg. The brute wan't four feet from the muzzle, and slap into him went wad and all, and down he tumbled like a felled ox. I seed he war as dead as a buck.

"Well, badly as I war fixed, I contrived to get loaded again, for I knowed that bars will fight for each other to the death; and I thought the other might attack me. It wan't to be seen at the time, but shortly after it come upon the ground from the direction of the crik.

"I watched it closely as it shambled up, having my rifle ready all the while. When it first set eyes on its dead comrade it gave a loud snort, and stopped. It appeared to be considerably surprised. It only halted a short spell, and then, with a loud roar, it run up to the carcass, and sniffed at it.

"I hain't the least o' a doubt that in two seconds more it would a-jumped me, but I war too quick for it, and sent a bullet right plum into one of its eyes, that come out again near the back o' its neck. That did the business, and I had the satisfaction to see it cowollop over nearly on top o' the other 'n.

"Well, I had killed the bars, but what o' that. That wouldn't get me from under the log; and what wi' the pain I was sufferin', and the poor prospect o' bein' relieved, I thought I mout as well have let them eat me.

"But a man don't die so long as he can help it, I b'lieve, and I determined to live it out while I could. At times I had hopes and shouted, and then I lost hope and lay still again.

"I grew as hungry as a famished wolf. The bars were lying right before me, but jest beyond reach, as if to tantylise me. I could have ate a collop raw if I could a-got hold of it, but how to reach it war the difeeculty.

"Needcesity they say is the mother o' invention; and I set myself to invent a bit. Thar war a piece o' rope I had brought along to help me wi' the trap, and that I got my claws on.

"I made a noose on one eend o' it, and after about a score o' trials I at last flung the noose over the head o' one o' the bars, and drew it tight. I then sot to work to pull the bar nearer. If that bar's neck wan't well stretched I don't know what you'd call stretchin', for I tugged at it about an hour afore I could get it within reach. I did get it at last, and then with my knife I cut out the bar's tongue, and ate it raw.

"I had satisfied one appetite, but another as bad, if not wusser, troubled me. That war thirst—my throat war as dry as a corn cob, and whar was the water to come from. It grew so bad at last that I thought I would die of it. I drawed the bar nearer me, and cut his juglar to see if thar war any relief from that quarter. Thar wan't. The blood war froze up thick as liver. Not a drop would run.

"I lay coolin' my tongue on the blade o' my knife an' chawin' a bullet, that I had taken from my pouch. I managed to put in the hul of the next day this away, now and then shoutin' as hard as I could. Towards the evenin' I grew hungry again, and ate a cut out o' the cheek o' the bar; but I thought I would a-choked for want o' water.

"I put in the night the best way I could. I had the owls again for company, and some varmint came up and smelt at the bars; but was frightened at my voice, and run away again. I suppose it war a fox or wolf, or some such thing, and but for me would a-made a meal off o' the bar's carcass.

"I won't trouble you with my reflexshuns all that night; but I can assure ye they war anything but pleasant. I thought of my ole mother, who had nobody but me, and that helped to keep up my spirits. I determined to cut away at the bar, and hold out as long as possible.

"As soon as day broke I set up my shoutin' again, restin' every fifeteen minutes or so, and then takin' afresh start. About an hour after sun-up, jest as I had finished a long spell o' screechin', I thought I heerd a voice. I listened a bit with my heart thumpin' against my ribs. Thar war no sound; I yelled louder than ever, and then listened. Thar war a voice.

"'Damn ye! what are ye hollowin' about?' cried the voice.

"I again shouted 'Holloa!'

"'Who the hell's thar?' inquired the voice.

"'Casey!' I called back, recognising the voice as that of a neighbour who lives up the crik; 'for God's sake this way.'

"'I'm a-comin',' he replied; ''Taint so easy to get through hyar—that you, Redwood? What the hell's the matter? Damn this brush!'

"I heard my neighbour breakin' his way through the thicket, and strange I tell ye all, but true it is, I couldn't believe I war goin' to get clar even then until I seed Casey standin' in front o' me.

"Well, of coorse, I was now set free again, but couldn't put a foot to the ground. Casey carried me home to the shanty, whar I lay for well nigh six weeks, afore I could go about, and damn the thing! I han't got over it yet."

So ended Redwood's story.

Chapter Twenty Three
The American Deer

During our next day's journey we fell in with and killed a couple of deer—a young buck and doe. They were the first of these animals we had yet seen, and that was considered strange, as we had passed through a deer country. They were of the species common to all parts of the United States' territory—the "red" or "fallow" deer (*Cervus Virginianus*). It may be here remarked that the common deer of the United States, sometimes called "red deer," is the fallow deer of English parks, that the "elk" of America is the red deer of Europe, and the "elk" of Europe is the "moose" of America. Many mistakes are made in relation to this family of animals on account of these misapplied names.

In North America there are six well-defined species of deer—the moose (*Cervus alces*); the elk (*Cervus Canadensis*); the caribou (*tarandus*); the black-tail or "mule" deer (*macrotis*); the long-tail (*leucurus*); and the Virginian, or fallow deer (*Virginianus*). The deer of Louisiana (*Cervus nemoralis*) is supposed by some to be a different species from any of the above; so also is the "mazama" of Mexico (*Cervus Mexicanus*). It is more probable that these two kinds are only varieties of the *Genus Virginianus*—the difference in colour, and other respects, resulting from a difference in food, climate, and such like causes.

It is probable, too, that a small species of deer exists in the Russian possessions west of the Rocky Mountains, quite distinct from any of the six mentioned above; but so little is yet known of the natural history of these wild territories, that this can only be taken as conjecture. It may be remarked, also that of the caribou (*Cervus tarandus*) there are two marked varieties, that may almost be regarded in the light of species. One, the larger, is known as the "woodland caribou," because it inhabits the more southern and wooded districts of the Hudson's Bay territory; the other, the "barren ground caribou," is the "reindeer" of the Arctic voyagers.

Of the six well-ascertained species, the last-mentioned (*Cervus Virginianus*) has the largest geographical range, and is the most generally known. Indeed, when the word "deer" is mentioned, it only is meant. It is the deer of the United States.

The "black-tails" and "long-tails" are two species that may be called new. Though long known to trappers and hunters, they have been but lately described by the scientific naturalist. Their *habitat* is the "far west" in California, Oregon, the high prairies, and the valleys of the Rocky Mountains. Up to a late period naturalists have had but little to do with these countries. For this reason their *fauna* has so long remained comparatively unknown.

The geographical disposition of the other four species is curious. Each occupies a latitudinal zone. That of the caribou, or rein deer, extends farthest north. It is not found within the limits of the United States.

The zone of the moose overlaps that of the caribou, but, on the other side, goes farther south, as this species is met with along the extreme northern parts of the United States.

The elk is next in order. His range "dovetails" into that of the moose, but the elk roves still farther into the temperate regions, being met with almost as far south as Texas.

The fourth, the common deer, embraces in his range the temperate and torrid zones of both North and South America, while he is not found in higher latitudes than the southern frontier of Canada.

The common deer, therefore, inhabits a greater area than any of his congeners, and is altogether the best-known animal of his kind. Most persons know him by sight. He is the smallest of the American species, being generally about five feet in length by three in height, and a little more than 100 pounds in weight. He is exceedingly well formed and graceful; his horns are not so large as those of the stag, but, like his, they are annually caducous, falling off in the winter and returning in the spring. They are rounded below, but in the upper part slightly flattened or palmated. The antlers do not rise upward, but protrude forward over the brow in a threatening manner. There is no regular rule, however, for their shape and "set," and their number also varies in different individuals. The horns are also present only in the male or buck; the doe is without them. They rise from a rough bony protuberance on the forehead, called the "burr." In the first year they grow in the shape of two short straight spikes; hence the name "spike-bucks" given to the animals of that age. In the second season a small antler appears on each horn, and the number increases until the fourth year, when they obtain a full head-dress of "branching honours." The antlers, or, as they are sometimes called, "points," often increase in number with the age of the animal, until as many as fifteen make their appearance. This, however, is rare. Indeed, the food of the animal has much to do with the growth of his horns. In an ill-fed specimen they do not grow to such size, nor branch so luxuriantly as in a well-fed fat buck.

We have said that the horns fall annually. This takes place in winter—in December and January. They are rarely found, however, as they are soon eaten up by the small-gnawing animals.

The new horns begin to grow as soon as the old ones have dropped off. During the spring and summer they are covered with a soft velvety membrane, and they are then described as being "in the velvet." The blood circulates freely through this membrane, and it is highly sensitive, so that a blow upon the horns at this season produces great pain. By the time the "rutting" season commences (in October), the velvet has peeled off, and the horns are then in order for battle—and they need be, for the battles of the bucks during this period are terrible indeed.—Frequently their horns get "locked" in such conflicts, and, being unable to separate them, the combatants remain in this situation until both perish by hunger, or fall a prey to their natural enemy—the wolf. Many pairs of horns have been found in the forest thus locked together, and there is not a museum in America without this singular souvenir of mutual destruction!

The hair of the American deer is thickly set and smooth on the surface. In winter it grows longer and is of a greyish hue; the deer is then, according to hunter phraseology, "in the grey." In the summer a new coat is obtained, which is reddish, or calf-coloured. The deer is then "in the red." Towards the end of August, or in autumn, the whole coat has a blue tinge. This is called "in the blue." At all times the animal is of a whitish appearance on the throat and belly and insides of the legs. The skin is toughest when "in the red," thickest "in the blue," and thinnest "in the grey." In the blue it makes the best buckskin, and is, therefore, most valuable when obtained in autumn.

The fawns of this species are beautiful little creatures; they are fawn-coloured, and showered all over with white spots which disappear towards the end of their first summer, when they gradually get into the winter grey.

The American deer is a valuable animal. Much of the buckskin of commerce is the product of its hides, and the horns are put to many uses. Its flesh, besides supplying the tables of the wealthy, has been for centuries almost the whole sustenance of whole nations of Indians. Its skins have furnished them with tents, beds, and clothing; its intestines with bowstrings, ball "raquets," and snow-shoes; and in the chase of this creature they have found almost their sole occupation as well as amusement.

With so many enemies, it is a matter of wonder that this species has not long been extirpated; not only has man been its constant and persevering destroyer, but it has a host of enemies besides, in the cougar, the lynxes, the wolverine, and the wolves.

The last are its worst foes. Hunters state that for one deer killed by themselves, five fall a prey to the wolves. These attack the young and feeble, and soon run them down. The old deer can escape from a wolf by superior speed; but in remote districts, where the wolves are numerous, they unite in packs of eight or ten, and follow the deer as hounds do, and even with a somewhat similar howling. They run by the nose, and unless the deer can reach water, and thus escape them, they will tire it down in the end.

Frequently the deer, when thus followed in winter, makes for the ice, upon which he is soon overtaken by his hungry pursuers.

Notwithstanding all this, the American deer is still common in most of the States, and in some of them even plentiful. Where the wolves have been thinned off by "bounty" laws, and the deer protected during the breeding season by legislative enactments, as is the case in New York, their number is said to be on the increase. The markets of all the great cities in America are supplied with venison almost as cheap as beef, which shows that the deer are yet far from being scarce.

The habits of this creature are well-known. It is gregarious in its natural *habitat*. The herd is usually led by an old buck, who watches over the safety of the others while feeding. When an enemy approaches, this sentinel and leader strikes the ground sharply with his hoofs, snorts loudly, and emits a shrill whistle; all the while fronting the danger with his horns set forward in a threatening manner. So long as he does not attempt to run, the others continue to browse with confidence; but the moment their leader starts to fly, all the rest follow, each trying to be foremost.

They are timid upon ordinary occasions, but the bucks in the rutting season are bold, and when wounded and brought "to bay," are not to be approached with impunity. They can inflict terrible blows, both with their hoofs and antlers; and hunters who have come too near them on such occasions have with difficulty escaped being gored to death.

They are foes to the snake tribe, and kill the most venomous serpents without being bitten. The rattle-snake hides from their attack. Their mode of destroying these creatures is similar to that employed by the peccary (*dicotyles*): that is, by pouncing down upon them with the four hoofs held close together, and thus crushing them to death. The hostility of the peccary to snakes is easily understood, as no sooner has it killed one than it makes a meal of it. With the deer, of course, such is not the case, as they are not carnivorous. Its enmity to the reptile race can be explained only by supposing that it possesses a knowledge of their dangerous qualities, and thinks they should therefore be got rid of.

The food of the American deer consists of twigs, leaves of trees, and grass. They are fonder of the tree-shoots than the grass; but their favourite morsels are the buds and flowers of *nymphae*, especially those of the common pond-lily. To get these, they wade into the lakes and rivers like the moose, and, like them, are good swimmers.

They love the shady forest better than the open ground, and they haunt the neighbourhood of streams. These afford them protection, as well as a means of quenching thirst. When pursued, their first thought is to make for water, in order to elude the pursuer, which they often succeed in doing, throwing both dogs and wolves off the scent. In summer, they seek the water to cool themselves, and get free from flies and mosquitoes, that pester them sadly.

They are fond of salt, and repair in great numbers to the salines, or salt springs, that abound in all parts of America. At these they lick up quantities of earth along with the salt efflorescence, until vast hollows are formed in the earth, termed, from this circumstance, salt "licks." The consequence of this "dirt-eating" is, that the excrement of the animal comes forth in hard pellets; and by seeing this, the hunters can always tell when they are in the neighbourhood of a "lick."

The does produce in spring—in May or June, according to the latitude. They bring forth one, two, and very rarely three fawns at a birth. Their attachment to their young is proverbial. The mothers treat them with the greatest tenderness, and hide them while they go to feed. The bleating of the fawn at once recalls the mother to its side. The hunter often imitates this with success, using either his own voice, or a "call," made out of a cane-joint. An anecdote, told by Parry, illustrates this maternal fondness:—"The mother, finding her young one could not swim as fast as herself, was observed to stop repeatedly, so as to allow, the fawn to come up with her; and, having landed first, stood watching it with trembling anxiety as the boat chased it to the shore. She was repeatedly fired at, but remained immovable, until her offspring landed in safety, when they both cantered out of sight." The deer to which Parry refers is the small "caribou;" but a similar affection exists between the mother and fawns of the common deer.

The American deer is hunted for its flesh, its hide, and "the sport." There are many modes of hunting it. The simplest and most common is that which is termed "still" hunting. In this, the hunter is armed with his rifle or deer-gun—a heavy fowling-piece—and steals forward upon the deer, as he would upon any other game. "Cover" is not so necessary as silence in such a hunt. This deer, like some antelopes, is of a "curious" disposition, and will sometimes allow the hunter to approach in full view without attempting to run off. But the slightest noise, such as the rustling of dry leaves, or the snapping of a stick, will alarm him. His sense of hearing is extremely acute. His nose, too, is a keen one, and he often scents the hunter, and makes off long before the latter has got within sight or range. It is necessary in "still" hunting to leave the dog at home; unless, indeed, he be an animal trained to the purpose.

Another species of hunting is "trailing" the deer in snow. This is done either with dogs or without them. The snow must be frozen over, so as to cut the feet of the deer, which puts them in such a state of fear and pain, that the hunter can easily get within shot. I have assisted in killing twenty in a single morning in this way; and that, too, in a district where deer were not accounted plentiful.

The "drive" is the most exciting mode of hunting deer; and the one practised by those who hunt for "the sport." This is done with hounds, and the horsemen who follow them also carry guns. In fact, there is hardly a species of hunting in America in which fire-arms are not used.

Several individuals are required to make up a "deer drive." They are generally men who know the "lay" of the country, with all its ravines and passes. One or two only accompany the hounds as "drivers," while the rest get between the place where the dogs are beating the cover and some river towards which it is "calculated" the startled game will run. They deploy themselves into a long line, which sometimes extends for miles through the forest. Each, as he arrives at his station, or "stand," as it is called, dismounts, ties his horse in a thicket, and takes his stand, "covering" himself behind a log or tree. The stands are selected with reference to the configuration of the ground, or by paths which the deer are accustomed to take; and as soon as all have so arranged themselves, the dogs at a distant point are set loose, and the "drive" begins.

The "stand men" remain quiet, with their guns in readiness. The barking of the dogs, afar off through the woods, usually admonishes them when a deer has been "put up;" and they watch with eager expectation, each one hoping that the game may come his way.

Hours are sometimes passed without the hunter either seeing or hearing a living thing but himself and his horse; and many a day he returns home from such a "chase" without having had the slightest glimpse of either buck, doe, or fawn.

This is discouraging; but at other times he is rewarded for his patient watching. A buck comes bounding forward, the hounds after him in full cry. At intervals he stops, and throws himself back on his haunches like a halted hare. His eyes are protruded, and watching backward. His beautiful neck is swollen with fear and rage, and his branching antlers tower high in the air. Again he springs forward, and approaches the silent hunter, who, with a beating heart, holds his piece in the attitude of "ready." He makes another of his pauses. The gun is levelled, the trigger pulled; the bullet speeds forth, and strikes into his broad chest, causing him to leap upward in the spasmodic effort of death.

The excitement of a scene like this rewards the hunter for his long and lonely vigil.

"Torch-hunting," or "fire-hunting," as it is sometimes termed, is another method of capturing the fallow deer. It is done by carrying a torch in a very dark night through woods where deer are known to frequent. The torch is made of pine-knots, well dried. They are not tied in bunches, as represented by some writers, but carried in a vessel of hard metal. A frying-pan with a long handle, as already stated, is best for the purpose.

The "knots" are kindled within the pan, and, if good ones, yield a blaze that will light the woods for a hundred yards around. The deer seeing this strange object, and impelled by curiosity, approaches within range; and the "glance" of his eyes, like two burning coals, betrays him to the hunter, who with his deadly rifle "sights" between the shining orbs and fire.

While we were on the subject of torch-hunting the doctor took up the cue, and gave us an account of a torch-hunt he had made in Tennessee.

"I will tell you of a 'torch-hunt,'" said he, "of which *pars magna fui*, and which ended with a 'catastrophe.' It took place in Tennessee, where I was for a while sojourning. I am not much of a hunter, as you all know; but happening to reside in a 'settlement,' where there were some celebrated hunters, and in the neighbourhood of which was an abundance of game, I was getting very fond of it. I had heard, among other things, of this 'torch-hunting,'—in fact, had read many interesting descriptions of it, but I had never witnessed the sport myself; and was therefore eager, above all things, to join in a torch-hunt.

"The opportunity at length offered. A party was made up to go hunting, of which I was one.

"There were six of us in all; but it was arranged that we should separate into three pairs, each taking its own torch and a separate course through the woods. In each pair one was to carry the light, while the other managed the 'shooting iron.' We were all to meet at an appointed rendezvous when the hunt was over.

"These preliminaries being arranged, and the torches made ready, we separated. My partner and I soon plunged into the deep forest.

"The night was dark as pitch—dark nights are the best—and when we entered the woods we had to grope our way. Of course, we had not yet set fire to our torch, as we had not reached the place frequented by the deer.

"My companion was an old hunter, and by right should have carried the gun; but it was arranged differently, out of compliment to me—the stranger, he held in one hand the huge frying-pan, while in a bag over his shoulder was a bushel or more of dry pine-knots.

"On arriving at the place where it was expected deer would be found, we set fire to our torch, and in a few moments the blaze threw its glaring circle around us, painting with vermilion tints the trunks of the great trees.

"In this way we proceeded onward, advancing slowly, and with as little noise as possible. We talked only in whispers, keeping our eyes turned upon all sides at once. But we walked and walked, up hill and down hill, for, I should say, ten miles at the least; and not a single pair of bright orbs answered to our luminary. Not a deer's eye reflected the blaze of our torch.

"We had kept the fire replenished and burning vividly to no purpose, until hardly a knot remained in the bag.

"I had grown quite tired in this fruitless search. So had my companion, and both of us felt chagrin and disappointment. We felt this the more keenly as there had been a 'supper-wager' laid between us and our friends, as to what party would kill the greatest number of deer, and we fancied once or twice that we heard shots far off in the direction the others had gone. We were likely to come back empty-handed, while they, no doubt, would bring a deer each, perhaps more.

"We were returning towards the point from which we had started, both of us in a most unamiable mood, when all at once an object right before us attracted my attention, and brought me to a sudden halt. I did not wait to ask any questions. A pair of small round circles glistened in the darkness like two little discs of fire. Of course they were eyes. Of course, they were the eyes of a deer.

"I could see no body, for the two luminous objects shone as if set in a ground of ebony. But I did not stay to scan in what they were set. My piece was up. I glanced hastily along the barrel. I sighted between the eyes. I pulled the trigger. I fired.

"As I did so, I fancied that I heard my companion shouting to me, but the report hindered me from hearing what he said.

"When the echoes died away, however, his voice reached me, in a full, clear tone, pronouncing these words:—

"'Tarnation, doctor! You've shot Squire Robbins's bull!'

"At the same time the bellowing of the bull, mingling with his own loud laugh, convinced me that the hunter had spoken the truth.

"He was a good old fellow, and promised to keep dark; but it was necessary to make all right with 'Squire Robbins.' So the affair soon got wind, and my torch-hunt became, for a time, the standing joke of the settlement."

Chapter Twenty Four
Deer Hunt in a "Dug-Out."

As we were now approaching the regions where the common fallow deer ceased to be met with, and where its place is supplied by two other species, these last became the subject of our talk. The species referred to are the "black-tails," and "long-tails" (*Cervus macrotis* and *leucurus*).

Ike and Redwood were well acquainted with both kinds, as they had often trapped beaver in the countries where these deer are found; and they gave us a very good account of the habits of these animals, which showed that both species were in many respects similar to the *Cervus Virginianus*. Their form, however, as well as their size, colour, and markings, leave no doubt of their being specifically distinct not only from the latter, but from each other. Indeed, there are two varieties of the black-tails, differing in some respects, although both have the dark hair upon the tail, and the long ears, which so much distinguish them from other deer. The great length of their ears gives to their heads something of a "mulish" look—hence they are often known among the trappers by the name of "mule deer." Ike and Redwood spoke of them by this name, although they also knew them as "black-tails," and this last is the designation most generally used. They receive it on account of the colour of the hair upon the upper side of their tail-tips, which is of a jetty blackness, and is very full and conspicuous.

The two species have been often confounded with each other, though in many respects they are totally unlike. The black-tails are larger, their legs shorter and their bodies more "chunky," and altogether of stouter build. In running, they bound with all their feet raised at once; while those of the long-tailed species run more like the common fallow deer—by trotting a few steps, then giving a bound, and trotting as before.

The ears of the black-tails stand up full half the height of their antlers, and their hair, of a reddish-brown colour, is coarser than the hair of the *Cervus Virginianus*, and more like the coat of the elk (*Cervus Canadensis*). Their hoofs, too, are shorter and wider, and in this respect there is also a similarity to the elk. The flesh of the black-tails is inferior to that of the fallow deer, while the long-tailed kind produces a venison very similar to the latter.

Both species inhabit woodlands occasionally, but their favourite *habitat* is the prairie, or that species of undulating country where prairie and forest alternate, forming a succession of groves and openings. Both are found only in the western half of the continent—that is, in the wild regions extending from the Mississippi to the Pacific. In longitude, as far east as the Mississippi, they are rarely seen; but as you travel westward, either approaching the Rocky Mountains, or beyond these to the shores of the Pacific, they are the common deer of the country. The black-tailed kind is more southern in its range. It is found in the Californias, and the valleys of the Rocky Mountains, as far south as Texas; while to the north it is met with in Oregon, and on the eastern side of the Rocky Mountains, as high as the fifty-fourth parallel. The long-tailed species is the most common deer of Oregon and the Columbia River, and its range also extends east of the Rocky Mountains, though not so far as the longitude of the Mississippi.

The hunter-naturalist, who had some years before made a journey to Oregon, and of course had become well acquainted with the habits of the *Cervus leucurus*, gave us a full account of them, and related a stirring adventure that had befallen him while hunting "long-tails" upon the Columbia.

"The long-tailed deer," began he, "is one of the smallest of the deer kind. Its weight rarely exceeds 100 pounds. It resembles in form and habits the common fallow deer, the chief distinction being the tail, which is a very conspicuous object. This appendage is often found to measure eighteen inches in length!

"While running, the tail is held erect, and kept constantly switching from side to side, so as to produce a singular and somewhat ludicrous effect upon the mind of the spectator.

"The gait of this animal is also peculiar. It first takes two ambling steps that resemble a trot, after these it makes a long bound, which carries it about twice the distance of the steps, and then it trots again. No matter how closely pursued, it never alters this mode of progression.

"Like the fallow deer, it produces spotted fawns, which are brought forth in the spring, and change their colour to that of the deer itself in the first winter. About the month of November they gather into herds, and remain together until April, when they separate, the females secreting themselves to bring forth their young.

"The long-tailed deer is often found in wooded countries; though its favourite haunts are not amid the heavy timber of the great forests, but in the park-like openings that occur in many parts of the Rocky Mountain valleys.

"Sometimes whole tracts of country are met with in these regions, whose surface exhibits a pleasing variety of woodland and prairie; sloping hills appear with coppices upon their crests and along their sides. Among these natural groves may be seen troops of the long-tailed deer, browsing along the declivities of the hills, and, by their elegant attitudes and graceful movements, adding to the beauty of the landscape.

"Some years ago I had an opportunity of hunting the long-tailed, deer. I was on my way across the Rocky Mountains to Fort Vancouver, when circumstances rendered it necessary that I should stop for some days at a small trading-post on one of the branches of the Columbia. I was, in fact, detained, waiting for a party of fur-traders with whom I was to travel, and who required some time to get their packs in readiness.

"The trading-post was a small place, with miserable accommodations, having scarcely room enough in its two or three wretched log-cabins to lodge half the company that happened at the time to claim its hospitality. As my business was simply to wait for my travelling companions, I was of course *ennuyé* almost to death in such a place. There was nothing to be seen around but packs of beaver, otter, mink, fox, and bear skins; and nothing to be heard but the incessant chattering of Canadian voyageurs, in their mixed jargon of French, English, and Indian. To make matters still more unpleasant, there was very little to eat, and nothing to drink but the clear water of the little mountain-stream upon which the fort was built.

"The surrounding country, however, was beautiful; and the lovely landscapes that on every side met the eye almost compensated for the discomforts of the post. The surface of the country was what is termed rolling—gentle undulations here and there rising into dome-shaped hills of low elevation. These were crowned with copses of shrubby trees, principally of the wild filbert or hazel (*corylus*), with several species of *rosa* and raspberry (rubus), and bushes of the june-berry (*amelanchier*), with their clusters of purplish-red fruit. The openings between were covered with a sward of short gramma grass, and the whole landscape presented the appearance of a cultivated park; so that one involuntarily looked along the undulating outlines of the hills for some noble mansion or lordly castle.

"It is just in such situations that the fallow deer delights to dwell; and these are the favourite haunts of its near congeners, the long-tails. I had ascertained this from the people at the post; and the fact that fresh venison formed our staple and daily food was proof sufficient that some species of deer was to be found in the neighbourhood. I was not long, therefore, after my arrival, in putting myself in train for a hunt.

"Unfortunately, the gentlemen of the company were too busy to go along with me; so also were the numerous *engagés*; and I set out, taking only my servant, a *bois brulé*, or half-breed, who happened, however, to be a good guide for such an expedition, as well as a first-rate hunter.

"Setting out, we kept down the stream for some distance, walking along its bank. We saw numerous deer-tracks in the mud, where the animals had gone to and from the water. These tracks were almost fresh, and many of them, as my servant averred, must have been made the previous night by the animals coming to drink—a common habit with them, especially in hot weather.

"But, strange to say, we walked a mile or more without getting a glimpse of a single deer, or any other sort of animal. I was becoming discouraged, when my man proposed that we should leave the stream, and proceed back among the hills. The deer, he believed, would be found there.

"This was resolved upon; and we accordingly struck out for the high ground. We soon climbed up from the river bottom, and threaded our way amidst the fragrant shrubbery of amelanchiers and wild-roses, cautiously scrutinising every new vista that opened before us.

"We had not gone far before we caught sight of several deer; we could also hear them at intervals, behind the copses that surrounded us, the males uttering a strange whistling sound, similar to that produced by blowing into the barrel of a gun, while this was occasionally replied to by the goat-like bleat of the females.

"Strange to say, however, they were all very shy, and notwithstanding much cautious crouching and creeping among the bushes, we wandered about for nearly two-thirds of the day without getting a shot at any of them.

"What had made them so wary we could not at the time, tell, but we afterwards learned that a large party of Flathead Indians had gone over the ground only a few days before, and had put the deer through a three days chase, from which they had not yet recovered. Indeed, we saw Indian 'sign' all along the route, and at one place came upon the head and horns of a fine buck, which, from some fancy or other of the hunter, had been left suspended from the branch of a tree, and had thus escaped being stripped by the wolves.

"At sight of this trophy, my companion appeared to be in ecstasies. I could not understand what there was in a worthless set of antlers to produce such joyful emotions; but as Blue Dick—such was the *soubriquet* of my servant—was not much given to idle exhibitions of feeling, I knew there must be something in it.

"'Now, master,' said he, addressing me, 'if I had something else, I could promise you a shot at the long-tails, shy as they are.'

"'Something else! What do you want?' I inquired.

"'Something that ought to grow about yar, else I'm mightily mistaken in the sign. Let me try down yonder,'—and Dick pointed to a piece of low swampy ground that lay to one side of our course.

"I assented, and followed him to the place.

"We had hardly reached the border of the wet ground, when an exclamation from my companion told me that the 'something' he wanted was in sight.

"'Yonder, master; the very weed: see yonder.'

"Dick pointed to a tall herbaceous plant that grew near the edge of the swamp. Its stem was fully eight feet in height, with large lobed leaves, and a wide-spreading umbel of pretty white flowers. I knew the plant well. It was that which is known in some places as master-wort, but more commonly by the name of cow parsnip. Its botanical name is *Heracleum lanatum*. I knew that its roots possessed stimulant and carminative properties; but that the plant had anything to do with deer-hunting, I was ignorant.

"Dick, however, was better acquainted with its uses in that respect; and his hunter-craft soon manifested itself.

"Drawing his knife from its sheath, he cut one of the joints from the stem of the heracleum, about six inches in length. This he commenced fashioning somewhat after the manner of a penny-trumpet.

"In a few minutes he had whittled it to the proper form and dimensions, after which he put up his knife, and applying the pipe to his lips, blew into it. The sound produced was so exactly like that which I had already heard to proceed from the deer, that I was startled by the resemblance.

"Not having followed his manoeuvres, I fancied for a moment that we had got into close proximity with one of the long-tails. My companion laughed, as he pointed triumphantly to his new made 'call.'

"'Now, master,' said he, 'we'll soon "rub out" one of the long-tail bucks.'

"So saying, he took up the antlers, and desired me to follow him.

"We proceeded as before, walking quickly but cautiously among the thickets, and around their edges. We had gone only a few hundred paces farther, when the hollow whistle of a buck sounded in our ears.

"'Now,' muttered Dick, 'we have him. Squat down, master, under the bush—so.'

"I did as desired, hiding myself under the leafy branches of the wild rose-trees. My companion cowered down beside me in such an attitude that he himself was concealed, while the buck's head and antlers were held above the foliage, and visible from several points where the ground was open.

"As soon as we were fairly placed, Dick applied the call to his lips, and blew his mimic note several times in succession. We heard what appeared to be an echo, but it was the response of a rival; and shortly after we could distinguish a hoof-stroke upon the dry turf, as if some animal was bounding towards us.

"Presently appeared a fine buck, at an opening between two copses, about one hundred paces from the spot where we lay. It had halted, thrown back upon its flanks until its haunches almost touched the ground, while its full large eye glanced over the opening, as if searching for some object.

"At this moment Dick applied the reed to his lips, at the same time moving the horns backward and forward, in imitation of a buck moving his head in a threatening manner.

"The stranger now perceived what appeared to him the branching horns of a rival, hearing, at the same time, the well-known challenge. This was not to be borne, and rising erect on all-fours, with his brow-antlers set forward, he accepted the challenge, and came bounding forward.

"At the distance of twenty paces or so, be again baited, as if still uncertain of the character of his enemy; but that halt was fatal to him, for by Dick's directions I had made ready my rifle, and taking sight at his breast, I pulled trigger. The result was as my companion had predicted, and the buck was 'rubbed out.'

"After skinning our game, and hanging the meat out of reach of the barking wolves, we proceeded as before; and soon after another buck was slain in a manner very similar to that described.

"This ended our day's hunt, as it was late before Dick had bethought him of the decoy; and taking the best parts of both the long-tails upon our shoulders, we trudged homeward to the post.

"Part of our road, as we returned, lay along the stream, and we saw several deer approaching the water, but, cumbered as we were, we failed in getting a shot. An idea, however, was suggested to my companion that promised us plenty of both sport and venison for the next hunt—which was to take place by night.

"This idea he communicated to me for my approval. I readily gave my consent, as I saw in the proposal the chances of enjoying a very rare sport. That sport was to be a fire-hunt; but not as usually practised among backwoodsmen, by carrying a torch through the woods. Our torch was to float upon the water, while we were snugly seated beside it; in other words, we would carry our torch in a canoe, and, floating down stream, would shoot the deer that happened to be upon the banks drinking or cooling their hoofs in the water. I had heard of the plan, but had never practised it, although I was desirous of so doing. Dick had often killed deer in this way, and therefore knew all about it. It was agreed, then, that upon the following night we should try the experiment.

"During the next day, Dick and I proceeded in our preparations without saying anything to any one. It was our design to keep our night-hunt a secret, lest we might be unsuccessful, and get laughed at for our pains. On the other hand, should we succeed in killing a goodly number of long-tails, it would be time enough to let it be known how we had managed matters.

"We had little difficulty in keeping our designs to ourselves. Every one was busy with his own affairs, and took no heed of our manoeuvres.

"Our chief difficulty lay in procuring a boat; but for the consideration of a few loads of powder, we at length borrowed an old canoe that belonged to one of the Flathead Indians—a sort of hanger-on of the post.

"This craft was simply a log of the cotton-wood, rudely hollowed out by means of an axe, and slightly rounded at the ends to produce the canoe-shape. It was that species of water craft popularly known throughout Western America as a 'dug-out,' a phrase which explains itself. It was both old and ricketty, but after a short inspection, Blue Dick declared it would do 'fust-rate.'

"Our next move was to prepare our torch. For this we had to make an excursion to the neighbouring hills, where we found the very material we wanted—the dry knots of the pitch-pine-tree.

"A large segment of birch-bark was then sought for and obtained, and our implements were complete.

"At twilight all was ready, and stepping into our dug-out, we paddled silently down stream.

"As soon as we had got out of the neighbourhood of the post, we lighted our torch. This was placed in a large frying-pan out upon the bow, and was in reality rather a fire of pine-knots than a torch. It blazed up brightly, throwing a glare over the surface of the stream, and reflecting in red light every object upon both banks. We, on the other hand, were completely hidden from view by means of the birch-bark screen, which stood up between us and the torch.

"As soon as we were fairly under way, I yielded up the paddle to Dick, who now assigned to himself the double office of guiding the dug-out and keeping the torch trimmed. I was to look to the shooting; so, placing my trusty rifle across my thighs, I sat alternately scanning both banks as we glided along.

"I shall never forget the romantic effect which was produced upon my mind during that wild excursion. The scenery of the river upon which we had launched our craft was at all times of a picturesque character: under the blaze of the pine-wood—its trees and rocks tinted with a reddish hue, while the rippling flood below ran like molten gold—the effect was heightened to a degree of sublimity which could not have failed to impress the dullest imagination. It was the autumn season, too, and the foliage, which had not yet commenced falling, had assumed those rich varied tints so characteristic of the American *sylva*—various hues of green and golden, and yellow and deep red were exhibited upon the luxuriant frondage that lined the banks of the stream, and here and there drooped like embroidered curtains down to the water's edge. It was a scene of that wild beauty, that picturesque sublimity, which carries one to the contemplation of its Creator.

"'Yonder!' muttered a voice, that roused me from my reverie. It was Dick who spoke; and in the dark shadow of the birch-bark I could see one of his arms extended, and pointing to the right bank.

"My eyes followed the direction indicated; they soon rested upon two small objects, that from the darker background of the foliage appeared bright and luminous. These objects were round, and close to each other; and at a glance I knew them to be the eyes of some animal, reflecting the light of our torch.

"My companion whispered me that they were the eyes of a deer. I took sight with my rifle, aiming as nearly as I could midway between the luminous spots. I pulled trigger, and my true piece cracked like a whip.

"The report was not loud enough to drown the noises that came back from the shore. There was a rustling of leaves, followed by a plunge, as of some body felling in the water.

"Dick turned the head of the dug-out, and paddled her up to the bank. The torch, blazing brightly, lit up the scene ahead of us, and our eyes were gratified by the sight of a fine buck, that had fallen dead into the river. He was about being drawn into the eddy of the current, but Dick prevented this, and, seizing him by the antlers, soon deposited him safely in the bottom of the dug-out.

"Our craft was once more headed down stream, and we scrutinised every winding of the banks in search of another pair of gleaming eyes. In less than half an hour these appeared, and we succeeded in killing a second long-tail—a doe—and dragged her also into the boat.

"Shortly after, a third was knocked over, which we found standing out in the river upon a small point of sand. This proved to be a young spike-buck, his horns not having as yet branched off into antlers.

"About a quarter of a mile farther down, a fourth, deer was shot at, and missed, the dug-out having grazed suddenly against a rock just as I was pulling trigger, thus rendering my aim unsteady.

"I need hardly say that this sport was extremely exciting; and we had got many miles from the post, without thinking either of the distance or the fact that we should be under the disagreeable necessity of paddling the old Flathead's canoe every inch of the way back again. Down stream it was all plain sailing; and Dick's duty was light enough, as it consisted merely in keeping the dug-out head foremost in the middle of the river. The current ran at the rate of three miles an hour, and therefore drifted us along with sufficient rapidity.

"The first thing that suggested a return to either of us, was the fact that our pine-knots had run out: Dick had just piled the last of them in the frying-pan.

"At this moment, a noise sounded in our ears that caused us some feelings of alarm: it was the noise of falling water. It was not new to us, for, since leaving the post, we had passed the mouths of several small streams that debouched into the one upon which we were, in most cases over a jumble of rocks, thus forming a series of noisy rapids. But that which we now heard was directly ahead of us, and must, thought we, be a rapid or fall of the stream itself; moreover, it sounded louder than any we had hitherto passed.

"We lost little time in conjectures. The first impulse of my companion, upon catching the sound, was to stop the progress of the dug-out, which in a few seconds he succeeded in doing; but by this time our torch had shown us that there was a sharp turning in the river, with a long reach of smooth water below. The cascade, therefore, could not be in our stream, but in some tributary that fell into it near the bend.

"On seeing this, Dick turned his paddle, and permitted the dug-out once more to float with the current.

"The next moment we passed the mouth of a good-sized creek, whose waters, having just leaped a fall of several feet, ran into the river, covered with white froth and bubbles. We could see the fall at a little distance, through the branches of the trees; and as we swept on, its foaming sheet reflected the light of our torch like shining metal.

"We had scarcely passed this point, when my attention was attracted by a pair of fiery orbs that glistened out of some low bushes upon the left bank of the river. I saw that they were the eyes of some animal, but what kind of animal I could not guess. I know they were not the eyes of a deer. Their peculiar scintillation, their lesser size, the wide space between them all convinced me they were not deer's eyes. Moreover, they moved at times, as if the head of the animal was carried about in irregular circles. This is never the case with the eyes of the deer, which either pass hurriedly from point to point, or remain with a fixed and steadfast gaze.

"I knew, therefore, it was no deer; but no matter what—it was some wild creature, and all such are alike the game of the prairie-hunter.

"I took aim, and pulled trigger. While doing so, I heard the voice of my companion warning me, as I thought, not to fire. I wondered at this admonition, but it was then too late to heed it, for it had been uttered almost simultaneously with the report of my rifle.

"I first looked to the bank, to witness the effect of my shot. To my great surprise, the eyes were still there, gleaming from the bushes as brightly as ever.

"Had I missed my aim? It is true, the voice of my companion had somewhat disconcerted me; but I still believed that my bullet must have sped truly, as it had been delivered with a good aim.

"As I turned to Dick for an explanation, a new sound fell upon my ears that explained all, at the same time causing me no slight feeling of alarm. It was a sound not unlike that sometimes uttered by terrified swine, but still louder and more threatening. I knew it well—I knew it was the snort of the grizzly bear!

"Of all American animals, the grizzly bear is the most to be dreaded. Armed or unarmed, man is no match for him, and even the courageous hunter of these parts shuns the encounter. This was why my companion had admonished me not to fire. I thought I had missed: it was not so. My bullet had hit and stung the fierce brute to madness; and a quick cracking among the bushes was immediately followed by a heavy plunge: the bear was in the water!

"'Good heavens, he's after us!' cried Dick in accents of alarm, at the same time propelling the dug-out with all his might.

"It proved true enough that the bear was after us, and the very first plunge had brought his nose almost up to the side of the canoe. However, a few well-directed strokes of the paddle set us in quick motion, and we were soon gliding rapidly down stream, followed by the enraged animal, that every now and then uttered one of his fierce snorts.

"What rendered our situation a terrible one was, that we could not now see the bear, nor tell how far he might be from us. All to the rear of the canoe was of a pitchy darkness, in consequence of the screen of birch-bark. No object could be distinguished in that direction, and it was only by hearing him that we could tell he was still some yards off. The snorts, however, were more or less distinct, as heard amid the varying roar of the waterfall; and sometimes they seemed as if the snout from which they proceeded was close up to our stern.

"We knew that if he once laid his paw upon the canoe, we should either be sunk or compelled to leap out and swim for it. We knew, moreover, that such an event would be certain death to one of us at least.

"I need hardly affirm, that my companion used his paddle with all the energy of despair. I assisted him as much as was in my power with the butt-end of my gun, which was now empty. On account of the hurry and darkness, I had not attempted to re-load it.

"We had shot down stream for a hundred yards or so, and were about congratulating ourselves on the prospect of an escape from the bear, when a new object of dread presented itself to our terrified imaginations. This object was the sound of falling water; but not as before, coming from some tributary stream. No. It was a fall of the river upon which we were floating, and evidently only a very short distance below us!

"We were, in fact, within less than one hundred yards of it. Our excitement, in consequence of being pursued by the bear, as well as the fact that the sough of the cascade above still filled our ears, had prevented us from perceiving this new danger until we had approached it.

"A shout of terror and warning from my companion seemed the echo of one I had myself uttered. Both of us understood the peril of our situation, and both, without speaking another word, set about attempting to stop the boat.

"We paddled with all our strength—he with the oar, whilst I used the flat butt of my rifle. We had succeeded in bringing her to a sort of equilibrium, and were in hopes of being able to force her toward the bank, when all at once we heard a heavy object strike against the stern. At the same moment, the bow rose up into the air, and a number of the burning pine-knots fell back into the bottom of the canoe. They still continued to blaze; and their light now falling towards the stern, showed us a fearful object. The bear had seized hold of the dug-out, and his fierce head and long curving claws were visible over the edge!

"Although the little craft danced about upon the water, and was likely to be turned keel upward, the animal showed no intention of relaxing its hold; but, on the contrary, seemed every moment mounting higher into the canoe.

"Our peril was now extreme. We knew it, and the knowledge half paralysed us.

"Both of us started up, and for some moments half sat, half crouched, uncertain how to act. Should we use the paddles, and get the canoe ashore, it would only be to throw ourselves into the jaws of the bear. On the other hand, we could not remain as we were, for in a few seconds we should be drifted over the falls; and how high these were we knew not. We had never heard of them: they might be fifty feet—they might be a hundred! High enough, they were, no doubt, to precipitate us into eternity.

"The prospect was appalling, and our thoughts ran rapidly. Quick action was required. I could think of no other than to lean sternward, and strike at the bear with my clubbed rifle, at the same time calling upon my companion to paddle for the shore. We preferred, under all circumstances, risking the chances of a land encounter with our grizzly antagonist.

"I had succeeded in keeping the bear out of the canoe by several well-planted blows upon the snout; and Dick was equally successful in forcing the dug-out nearer to the bank, when a sharp crack reached my ears, followed by a terrified cry from my companion.

"I glanced suddenly round, to ascertain the cause of these demonstrations. Dick held in his hands a short round stick, which I recognised as the shaft of the paddle. The blade had snapped off, and was floating away on the surface!

"We were now helpless. The *manège* of the canoe was no longer possible. Over the falls she must go!

"We thought of leaping out, but it was too late. We were almost upon the edge, and the black current that bore our craft swiftly along would have carried our bodies with like velocity. We could not make a dozen strokes before we should be swept to the brink: it was too late.

"We both saw this; and each knew the feelings of the other, for we felt alike. Neither spoke; but, crouching down and holding the gunwales of the canoe, we awaited the awful moment.

"The bear seemed to have some apprehension as well as ourselves; for, instead of continuing his endeavours to climb into the canoe, he contented himself with holding fast to the stern, evidently under some alarm.

"The torch still blazed, and the canoe was catching fire; perhaps this it was that alarmed the bear.

"The last circumstance gave us at the moment but little concern; the greater danger eclipsed the less. We had hardly noticed it, when we felt that we were going over!

"The canoe shot outward as if propelled by some projectile force; then came a loud crash, as though we had dropped upon a hard rock. Water, and spray, and froth were dashed over our bodies; and the next moment, to our surprise as well as delight, we felt ourselves still alive, and seated in the canoe, which was floating gently in still smooth water.

"It was quite dark, for the torch had been extinguished; but even in the darkness we could perceive the bear swimming and floundering near the boat. To our great satisfaction, we saw him heading for the shore, and widening the distance between himself and us with all the haste he could make. The unexpected precipitation over the falls had cooled his courage, if not his hostility.

"Dick and I headed the canoe, now half full of water, for the opposite bank, which we contrived to reach by using the rifle and our hands for paddles. Here we made the little vessel fast to a tree, intending to leave it there, as we could not by any possibility get it back over the fall. Having hung our game out of reach of the wolves, we turned our faces up-stream, and, after a long and wearisome walk, succeeded in getting back to the post.

"Next morning, a party went down for the venison, with the intention also of carrying the canoe back over the fall. The craft, however, was found to be so much injured, that it would not hang together during the portage, and was therefore abandoned. This was no pleasant matter to me, for it afterwards cost me a considerable sum before I could square with the old Flathead for his worthless dug-out."

Chapter Twenty Five
Old Ike and the Grizzly

A—'s adventure ending in a grizzly bear story, drew the conversation upon that celebrated animal, and we listened to the many curious facts related about it, with more than usual interest.

The grizzly bear (*Ursus ferox*) is, beyond all question, the most formidable of the wild creatures inhabiting the continent of America—jaguar and cougar not excepted. Did he possess the swiftness of foot of either the lion or tiger of the Old World, he would be an assailant as dangerous as either; for he is endowed with the strength of the former, and quite equals the latter in ferocity. Fortunately, the horse outruns him; were it not so, many a human victim would be his, for he can easily overtake a man on foot. As it is, hundreds of well-authenticated stories attest the prowess of this fierce creature. There is not a "mountain-man" in America who cannot relate a string of perilous adventures about the "grizzly bar;" and the instances are far from being few, in which human life has been sacrificed in conflicts with this savage beast.

The grizzly bear is an animal of large dimensions; specimens have been killed and measured quite equal to the largest size of the polar bear, though there is much variety in the sizes of different individuals. About 500 pounds might be taken as the average weight.

In shape, the grizzly bear is a much more compact animal than either the black or polar species: his ears are larger, his arms stouter, and his aspect fiercer. His teeth are sharp and strong; but that which his enemies most dread is the armature of his paws. The paws themselves are so large, as frequently to leave in the mud a track of twelve inches in length, by eight in breadth; and from the extremities of these formidable fists protrude horn-like claws full six inches long! Of course, we are speaking of individuals of the largest size.

These claws are crescent-shaped, and would be still longer, but in all cases nearly an inch is worn from their points.

The animal digs up the ground in search of marmots, burrowing squirrels, and various esculent roots; and this habit accounts for the blunted condition of his claws. They are sharp enough, notwithstanding, to peel the hide from a horse or buffalo, or to drag the scalp from a hunter—a feat which has been performed by grizzly bears on more than one occasion.

The colour of this animal is most generally brownish, with white hairs intermixed, giving that greyish or grizzled appearance—whence the trivial name, grizzly. But although this is the most common colour of the species, there are many varieties. Some are almost white, others yellowish red, and still others nearly black. The season, too, has much to do with the colour; and the pelage is shaggier and longer than that of the *Ursus Americanus*. The eyes are small in proportion to the size of the animal, but dark and piercing.

The geographical range of the grizzly bear is extensive. It is well-known that the great chain of the Rocky Mountains commences on the shores of the Arctic Ocean, and runs southwardly through the North-American continent. In those mountains, the grizzly bear is found, from their northern extremity, at least as far as that point where the Rio Grande makes its great bend towards the Gulf of Mexico.

In the United States and Canada, this animal has never been seen in a wild state. This is not strange. The grizzly bear has no affinity with the forest. Previous to the settling of these territories, they were all forest-covered. The grizzly is rarely found under heavy timber, like his congener the black bear; and, unlike the latter, he is not a tree-climber. The black bear "hugs" himself up a tree, and usually destroys his victim by compression. The grizzly does not possess this power, so as to enable him to ascend a tree-trunk; and for such a purpose, his huge dull claws are worse than useless. His favourite haunts are the thickets of *Corylus rubus*, and *Amelanchiers*, under the shade of which he makes his lair, and upon the berries of which he partially subsists. He lives much by the banks of streams, hunting among the willows, or wanders along the steep and rugged bluffs, where scrubby pine and dwarf cedar (*Juniperus prostrata*), with its rooting branches, forms an almost impenetrable underwood. In short, the grizzly bear of America is to be met with in situations very similar to those which are the favourite haunts of the African lion, which, after all, is not so much the king of the forest, as of the mountain and the open plain.

The grizzly bear is omnivorous. Fish, flesh, and fowl are eaten by him apparently with equal relish. He devours frogs, lizards, and other reptiles.

He is fond of the larvae of insects; these are often found in large quantities adhering to the under sides of decayed logs. To get at them, the grizzly bear will roll over logs of such size and weight, as would try the strength of a yoke of oxen.

He can "root" like a hog, and will often plough up acres of prairie in search of the wapatoo and Indian turnip. Like the black bear, he is fond of sweets; and the wild-berries, consisting of many species of currant, gooseberry, and service berry, are greedily gathered into his capacious maw.

He is too slow of foot to overtake either buffalo, elk, or deer, though he sometimes comes upon these creatures unawares; and he will drag the largest buffalo to the earth, if he can only get his claws upon it.

Not unfrequently he robs the panther of his repast, and will drive a whole pack of wolves from the carrion they have just succeeded in killing.

Several attempts have been made to raise the young grizzlies, but these have all been abortive, the animals proving anything but agreeable pets. As soon as grown to a considerable size, their natural ferocity displays itself, and their dangerous qualities usually lead to the necessity for their destruction.

For a long time the great polar bear has been the most celebrated animal of his kind; and most of the bear-adventures have related to him. Many a wondrous tale of his prowess and ferocity has been told by the whaler and arctic voyager, in which this creature figures as the hero. His fame, however, is likely to be eclipsed by his hitherto less-known congener—the grizzly. The golden lure which has drawn half the world to California, has also been the means of bringing this fierce animal more into notice; for the mountain-valleys of the Sierra Nevada are a favourite range of the species. Besides, numerous "bear scrapes" have occurred to the migrating bands who have crossed the great plains and desert tracts that stretch from the Mississippi to the shores of the South Sea. Hundreds of stories of this animal, more or less true, have of late attained circulation through the columns of the press and the pages of the traveller's note-book, until the grizzly bear is becoming almost as much an object of interest as the elephant, the hippopotamus, or the king of beasts himself.

Speaking seriously, he is a dangerous assailant. White hunters never attack him unless when mounted and well armed; and the Indians consider the killing a grizzly bear a feat equal to the scalping of a human foe. These never attempt to hunt him, unless when a large party is together; and the hunt is, among some tribes, preceded by a ceremonious feast and a bear-dance.

It is often the lot of the solitary trapper to meet with this four-footed enemy, and the encounter is rated as equal to that with two hostile Indians.

Of course, both Redwood and old Ike had met with more than one "bar scrape," and the latter was induced to relate one of his best.

"Strengers," began he, "when you scare up a grizzly, take my advice, and gie 'im a wide berth—that is, unless yur unkimmun well mounted. Ov coorse, ef yur critter kin be depended upon, an' thur's no brush to 'tangle him, yur safe enuf; as no grizzly, as ever I seed, kin catch up wi' a hoss, whur the ground's open an' clur. F'r all that, whur the timmer's clost an' brushy, an' the ground o' that sort whur a hoss mout stummel, it are allers the safest plan to let ole Eph'm slide. I've seed a grizzly pull down as good a hoss as ever tracked a parairy, whur the critter hed got bothered in a thicket. The fellur that straddled him only saved himself by hookin' on to the limb o' a tree. 'Twant two minnits afore this child kim up—hearin' the rumpus. I hed good sight o' the bar, an' sent a bullet—sixty to the pound—into the varmint's brain-pan, when he immediately cawalloped over. But 'twur too late to save the hoss. He wur rubbed out. The bar had half skinned him, an' wur tarrin' at his guts! Wagh!"

Here the trapper unsheathed his clasp-knife, and having cut a "chunk" from a plug of real "Jeemes's River," stuck it into his cheek, and proceeded with his narration.

"I reck'n, I've seed a putty consid'able o' the grizzly bar in my time. Ef them thur chaps who writes about all sorts o' varmint hed seed as much o' the grizzly as I hev, they mout a gin a hul book consarnin' the critter. Ef I hed a plug o' bacca for every grizzly I've rubbed out, it 'ud keep my jaws waggin' for a good twel'month, I reck'n. Ye-es, strengers, I've done some bar-killin'—I hev that, an' no mistake! Hain't I, Mark?

"Wal, I wur a-gwine to tell you ov a sarcumstance that happened to this child about two yeern ago. It wur upon the Platte, atween Chimbly Rock an' Laramies'.

"I wur engaged as hunter an' guide to a carryvan o' emigrant folks that wur on thur way to Oregon.

"Ov coorse I allers kept ahead o' the carryvan, an' picked the place for thur camp.

"Wal, one arternoon I hed halted whur I seed some timmer, which ur a scace article about Chimbly Rock. This, thort I, 'll do for campin'-ground; so I got down, pulled the saddle off o' my ole mar, an' staked the critter upon the best patch o' grass that wur near, intendin' she shed hev her gut-full afore the camp cattle kim up to bother her.

"I hed shot a black-tail buck, an' after kindlin' a fire, I roasted a griskin' o' him, an' ate it.

"Still thur wan't no sign o' the carryvan, an' arter hangin' the buck out o' reach o' the wolves, I tuk up my rifle, an' set out to rackynoiter the neighbourhood.

"My mar bein' some'at jaded, I let her graze away, an' went afoot; an' that, let me tell you, strengers, ar about the foolichest thing you kin do upon a parairy. I wan't long afore I proved it; but I'll kum to that by 'm by.

"Wal, I fust clomb a conside'able hill, that gin me a view beyont. Thur war a good-sized parairy layin' torst the south an' west. Thur wur no trees 'ceptin' an odd cotton-wood hyur an' thur on the hillside.

"About a mile off I seed a flock of goats—what you'd call antelopes, though goats they ur, as sure as goats is goats.

"Thur waunt no kiver near them—not a stick, for the parairy wur as bar as yur hand; so I seed, at a glimp, it 'ud be no use a tryin' to approach, unless I tuk some plan to decoy the critters.

"I soon thort o' a dodge, an' went back to camp for my blanket, which wur a red Mackinaw. This I knew 'ud be the very thing to fool the goats with, an' I set out torst them.

"For the fust half-a-mile or so, I carried the blanket under my arm. Then I spread it out, an' walked behind it until I wur 'ithin three or four hundred yards o' the animals. I kept my eye on 'em through a hole in the blanket. They wur a-growin' scary, an' hed begun to run about in circles; so when I seed this, I knew it wur time to stop.

"Wal, I hunkered down, an' still keepin' the blanket spread out afore me, I hung it upon a saplin' that I had brought from the camp. I then stuck the saplin' upright in the ground; an' mind ye, it wan't so easy to do that, for the parairy wur hard friz, an' I hed to dig a hole wi' my knife. Howsomdever, I got the thing rigged at last, an' the blanket hangin' up in front kivered my karkidge most complete. I hed nothin' more to do but wait till the goats shed come 'ithin range o' my shootin'-iron.

"Wal, that wan't long. As ye all know, them goats is a mighty curious animal—as curious as weemen is—an' arter runnin' backward an' forrard a bit, an' tossin' up thur heads, an' sniffin' the air, one o' the fattest, a young prong-horn buck, trotted up 'ithin fifty yards o' me.

"I jest squinted through the sights, an' afore that goat hed time to wink twice, I hit him plum atween the eyes. Ov coorse he wur throwed in his tracks.

"Now, you'd a-jumped up, an' frightened the rest away—that's what you'd a done, strengers. But you see I knowd better. I knowd that so long's the critters didn't see my karkidge, they wan't a-gwine to mind the crack o' the gun. So I laid still, in behopes to git a wheen more o' them.

"As I hed calc'lated at fust, they didn't run away, an' I slipped in my charge as brisk as possible. But jest as I wur raisin' to take sight on a doe that hed got near enough, the hull gang tuk scare, an' broke off as ef a pack of paraïry-wolves wur arter 'em.

"I wur clean puzzled at this, for I knowd I hedn't done anythin' to frighten 'em, but I wan't long afore I diskivered the pause o' thur alarm. Jest then I heerd a snift, like the coughin' o' a glandered hoss; an' turnin' suddintly round, I spied the biggest bar it hed ever been my luck to set eyes on. He wur comin' direct torst me, an' at that minnit wan't over twenty yards from whur I lay. I knowd at a glimp he wur a grizzly!

"'Tain't no use to say I wan't skeart; I wur skeart, an' mighty bad skeart, I tell ye.

"At fust, I thort o' jumpin' to my feet, an' makin' tracks; but a minnit o' reflexshun showed me that 'ud be o' little use. Thur wur a half o' mile o' clur paraïry on every side o' me, an' I knowd the grizzly laid catch up afore I hed made three hundred yards in any direction. I knowd, too, that ef I started, the varmint 'ud be sartin to foller. It wur plain to see the bar meant mischief; I kud tell that from the glint o' his eyes.

"Thur wan't no time to lose in thinkin' about it. The brute wur still comin' nearer; but I noticed that he wur a-gwine slower an' slower, every now an' agin risin' to his hind-feet, clawin' his nose, an' sniffin' the air.

"I seed that it wur the red blanket that puzzled him; an' seein' this, I crep' closter behint it, an' cached as much o' my karkidge as it 'ud kiver.

"When the bar hed got 'ithin about ten yards o' the spot, he kim to a full stop, an' reared up as he hed did several times, with his belly full torst me. The sight wur too much for this niggur, who never afore had been bullied by eyther Injun or bar.

"'Twur a beautiful shot, an' I kudn't help tryin' it, ef 't hed been my last; so I poked my rifle through the hole in the blanket, an' sent a bullet atween the varmint's ribs.

"That wur, perhaps, the foolichest an' wust shot this child ever made. Hed I not fired it, the bar mout a gone off, feard o' the blanket; but I did fire, an' my narves bein' excited, I made a bad shot.

"I had ta'en sight for the heart, an' I only hit the varmint's shoulder.

"Ov coorse, the bar bein' now wounded, bekim savage, and cared no longer for the blanket. He roared out like a bull, tore at the place whur I hed hit him, an' then kim on as fast as his four legs 'ud carry him.

"Things looked squally. I throwed away my emp'y gun, an' drawed my bowie, expectin' nothin' else than a regular stand-up tussle wi' the bar. I knowd it wur no use turnin' tail now; so I braced myself up for a desp'rate fight.

"But jest as the bar hed got 'ithin ten feet o' me, an idee suddintly kim into my head. I hed been to Santa Fé, among them yaller-hided Mexikins, whur I hed seed two or three bull-fights. I hed seed them mattydoors fling thur red cloaks over a bull's head, jest when you'd a thort they wur a-gwine to be gored to pieces on the fierce critter's horns.

"Jest then, I remembered thur trick; an' afore the bar cud close on me, I grabbed the blanket, spreadin' it out as I tuk holt.

"Strangers, that wur a blanket an' no mistake! It wur as fine a five-point Mackinaw as ever kivered the hump-ribs o' a nor'-west trader. I used to wear it Mexikin-fashun when it rained; an' in coorse, for that purpose, thur wur a hole in the middle to pass the head through.

"Wal, jest as the bar sprung at me, I flopped the blanket straight in his face. I seed his snout a passin' through the hole, but I seed no more; for I feeled the critter's claws touchin' me, an' I let go.

"Now, thunk I, wur my time for a run. The blanket mout blin' him a leetle, an' I mout git some start.

"With this thort, I glid past the animal's rump, an' struck out over the parairy.

"The direction happened to be that that led torst the camp, half a mile off; but thur wur a tree nearer, on the side o' the hill. Ef I kud reach that, I knowd I 'ud be safe enuf, as the grizzly bar it don't climb.

"For the fust hundred yards I never looked round; then I only squinted back, runnin' all the while.

"I kud jest see that the bar appeared to be still a tossin' the blanket, and not fur from whur we hed parted kumpny.

"I thort this some'at odd; but I didn't stay to see what it meant till I hed put another hundred yards atween us. Then I half turned, an' tuk a good look; an' if you believe me, strangers, the sight I seed thur 'ud a made a Mormon larf. Although jest one minnit afore, I wur putty nigh skeart out o' my seven senses, that sight made me larf till I wur like to bring on a colic.

"Thur wur the bar wi' his head right a-through the blanket. One minnit, he 'ud rear up on his hind-feet, an' then the thing hung roun' him like a Mexikin greaser. The next minnit, he 'ud be down on all-fours, an' tryin' to foller me; an' then the Mackinaw 'ud trip him up, an' over he 'ud whammel, and kick to get free—all the while routin' like a mad buffalo. Jehosophat! it wur the funniest sight this child ever seed. Wagh!

"Wal, I watched the game awhile—only a leetle while; for I knowd that if the bar could git clur o' the rag, he mout still overtake me, an' drive me to the tree. That I didn't wan't, eyther, so I tuk to my heels agin' and soon reached camp.

"Thur I saddled my mar, an' then rid back to git my gun, an', perhaps, to give ole Eph'm a fresh taste o' lead.

"When I clomb the hill agin, the bar wur still out on the parairy, an' I cud see that the blanket wur a-hanging around 'im. Howsomdever, he wur makin' off torst the hills, thinkin', maybe, he'd hed enuf o' my kumpny.

"I wan't a-gwine to let 'im off so easy, for the skear he hed 'gin me; besides, he wur traillin' my Mackinaw along wi' 'im. So I galluped to whur my gun lay, an' havin' rammed home a ball, I then galluped arter ole grizzly.

"I soon overhauled him, an' he turned on me as savagerous as ever. But this time, feeling secure on the mar's back, my narves wur steadier; an' I shot the bar plum through the skull, which throwed him in his tracks wi' the blanket wropped about 'im.

"But sich a blanket as that wur then—ay, sich a blanket! I never seed sich a blanket! Thur wunt a square foot o' it that wan't torn to raggles. Ah, strangers, you don't know what it are to lose a five-point Mackinaw; no, that you don't. Cuss the bar!"

Chapter Twenty Six
A Battle with Grizzly Bears

As adventure with grizzly bears which had befallen the "captain" was next related. He had been travelling with a strange party—the "scalp-hunters,"—in the mountains near Santa Fé, when they were overtaken by a sudden and heavy fall of snow that rendered farther progress impossible. The "canon," a deep valley in which they had encamped, was difficult to get through at any time, but now the path, on account of the deep soft snow, was rendered impassable. When morning broke they found themselves fairly "in the trap."

"Above and below, the valley was choked up with snow five fathoms deep. Vast fissures—*barrancas*—were filled with the drift; and it was perilous to attempt penetrating in either direction. Two men had already disappeared.

"On each side of our camp rose the walls of the canon, almost vertical, to the height of a hundred feet. These we might have climbed had the weather been soft, for the rock was a trap formation, and offered numerous seams and ledges; but now there was a coating of ice and snow upon them that rendered the ascent impossible. The ground had been frozen hard before the storm came on, although it was now freezing no longer, and the snow would not bear our weight. All our efforts to get out of the valley proved idle; and we gave them over, yielding ourselves, in a kind of reckless despair, to wait for—we scarce knew what.

"For three days we sat shivering around the fires, now and then casting looks of gloomy inquiry around the sky. The same dull grey for an answer, mottled with flakes slanting earthward, for it still continued to know. Not a bright spot cheered the aching eye.

"The little platform on which we rested—a space of two or three acres—was still free from the snow-drift, on account of its exposure to the wind. Straggling pines, stunted and leafless, grew over its surface, in all about fifty or sixty trees. From these we obtained our fires; but what were fires when we had no meat to cook upon them!

"We were now in the third day without food! Without food, though not absolutely without eating—the men had bolted their gun-covers and the cat-skin flaps of their bullet-pouches, and were now seen—the last shift but one—stripping the *parflèche* from the soles of their moccasins!

"The women, wrapped in their *tilmas*, nestled closely in the embrace of father, brother, husband, and lover; for all these affections were present. The last string of *tasajo*, hitherto economised for their sake, had been parcelled out to them in the morning. That was gone, and whence was their next morsel to come? At long intervals, '*Ay da mi! Dios de mi alma!*' were heard only in low murmurs, as some colder blast swept down the canon. In the faces of those beautiful creatures might be read that uncomplaining patience—that high endurance—so characteristic of the Hispano-Mexican women.

"Even the stern men around them bore up with less fortitude. Rude oaths were muttered from time to time, and teeth ground together, with that strange wild look that heralds insanity. Once or twice I fancied that I observed a look of still stranger, still wilder expression, when the black ring forms around the eye—when the muscles twitch and quiver along gaunt, famished jaws—when men gaze guilty-like at each other. O God! it was fearful! The half-robber discipline, voluntary at the best, had vanished under the levelling-rod of a common suffering, and I trembled to think—

"'It clars a leetle, out tharawa!'

"It was the voice of the trapper, Garey, who had risen and stood pointing toward the East.

"In an instant we were all upon our feet, looking in the direction, indicated. Sure enough, there was a break in the lead-coloured sky—a yellowish streak, that widened out as we continued gazing—the flakes fell lighter and thinner, and in two hours more it had ceased snowing altogether.

"Half-a-dozen of us, shouldering our rifles, struck down the valley. We would make one more attempt to trample a road through the drift. It was a vain one. The snow was over our heads, and after struggling for two hours, we had not gained above two hundred yards. Here we caught a glimpse of what lay before us. As far as the eye could reach, it rested upon the same deep impassable masses. Despair and hunger paralysed our exertions, and, dropping off one by one, we returned to the camp. We fell down around the fires in sullen silence. Garey continued pacing back and forth, now glancing up at the sky, and at times kneeling down, and running his hand over the surface of the snow. At length he approached the fire, and in his slow, drawling manner, remarked—

"'It's a-gwine to friz, I reckin.'

"'Well! and if it does?' asked one of his comrades, without caring for an answer to the question.

"'Wal, an iv it does,' repeated the trapper, 'we'll walk out o' this hyar jug afore sun-up, an' upon a good hard trail too.'

"The expression of every face was changed, as if by magic. Several leaped to their feet. Godé, the Canadian, skilled in snow-craft, ran to a bank, and drawing his hand along the combing, shouted back—

"'C'est vrai; il gèle; il gèle!'

"A cold wind soon after set in, and, cheered by the brightening prospect, we began to think of the fires, that, during our late moments of reckless indifference, had been almost suffered to burn out. The Delawares, seizing their tomahawks, commenced hacking at the pines, while others dragged forward the fallen trees, lopping off their branches with the keen scalping-knife.

"At this moment a peculiar cry attracted our attention, and, looking around, we perceived one of the Indians drop suddenly upon his knees, striking the ground with his hatchet.

"'What is it? what is it?' shouted several voices, in almost as many languages.

"'*Yam-yam! yam-yam!*' replied the Indian, still digging at the frozen ground.

"'The Injun's right; it's *man-root!*' said Garey, picking up some leaves which the Delaware had chopped off.

"I recognised a plant well-known to the mountain-men—a rare, but wonderful convolvulus, the *Iponea leptophylla*. The name of 'man-root' is given to it by the hunters from the similarity of its root in shape, and sometimes in size, to the body of a man. It is esculent, and serves to sustain human life.

"In an instant, half-a-dozen men were upon their knees, chipping and hacking the hard clay, but their hatchets glinted off as from the surface of a rock.

"'Look hyar!' cried Garey; 'ye're only spoilin' yer tools. Cut down a wheen o' these pine saplin's, and make a fire over him!'

"The hint was instantly followed, and in a few minutes a dozen pieces of pine were piled upon the spot, and set on fire.

"We stood around the burning branches with eager anticipation. Should the root prove a 'full-grown man,' it would make a supper for our whole party; and with the cheering idea of supper, jokes were ventured upon—the first we had heard for some time—the hunters tickled with the novelty of unearthing the 'old man' ready roasted, and speculating whether he would prove a 'fat old hoss.'

"A hollow crack sounded from above, like the breaking of a dead tree. We looked up. A large object—an animal—was whirling outward and downward from a ledge that projected half-way up the cliff. In an instant it struck the earth, head foremost, with a loud 'bump,' and, bounding to the height of several feet, came back with a somersault on its legs, and stood firmly.

"An involuntary 'hurrah!' broke from the hunters, who all recognised, at a glance, the 'Carnero cimmaron,' or 'bighorn.' He had cleared the precipice at two leaps, alighting each time on his huge crescent-shaped horns.

"For a moment, both parties—hunters and game—seemed equally taken by surprise, and stood eyeing each other in mute wonder. It was but for a moment. The men made a rush for their rifles, and the animal, recovering from his trance of astonishment, tossed back his horns, and bounded across the platform. In a dozen springs he had reached the selvedge of the snow, and plunged into its yielding bank; but, at the same instant, several rifles cracked, and the white wreath was crimsoned behind him. He still kept on, however, leaning and breaking through the drift.

"We struck into his track, and followed with the eagerness of hungry wolves. We could tell by the numerous *goûts* that he was shedding his life-blood, and about fifty paces farther on we found him dead.

"A shout apprised our companions of our success, and we had commenced dragging back the prize, when wild cries reached us from the platform,—the yells of men, the screams of women, mingled with oaths and exclamations of terror!

"We ran on towards the entrance of the track. On reaching it, a sight was before us that caused the stoutest to tremble. Hunters, Indians, and women were running to and fro in frantic confusion, uttering their varied cries, and pointing upward. We looked in that direction—a row of fearful objects stood upon the brow of the cliff. We knew our enemy at a glance,— the dreaded monsters of the mountains—the grizzly bears!

"There were; five of them—five in sight—there might be others in the background. Five were enough to destroy our whole party, caged as we were, and weakened by famine.

"They had reached the cliff in chase of the cimmaron, and hunger and disappointment were visible in their horrid aspects. Two of them had already crawled close to the scarp, and were pawing over and snuffing the air, as if searching for a place to descend. The other three reared themselves up on their hams, and commenced manoeuvring with their forearms, in a human-like and comical pantomime!

"We were in no condition to relish this amusement. Every man hastened to arm himself, those who had emptied their rifles hurriedly re-loading them.

"'For your life don't!' cried Garey, catching at the gun of one of the hunters.

"The caution came too late: half-a-dozen bullets were already whistling upwards.

"The effect was just what the trapper had anticipated. The bears, maddened by the bullets, which had harmed them no more than the pricking of as many pins, dropped to their all-fours again, and, with fierce growls, commenced descending the cliff.

"The scene of confusion was now at its height. Several of the men, less brave than their comrades, ran off to hide themselves in the snow, while others commenced climbing the low pine-trees!

"'Caché the gals!' cried Garey. 'Hyar, yer darned Spanish greasers! if yer won't light, hook on to the weemen a wheen o' yer, and toat them to the snow. Cowardly slinks,—wagh!'

"'See to them, doctor,' I shouted to the German, who, I thought, might be best spared from the fight; and the next, moment, the doctor, assisted by several Mexicans, was hurrying the terrified girls towards the spot where we had left the cimmaron.

"Many of us knew that to hide, under the circumstances, would be worse than useless. The fierce but sagacious brutes would have discovered, us one by one, and destroyed, us in detail. 'They must, be met and fought!' that was the word; and we resolved to carry it into execution.

"There were about a dozen of us who 'stood up to it'—all the Delaware and Shawanoes, with Garey and the mountain-men.

"We kept firing at the bears as they ran along the ledges in their zigzag descent, but our rifles were out of order, our fingers were numbed with cold, and our nerves weakened with hunger. Our bullets drew blood from the hideous brutes, yet not a shot proved deadly. It only stung them into fiercer rage.

"It was a fearful moment when the last shot was fired, and still not an enemy the less. We flung away the guns, and, clutching the hatchets and hunting-knives, silently awaited our grizzly foes.

"We had taken our stand close to the rock. It was our design to have the first blow, as the animals, for the most part, came stern-foremost down the cliff. In this we were disappointed. On reaching a ledge some ten feet from the platform, the foremost bear halted, and, seeing our position, hesitated to descend. The next moment, his companions, maddened with wounds, came tumbling down upon the same ledge, and, with fierce growls, the five huge bodies were precipitated into our midst.

"Then came the desperate struggle, which I cannot describe,—the shouts of the hunters, the wilder yells of our Indian allies, the hoarse worrying of the bears, the ringing of tomahawks from skulls like flint, the deep, dull 'thud' of the stabbing-knife, and now and then a groan, as the crescent claw tore up the clinging muscle. O God! it was a fearful scene!

"Over the platform bears and men went rolling and struggling, in the wild battle of life and death. Through the trees, and into the deep drift, staining the snow with their mingled blood! Here, two or three men were engaged with a single foe—there, some brave hunter stood battling alone. Several were sprawling upon the ground. Every moment, the bears were lessening the number of their assailants!

"I had been struck down at the commencement of the struggle. On regaining my feet, I saw the animal that had felled me hugging the prostrate body of a man.

"It was Godé. I leaned over the bear, clutching its shaggy skin. I did this to steady myself; I was weak and dizzy; so were we all. I struck with all my force, stabbing the animal on the ribs.

"Letting go the Frenchman, the bear turned suddenly, and reared upon me. I endeavoured to avoid the encounter, and ran backward, fending him off with my knife.

"All at once I came against the snow-drift, and fell over on my back. Next moment, the heavy body was precipitated upon me, the sharp claws pierced deep into my shoulder,—I inhaled the monster's fetid breath; and striking wildly with my right arm, still free, we rolled over and over in the snow.

"I was blinded by the dry drift. I felt myself growing weaker and weaker; it was the loss of blood. I shouted—a despairing shout—but it could not have been heard at ten paces' distance. Then there was a strange hissing sound in my ears,—a bright light flashed across my eyes; a burning object passed over my face, scorching the skin; there was a smell as of singeing hair; I could hear voices, mixed with the roars of my adversary; and all at once the claws were drawn out of my flesh, the weight was lifted from my breast, and I was alone!

"I rose to my feet, and, rubbing the snow out of my eyes, looked around. I could see no one. I was in a deep hollow made by our struggles, but I was alone!

"The snow all around me was dyed to a crimson; but what had become of my terrible antagonist? Who had rescued me from his deadly embrace?

"I staggered forward to the open ground. Here a new scene met my gaze: a strange-looking man was running across the platform, with a huge firebrand,—the bole of a burning pine-tree,—which he waved in the air. He was chasing one of the hears, that, growling with rage and pain, was making every effort to reach the cliffs. Two others were already half-way up, and evidently clambering with great difficulty, as the blood dripped back from their wounded flanks.

"The bear that was pursued soon took to the rocks, and, urged by the red brand scorching his shaggy hams, was soon beyond the reach of his pursuer. The latter now made towards a fourth, that was still battling with two or three weak antagonists. This one was 'routed' in a twinkling, and with yells of terror followed his comrades up the bluff. The strange man looked around for the fifth. It had disappeared. Prostrate, wounded men were strewed over the ground, but the bear was nowhere to be seen. He had doubtless escaped through the snow.

"I was still wondering who was the hero of the firebrand, and where he had come from. I have said he was a strange-looking man. He was so— and like no one of our party that I could think of. His head was bald,— no, not bald, but naked,—there was not a hair upon it, crown or sides, and it glistened in the clear light like polished ivory. I was puzzled beyond expression, when a man—Garey—who had been felled upon the platform by a blow from one of the bears, suddenly sprang to his feet, exclaiming,—

"'Go it, Doc! Three chyars for the doctor!'

"To my astonishment, I now recognised the features of that individual, the absence of whose brown locks had produced such a metamorphosis as, I believe, was never effected by means of borrowed hair.

"'Here's your scalp, Doc,' cried Garey, running up with the wig, 'by the livin' thunder! yer saved us all;' and the hunter seized the German in his wild embrace.

"Wounded men were all around, and commenced crawling together. But where was the fifth of the bears? Four only had escaped by the cliff.

"'Yonder he goes!' cried a voice, as a light spray, rising above the snow-wreath, showed that some animal was struggling through the drift.

"Several commenced loading their rifles, intending to follow, and, if possible, secure him. The doctor armed himself with a fresh pine; but before these, arrangements were completed, a strange cry came from the spot, that caused our blood to run cold again. The Indians leaped to their feet, and, seizing their tomahawks, rushed to the gap. They knew the meaning of that cry—it was the death-yell of their tribe!

"They entered the road that we had trampled down in the morning, followed by those who had loaded their guns. We watched them from the platform with anxious expectation, but before they had reached the spot, we could see that, the 'stoor' was slowly settling down. It was plain that the struggle had ended.

"We still stood waiting in breathless silence, and watching the floating spray that noted their progress through the drift. At length they had reached the scene of the struggle. There was an ominous stillness, that lasted for a moment, and then the Indian's fate was announced in the sad, wild note that came wailing up the valley. It was the dirge of a Shawano warrior!

"They had found their brave comrade dead, with his scalping-knife buried in the heart of his terrible antagonist!

"It was a costly supper, that bear-meat, but, perhaps, the sacrifice had saved many lives. We would keep the 'cimmaron' for to-morrow; next day, the man-root; and the next,—what next? Perhaps—the man!

"Fortunately, we were not, driven to this extremity. The frost, had again set in, and the surface of the snow, previously moistened by the sun and rain, soon became caked into ice strong enough to bear us, and upon its firm crust we escaped out of the perilous pass, and gained the warmer region of the plains in safety."

Chapter Twenty Seven
The Swans of America

In our journey we had kept far enough to the north to avoid the difficult route of the Ozark Hills; and we at length encamped upon the Marais de Cygnes, a branch of the Osage River. Beyond this we expected to fall in with the buffalo, and of course we were full of pleasant anticipation. Near the point where we had pitched our camp, the banks of the river were marshy, with here and there small lakes of stagnant water. In these a large number of swans, with wild geese and other aquatic birds, were swimming and feeding.

Of course our guns were put in requisition, and we succeeded in killing a brace of swans, with a grey goose (Anser *Canadensis*), and a pair of ducks. The swans were very large ones—of the Trumpeter species—and one of them was cooked for supper. It was in excellent condition, and furnished a meal for the whole of our party! The other swan, with the goose and ducks, were stowed away for another occasion.

While "discussing" the flesh of this great and noble bird, we also discussed many of the points in its natural history.

"White as a swan" is a simile old as language itself. It would, no doubt, puzzle an Australian, used to look upon those beautiful and stately birds as being of a very different complexion. The simile holds good, however, with the North-American species, all three of which—for there are three of them—are almost snow-white.

We need not describe the form or general appearance of the swan. These are familiar to every one. The long, upright, and gracefully-curving neck; the finely-moulded breast, the upward-tending tail-tip, the light "dip," and easy progression through the water, are points that everybody has observed, admired, and remembered. These are common to all birds of the genus *Cygnus*, and are therefore not peculiar to the swans of America.

Many people fancy there are but two kinds of swans—the white and black. It is not long since the black ones have been introduced to general notoriety, as well as to general admiration. But there are many distinct species besides—species differing from each other in size, voice, and other peculiarities. In Europe alone, there are four native swans, specifically distinct.

It was long believed that the common American swan (*Cygnus Americanus*) was identical with the common European species, so well-known in England. It is now ascertained, however, not only that these two are specifically distinct, but that in North America there exist two other species, differing from the *Cygnus Americanus*, and from each other. These are the Trumpeter (*Cygnus buccinnator*) and the small swan of Bewick (*Cygnus Bewickii*), also an inhabitant of European countries.

The common American species is of a pure white, with black hill, logs, and feet. A slight tinge of brownish red is found on some individuals on the crown of the head, and a small patch of orange-yellow extends from the angles of the mouth to the eye. On the base of the bill is a fleshy tubercle or knob, and the upper mandible is curved at the tip.

The young of this species are of a bluish-grey colour, with more of the brown-red tinge upon the head. The naked yellow patch, extending from the angles of the mouth to the eye, in the young birds, is covered with feathers, and their bills are flesh-coloured. This description answers in every respect for the swan of Bewick; but the latter species is only three-fourths the size of the former; and, besides, it has only eighteen tail feathers, while the American swan has twenty. Their note is also entirely unlike.

The "Trumpeter" is different from either. He is the largest, being frequently met with of nearly six feet in length, while the common swan rarely exceeds five. The bill of the Trumpeter is not tuberculated; and the yellow patch under the eye is wanting. The bill, legs, and feet are entirely black. All the rest is white, with the exception of the head, which is usually tinged with chestnut or red-brown. When young, he is of a greyish-white, with a yellow mixture, and the head of deeper red-brown. His tail feathers are twenty-four in number; but there is a material difference between him and his congeners in the arrangement of the windpipe. In the Trumpeter this enters a protuberance that stands out on the dorsal aspect of the sternum, which is wanting in both the other kinds. It may be that this arrangement has something to do with his peculiar note, which differs altogether from that of the others. It is much fuller and louder, and at a distance bears a considerable resemblance to the trumpet or French horn. Hence the trivial name by which this species is known to the hunters.

All the American swans are migratory—that is, they pass from north to south, every autumn, and back again from south to north in the beginning of spring.

The period of their migration is different with the three species. The Trumpeter is the earliest, preceding all other birds, with the exception of the eagles. The *Cygnus Americanus* comes next; and, lastly, the small swans, that are among the very latest of migratory birds.

The Trumpeters seek the north at the breaking up of the ice. Sometimes they arrive at a point in their journey where this has not taken place. In such cases they fly back again until they reach some river or lake from which the ice has disappeared, where they remain a few days, and wait the opening of the waters farther north. When they are thus retarded and sent back, it is always in consequence of some unusual and unseasonable weather.

The swans go northward to breed. Why they do so is a mystery. Perhaps they feel more secure in the inhospitable wastes that lie within the Arctic circle. The Trumpeters breed as far south as latitude 61 degrees, but most of them retire within the frigid zone.

The small swans do not nest so far south, but pursue their course still onward to the Polar Sea. Here they build immense nests by raising heaps of peat moss, six feet in length by four in width, and two feet high. In the top of these heaps is situated the nest, which consists of a cavity a foot deep, and a foot and a half in diameter.

The Trumpeters and American swans build in marshes and the islands of lakes. Where the muskrat (*Fiber zibethicus*) abounds, his dome-shaped dwelling—at that season, of course, deserted—serves often as the breeding-place boll? for the swans and wild geese. On the top of this structure, isolated in the midst of great marshes, these birds are secure from all their enemies—the eagle excepted.

The eggs of the Trumpeter are very large, one of them being enough to make a good meal for a man. The eggs of the American species are smaller and of a greenish appearance, while those of the Bewick swan are still smaller and of a brownish-white colour, with a slight clouding of darker hue.

Six or seven eggs is the usual "setting." The cygnets, when half or full-grown, are esteemed good eating, and are much sought after by the hunters and Indians of the fur countries.

When the cygnets are full-grown, and the frost makes its appearance upon the lakes and rivers of the hyperborean regions, the swans begin to shift southwards. They do not migrate directly, as in the spring, but take more time on their journey, and remain longer in the countries through which they pass. This no doubt arises from the fact that a different motive or instinct now urges them. In the spring they are under the impulse of philo-progenitiveness. Now they range from lake to lake and stream to stream in search only of food. Again, as in the spring, the Trumpeters lead the van—winging their way to the great lakes, and afterwards along the Atlantic coast, and by the line of the Mississippi, to the marshy shores of the Mexican Sea.

It may be remarked that this last-mentioned species—the Trumpeter— is rare upon the Atlantic coast, where the common swan is seen in greatest plenty. Again, the Trumpeter docs not appear on the Pacific or by the Colombia River, where the common swan is met with, but the latter is there outnumbered by the small species (*Cygnus Bewickii*) in the ratio of five to one. This last again is not known in the fur countries of the interior, where the *Cygnus Americanus* is found, but where the Trumpeter exists in greatest numbers. Indeed the skins of the Trumpeter are those which are mostly exported by the Hudson's Bay Company, and which form an important article of their commerce.

The swan is eagerly hunted by the Indians who inhabit the fur countries. Its skin brings a good price from the traders, and its quills are valuable. Besides, the flesh is a consideration with these people, whose life, it must be borne in mind, is one continuous struggle for food; and who, for one-half the year, live upon the very verge of starvation.

The swan, therefore, being a bird that weighs between twenty and thirty pounds, ranks among large game, and is hunted with proportionate ardour. Every art the Indian can devise is made use of to circumvent these great birds, and snares, traps, and decoys of all kinds are employed in the pursuit.

But the swans are among the shyest of God's creatures. They fly so rapidly, unless when beating against the wind, that it requires a practised shot to hit them on the wing. Even when moulting their feathers, or when young, they can escape—fluttering over the surface of the water faster than a canoe can be paddled.

The most usual method of hunting them is by snares. These are set in the following manner:—

A lake or river is chosen, where it is known the swans are in the habit of resting for some time on their migration southward—for this is the principal season of swan-catching.

Some time before the birds make their appearance, a number of wicker hedges are constructed, running perpendicularly out from the bank, and at the distance of a few yards from each other. In the spaces between, as well as in openings left in the fences themselves, snares are set. These snares are made of the intestines of the deer, twisted into a round shape, and looped.

They are placed so that several snares may embrace the opening, and the swans cannot pass through without being caught.

The snare is fastened to a stake, driven into the mud with sufficient firmness to hold the bird when caught and struggling. That the snare may not be blown out of its proper place by the wind, or carried astray by the current, it is attached to the wattles of the hedge by some strands of grass. These, of course, are easily broken, and give way the moment a bird presses against the loop.

The fences or wattle-hedges are always constructed projecting out from the shore—for it is known that the swans must keep close in to the land while feeding. Whenever a lake or river is sufficiently shallow to make it possible to drive in stakes, the hedges are continued across it from one side to the other.

Swans are also snared upon their nests. When a nest is found, the snare is set so as to catch the bird upon her return to the eggs. These birds, like many others, have the habit of entering the nest on one side, and going out by the other, and it is upon the entrance side that the snare is set.

The Indians have a belief that if the hands of the persons setting the snare be not clean, the bird will not approach it, but rather desert her eggs, even though she may have been hatching them for some time.

It is, indeed, true that this is a habit of many birds, and may be so of the wild swan. Certain it is that the nest is always reconnoitred by the returning bird with great caution, and any irregularity appearing about it will render her extremely shy of approaching it.

Swans are shot, like other birds, by "approaching" them under cover. It requires very large shot to kill them—the same that is used for deer, and known throughout America as "buck-shot." In England this size of shot is termed "swan shot."

It is difficult to get within range of the wild swan, he is by nature a shy bird; and his long neck enables him to see over the sedge that surrounds him. Where there happens to be no cover—and this is generally the case where he haunts—it is impossible to approach him.

Sometimes the hunter floats down upon him with his canoe hidden by a garniture of reeds and bushes. At other times he gets near enough in the disguise of a deer or other quadruped—for the swan, like most wild birds, is less afraid of the lower animals than of man.

During the spring migration, when the swan is moving northward, the hunter, hidden under some rock, bank, or tree, frequently lures him from his high flight by the imitation of his well-known "hoop." This does not succeed so well in the autumn.

When the swans arrive prematurely on their spring journey, they resort sometimes in considerable flocks to the springs and waterfalls, all other places being then ice-bound. At this time the hunters concealing themselves in the neighbourhood, obtain the desired proximity, and deal destruction with their guns.

A— related an account of a swan hunt by torch-light, which he had made some years before.

"I was staying some days," said he, "at a remote, settlement upon one of the streams that run into the Red river of the north, it was in the autumn season, and the Trumpeter-swans had arrived in the neighbourhood on their annual migration to the south. I had been out several times after them with my gun, but was unable to get a shot at them in consequence of their shyness. I had adopted every expedient I could think of—calls, disguises, and decoys—but all to no purpose. I resolved, at length, to try them by torch-light.

"It so happened that none of the hunters, at the settlement had ever practised this method; but as most of them had succeeded, by some means or other, in decoying and capturing several swans by other means, my hunter-pride was touched, and I was most anxious to show that I could kill swans as well as they. I had never seen Swans shot by torch-light, but I had employed the plan for killing deer, as you already know, and I was determined to make a trial of it upon the swans.

"I set secretly about it, resolved to steal a march upon my neighbours, if possible. My servant alone was admitted into my confidence, and we proceeded to make the necessary arrangements.

"These were precisely similar to those already described in my limit of the long-tails, except that the canoe, instead of being 'a dug-out,' was a light craft of birch-bark, such as are in use among the Chippowas and other Indians of the northern countries. The canoe was obtained from a settler, and tilled with torch-wood and other necessary articles, but these were clandestinely put on board.

"I was now ready, and a dark night was all that was wanted to enable me to carry out my plan.

"Fortunately I soon obtained this to my heart's satisfaction. A night arrived as dark as Erebus; and with my servant using the paddle, we pushed out and shot swiftly down stream.

"As soon as we had cleared the 'settlement,' we lit our pine-knots in the frying-pan. The blaze refracted from the concave and blackened surface of the bark, cast a brilliant light over the semicircle ahead of us, at the same time that we, behind the screen of birch-bark, were hid in utter darkness. I had heard that the swans, instead of being frightened by torch-light, only became amazed, and even at times curious enough to approach it, just as the deer and some other animals do. This proved to be correct, as we had very soon a practical illustration of it.

"We had not gone a mile down the river when we observed several white objects within the circle of our light; and paddling a little nearer, we saw that they were swans. We could distinguish their long, upright necks; and saw that they had given up feeding, and were gazing with wonder at the odd object that was approaching them.

"There were five of them in the flock; and I directed my servant to paddle towards that which seemed nearest, and to use his oar with as much silence as possible. At the same time I looked to the caps of my double-barrelled gun.

"The swans for a time remained perfectly motionless, sitting high in the water, with their long necks raised far above the surface. They appeared to be more affected by surprise than fear.

"When we had got within about a hundred yards of them, I saw that they began to move about, and close in to one another; at the same time was heard proceeding from them a strange sound resembling very much the whistle of the fallow deer. I had heard of the singing of the swan, as a prelude to its death, and I hoped that which now reached my ears was a similar foreboding.

"In order to make it so, I leaned forward, levelled my double-barrel—both barrels being cocked—and waited the *moment*.

"The birds had 'clumped' together, until their long serpent-like necks crossed each other. A few more noiseless strokes of the paddle brought me within reach, and aiming for the heads of three that 'lined,' I pulled both triggers at once.

"The immense recoil flung me back, and the smoke for a moment prevented us from seeing the effect.

"As soon as it had been wafted aside, our eyes were feasted by the sight of two large white objects floating down the current, while a third, evidently wounded, struggled along the surface, and beating the water into foam with its broad wings.

"The remaining two had risen high into the air, and were heard uttering their loud trumpet-notes as they winged their flight through the dark heavens.

"We soon bagged our game, both dead and wounded, and saw that they were a large 'gander' and two young birds.

"It was a successful beginning; and having replenished our torch, we continued to float downward in search of more. Half a mile farther on, we came in sight of three others, one of which we succeeded in killing.

"Another 'spell' of paddling brought us to a third flock, out of which I got one for each barrel of my gun; and a short distance below I succeeded in killing a pair of the grey wild geese.

"In this way we kept down the river for at least ten miles I should think, killing both swans and geese as we went. Indeed, the novelty of the thing, the wild scenery through which we passed—rendered more wild and picturesque by the glare of the torch—and the excitement of success, all combined to render the sport most attractive; and but that our 'pine-knots' had run out, I would have continued it until morning.

"The failure of these at length brought our shooting to a termination, and we were compelled to put about, and undertake the much less pleasant, and much more laborious, task, of paddling ten miles up-stream. The consciousness, however, of having performed a great feat—in the language of the Canadian hunters, a grand 'coup,' made the labour seem more light, and we soon arrived at the settlement, and next morning triumphantly paraded our game-bag in front of our 'lodge.'

"Its contents were twelve trumpeter-swans, besides three of the 'hoopers.' We had also a pair of Canada geese; a snow-goose, and three brant,—these last being the produce of a single shot.

"The hunters of the settlement were quite envious, and could not understand what means I had employed to get up such a 'game-bag.' I intended to have kept that for some time a secret; but the frying-pan and the piece of blackened bark were found, and these betrayed my stratagem; so that on the night after, a dozen canoes, with torches at their bows, might have been seen floating down the waters of the stream."

Chapter Twenty Eight
Hunting the Moose

While crossing the marshy bottom through which our road led, a singular hoof-track was observed in the mud. Some were of opinion that it was a track of the great moose-deer, but the hunter-naturalist, better informed, scouted the idea—declaring that moose never ranged, so far to the south. It was no doubt a very large elk that had made the track, and to this conclusion all at length came.

The great moose-deer, however, was an interesting theme, and we rode along conversing upon it.

The moose (*Cervus alces*) is the largest of the deer kind. The male is ordinarily as large as a mule; specimens have been killed of still greater dimensions. One that has been measured stood seventeen bands, and weighed 1200 pounds; it was consequently larger than most horses. The females are considerably smaller than the males.

The colour of the moose, like that of other animals of the deer kind, varies with the season; it varies also with the sex. The male is tawny-brown over the back, sides, head, and thighs; this changes to a darker hue in winter, and in very old animals it is nearly black; hence the name "black elk," which is given in some districts to the moose. The under parts of the body are light-coloured, with a tinge of yellow or soiled white.

The female is of a sandy-brown colour above, and beneath almost white. The calves are sandy-brown, but never spotted, as are the fawns of the common deer.

The moose is no other than the elk of Northern Europe; but the elk of America (*Cervus Canadensis*), as already stated, is altogether a different animal. These two species may be mistaken for each other, in the season when their antlers are young, or in the velvet; then they are not unlike to a superficial observer. But the animals are rarely confounded—only the names. The American elk is not found indigenous in the eastern hemisphere, although he is the ornament of many a lordly park.

The identity of the moose with the European elk is a fact that leads to curious considerations. A similar identity exists between the caribou of Canada and the reindeer of Northern Europe—they are both the *Cervus tarandus* of Pliny. So also with the polar hear of both hemispheres, the arctic, fox, and several other animals. Hence we infer, that there existed at some period either a land connection, or some other means of communication, between the northern parts of both continents.

Besides being the largest, the moose is certainly the most ungraceful of the deer family. His head is long, out of all proportion; so, too, are his legs; while his neck is short in an inverse ratio. His ears are nearly a foot in length, asinine, broad, and slouching; his eyes are small; and his muzzle square, with a deep *sulcus* in the middle, which gives it the appearance of being bifid. The upper lip overhangs the under by several inches, and is highly prehensile. A long tuft of coarse hair grows out of an excrescence on the throat, in the angle between the head and neck. This tuft is observed both in the male and female, though only when full-grown. In the young, the excrescence is naked.

An erect mane, somewhat resembling that of a cropped Shetland pony, runs from the base of the horns over the withers, and some way down the back. This adds to the stiff and ungainly appearance of the animal.

The horns of the moose are a striking characteristic: they are palmated or flattened out like shovels, while along the edge rise the points or antlers. The width from horn to horn at their tops is often more than four feet, and the breadth of a single one, antlers included, is frequently above thirty inches. A single pair has been known to weigh as much as 60 pounds avoirdupois!

Of course this stupendous head-dress gives the moose quite an imposing appearance; and it is one of the wonders of the naturalist what can be its object.

The horns are found only on the males, and attain their full size only when these have reached their seventh year. In the yearlings appear two knobs, about an inch in length; in two-year-olds, these knobs have become spikes a foot high; in the third year they begin to palmate, and antlers rise along their edges; and so on, until the seventh year, when they become fully developed. They are annually caducous, however, as with the common deer, so that these immense appendages are the growth of a few weeks!

The haunts and habits of the moose differ materially from those of other deer. He cannot browse upon level ground without kneeling or widening his legs to a great extent: this difficulty arises from the extreme length of his legs, and the shortness of his neck. He can do better upon the sides of steep hills, and he is often seen in such places grazing *upward*.

Grass, however, is not his favourite food: he prefers the twigs and leaves of trees—such as birch, willow, and maple. There is one species of the last of which he is extremely fond; it is that known as striped maple (*Acer striatum*), or, in the language of hunters, "moose-wood." He peels off the bark from old trees of this sort, and feeds upon it, as well as upon several species of mosses with which the arctic regions abound. It will be seen that in these respects he resembles the giraffe: he may be regarded as the giraffe of the frigid zone.

The moose loves the forest; he is rarely found in the open ground—on the prairie, never.

On open level ground, he is easily overtaken by the hunter, as he makes but a poor run in such a situation. His feet are tender, and his wind short; besides, as we have already said, he cannot browse there without great inconvenience. He keeps in the thick forest and the impenetrable swamp, where he finds the food most to his liking.

In summer, he takes to the water, wading into lakes and rivers, and frequently swimming across both. This habit renders him at that season an easy prey to his enemies, the Indian hunters, for in the water he is easily killed. Nevertheless, he loves to bury himself in the water, because along the shores of lakes and margins of rivers he finds the tall reed-grass, and the pond-lily—the latter a particular favourite with him. In this way, too, he rids himself of the biting gnats and stinging mosquitoes that swarm there; and also cools his blood, fevered by parasites, larvae, and the hot sun.

The female moose produces one, two, and sometimes three calves at a birth; this is in April or May. The period of gestation is nine-months.

During the summer, they are seen in families—that is, a bull, a cow, and two calves. Sometimes the group includes three or four cows; but this is rare.

Occasionally, when the winter comes on, several of these family parties unite, and form herds of many individuals. When the snow is deep, one of these herds will tread down a space of several acres, in which they will be found browsing on the bark and twigs of the trees. A place of this sort is termed by the hunters a "moose-yard;" and in such a situation the animals become an easy prey. They are shot down on the spot, and those that attempt to escape through the deep snow are overtaken and brought to bay by dogs. This can only happen, however, when the snow is deep and crusted with frost; otherwise, the hunters and their dogs, as well as their heavier game, would sink in it. When the snow is of old standing, it becomes icy on the surface through the heat of the sun, rain, and frost; then it will bear the hunter, but not the deer. The latter break through it, and as these animals are tender-hoofed, they are lacerated at every jump. They soon feel the pain, give up the attempt to escape, and come to bay.

It is dangerous for dogs to approach them when in this mood. They strike with the hoofs of their forefeet, a single blow of which often knocks the breath out of the stoutest deer-hound. There are many records of hunters having been sacrificed in a similar manner.

Where the moose are plentiful, the Indians hunt them by pounding. This is done simply by inclosing a large tract of woods, with a funnel-shaped entrance leading into the inclosure. The wide mouth of the entrance embraces a path which the deer habitually take; upon this they are driven by the Indians, deployed in a wide curve, until they enter the funnel, and the pound itself. Here there are nooses set, in which many are snared, while others are shot down by the hunters who follow. This method is more frequently employed with the caribou, which are much smaller, and more gregarious than the moose-deer.

We have already said that the moose are easily captured in summer, when they resort to the lakes and rivers to wade and swim. The biting of gnats and mosquitoes renders them less fearful of the approach of man. The Indians then attack them in their canoes, and either shoot or spear them while paddling alongside.

They are much less dangerous to assail in this way than the elk or even the common deer (*Cervus Virginianus*), as the latter, when brought in contact with the frail birch-canoe, often kick up in such a manner as to upset it, or break a hole through its side. On the contrary, the moose is frequently caught by the antlers while swimming, and in this way carried alongside without either difficulty or danger.

Although in such situations these huge creatures are easily captured, it is far otherwise as a general rule. Indeed, few animals are more shy than the moose. Its sight is acute; so, too, with its sense of smell; but that organ in which it chiefly confides is the ear. It can hear the slightest noise to a great distance; and the hunter's foot among the dead leaves, or upon the frozen snow-crust, often betrays him long before he can creep within range. They are, however, frequently killed by the solitary hunter stealing upon them, or "approaching," as it is termed. To do this, it is absolutely necessary to keep to leeward of them, else the wind would carry to their quick ears even the cautious tread of the Indian hunter.

There is one other method of hunting the moose often practised by the Indians—that is, trailing them with *rackets*, or snow-shoes, and running them down. As I had partaken of this sport I was able to give an account of it to my companions.

"In the winter of 18—, I had occasion to visit a friend who lived in the northern part of the state of Maine. My friend was a backwood settler; dwelt in a comfortable log-house; raised corn, cattle, and hogs; and for the rest, amused himself occasionally with a hunt in the neighbouring woods. This he could do without going far from home, as the great forests of pine, birch, and maple trees on all sides surrounded his solitary clearing, and his nearest neighbour was about twenty miles off. Literally, my friend lived in the woods, and the sports of the chase were with him almost a necessity; at all events, they were an everyday occupation.

"Up to the time of my visit, I had never seen a moose, except in museums. I had never been so far north upon the American Continent; and it must be remembered, that the geographical range of the moose is confined altogether to the cold countries. It is only in the extreme northern parts of the United States that he appears at all. Canada, with the vast territories of the Hudson's Bay Company, even to the shores of the Arctic Sea, is the proper *habitat* of this animal.

"I was familiar with bears; cougars I had killed; elk and fallow deer I had driven; 'coons and 'possums I had treed; in short, I had been on hunting terms with almost every game in America except the moose. I was most eager, therefore, to have a shot at one of these creatures, and I well remember the delight I experienced when my friend informed me there were moose in the adjacent woods.

"On the day after my arrival, we set forth in search of them, each armed with a hunting-knife and a heavy deer-gun. We went afoot; we could not go otherwise, as the snow lay to the depth of a yard, and a horse would have plunged through it with difficulty. It was an old snow, moreover, thickly crusted, and would have maimed our horses in a few minutes. We, with our broad rackets, could easily skim along without sinking below the surface.

"I know not whether you have ever seen a pair of rackets, or Indian snow-shoes, but their description is easy. You have seen the rackets used in ball-play. Well, now, fancy a hoop, not of circular form, but forced into an elongated pointed ellipse, very much after the shape of the impression that a capsized boat would make in snow; fancy this about three feet long, and a foot across at its widest, closely netted over with gut or deer-thong, with bars in the middle to rest the foot upon, and a small hole to allow play to the toes, and you will have some idea of a snow-shoe. Two of these—right and left—make a pair. They are simply strapped on to your boots, and then their broad surface sustains you, even when the snow is comparatively soft, but perfectly when it is frozen.

"Thus equipped, my friend and I set out *à pied*, followed by a couple of stout deer-hounds. We made directly for a part of the woods where it was known to my friend that the striped maple grew in great plenty. It has been stated already, that the moose are particularly fond of these trees, and there we would be most likely to fall in with them.

"The striped maple is a beautiful deciduous little tree or shrub, growing to the height of a dozen feet or so in its natural *habitat*. When cultivated, it often reaches thirty feet. There is one at Schonbrunn, near Vienna, forty feet high, but this is an exception, and is the largest known. The usual height is ten or twelve feet, and it is more often the underwood of the forest than the forest itself. When thus situated, under the shade of loftier trees, it degenerates almost to the character of a shrub.

"The trunk and branches of the striped maple are covered with a smooth green bark, longitudinally marked with light and dark stripes, by which the tree is easily distinguished from others, and from which it takes its name. It has other trivial names in different parts of the country. In New York state, it is called 'dogwood;' but improperly so, as the real dogwood (*Cornus florida*) is a very different tree. It is known also as 'false dogwood,' and 'snake-barked maple.' The name 'moose-wood' is common among the hunters and frontiers-men for reasons already given. Where the striped maple is indigenous, it is one of the first productions that announces the approach of spring. Its buds and leaves, when beginning to unfold, are of a roseate hue, and soon change to a yellowish green; the leaves are thick, cordate, rounded at the base, with three sharp lobes at the other extremity, and finely serrated. They are usually four or five inches in length and breadth. The tree flowers in May and June, and its flowers are yellow-green, grouped on long peduncles. The fruit, like all other maples, consists of *samarae* or 'keys;' it is produced in great abundance, and is ripe in September or October.

"The wood is white and finely grained; it is sometimes used by cabinet-makers as a substitute for holly, in forming the lines with which they inlay mahogany.

"In Canada, and those parts of the United States where it grows in great plenty, the farmers in spring turn out their cattle and horses to feed upon its leaves and young shoots, of which these animals are extremely fond; the more so, as it is only in very cold regions that it grows, and the budding of its foliage even precedes the springing of the grass. Such is the tree which forms the favourite browsing of the moose.

"To return to my narrative.

"After we had shuffled about two miles over the snow, my friend and I entered a tract of heavy timber, where the striped maple formed the underwood. It did not grow regularly, but in copses or small thickets. We had already started some small game, but declined following it, as we were bent only on a moose-chase.

"We soon fell in with signs that indicated the propinquity of the animals we were in search of. In several of the thickets, the maples were stripped of their twigs and bark, but this had been done previous to the falling of the snow. As yet, there were no tracks: we were not long, however, before this welcome indication was met with. On crossing a glade where there was but little snow, the prints of a great split hoof were seen, which my friend at once pronounced to be those of the moose.

"We followed this trail for some distance, until it led into deeper snow and a more retired part of the forest. The tracks were evidently fresh ones, and those, as my friend asserted, of an old bull.

"Half-a-mile farther on, they were joined by others; and the trail became a broken path through the deep snow, as if it had been made by farm-cattle following each other in single file. Four moose had passed, as my friend—skilled in woodcraft—confidently asserted, although I could not have told that from the appearance of the trail. He went still farther in his 'reckoning,' and stated that they were a bull, a cow, and two nine-months' calves.

"'You shall soon see,' he said, perceiving that I was somewhat incredulous. 'Look here!' he continued, bending down and pressing the broken snow with his fingers; 'they are quite fresh—made within the hour. Speak low—the cattle can't be far off. Yonder, as I live! yonder they are—hush!'

"My friend, as he spoke, pointed to a thicket about three hundred yards distant; I looked in that direction, but at first could perceive nothing more than the thickly-growing branches of the maples.

"After a moment, however, I could trace among the twigs the long dark outlines of a strange animal's back, with a huge pair of palmated horns rising above the underwood. It was the bull-moose—there was no mistaking him for any other creature. Near him other forms—three of them—were visible: these were of smaller stature, and I could see that they were hornless. They were the cow and calves; and the herd was made up, as my companion had foretold, of these four individuals.

"We had halted on the moment, each of us holding one of the dogs, and endeavouring to quiet them, as they already scented the game. We soon saw that it was of no use remaining where we were, as the herd was fully three hundred yards from us, far beyond the reach of even our heavy deer-guns.

"It would be of no use either to attempt stealing forward. There was no cover that would effectually conceal us, for the timber around was not large, and we could not, therefore, make shift with the tree-trunks.

"There was no other mode, then, but to let the dogs free of their leashes, and dash right forward. We knew we should not get a shot until after a run; but this would not be long, thought we, as the snow was in perfect order for our purpose.

"Our dogs were therefore unleashed, and went off with a simultaneous 'gowl,' while my friend and I followed as fast as we could.

"The first note of the deer-hounds was a signal for the herd, and we could hear their huge bodies crashing through the underwood, as they started away.

"They ran across some open ground, evidently with the intention of gaining the heavy timber beyond. On this ground there was but little snow; and as we came out through the thicket we had a full view of the noble game. The old bull was in the lead, followed by the others in a string. I observed that none of them galloped—a gait they rarely practise—but all went in a shambling trot, which, however, was a very fast one, equal to the speed of a horse. They carried their heads horizontally, with their muzzles directed forward, while the huge antlers of the bull leaned back upon his shoulders as he ran. Another peculiarity that struck me—the divisions of their great split hoofs, as they lifted them from the ground, met with a cracking sound, like the bursting of percussion-caps; and the four together rattled as they ran, as though a string of Christmas crackers had been touched off. I have often heard a similar cracking from the hoofs of farm-cattle; but with so many hoofs together, keeping up the fire incessantly, it produced a very odd impression upon me.

"In a short time they were out of sight, but we could hear the baying of the dogs as the latter closed upon them, and we followed, guided by the trail they had made.

"We had skated along for nearly a mile, when the howl of the hounds began to sound through the woods with more abrupt and fiercer echoes. We knew by this that the moose had been brought to bay, and we hurried forward, eager to have a shot.

"On arriving at the place, we found that only the old bull had made stand, and he was successfully engaged in keeping off the dogs, both with feet and horns. The others had gone forward, and were out of view.

"The bull, on seeing us approach, once more took the trot, and, followed by the dogs, was soon out of sight.

"On reaching the spot where he had made his temporary halt, we found that his trail there parted from that of the other three, as he had taken almost an opposite direction. Whether he had done so considerately, in order to lead the dogs away from his weaker companions, I know not; perhaps our sudden appearance had terrified him into confusion, and he had struck out without looking before him.

"We did not reflect on these points at the time. My friend, who probably was thinking more about the meat than the sport, without halting a moment, followed the trail of the cow and calves; while I, guided by different motives, took after the bull. I was in too great a hurry to heed some admonitions which were given by my friend as we parted company. As our trails separated, I heard him shouting to me to mind what I was about; but the courses we followed soon carried us beyond earshot or sight of each other.

"I followed the chase about half a mile farther, guided by the tracks, as well as by the baying of the hounds. Again this assumed the fierce angry tone that denoted a battle going on between the dogs and the deer.

"As I neared the spot, the voices of the former seemed to grow feebler; then there was a continued howling, as if the hounds were being roughly handled, and one of them I noticed was altogether silent.

"On arriving on the scene, which I did soon after, I learned the cause of this change of tune. One of the dogs met me running back on the trail on three legs only, and woefully mangled. The moose was standing in a snow-pit, which had been trodden out by the animals while battling, and near his feet lay the other dog, mutilated in a most fearful manner, and evidently quite dead. The bull, in his rage, still continued to assail the dead body of the hound, rising and pouncing down upon it with his fore-hoofs until the ribs cracked under the concussion!

"On seeing me, he again struck into the snow, and made off; I saw, however, that his limbs were much lacerated by the frozen crust, and that he ran slowly, leaving red tracks behind him.

"I did not stop by the dogs—one being dead, and the survivor but little better—but kept on after the game.

"We had now got into a tract where the snow lay of more than usual depth, and my snow-shoes enabled me to skim along faster than the moose himself, that I could easily perceive was growing feebler at every plunge. I saw that I was gaining upon him, and would soon be alongside. The woods through which we were passing were pretty open, and I could note every movement of the chase.

"I had got within a hundred yards of him, and was thinking of firing at him as he ran, when all at once he came to a stop, and wheeling suddenly round, stood facing me. His huge antlers were thrown back until they touched his withers; his mane stood erect; all the hair upon his body seemed to bristle forward; and his whole attitude was one of rage and defiance: he was altogether as formidable-looking an enemy as it had ever been my lot to encounter.

"My first thought, on getting near enough, was to raise my rifle and fire, which I did. I aimed for his chest, that was fair before me; but I shot wide, partly because my fingers were numbed with cold, and partly because the sun at the moment flashed in my eyes as I glanced along the barrel. I hit the moose, however, but in a part that was not mortal—in the shoulder.

"The shot enraged him, and without waiting for me to re-load, he dashed madly forward and towards me; a few plunges brought him up, and I had no resource but to get behind a tree.

"Fortunately there were some large pines in the neighbourhood, and behind one of these I took shelter—not, however, before the enraged animal had almost impaled me upon his antlers. As I slipped behind the trunk, he was following me so close that his horns came in contact with the tree, causing it to vibrate by the terrific shock. He himself drew back a pace or two, and then stopped and stood fast, eyeing the tree with sullen rage; his eyes glared, and his long stiff hair seemed to quiver as he threatened.

"In the hope that he would allow me time, I again bethought me of re-loading my gun. What was my chagrin to find that I had not a grain of powder about me! My friend and I had started with but one powder-flask, and that he had carried with him. My gun was as useless as a bar of iron.

"What was to be done? I dared not, approach the bull with my knife: my life would not have been worth five minutes' purchase. His horns and great sharp hoofs were weapons superior to mine. He might throw me down at the first outset, gore me to death, or trample me in the snow. I dared not risk such an encounter.

"After reflecting for some time, I concluded that it would be wiser for me to leave the moose where he was, and take the back track without him. But how was I to get away from the spot? I was still behind the tree, and the enraged bull was within three feet of it on the other side, without showing any symptoms of retiring. Should I step either to one side or the other, he would launch himself upon me, and the result would be my certain destruction.

"I now began to perceive that I was in a fix—regularly 'treed,' in fact; and the knowledge was anything but cheering. I did not know how long I might be kept so; perhaps the moose might not leave me at all, or until hunger had done its work. The wound I had given him had certainly rendered him desperate and vengeful, and he appeared as if determined to protract the siege indefinitely.

"After remaining nearly an hour in this situation, I began to grow angry and impatient. I had shouted to frighten the bull, but to no purpose; I had shouted, and at the top of my voice, in hopes that I might be heard by my friend, but there was no response except the echoes of my own voice borne hoarsely through the aisles of the winter forest. I grew impatient of my odd captivity, and determined to stand it no longer.

"On stealing a glance behind me, I perceived a tree as large as the one which sheltered me. I resolved to make for that one, as it would at least not render my situation worse should I reach it in safety. This I effected, but not without having my speed put to the test, for the moose followed so close as almost to touch me with his brow-antlers. Once behind this new tree, I was no better off than before, except that it brought me some twenty paces nearer home. The moose—still stood in front of me only a few feet distant, and threatening as fiercely as ever.

"After waiting some minutes for my breath, I selected a third tree in the right direction, and made for it in a similar manner, the moose following as before.

"Another rest and another run brought me behind a fresh tree, and another and another, until I must have made a full mile through the woods, still followed by my implacable and untiring enemy. I knew, however, that I was going homeward, for I guided myself by the trail which we had made in the chase.

"I was in hopes that I might make the whole back-journey in this way, when all at once I perceived that the heavy timber came to an end, and a wide, almost open tract intersected the country, over this the trees were small stunted pines, far apart, and offering no hope of shelter from my relentless persecutor.

"I had no alternative now but to remain where I was, and await the arrival of my friend, who, I presumed, would come after me as soon as he had finished his own hunt.

"With this dubious hope, I kept my stand, although I was ready to drop with fatigue. To add to my misery, it commenced snowing. I saw this with feelings akin to terror, for I knew that the snow would soon blind the trail;

and how, then, was my friend to follow it, and find me? The bull still stood before me in the same threatening attitude, occasionally snorting, striking the ground with his hoofs, and ready to spring after me whenever I should move. Ever as I changed the attitude of my body, he would start forward again, until I could almost touch him with the muzzle of my gun.

"These manoeuvres on his part suggested to me an experiment, and I wondered that I had not thought of it before. I was not long in resolving to carry it out. I was armed with a stout hunting-knife, a bowie; it was pointed as sharp as a needle; and could I only have ventured near enough to the bull, I would soon have settled the dispute with him. The idea now occurred to me of converting my bowie into a lance by splicing it upon the barrel of my gun. With this I had hopes of being able to reach my powerful assailant without coming within range either of his hoofs or horns.

"The lance was soon made, a pair of buckskin gaiters which I wore furnished me with thongs. My gun happened to be a long rifle; and the knife, spliced firmly to the muzzle, rendered it a formidable weapon, so that in a few minutes I stood in a better attitude than I had assumed for hours before.

"The affair soon came to an issue. As I had anticipated, by showing myself a little to one side of the tree, the bull sprang forward, and I was enabled, by a dexterous thrust, to plant the knife between his ribs. It entered his heart, and the next moment I saw him rolling over, and kicking the crimsoned snow around him in the struggles of death.

"I had scarcely completed my victory, when a loud whoop sounded in my ears, and looking up, I saw my friend making towards me across the open ground. He had completed his chase, having killed all three, cut them up, and hung their meat upon the trees, to be sent for on our return to the house.

"By his aid the bull was disposed of in a similar manner; and being now satisfied with our day's sport—though my friend very much regretted the loss of his fine dog—we commenced shuffling homeward."

Chapter Twenty Nine
The Prairie-Wolf and Wolf-Killer

After crossing the Marais de Cygnes River the country became much more open. There was a mixture of timber and prairie-land—the latter, however, constantly gaining the ascendancy as we advanced farther west. The openings became larger, until they assumed the appearance of vast meadows, inclosed by groves, that at a distance resembled great hedges. Now and then there were copses that stood apart from the larger tracts of forests, looking like islands upon the surface of a green sea, and by the name of "islands" these detached groves are known among the hunters and other denizens of prairie-land. Sometimes the surface was undulating or, as it is there termed, "rolling," and our road was varied, ascending or descending, as we crossed the gentle declivities. The timber through which we had up to this time been passing consisted of ash, burr oak, black walnut, chestnut oak, buck eye, the American elm, hickory, hackberry, sumach, and, in low moist places, the sycamore, and long-leaved willow. These trees, with many others, form the principal growth of the large forests, upon the banks of the Mississippi, both cast and west.

As we advanced westward, Besançon called our attention to the fact, that all these kinds of timber, one by one, disappeared from the landscape, and in their place a single species alone made up the larger growth of the forest. This was the celebrated "cotton-wood," a species of poplar (*Populus angulatus*). I say celebrated, because, being almost the only tree of large size which is found throughout the region of the great plains, it is well-known to all hunters and prairie travellers, who regard it with a peculiar veneration. A grove of cotton-wood is always a glad sight to those who traverse the limitless levels of the prairie. It promises shelter from the wind or sun, wood for the camp-fire, and, above all, water to slake the thirst. As the ocean mariner regards the sight of the welcome port, with similar feelings of joy the mariner of the "prairie-sea" beholds, over the broad waste, the silvery foliage of the cotton-wood grove, regarding it as his temporary home—his place of rest and refuge.

After travelling through hundreds of small prairies, separated from each other by groves of cotton-wood, we arrived at a high point on the waters of the "Little Osage," another tributary of the larger river of that name. As yet we had met with no traces of the buffalo, and were beginning to doubt the correctness of the information we had received at Saint Louis, when we fell in with a band of Kansas Indians—a friendly tribe—who received us in the most courteous manner. From them we learned that the buffalo had been upon the Little Osage at an earlier period in that same year, but that harassed and decimated by their own hunters, they had roamed much farther west, and were now supposed to be on the other side of the "Neosho," or Grand River—a northern tributary of the Arkansas.

This was anything but pleasant news. We should have at least another hundred miles to travel before coming up with our game; but there was no thought of going back, until we had done so. No. One and all declared that rather than give up the object of our expedition, we would travel on to the Rocky Mountains themselves, risking the chances of being scalped by hostile Indians.

There was a good deal of bravado in this, it is true; but we were fully determined that we would not go back without our buffalo-hunt.

Thanking our Kansas friends for their courtesy, we parted from them, and headed westward for the Neosho.

As we proceeded, timber became scarce, until at length it was found only on the banks of streams widely distant from each other. Sometimes not a tree was in sight for the whole day's journey. We were now fairly on the prairies.

We crossed the Neosho at length—still no buffalo.

We kept on, and crossed several other large streams, all flowing south-eastwardly to the Arkansas. Still no buffalo.

We began to yearn exceedingly for a sight of the great game. The few deer that were killed from time to time offered us but poor sport, and their meat was not sufficient for our supply.

Of bacon we were heartily tired, and we longed for fresh buffalo-beef. The praises lavished by our guides upon the delicacy of this viand—their talk over the camp-fire, about "fat cow" and "*boudins*" and "hump-ribs," quite tantalised our palates, and we were all eager to try our teeth upon these vaunted tit-bits. No buffalo appeared yet, and we were forced to chew our bacon, as well as our impatience, for several days longer.

A great change now took place in the appearance of the country. The timber became still more scarce, and the soil drier and more sandy. Species of cactus (*opuntia*) appeared along the route, with several other plants new to the eyes of most of us, and which to those of Besançon were objects of extreme interest. But that which most gratified us was the appearance of a new herbage, different entirely from what we had been passing over, and this was hailed by our guides with exclamations of joy. It was the celebrated "buffalo grass." The trappers declared we should not have much farther to go until we found the buffaloes themselves, for, wherever this grass existed in plenty, the buffalo, unless driven off by hunting, were sure to be found.

The buffalo grass is a short grass, not more than a few inches in height, with crooked and pointed culms, often throwing out suckers that root again, and produce other leaves and culms, and in this way form a tolerably thick sward. When in flower or seed, it is headed by numerous spikes of half an inch in length, and on these the spikelets are regular and two rowed.

It is a species of *Sesleria* (*Sesleria dactyloides*), but Besançon informed us that it possesses characters that cause it to differ from the genus, and to resemble the *Chondrosium*.

The buffalo grass is not to be confounded with, another celebrated grass of the Texan and North Mexican prairies, the "gramma" of the Spaniards. This last is a true Chondrosium, and there are several species of it. The *Chondrosium foeneum* is one of the finest fodders in the world for the food of cattle, almost equal to unthrashed oats.

The buffalo grass forms the favourite and principal fodder of the buffaloes whenever it is in season, and these animals roam over the prairies in search of it.

Of course with this knowledge we were now on the *qui vive*. At every new rise that we made over the swells of the prairie our eyes were busy, and swept the surface on every side of us, and in the course of a few days we encountered several false alarms.

There is an hallucination peculiar to the clear atmosphere of these regions. Objects are not only magnified, but frequently distorted in their outlines, and it is only an old hunter that knows a buffalo when he sees one. Brothers a bush is often taken for a wild bull, and with us a brace of carrion crows, seated upon the crest of a ridge, were actually thought to be buffaloes, until they suddenly took wing and rose into the air, thus dispelling the illusion!

Long before this time we had encountered that well-known animal of the great plains—the "prairie-wolf,"—(*Lupus latrans*).

The prairie-wolf inhabits the vast and still unpeopled territories that lie between the Mississippi River and the shores of the Pacific Ocean. Its range extends beyond what is strictly termed "the prairies." It is found in the wooded and mountainous ravines of California and the Rocky Mountain districts. It is common throughout the whole of Mexico, where it is known as the "coyote." I have seen numbers of this species on the battle-field, tearing at corpses, as far south as the valley of Mexico itself. Its name of prairie-wolf is, therefore, in some respects inappropriate, the more so as the larger wolves are also inhabitants of the prairie. No doubt this name was given it, because the animal was first observed in the prairie country west of the Mississippi by the early explorers of that region. In the wooded countries east of the great river, the common large wolf only is known.

Whatever doubt there may be of the many varieties of the large wolf being distinct species, there can be none with regard to the *Lupus latrans*. It differs from all the others in size, and in many of its habits. Perhaps it more nearly resembles the jackal than any other animal. It is the New World representative of that celebrated creature.

In size, it is just midway between the large wolf and fox. With much of the appearance of the former, it combines all the sagacity of the latter. It is usually of a greyish colour, lighter or darker, according to circumstances, and often with a tinge of cinnamon or brown.

As regards its cunning, the fox is "but a fool to it." It cannot be trapped. Some experiments made for the purpose, show results that throw the theory of instinct quite into the background. It has been known to burrow under a "dead fall," and drag off the bait without springing the trap. The steel-trap it avoids, no matter how concealed; and the cage-trap has been found "no go."

Farther illustrations of the cunning of the prairie-wolf might be found in its mode of decoying within reach the antelopes and other creatures on which it preys. Of course this species is as much fox as wolf, for in reality a small wolf is a fox, and a large fox is a wolf. To the traveller and trapper of the prairie regions, it is a pest. It robs the former of his provisions—often stealing them out of his very tent; it unbaits the traps of the latter, or devours the game already secured in them.

It is a constant attendant upon the caravans or travelling-parties that cross prairie-land. A pack of prairie-wolves will follow such a party for hundreds of miles, in order to secure the refuse left at the camps. They usually he down upon the prairie, just out of range of the rifles of the travellers; yet they do not observe this rule always, as they know there is not much danger of being molested. Hunters rarely shoot them, not deeming their hides worth having, and not caring to waste a charge upon them.

They are more cautious when following a caravan of California emigrants, where there are plenty of "greenhorns" and amateur-hunters ready to fire at anything.

Prairie-wolves are also constant attendants upon the "gangs" of buffalo. They follow these for hundreds of miles—in fact, the outskirts of the buffalo herd are, for the time being, their home. They he down on the prairie at a short distance from the buffaloes, and wait and watch, in hopes that some of these animals may get disabled or separated from the rest, or with the expectation that a cow with her new-dropped calf may fall into the rear. In such cases, the pack gather round the unfortunate individual, and worry it to death. A wounded or superannuated bull sometimes "falls out," and is attacked. In this case the fight is more desperate, and the bull is sadly mutilated before he can be brought to the ground. Several wolves, too, are laid *hors de combat* during the struggle.

The prairie traveller may often look around him without seeing a single wolf; but let him fire off his gun, and, as if by magic, a score of them will suddenly appear. They start from their hiding-places, and rush forward in hopes of sharing in the produce of the shot.

At night, they enliven the prairie-camp with their dismal howling, although most travellers would gladly dispense with such music. Their note is a bark like that of a terrier-dog repeated three times, and then prolonged into a true wolf's howl. I have heard farm-house dogs utter a very similar bark. From this peculiarity, some naturalists prefer calling them the "barking wolf," and that (*Lupus latrans*) is the specific appellation given by Say, who first described them.

Prairie-wolves have all the ferocity of their race, but no creature could be more cowardly. Of course no one fears them under ordinary circumstances, but they have been known to make a combined attack upon persons disabled, and in severe weather, when they themselves were rendered unusually savage by hunger, as already stated. But they are not regarded with fear either by traveller or hunter; and the latter disdains to waste his charge upon such worthless game.

Our guide, Ike, was an exception to this rule. He was the only one of his sort that shot prairie-wolves, and he did so "on sight." I believe if it had been the last bullet in his pouch, and an opportunity had offered of sending it into a prairie-wolf, he would have despatched the leaden missile. We asked him how many he had killed in his time. He drew a small notched stick from his "possible sack," and desired us to count the notches upon it. We did so. There were one hundred and forty-five in all.

"You have killed one hundred and forty-five, then?" cried we, astonished at the number.

"Yes, i'deed," replied he, with a quiet chuckle, "that many dozen; for every 'un of them nutches count twelve. I only make a nutch when I've throwed the clur dozen."

"A hundred and forty-five dozen!" we repeated in astonishment; and yet I have no doubt of the truth of the trapper's statement, for he had no interest in deceiving us. I am satisfied from what I knew of him, that he had slain the full number stated—one thousand seven hundred and forty!

Of course we became curious to learn the cause of his antipathy to the prairie-wolves; for we knew he had an antipathy, and it was that that had induced him to commit such wholesale havoc among these creatures. It was from this circumstance he had obtained the soubriquet of "wolf-killer." By careful management, we at last got him upon the edge of the stray, and quietly pushed him into it. He gave it to us as follows:—

"Wal, strengers, about ten winters agone, I wur travellin' from Bent's Fort on the Arkensaw, to 'Laramie on the Platte, all alone by myself. I had undertuk the journey on some business for Bill Bent—no matter now what.

"I had crossed the divide, and got within sight o' the Black Hills, when one night I had to camp out on the open parairy, without either bush or stone to shelter me.

"That wur, perhaps, the coldest night this nigger remembers; thur wur a wind kim down from the mountains that wud a froze the bar off an iron dog. I gathered my blanket around me, but that wind whistled through it as if it had been a rail-fence.

"'Twan't no use lyin' down, for I couldn't a sleep, so I sot up.

"You may ask why I hadn't a fire? I'll tell you why. Fust, thur wan't a stick o' timber within ten mile o' me; and, secondly, if thur had been I dasen't a made a fire. I wur travellin' as bad a bit o' Injun ground as could been found in all the country, and I'd seen Injun sign two or three times that same day. It's true thur wur a good grist o' buffler-chips about, tol'ably dry, and I mout have made some sort o' a fire out o' that; an' at last I did make a fire arter a fashion. I did it this a way.

"Seeing that with the cussed cold I wan't again' to get a wink o' sleep, I gathered a wheen o' the buffler-chips. I then dug a hole in the ground with my bowie, an' hard pickin' that wur; but I got through the crust at last, and made a sort o' oven about a fut, or a fut and a half deep. At the bottom I laid some dry grass and dead branches o' sage plant, and then settin' it afire, I piled the buffler-chips on top. The thing burnt tol'able well, but the smoke o' the buffler-dung would a-choked a skunk.

"As soon as it had got fairly under way, I hunkered, an' sot down over the hole, in sich a position as to catch all the heat under my blanket, an' then I was comf'table enough. Of coorse no Injun kud see the smoke arter night, an it would a tuk sharp eyes to have sighted the fire, I reckon.

"Wal, strengers, the critter I rode wur a young mustang colt, about half-broke. I had bought him from a Mexikin at Bent's only the week afore, and it wur his fust journey, leastwise with me. Of coorse I had him on the lariat; but up to this time I had kept the eend o' the rope in my hand, because I had that same day lost my picket pin; an' thinkin' as I wan't agoin' to sleep, I mout as well hold on to it.

"By 'm by, however, I begun to feel drowsy. The fire 'atween my legs promised to keep me from freezin', an' I thort I mout as well take a nap. So I tied the lariat round my ankles, sunk my head atween my knees, an' in the twinklin' o' a goat's tail I wur sound. I jest noticed as I wur goin' off, that the mustang wur out some yards, nibbling away at the dry grass o' the parairy.

"I guess I must a slep about an hour, or tharabouts—I won't be sartint how long. I only know that I didn't wake o' my own accord. I wur awoke; an' when I did awoke, I still thort I wur a-dreamin'. It would a been a rough dream; but unfort'nately for me, it wan't a dream, but a jenwine reality.

"At fust, I cudn't make out what wur the matter wi' me, no how; an' then I thort I wur in the hands o' the Injuns, who were draggin' me over the parairy; an' sure enough I wur a draggin' that a way, though not by Injuns. Once or twice I lay still for jest a second or two, an' then away I went agin, trailin' and bumpin' over the ground, as if I had been tied to the tail o' a gallopin' hoss. All the while there wur a yellin' in my ears as if all the cats an' dogs of creation were arter me.

"Wal, it wur some time afore I compre'nded what all this rough usage meant. I did at last. The pull upon my ankles gave me the idea. It wur the lariat that wur round them. My mustang had stampedoed, and wur draggin' me at full gallop acrosst the parairy!

"The barkin', an' howlin', an' yelpin' I heerd, wur a pack o' parairy-wolves. Half-famished, they had attacked the mustang, and started him.

"All this kim into my mind at once. You'll say it wur easy to lay hold on the rope, an' stop the hoss. So it mout appear; but I kin tell you that it ain't so easy a thing. It wan't so to me. My ankles wur in a noose, an' wur drawed clost together. Of coorse, while I wur movin' along, I couldn't get to my feet; an' whenever the mustang kim to a halt, an' I had half gathered myself, afore I laid reach the rope, away went the critter agin, flingin' me to the ground at full length. Another thing hindered me. Afore goin' to sleep, I had put my blanket on Mexikin-fashion—that is, wi' my head through a slit in the centre—an' as the drag begun, the blanket flopped about my face, an' half-smothered me. Prehaps, however, an' I thort so arterwurd, that blanket saved me many a scratch, although it bamfoozled me a good bit.

"I got the blanket off at last, arter I had made about a mile, I reckon, and then for the fust time I could see about me. Such a sight! The moon wur up, an' I kud see that the ground wur white with snow. It had snowed while I wur asleep; but that wan't the sight—the sight war, that clost up an' around me the hul parairy wur kivered with wolves—cussed parairy-wolves! I kud see their long tongues lollin' out, an' the smoke steamin' from their open mouths.

"Bein' now no longer hampered by the blanket, I made the best use I could o' my arms. Twice I got hold o' the lariat, but afore I kud set myself to pull up the runnin' hoss, it wur jerked out o' my hand agin.

"Somehow or other, I had got clutch o' my bowie, and at the next opportunity I made a cut at the rope, and heerd the clean 'snig' o' the knife. Arter that I lay quiet on the parairy, an' I b'lieve I kinder sort o' fainted.

"'Twan't a long faint no how; for when I got over it, I kud see the mustang about a half a mile off, still runnin' as fast as his legs could carry him, an' most of the wolves howlin' arter him. A few of these critters had gathered about me, but gettin' to my feet, I made a dash among them wi' the shinin' bowie, an' sent them every which way, I reckon.

"I watched the mustang until he wur clur out o' sight, an' then I wur puzzled what to do. Fust, I went back for my blanket, which I soon rekivered, an' then I follered the back track to get my gun an' other traps whur I had camped. The trail wur easy, on account o' the snow, an' I kud see whur I had slipped through it all the way.

"Having got my possibles, I then tuk arter the mustang, and follered for at least ten miles on his tracks, but I never see'd that, mustang agin. Whether the wolves hunted him down or not, I can't say, nor I don't care if they did, the scarey brute! I see'd their feet all the way arter him in the snow, and I know'd it wur no use follering further. It wur plain I wur put down on the parairy, so I bundled my possibles, and turned head for Laramies afoot. I had a three days' walk o' it, and prehaps I didn't cuss a few!

"I wur right bad used. Thur wan't a bone in my body that didn't ache, as if I had been passed through a sugar-mill; and my clothes and skin were torn consid'ably. It mout a been wuss but for the blanket an' the sprinkle o' snow that made the ground a leetle slickerer.

"Howsomever, I got safe to the Fort, whur I wur soon rigged out in a fresh suit o' buckskin an' a hoss.

"But I never arterward see'd a parairy-wolf within range o' my rifle, that I didn't let it into him, an' as you see, I've throwed a good wheen in their tracks since then. Wagh! Hain't I, Mark?"

Chapter Thirty
Hunting the Tapir

At one of our prairie-camps our English comrade furnished us with the following account of that strange creature, the tapir.

"No one who has turned over the pages of a picture-book of mammalia will be likely to forget the odd-looking animal known as the tapir. Its long proboscis-like snout, its stiff-maned neck, and clumsy hog-like body, render the *tout ensemble* of this creature so peculiar, that there is no mistaking it for any other animal.

"When full-grown, the tapir, or anta, as it is sometimes called, is six feet in length by four in height—its weight being nearly equal to that of a small bullock. Its teeth resemble those of the horse; but instead of hoofs, its feet are toed—the fore ones having four toes, while the hind-feet have only three each. The eyes are small and lateral, while the ears are large and pointed. The skin is thick, somewhat like that of the hippopotamus, with a very thin scattering of silky hairs over it; but along the ridge of the neck, and upon the short tail, the hairs are longer and more profuse. The upper jaw protrudes far beyond the extremity of the under one. It is, moreover, highly prehensile, and enables the tapir to seize the roots upon which it feeds with greater ease. In fact, it plays the part of the elephant's proboscis to a limited degree.

"Although the largest quadruped indigenous to South America, the tapir is not very well-known to naturalists. Its haunts are far beyond the borders of civilisation. It is, moreover, a shy and solitary creature, and its active life is mostly nocturnal; hence no great opportunity is offered for observing its habits. The chapter of its natural history is therefore a short one.

"The tapir is an inhabitant of the tropical countries of America, dwelling near the banks of rivers and marshy lagoons. It is the American representative of the rhinoceros and hippopotamus, or, more properly, of the *mäiba*, or Indian tapir (*Tapirus Indicus*) of Sumatra, which has but lately become known to naturalists. The latter, in fact, is a near congener, and very much, resembles the tapir of South America.

"The tapir is amphibious—that is, it frequents the water, can swim and dive well, and generally seeks its food in the water or the soft marshy sedge; but when in repose, it is a land animal, making its haunt in thick coverts of the woods, and selecting a dry spot for its lair. Here it will remain couched and asleep during the greater part of the day. At nightfall, it steals forth, and following an old and well-used path, it approaches the bank of some river, and plunging in, swims off in search of its food—the roots and stems of several species of water-plants. In this business it occupies most of the hours of darkness; but at daybreak, it swims back to the place where it entered the water, and going out, takes the 'backtrack' to its lair, where it sleeps until sunset again warns it forth.

"Sometimes during rain, it leaves its den even at midday. On such occasions, it proceeds to the river or the adjacent swamp, where it delights to wallow in the mud, after the manner of hogs, and often for hours together. Unlike the hog, however, the tapir is a cleanly animal. After wallowing, it never returns to its den until it has first plunged into the clear water, and washed the mud thoroughly from its skin.

"It usually travels at a trot, but when hard pressed it can gallop. Its gallop is peculiar. The fore-legs are thrown far in advance, and the head is carried between them in a very awkward manner, somewhat after the fashion of a frolicsome donkey.

"The tapir is strictly a vegetable feeder. It lives upon flags and roots of aquatic plants. Several kinds of fruits, and young succulent branches of trees, form a portion of its food.

"It is a shy, timid animal, without any malice in its character; and although possessed of great strength, never uses it except for defence, and then only in endeavours to escape. It frequently suffers itself to be killed without making any defence, although with its great strength and well-furnished jaws it might do serious hurt to an enemy.

"The hunt of the tapir is one of the amusements, or rather employments, of the South-American Indians. Not that the flesh of this animal is so eagerly desired by them: on the contrary, it is dry, and has a disagreeable taste, and there are some tribes who will not eat of it, preferring the flesh of monkeys, macaws, and the armadillo. But the part most prized is the thick, tough skin, which is employed by the Indians in making shields, sandals, and various other articles. This is the more valuable in a country where the thick-skinned and leather-yielding mammalia are almost unknown.

"Slaying the tapir is no easy matter. The creature is shy; and, having the advantage of the watery clement, is often enabled to dive beyond the reach of pursuit, and thus escape by concealing itself. Among most of the native tribes of South America, the young hunter who has killed a tapir is looked upon as having achieved something to be proud of.

"The tapir is hunted by bow and arrow, or by the gun. Sometimes the 'gravatana,' or blow-tube, is employed, with its poisoned darts. In any case, the hunter either lies in wait for his prey, or with a pack of dogs drives it out of the underwood, and takes the chances of a 'flying shot.'

"When the trail of a tapir has been discovered, its capture becomes easy. It is well-known to the hunter that this animal, when proceeding from its lair to the water and returning, always follows its old track until a beaten-path is made, which is easily discernible.

"This path often betrays the tapir, and leads to its destruction.

"Sometimes the hunter accomplishes this by means of a pitfall, covered with branches and palm-leaves; at other times, he places himself in ambuscade, either before twilight or in the early morning, and shoots the unsuspecting animal as it approaches on its daily round.

"Sometimes, when the whereabouts of a tapir has been discovered, a whole tribe sally out, and take part in the hunt. Such a hunt I myself witnessed on one of the tributaries of the Amazon.

"In the year 18—, I paid a visit to the Jurunas up the Xingu. Their *Malaccas* (palm-hut villages) lie beyond the falls of that river. Although classed as 'wild Indians,' the Jurunas are a mild race, friendly to the traders, and collect during a season considerable quantities of *seringa* (Indian-rubber), sarsaparilla, as well as rare birds, monkeys, and Brazil-nuts—the objects of Portuguese trade.

"I was about to start back for Para, when nothing would serve the *tuxava*, or chief of one of the maloccas, but that I should stay a day or two at his village, and take part in some festivities. He promised a tapir-hunt.

"As I knew that among the Jurunas were some skilled hunters, and as I was curious to witness an affair of this kind, I consented. The hunt was to come off on the second day of my stay.

"The morning arrived, and the hunters assembled, to the number of forty or fifty, in an open space by the malocca; and having got their arms and equipments in readiness, all repaired to the *praya*, or narrow beach of sand, which separated the river from the thick underwood of the forest. Here some twenty or thirty *ubas* (canoes hollowed out of tree-trunks) floated on the water, ready to receive the hunters. They were of different sizes; some capable of containing half a dozen, while others were meant to carry only a single person.

"In a few minutes the ubas were freighted with their living cargoes, consisting not only of the hunters, but of most of the women and boys of the malocca, with a score or two of dogs.

"These dogs were curious creatures to look at. A stranger, ignorant of the customs of the Jurunas, would have been at some loss to account for the peculiarity of their colour. Such dogs I had never seen before. Some were of a bright scarlet, others were yellow, others blue, and some mottled with a variety of tints!

"What could it mean? But I knew well enough. *The dogs were dyed*!

"Yes, it is the custom among many tribes of South-American Indians to dye not only their own bodies, but the hairy coat of their dogs, with brilliant colours obtained from vegetable juices, such as the huitoc, the yellow raucau (*annato*), and the blue of the wild indigo. The light grey, often white, hair of these animals favours the staining process; and the effect produced pleases the eye of their savage masters.

"On my eye the effect was strange and fantastical. I could not restrain my laughter when I first scanned these curs in their fanciful coats. Picture to yourself a pack of scarlet, and orange, and purple dogs!

"Well, we were soon in the ubas, and paddling up-stream. The tuxava and I occupied a canoe to ourselves. His only arms were a light fusil, which I had given him as a present. It was a good piece, and he was proud of it. This was to be its first trial. I had a rifle for my own weapon. The rest were armed variously: some had guns, others the native bow and arrows; some carried the gravatana, with arrows dipped in curari poison; some had nothing but machetes, or cutlasses—for clearing the underwood, in case the game had to be driven from the thickets.

"There was a part of the river, some two or three miles above the malocca, where the channel was wider than elsewhere—several miles in breadth at this place. Here it was studded with islands, known to be a favourite resort of the tapirs. This was to be the scene of our hunt.

"We approached the place in about an hour; but on the way I could not help being struck with the picturesqueness of our party. No 'meet' in the hunting-field of civilised countries could have equalled us in that respect. The ubas, strung out in a long irregular line, sprang up-stream in obedience to the vigorous strokes of the rowers, and these sang in a sort of irregular concert as they plied their paddles. The songs were improvised: they told the feats of the hunters already performed, and promised others yet to be done. I could hear the word 'tapira' (tapir), often repeated. The women lent their shrill voices to the chorus; and now and then interrupted the song with peals of merry laughter. The strange-looking flotilla—the bronzed bodies of the Indians, more than half nude—their waving black hair—their blue-head belts and red cotton armlets—the bright *tangas* (aprons) of the women—their massive necklaces—the macaw feathers adorning the heads of the hunters—their odd arms and equipments—all combined to form a picture which, even to me, accustomed to such sights, was full of interest.

"At length we arrived among the islands, and then the noises ceased. The canoes were paddled as slowly and silently as possible.

"I now began to understand the plan of the hunt. It was first to discover an island upon which a tapir was supposed to be, and then encompass it with the hunters in their canoes, while a party landed with the dogs, to arouse the game and drive it toward the water.

"This plan promised fair sport.

"The canoes now separated; and in a short while each of them were seen coursing quietly along the edge of some islet, one of its occupants leaning inward, and scrutinising the narrow belt of sand that bordered the water.

"In some places no such sand-belt appeared. The trees hung over, their branches even dipping into the current, and forming a roofed and dark passage underneath. In such places a tapir could have hidden himself from the sharpest-eyed hunters, and herein lies the chief difficulty of this kind of hunt.

"It was not long before a low whistle was heard from one of the ubas, a sign for the others to come up. The traces of a tapir had been discovered.

"The chief, with a stroke or two of his palm-wood paddle, brought our canoe to the spot.

"There, sure enough, was the sign—the tracks of a tapir in the sand—leading to a hole in the thick underwood, where a beaten-path appeared to continue onward into the interior of the island, perhaps to the tapir-den. The tracks were fresh—had been made that morning in the wet sand—no doubt the creature was in its lair.

"The island was a small one, with some five or six acres of surface. The canoes shot off in different directions, and in a few minutes were deployed all around it. At a given signal, several hunters leaped ashore, followed by their bright-coloured assistants—the dogs; and then the chopping of branches, the shouts of the men, and the yelping of their canine companions, were all heard mingling together.

"The island was densely wooded. The *uaussu* and *piriti* palms grew so thickly, that their crowned heads touched each other, forming a close roof. Above these, rose the taller summits of the great forest trees, *cedrelas*, *zamangs*, and the beautiful long-leaved silk-cotton (*bombax*); but beneath, a perfect net-work of sipos or creepers and llianas choked up the path, and the hunters had to clear every step of the way with their machetes. Even the dogs, with all their eagerness, could make only a slow and tortuous advance among the thorny vines of the smilax, and the sharp spines that covered the trunks of the palms.

"In the circle of canoes that surrounded the island, there was perfect silence; each had a spot to guard, and each hunter sat, with arms ready, and eyes keenly fixed on the foliage of the underwood opposite his station.

"The uba of the chief had remained to watch the path where the tracks of the tapir had been observed. We both sat with guns cocked and ready; the dogs and hunters were distinctly heard in the bushes approaching the centre of the islet. The former gave tongue at intervals, but their yelping grew louder, and was uttered with a fiercer accent. Several of them barked at once, and a rushing was heard towards the water.

"It came in our direction, but not right for us; still the game was likely to issue at a point within range of our guns. A stroke of the paddle brought us into a better position. At the same time several other canoes were seen shooting forward to the spot.

"The underwood crackled and shook; reddish forms appeared among the leaves; and the next moment a dozen animals, resembling a flock of hogs, tumbled out from the thicket, and flung themselves with a splashing into the water.

"'No—tapir no—capivara,' cried the chief; but his voice was drowned by the reports of guns and the twanging of bowstrings. Half a dozen of the capivaras were observed to fall on the sandy margin, while the rest plunged forward, and, diving beyond the reach of pursuit, were seen no more.

"This was a splendid beginning of the day's sport; for half a dozen at a single volley was no mean game, even among Indians.

"But the nobler beast, the tapir, occupied all our thoughts; and leaving the capivaras to be gathered in by the women, the hunters got back to their posts in a few seconds.

"There was no doubt that a tapir would be roused. The island had all the appearance of being the haunt of one or more of these creatures, besides the tracks were evidence of their recent presence upon the spot. The beating, therefore, proceeded as lively as ever, and the hunters and dogs now penetrated to the centre of the thicket.

"Again the quick angry yelping of the latter fell upon the ear; and again the thick cover rustled and shook.

"'This time the tapir,' said the chief to me in an undertone, adding the next moment in a louder voice, 'Look yonder!'

"I looked in the direction pointed out. I could perceive something in motion among the leaves—a dark brown body, smooth and rounded, the body of a tapir!

"I caught only a glimpse of it, as it sprang forward into the opening. It was coming at full gallop, with its head carried between its knees. The dogs were close after, and it looked not before it, but dashed out and ran towards us as though blind.

"It made for the water, just a few feet from the bow of our canoe. The chief and I fired at the same time. I thought my bullet took effect, and so thought the chief did his; but the tapir, seeming not to heed the shots, plunged into the stream, and went under.

"The next moment the whole string of dyed dogs came sweeping out of the thicket, and leaped forward to where the game had disappeared.

"There was blood upon the water. The tapir is hit, then, thought I; and was about to point out the blood to the chief, when on turning I saw the latter poising himself knife in hand, near the stern of the canoe. He was about to spring out of it. His eye was fixed on some object under the water.

"I looked in the same direction. The waters of the Xingu are as clear as crystal: against the sandy bottom, I could trace the dark brown body of the tapir. It was making for the deeper channel of the river, but evidently dragging itself along with difficulty. One of its legs was disabled by our shots.

"I had scarcely time to get a good view of it before the chief sprang into the air, and dropped head foremost into the water. I could see a struggle going on at the bottom—turbid water came to the surface—and then up came the dark head of the savage chief.

"'Ugh!' cried he, as he shook the water from his thick tresses, and beckoned me to assist him—'Ugh! Senhor, you eat roast tapir for dinner. Si—bueno—here tapir.'

"I pulled him into the boat, and afterwards assisted to haul up the huge body of the slain tapir.

"As was now seen, both our shots had taken effect; but it was the rifle-bullet that had broken the creature's leg, and the generous savage acknowledged that he would have had but little chance of overtaking the game under water, had it not been previously crippled.

"The hunt of the day proved a very successful one. Two more tapirs were killed; several capivaras; and a paca—which is an animal much prized by the Indians for its flesh, as well as the teeth—used by them in making their blow-guns. We also obtained a pair of the small peccaries, several macaws, and no less than a whole troop of guariba monkeys. We returned to the malocca with a game-bag as various as it was full, and a grand dance of the Juruna women wound up the amusements of the day."

Chapter Thirty One
The Buffaloes at last

The long looked for day at length arrived when the game were to be met with, and I had myself the "distinguished honour" of being the first not only to see the great buffalo, but to throw a couple of them "in their tracks." This incident, however, was not without an "adventure," and one that was neither very pleasant nor without peril. During several late days of our journey we had been in the habit of straggling a good deal in search of game—deer if we could find it, but more especially in hopes of falling in with the buffalo. Sometimes we went in twos or threes, but as often one of the party rode off alone to hunt wherever his inclination guided him. Sometimes these solitary expeditions took place while the party was on the march, but oftener during the hours after we had pitched our night-camp.

One evening, after we had camped as usual, and my brave horse had eaten his "bite" of corn, I leaped into the saddle and rode off in hopes of finding something fresh for supper. The prairie where we had halted was a "rolling" one, and as the camp had been fixed on a small stream, between two great swells, it was not visible at any great distance. As soon, therefore, as I had crossed one of the ridges, I was out of sight of my companions. Trusting to the sky for my direction, I continued on.

After riding about a mile, I came upon buffalo "sign," consisting of several circular holes in the ground, five or six feet in diameter, known as buffalo wallows I saw at a glance that the sign was fresh. There were several wallows; and I could tell by the tracks, in the dusk, there had been bulls in that quarter. So I continued on in hopes of getting a sight of the animals that had been wallowing.

Shortly after, I came to a place where the ground was ploughed up, as if a drove of hogs had been rooting it. Here there had been a terrible fight among the bulls—it was the rutting season, when such conflicts occur. This augured well. Perhaps they are still in the neighbourhood, reasoned I, as I gave the spur to my horse, and galloped forward with more spirit.

I had ridden full five miles from camp, when my attention was attracted by an odd noise ahead of me. There was a ridge in front that prevented me from seeing what produced the noise; but I knew what it was—it was the bellowing of a buffalo-bull.

At intervals, there were quick shocks, as of two hard substances coming in violent contact with each other.

I mounted the ridge with caution, and looked over its crest. There was a valley beyond; a cloud of dust was rising out of its bottom, and in the midst of this I could distinguish two huge forms—dark and hirsute.

I saw at once that they were a pair of buffalo-bulls engaged in a fierce fight. They were alone; there were no others in sight, either in the valley or on the prairie beyond.

I did not halt longer than to see that the cap was on my rifle, and to cock the piece. Occupied as the animals were, I did not imagine they would heed me: or, if they should attempt flight, I knew I could easily overtake one or other; so, without farther hesitation or precaution, I rode towards them.

Contrary to my expectation, they both "winded" me, and started off. The wind was blowing freshly towards them, and the sun had thrown my shadow between them, so as to draw their attention.

They did not run, however, as if badly scared; on the contrary, they went off, apparently indignant at being disturbed in their fight; and every now and then both came round with short turnings, snorted, and struck the prairie with their hoofs in a violent and angry manner.

Once or twice, I fancied they were going to charge upon me; and had I been otherwise than well mounted, I should have been very chary of risking such an encounter. A more formidable pair of antagonists, as far as appearance went, could not have been well conceived. Their huge size, their shaggy fronts, and fierce glaring eyeballs, gave them a wild and malicious seeming, which was heightened by their bellowing, and the threatening attitudes in which they continually placed themselves.

Feeling quite safe in my saddle, I galloped up to the nearest, and sent my bullet into his ribs. It did the work. He fell to his knees—rose again—spread out his legs, as if to prevent a second fall—rocked from side to side like a cradle—again came to his knees; and after remaining in this position for some minutes, with the blood running from his nostrils, rolled quietly over on his shoulder, and lay dead.

I had watched these manoeuvres with interest, and permitted the second bull to make his escape; a side-glance had shown me the latter disappearing over the crest of the swell.

I did not care to follow him, as my horse was somewhat jaded, and I knew it would cost me a sharp gallop to come up with him again; so I thought no more of him at that time, but alighted, and prepared to deal with the one already slain.

There stood a solitary tree near the spot—it was a stunted cotton-wood. There were others upon the prairie, but they were distant; this one was not twenty yards from the carcass. I led my horse up to it, and taking the trail-rope from the horn of the saddle, made one end fast to the bit-ring, and the other to the tree. I then went back, drew my knife, and proceeded to cut up the buffalo.

I had hardly whetted my blade, when a noise from behind caused me to leap to an upright attitude, and look round; at the first glance, I comprehended the noise. A huge dark object was passing the crest of the ridge, and rushing down the hill towards the spot where I stood. It was the buffalo-bull, the same that had just left me.

The sight, at first thought, rather pleased me than otherwise. Although I did not want any more meat, I should have the triumph of carrying two tongues instead of one to the camp. I therefore hurriedly sheathed my knife, and laid hold of my rifle, which, according to custom, I had taken the precaution to re-load.

I hesitated a moment whether to run to my horse and mount him, or to fire from where I stood. That question, however, was settled by the buffalo. The tree and the horse were to one side of the direction in which he was running, but being attracted by the loud snorting of the horse, which had begun to pitch and plunge violently, and deeming it perhaps a challenge, the buffalo suddenly swerved from his course, and ran full tilt upon the horse. The latter shot out instantly to the full length of the trail-rope—a heavy "pluck" sounded in my ears, and the next instant I saw my horse part from the tree, and scour off over the prairie, as if there had been a thistle under his tail. I had knotted the rope negligently upon the bit-ring, and the knot had "come undone."

I was chagrined, but not alarmed as yet. My horse would no doubt follow back his own trail, and at the worst I should only have to walk to the camp. I should have the satisfaction of punishing the buffalo for the trick he had served me; and with this design I turned towards him.

I saw that he had not followed the horse, but was again heading himself in my direction.

Now, for the first time, it occurred to me that I was in something of a scrape. The bull was coming furiously on. Should my shot miss, or even should it only wound him, how was I to escape? I knew that he could overtake me in a three minutes' stretch; I knew that well.

I had not much time for reflection—not a moment, in fact: the infuriated animal was within ten paces of me. I raised my rifle, aimed at his fore-shoulder, and fired.

I saw that I had hit him; but, to my dismay, he neither fell nor stumbled, but continued to charge forward more furiously than ever.

To re-load was impossible. My pistols had gone off with my horse and holsters. Even to reach the tree was impossible; the bull was between it and me.

To make off in the opposite direction was the only thing that held out the prospect of five minutes' safety; I turned and ran.

I can run as fast as most men, and upon that occasion I did my best. It would have put "Gildersleeve" into a white sweat to have distanced me; but I had not been two minutes at it, when I felt conscious that the buffalo gained upon me, and was almost treading upon my heels! I knew it only by my ears—I dared not spare time to look back.

At this moment, an object appeared before me, that promised, one way or another, to interrupt the chase; it was a ditch or gully, that intersected my path at right angles. It was several feet in depth, dry at the bottom, and with perpendicular sides.

I was almost upon its edge before I noticed it, but the moment it came under my eye, I saw that it offered the means of a temporary safety at least. If I could only leap this gully, I felt satisfied that the buffalo could not.

It was a sharp leap—at least, seventeen feet from cheek to cheek; but I had done more than that in my time; and, without halting in my gait, I ran forward to the edge, and sprang over.

I alighted cleverly upon the opposite bank, where I stopped, and turned round to watch my pursuer.

I now ascertained how near my end I had been: the bull was already up to the very edge of the gully. Had I not made my leap at the instant I did, I should have been by that time dancing upon his horns. He himself had balked at the leap; the deep chasm-like cleft had cowed him. He saw that he could not clear it; and now stood upon the opposite bank with head lowered, and spread nostrils, his tail lashing his brown flanks, while his glaring black eyes expressed the full measure of his baffled rage.

I remarked that my shot had taken effect in his shoulder, as the blood trickled from his long hair.

I had almost begun to congratulate myself on having escaped, when a hurried glance to the right, and another to the left, cut short my happiness. I saw that on both sides, at a distance of less than fifty paces, the gully shallowed out into the plain, where it ended; at either end it was, of course, passable.

The bull observed this almost at the same time as myself; and, suddenly turning away from the brink, he ran along the edge of the chasm, evidently with the intention of turning it.

In less than a minute's time we were once more on the same side, and my situation appeared as terrible as ever; but, stepping back for a short run, I re-leaped the chasm, and again we stood on opposite sides.

During all these manoeuvres I had held on to my rifle; and, seeing now that I might have time to load it, I commenced feeling for my powder-horn. To my astonishment, I could not lay my hands upon it: I looked down to my breast for the sling—it was not there; belt and bullet-pouch too—all were gone! I remembered lifting them over my head, when I set about cutting the dead bull. They were lying by the carcass.

This discovery was a new source of chagrin; but for my negligence, I could now have mastered my antagonist.

To reach the ammunition would be impossible; I should be overtaken before I had got half-way to it.

I was not allowed much time to indulge in my regrets; the bull had again turned the ditch, and was once more upon the same side with me, and I was compelled to take another leap.

I really do not remember how often I sprang backwards and forwards across that chasm; I should think a dozen times at least, and I became wearied with the exercise. The leap was just as much as I could do at my best; and as I was growing weaker at each fresh spring, I became satisfied that I should soon leap short, and crush myself against the steep rocky sides of the chasm.

Should I fall to the bottom, my pursuer could easily reach me by entering at either end, and I began to dread such a finale. The vengeful brute showed no symptoms of retiring; on the contrary, the numerous disappointments seemed only to render him more determined in his resentment.

An idea now suggested itself to my mind, I had looked all round to see if there might not be something that offered a better security. There were trees, but they were too distant: the only one near was that to which my horse had been tied. It was a small one, and, like all of its species (it was a cotton-wood), there were no branches near the root.

I knew that I could clamber up it by embracing the trunk, which was not over ten inches in diameter. Could I only succeed in reaching it, it would at least shelter me better than the ditch, of which I was getting heartily tired.

But the question was, could I reach it before the bull?

It was about three hundred yards off. By proper manoeuvring, I should have a start of fifty. Even, with that, it would be a "close shave;" and it proved so.

I arrived at the tree, however, and sprang up it like a mountebank; but the hot breath of the buffalo steamed after me as I ascended, and the concussion of his heavy skull against the trunk almost shook me back upon his horns.

After a severe effort of climbing, I succeeded in lodging myself among the branches.

I was now safe from all immediate danger, but how was the affair to end?

I knew from the experience of others, that my enemy might stay for hours by the tree—perhaps for days!

Hours would be enough. I could not stand it long. I already hungered, but a worse appetite began to torture me: thirst. The hot sun, the dust, the violent exercise of the past hour, all contributed to make me thirsty. Even then, I would have risked life for a draught of water. What would it come to should I not be relieved?

I had but one hope—that my companions would come to my relief; but I knew that that would not be before morning. They would miss me of course. Perhaps my horse would return to camp—that would send them out in search for me—but not before night had fallen. In the darkness they could not follow my trail. Could they do so in the light?

This last question, which I had put to myself, startled me. I was just in a condition to look upon the dark side of everything, and it now occurred to me that they might not be able to find me!

There were many possibilities that they might not. There were numerous horse-trails on the prairie, where Indians had passed. I saw this when tracking the buffalo. Besides, it might rain in the night, and obliterate them all—my own with the rest. They were not likely to find me by chance. A circle of ten miles diameter is a large tract. It was a rolling prairie, as already stated, full of inequalities, ridges with valleys between. The tree upon which I was perched stood in the bottom of one of the valleys—it could not be seen from any point over three hundred yards distant. Those searching for me might pass within hail without perceiving either the tree or the valley.

I remained for a long time busied with such gloomy thoughts and forebodings. Night was coming on, but the fierce and obstinate brute showed no disposition to raise the siege. He remained watchful as ever, walking round and round at intervals, lashing his tail, and uttering that snorting sound so well-known, to the prairie-hunter, and which so much resembles the grunting of hogs when suddenly alarmed. Occasionally he would bellow loudly like the common bull.

While watching his various manoeuvres, an object on the ground drew my attention—it was the trail-rope left by my horse. One end of it was fastened round the trunk by a firm knot—the other lay far out upon the prairie, where it had been dragged. My attention had been drawn to it by the bull himself, that in crossing over it had noticed it, and now and then pawed it with his hoofs.

All at once a bright idea flashed upon me—a sudden hope arose within me—a plan of escape presented itself, so feasible and possible, that I leaped in my perch as the thought struck me.

The first step was to get possession of the rope. This was not such an easy matter. The rope was fastened around the tree, but the knot had slipped down the trunk and lay upon the ground. I dared not descend for it.

Necessity soon suggested a plan.

My "picker"—a piece of straight wire with a ring-end—hung from one of my breast buttons. This I took hold of, and bent into the shape of a grappling-hook. I had no cord, but my knife was still sate in its sheath; and, drawing this, I cut several thongs from the skirt or my buckskin shirt, and knotted them together until they formed a string long enough to reach the ground. To one end I attached the picker; and then letting it down, I commenced angling for the rope.

After a few transverse drags, the hook caught the latter, and I pulled it up into the tree, taking the whole of it in until I held the loose end in my hands. The other end I permitted to remain as it was; I saw it was securely knotted around the trunk, and that was just what I wanted.

It was my intention to lasso the bull; and for this purpose I proceeded to make a running-noose on the end of the trail-rope.

This I executed with great care, and with all my skill. I could depend upon the rope; it was raw hide, and a hotter was never twisted; but I knew that if anything should chance to slip at a critical moment, it might cost me my life. With this knowledge, therefore, I spliced the eye, and made the knot as firm as possible, and then the loop was reeved through, and the thing was ready.

I could throw a lasso tolerably well, but the branches prevented me from winding it around my head. It was necessary, therefore, to get the animal in a certain position under the tree, which, by shouts and other demonstrations, I at length succeeded in effecting.

The moment of success had arrived. He stood almost directly below me. The noose was shot down—I had the gratification to see it settle around his neck; and with a quick jerk I tightened it. The rope ran beautifully through the eye, until both eye and loop were buried beneath the shaggy hair of the animal's neck. It embraced his throat in the right place, and I felt confident it would hold.

The moment the bull felt the jerk upon his throat, he dashed madly out from the tree, and then commenced running in circles around it.

Contrary to my intention, the rope had slipped from my hands at the first drag upon it. My position was rather an unsteady one, for the branches were slender, and I could not manage matters as well as I could have wished.

But I now felt confident enough. The bull was tethered, and it only remained for me to get out beyond the length of his tether, and take to my heels.

My gun lay on one side, near the tree, where I had dropped it in my race: this, of course, I meant to carry off with me.

I waited then until the animal, in one of his circles, had got round to the opposite side, and slipping silently down the trunk, I sprang out, picked up my rifle, and ran.

I knew the trail-rope to be about twenty yards in length, but I ran a hundred, at least, before making halt. I had even thoughts of continuing on, as I still could not help some misgivings about the rope.

The bull was one of the largest and strongest. The rope might break, the knot upon the tree might give way, or the noose might slip over his head.

Curiosity, however, or rather a desire to be assured of my safety, prompted me to look around, when, to my joy, I beheld the huge monster stretched upon the plain. I could see the rope as taut as a bow-string; and the tongue protruding from the animal's jaws showed me that he was strangling himself as fast as I could desire.

At the sight, the idea of buffalo-tongue for supper returned in all its vigour; and it now occurred to me that I should eat that very tongue, and no other.

I immediately turned in my tracks, ran towards my powder and balls—which, in my eagerness to escape, I had forgotten all about—seized the horn and pouch, poured in a charge, rammed down a bullet, and then stealing nimbly up behind the still struggling bull, I placed the muzzle within three feet of his brisket, and fired. He gave a death-kick or two, and then lay quiet: it was all over with him.

I had the tongue from between his teeth in a twinkling; and proceeding to the other bull, I finished the operations I had commenced upon him. I was too tired to think of carrying a very heavy load; so I contented myself with the tongues, and slinging these over the barrel of my rifle, I shouldered it, and set out to grope my way back to camp.

The moon had risen, and I had no difficulty in following my own trail; but before I had got half-way, I met several of my companions shouting, and at intervals firing off their guns.

My horse had got back a little before sunset. His appearance had, of course, produced alarm, and the camp had turned out in search of me.

Several who had a relish for fresh meat galloped back to strip the two bulls of the remaining tit-bits; but before midnight all had returned; and to the accompaniment of the hump-ribs spurting in the cheerful blaze, I recounted the details of my adventure.

Chapter Thirty Two
The Bison

The bison—universally, though improperly, called buffalo—is, perhaps, the most interesting animal in America. Its great size and strength—the prodigious numbers in which it is found—its peculiar *habitat*—the value of its flesh and hide to the traveller, as well as to the many tribes of Indians—the mode of its chase and capture—all these circumstances render the buffalo an interesting and highly-prized animal.

Besides, it is the largest ruminant indigenous to America, exceeding in weight even the moose-deer, which latter, however, equals it in height. With the exception of the musk-ox, it is the only indigenous animal of the bovine tribe, but the latter being confined to a very limited range, near the Arctic Sea, has been less subject to the observation and attention of the civilised world. The buffalo, therefore, may be regarded as the representative of the ox in America.

The appearance of the animal is well-known; pictorial illustration has rendered it familiar to the eyes of every one. The enormous head, with its broad triangular front—the conical hump on the shoulders—the small but brilliantly-piercing eyes—the short black horns, of crescent shape—the profusion of shaggy hair about, the neck and foreparts of the body—the disproportioned bulk of the smaller hind-quarters—the short tail, with its tufted extremity; all these are characteristics. The hind-quarters are covered with a much shorter and smoother coat of hair, which adds to their apparent disproportion, and this, with the long hirsute covering of the breast, neck, hump, and shoulders, gives to the buffalo—especially when seen in a picture—a somewhat lion-like figure. The naked tail, with its tuft at the end, strengthens this similarity.

Some of the characteristics above enumerated belong only to the bull. The cow is less shaggy in front, has a smaller head, a less fierce appearance, and is altogether more like the common black cattle.

The buffalo is of a dark brown colour—sometimes nearly black—and sometimes of a burnt or liver hue; but this change depends on the season. The young coat of hair is darker, but changes as the season advances. In autumn it is nearly black, and then the coat of the animal has a shiny appearance; but as winter comes on, and the hair lengthens, it becomes lighter and more bleached-like. In the early part of summer it has a yellowish brown hue, and at this time, with rubbing and wallowing, part of it has already come off, while large flakes hang raggled and loose from the flanks, ready at any moment to drop off.

In size, the American buffalo competes with the European species (*Bos aurochs*), now nearly extinct. These animals differ in shape considerably, but the largest individuals of each species would very nearly balance one another in weight. Either of them is equal in size and weight to the largest specimens of the common ox—prize oxen, of course, excepted.

A full-grown buffalo-bull is six feet high at the shoulders, eight feet from the snout to the base of the tail, and will weigh about 1500 pounds.

Rare individuals exist whose weight much exceeds this. The cows are, of course, much smaller than the bulls, and scarcely come up to the ordinary standard of farm-cattle.

The flesh of the buffalo is juicy and delicious, equal, indeed superior, to well-fed beef. It may be regarded as beef with a *game flavour*.

Many people—travellers and hunters—prefer it to any other species of meat.

The flesh of the cow, as may be supposed, is more tender and savoury than that of the bull; and in a hunt when "meat" is the object, the cow is selected as a mark for the arrow or bullet.

The parts most esteemed are the tongue, the "hump-ribs" (the long spinous processes of the first dorsal vertebra), and the marrow of the shank bones. "Boudins" (part of the intestines) are also favourite "tit-bits" among the Indians and trappers.

The tongues, when dried, are really superior to those of common beeves, and, indeed, the same may be said of the other parts, but there is a better and worse in buffalo-beef, according to the age and sex of the animal. "Fat cow" is a term for the super-excellent, and by "poor bull," or "old bull," is meant a very unpalatable article, only to be eaten by the hunter in times of necessity.

The range of the buffalo is extensive, though not as it once was. It is gradually being restricted by hunter-pressure, and the encroachments of civilisation. It now consists of a longitudinal strip, of which the western boundary may be considered the Rocky Mountains, and the eastern the Mississippi River, though it is only near the head waters of the latter that the range of this animal extends so far east. Below the mouth of the Missouri no buffalo are found near the Mississippi, nor within two hundred miles of it—not, in fact, until you have cleared the forests that fringe this stream, and penetrated a good distance into the prairie tract. At one period, however, they roamed as far to the east as the Chain of the Alleghanies.

In Texas, the buffalo yet extends its migrations to the head waters of the Brazos and Colorado, but it is not a Mexican animal. Following the Rocky Mountains from the great bend of the Rio Grande, northward, we find no buffalo west of them until we reach the higher latitudes near the sources of the Saskatchewan. There they have crossed the mountains, and are now to be met with in some of the plains that lie on the other side. This, however, is a late migration, occasioned by hunter-pressure upon the eastern slope. The same has been observed at different periods, at other points in the Rocky Mountain chain, where the buffalo had made a temporary lodgment on the Pacific side of the mountains, but where they are now entirely extinct. It is known, from the traditional history of the tribes on the west side, that the buffalo was only a newcomer among them, and was not indigenous to that division of the Continent.

Following the buffaloes north, we find their range co-terminous with the prairies. The latter end in an angle between the Peace River and the great Slave Lake, and beyond this the buffalo does not run. There is a point, however, across an arm of the Slave Lake where buffalo are found. It is called Slave Point, and although contiguous to the primitive rocks of the "Barren Grounds" it is of a similar geology (*stratified* limestone) with the buffalo prairies to the west. This, to the geologist, is an interesting fact.

From the Slave Lake, a line drawn to the head waters of the Mississippi, and passing through Lake Winnipeg, will shut in the buffalo country along the north-east. They are still found in large bands upon the western shores of Winnipeg, on the plains of the Saskatchewan and the Red River of the north. In fact, buffalo-hunting is one of the chief employments of the inhabitants of that half-Indian colony known as the "Red River Settlements."

One of the most singular facts in relation to the buffalo is their enormous numbers. Nothing but the vast extent of their pasturage could have sustained such droves as have from time to time been seen. Thousands frequently feed together, and the plain for miles is often covered with a continuous drove. Sometimes they are seen strung out into a long column, passing from place to place, and roads exist made by them that resemble great highways. Sometimes these roads, worn by the rains, form great hollows that traverse the level plain, and they often guide the thirsty traveller in the direction of water.

Another curious fact about the buffalo is their habit of wallowing. The cause of this is not well-ascertained. It may be that they are prompted to it, as swine are, partly to cool their blood by bringing their bodies in contact with the colder earth, and partly to scratch themselves as other cattle do, and free their skins from the annoying insects and parasites that prey upon them. It must be remembered that in their pasturage no trees or "rubbing posts" are to be found, and in the absence of these they are compelled to resort to wallowing. They fling themselves upon their sides, and using their hunch and shoulder as a pivot, spin round and round for hours at a time. In this rotatory motion they aid themselves by using the legs freely. The earth becomes hollowed out and worn into a circular basin, often of considerable depth, and this is known as a "buffalo wallow." Such curious circular concavities are seen throughout the prairies where these animals range; sometimes grown over with grass, sometimes freshly hollowed out, and not unfrequently containing water, with which the traveller assuages his thirst, and so, too, the buffalo themselves. This has led to the fanciful idea of the early explorers that there existed on the American Continent an animal who *dug its own wells*!

The buffaloes make extensive migrations, going in large "gangs." These are not periodical, and are only partially influenced by climate. They are not regular either in their direction. Sometimes the gangs will be seen straying southward, at other times to the north, east, or west.

The search of food or water seems partially to regulate these movements, as with the passenger-pigeon, and some other migratory creatures.

At such times the buffaloes move forward in an impetuous march which nothing seems to interrupt. Ravines are passed, and waterless plains traversed, and rivers crossed without hesitation. In many cases broad streams, with steep or marshy banks, are attempted, and thousands either perish in the waters or become mired in the swamp, and cannot escape, but die the most terrible of deaths. Then is the feast of the eagles, the vultures, and the wolves. Sometimes, too, the feast of the hunter; for when the Indians discover a gang of buffaloes in a difficulty of this kind, the slaughter is immense.

Hunting the buffalo is, among the Indian tribes, a profession rather than a sport. Those who practise it in the latter sense are few indeed, as, to enjoy it, it is necessary to do as we had done, make a journey of several hundred miles, and risk our scalps, with no inconsiderable chance of losing them. For these reasons few amateur-hunters ever trouble the buffalo.

The true professional hunters—the white trappers and Indians—pursue these animals almost incessantly, and thin their numbers with lance, rifle, and arrow.

Buffalo-hunting is not all sport without peril. The hunter frequently risks his life; and numerous have been the fatal results of encounters with these animals. The bulls, when wounded, cannot be approached, even on horseback, without considerable risk, while a dismounted hunter has but slight chance of escaping.

The buffalo runs with a gait apparently heavy and lumbering—first heaving to one side, then to the other, like a ship at sea; but this gait, although not equal in speed to that of a horse, is far too fast for a man on foot, and the swiftest runner, unless favoured by a tree or some other object, will be surely overtaken, and either gored to death by the animal's horns, or pounded to a jelly under its heavy hoofs. Instances of the kind are far from being rare, and could amateur-hunters only get at the buffalo, such occurrences would be fearfully common. An incident illustrative of these remarks is told by the traveller and naturalist Richardson, and may therefore be safely regarded as a fact.

"While I resided at Charlton House, an incident of this kind occurred. Mr Finnan McDonald, one of the Hudson's Bay Company's clerks, was descending the Saskatchewan in a boat, and one evening, having pitched his tent for the night, he went out in the dusk to look for game.

"It had become nearly dark when he fired at a bison bull, which was galloping over a small eminence; and as he was hastening forward to see if the shot had taken effect, the wounded beast made a rush at him. He had the presence of mind to seize the animal by the long hair on his forehead, as it struck him on the side with its horn, and being a remarkably tall and powerful man, a struggle ensued, which continued until his wrist was severely sprained, and his arm was rendered powerless; he then fell, and after receiving two or three blows, became senseless.

"Shortly after, he was found by his companions lying bathed in blood, being gored in several places; and the bison was couched beside him, apparently waiting to renew the attack, had he shown any signs of life. Mr McDonald recovered from the immediate effects of the injuries he received, but died a few months after." Dr Richardson adds:—"Many other instances might be mentioned of the tenaciousness with which this animal pursues its revenge; and I have been told of a hunter having been detained for many hours in a tree, by an old bull which had taken its post below to watch him."

The numbers of the buffalo, although still very great, are annually on the decrease. Their woolly skins, when dressed, are of great value as an article of commerce. Among the Canadians they are in general use; they constitute the favourite wrappers of the traveller in that cold climate: they line the cariole, the carriage, and the sleigh. Thousands of them are used in the northern parts of the United States for a similar purpose. They are known as buffalo-robes, and are often prettily trimmed and ornamented, so as to command a good price. They are even exported to Europe in large quantities.

Of course this extensive demand for the robes causes a proportionate destruction among the buffaloes. But this is not all. Whole tribes of Indians, amounting to many thousands of individuals, subsist entirely upon these animals, as the Laplander upon the reindeer, or the Guarani Indian upon the *moriché* palm. Their blankets are buffalo-robes, part of their clothing buffalo-leather, their tents are buffalo-hides, and buffalo-beef is their sole food for three parts of the year. The large prairie tribes—as the Sioux, the Pawnees, the Blackfeet, the Crows, the Chiennes, the Arapahoes, and the Comanches, with several smaller bands—live upon the buffalo. These tribes, united, number at least 100,000 souls. No wonder the buffalo should be each year diminishing in numbers!

It is predicted that in a few years the race will become extinct. The same has been often said of the Indian. The *soi-disant* prophet is addicted to this sort of melancholy foreboding, because he believes by such babbling he gains a character for philanthropic sympathy; besides, it has a poetic sound. Believe me, there is not the slightest danger of such a destiny for the Indian: his race is not to become extinct; it will be on the earth as long as that of either black or white. Civilisation is removing the seeds of decay; civilisation will preserve the race of the red man yet to multiply. Civilisation, too, may preserve the buffalo. The hunter races must disappear, and give place to the more useful agriculturist. The prairies are wide—vast expanses of that singular formation must remain in their primitive wildness, at least for ages, and these will still be a safe range for the buffalo.

Chapter Thirty Three
Trailing the Buffalo

After a breakfast of fresh buffalo-meat we took the road in high spirits. The long-expected sport would soon come off. Every step showed us "buffalo sign"—tracks, wallows, fresh ordure. None of the animals were yet in sight, but the prairie was filled with undulations, and no doubt "a gang" would be found in some of the valleys.

A few miles farther on, and we came suddenly upon a "buffalo road," traversing the prairie nearly at right angles to our own direction. This caused a halt and consultation. Should we follow the road? By all means thought every one. The tracks were fresh—the road a large one—thousands of buffaloes must have passed over it; where were they now? They might be a hundred miles off, for when these animals get upon one of those regular roads they often journey at great speed, and it is difficult to overtake them. When merely browsing over the prairie the case is different. Then they travel only a few miles a day, and a hunter trailing them soon comes up with the gang.

Ike and Redwood were consulted as to what was best to be done. They had both closely examined the trail, bending down to the ground, and carefully noting every symptom that would give them a clue to the condition of the herd—its numbers—its time of passing—the rate of its speed, etcetera.

"Thur's a good grist o' 'em," said Ike, "leastways a kupple o' thousand in the gang—thur's bulls, cows, yearlins, an' young calf too, so we'll have a choice o' meat—either beef or veal. Kin we do better than foller 'em up? Eh, Mark?"

"Wal! I don't think we can, ole boss," replied Redwood. "They passed hyur yesterday, jest about noon—that is the thick o' the drove passed then."

"How do you tell that?" inquired several.

"Oh, that's easy made out," replied the guide, evidently regarding the question as a very simple one; "you see most o' these hyur tracks is a day old, an' yet thur not two."

"And why not?"

"Why how could they be two," asked the guide in astonishment, "when it rained yesterday before sun-up? Thur made since the rain, yu'll admit that?"

We now remembered the rain, and acknowledged the truth of this reasoning. The animals must have passed since it rained; but why not immediately after, in the early morning? How could Redwood tell that it was the hour of noon? How?

"Easy enough, comrades," replied he.

"Any greenhorn mout do that," added Ike. The rest, however, were puzzled and waited the explanation.

"I tells this a way," continued the guide. "Ef the buffler had passed by hyur, immediately after the rain, thar tracks wud a sunk deeper, and thar wud a been more mud on the trail. As thar ain't no great slobber about, ye see, I make my kalklations that the ground must a been well dried afore they kim along, and after such a wet, it could not a been afore noon at the least—so that's how I know the buffler passed at that hour."

We were all interested in this craft of our guides, for without consulting each other they had both arrived at the same conclusion by the same process of mental logic. They had also determined several other points about the buffalo—such as that they had not all gone together, but in a straggling herd; that some had passed more rapidly than the rest; that no hunters were after them; and that it was probable they were not bound upon any distant migration, but only in search of water; and the direction they had taken rendered this likely enough. Indeed most of the great buffalo roads lead to watering-places, and they have often been the means of conducting the thirsty traveller to the welcome rivulet or spring, when otherwise he might have perished upon the dry plain. Whether the buffalo are guided by some instinct towards water, is a question not satisfactorily solved. Certain it is, that their water paths often lead in the most direct route to streams and ponds, of the existence of which they could have known nothing previously. It is certain that many of the lower animals possess either an "instinct," or a much keener sense in these matters than man himself. Long before the thirsty traveller suspects the propinquity of water, his sagacious mule, by her joyful hinney, and suddenly altered bearing, warns him of its presence.

We now reasoned that if the buffalo had been making to some watering-place, merely for the purpose of drinking and cooling their flanks, they would, of course, make a delay there, and so give us a chance of coming up. They had a day the start of us, it is true, but we should do our best to overhaul them. The guides assured us we were likely to have good sport before we came up with the great gang. There were straggling groups they had no doubt, some perhaps not over thirsty, that had hung in the rear. In high hopes, then, we turned our heads to the trail, and travelled briskly forward.

We had not gone many hundred yards when a very singular scene was presented to our eyes. We had gained the crest of a ridge, and were looking down into a little valley through which ran the trail. At the bottom of the valley a cloud of dust was constantly rising upward, and very slowly moving away, as the day was quite calm. Although there had been rain a little over thirty hours before, the ground was already parched and dry as pepper. But what caused the dust to rise? Not the wind—there was none. Some animal then, or likely more than one!

At first we could perceive no creature within the cloud, so dun and thick was it; but after a little a wolf dashed out, ran round a bit, and then rushed in again, and then another and another, all of them with open jaws, glaring eyes, manes erect, and tails switching about in a violent and angry manner. Now and then we could only see part of their bodies, or their bushy tails flung upward, but we could hear by their yelping barks that they were engaged in a fierce contest either among themselves, or with some other enemy. It was not among themselves, as Ike and Redwood both affirmed.

"An old bull's the game," said they; and without waiting a moment, the two trappers galloped forward, followed closely by the rest of our party. We were soon in the bottom of the little valley. Ike already cracking away at the wolves—his peculiar enemies. Several others, led away by the excitement, also emptied their pieces at these worthless creatures, slaying a number of them, while the rest, nearly a dozen in all, took to their heels, and scampered off over the ridges.

The dust gradually began to float off, and through the thinner cloud that remained we now saw what the wolves had been at. Standing in the centre of a ring, formed by its own turnings and struggles, was the huge form of a buffalo-bull. Its shape indicated that it was a very old one, lank, lean, and covered with long hair, raggled and torn into tufts. Its colour was that of the white dust, but red blood was streaming freshly down its hind flanks, and from its nose and mouth. The cartilage of the nose was torn to pieces by the fierce enemies it had so lately encountered, and on observing it more closely we saw that its eyes were pulled out of their sockets, exhibiting a fearful spectacle. The tail was eaten off by repeated wrenches, and the hind-quarters were sadly mangled. Spite of all this mutilation, the old bull still kept his feet, and his prowess had been proved, for no less than five wolves lay around, that he had "rubbed out" previous to our arrival. He was a terrible and melancholy spectacle—that old bull, and all agreed it would be better to relieve him by a well-aimed bullet. This was instantly fired at him; and the animal, after rocking about a while on his spread legs, fell gently to the earth.

Of course he had proved himself too tough to be eatable by anything but prairie-wolves, and we were about to leave him as he lay. Ike, however, had no idea of gratifying these sneaking creatures at so cheap a rate. He was determined they should not have their dinner so easily, so taking out his knife he extracted the bladder, and some of the smaller intestines from the buffalo. These he inflated in a trice, and then rigging up a sapling over the body, he hung them upon it, so that the slightest breeze kept them in motion. This, as we had been already assured, was the best mode of keeping wolves at a distance from any object, and the hunter, when wolves are near, often avails himself of it to protect the venison or buffalo-meat which he is obliged to leave behind him.

The guide having rigged his "scare wolf," mounted his old mare, and again joined us, muttering his satisfaction as he rode along.

We had not travelled much farther when our attention was attracted by noises in front, and again from a ridge we beheld a scene still more interesting than that we had just witnessed. As before, the actors were buffalo and wolves, but this time there was very little dust, as the contest was carried on upon the green turf—and we could see distinctly the manoeuvres of the animals.

There were three buffaloes—a cow, her calf, and a large bull that was acting as their champion and protector. A pack of wolves had gathered around them, in which there were some of the larger species, and these kept up a continuous attack, the object of which was to destroy the calf, and its mother if possible. This the bull was using all his endeavours to prevent, and with considerable success too, as already several of the wolves were down, and howling with pain. But what rendered the result doubtful was that fresh wolves were constantly galloping up to the spot, and the buffaloes would likely have to yield in time. It was quite amusing to see the efforts made by the cunning brutes, to separate the calf front its protector. Sometimes they would get it a few feet to the one side, and fling it to the ground; but before they could do it any great injury, the active bull, and the cow as well, would rush forward upon them, scattering the cowardly creatures like a flock of birds. Then the calf would place itself between the old ones, and would thus remain for a while, until the wolves, having arranged some new plan, would recommence the attack, and drive it forth again. Once the position was strikingly in favour of the buffaloes. This position, which seemed in the hurry of the conflict to turn up accidentally, was in fact the result of design, for the old ones every now and then endeavoured to renew it, but were hindered by the stupidity of the calf. The latter was placed between them in such a way that the heads of the bull and cow were in opposite directions, and thus both flanks were guarded. In this way the buffaloes might have held their ground, but the silly calf when closely menaced by the wolves foolishly started out, rendering it necessary for its protectors to assume a new attitude of defence.

It was altogether a singular conflict, a touching picture of parental fondness. The end of it was easily guessed. The wolves would tire out the old ones, and get hold of the calf of course, although they might spend a long time about it. But the great herd was distant, and there was no hope for the cow to get her offspring back to its protection. It would certainly be destroyed.

Notwithstanding our sympathy for the little family thus assailed, we were not the less anxious to do for them just what the wolves wished to do—kill and eat them. With this intent we all put spur to our horses, and galloped right forward to the spot.

Not one of the animals—neither wolves nor buffaloes—took any notice of us until we were within a few yards of them. The wolves then scampered off, but already the cracking rifles and shot-guns were heard above the shouts of the charging cavalcade, and both the cow and calf were seen sinking to the earth. Not so the huge bull. With glaring eyeballs he glanced around upon his new assailants, and then, as if aware that farther strife was useless, he stretched forth his neck, and breaking through the line of horsemen, went off in full flight.

A fresh touch of the spur, with a wrench of the bridle-rein, brought our horses round, and set their heads after him, and then followed as fine a piece of chasing as I remember to have taken part in. The whole eight of us swept over the plain in pursuit, but as we had all emptied our pieces on first charging up, there was not one ready to deliver a shot even should we overtake the game. In the quick gallop no one thought of re-loading. Our pistols, however, were still charged, and these were grasped and held in readiness.

It was one of the most exciting chases. There before us galloped the great game, under full view, with neither brake nor bush to interrupt the pleasure of our wild race. The bull proved to be one of the fastest of his kind—for there is a considerable difference in this respect. He led us nearly half-a-mile across the ridges before even the best of our horses could come up, and then just as we were closing in upon him, before a shot had been fired, he was seen to give a sudden lounge forward and tumble over upon the ground.

Some of us fancied he had only missed his footing and stumbled; but no motion could be perceived as we rode forward, and on coming up he was found to be quite dead! A rifle-bullet had done the work—one that had been fired in the first volley; and his strong fast run was only the last spasmodic effort of his life.

One or two remained by the dead bull to get his hide and the "tit-bits" of his meat, while the rest rode back to recover the more precious cow and calf. What was our chagrin to find that the rascally wolves had been before us! Of the tender calf, not a morsel remained beyond a few tufts of hairy skin, and the cow was so badly torn and mutilated that she was not worth cutting up! Even the tongue, that most delicate bit, had been appropriated by the sneaking thieves, and eaten out to the very root.

As soon as they had observed us coming back, they had taken to their heels, each carrying a large piece with him, and we could now see them out upon the prairie devouring the meat before our very eyes. Ike was loud in his anathemas, and but that the creatures were too cunning for him, would have taken his revenge upon the spot. They kept off, however, beyond range of either rifle or double-barrel, and Ike was forced to nurse his wrath for some other occasion.

We now went back to the bull, where we encamped for the night. The latter, tough as he was, furnished us an excellent supper from his tongue, hump-ribs, boudins, and marrow bones, and we all lay down to sleep and dream of the sports of to-morrow.

Chapter Thirty Four
Approaching the Buffalo

Next morning, just as we were preparing to resume our journey, a gang of buffalo appeared upon one of the swells, at the distance of a mile or a mile and a half from our camp. There were about a dozen of them, and, as our guides asserted, they were all cows. This was just what we wanted, as the flesh of the cows is much more delicate than that of the bulls, and were eager to lay in a stock of it.

A hurried consultation was held, in which it was debated as to the best manner of making an attack upon the herd. Some advised that we should ride boldly forward, and overtake the cows by sheer swiftness, but this mode was objected to by others. The cows are at times very shy. They might break off long before we were near, and give our horses such a gallop as would render them useless for the rest of the day. Besides, our animals were in no condition for such exercise. Our stock of corn had run out, and the grass feeding and hard travelling had reduced most of them to skeletons. A hard gallop was therefore to be avoided if possible.

Among those who counselled a different course wore the guides Ike and Redwood. These men thought it would be much better to try the cows by "approaching," that is, by endeavouring to creep up, and get a shot when near enough. The ground was favourable enough for it, as there were here and there little clumps of cactus plants and bushes of the wild sage (*artemisia*), behind which a hunter might easily conceal himself. The trappers farther alleged that the herd would not be likely to make off at the first shot, unless the hunter discovered himself. On the contrary, one after another might fall, and not frighten the rest, so long as these did not get to leeward, and detect the presence of their enemy by the scent.

The wind was in our favour, and this was a most important consideration. Had it been otherwise the game would have "winded" us at a mile's distance, as they can recognise the smell of man, and frequently comprehend the danger of being near such an enemy. Indeed, it is on their great power of scent that the buffalo most commonly rely for warning. The eyes of these creatures, and particularly the bulls, are so covered with the shaggy hair hanging over them, that individuals are often seen quite blinded by it, and a hunter, if he keep silent enough, may walk up and lay his hand upon them, without having been previously noticed. This, however, can only occur when the hunter travels against the wind. Otherwise he finds the buffalo as shy and difficult to approach as most game, and many along spoil of crouching and crawling has been made to no purpose—a single sniff of the approaching enemy proving enough to startle the game, and send it off in wild flight.

Ike and his brother trapper urged that if the approach should prove unsuccessful there would still be time to "run" the herd, as those who did not attempt the former method might keep in their saddles, and be ready to gallop forward.

All this was feasible enough; and it was therefore decided that the "approach" should have a trial. The trappers had already prepared themselves for this sort of thing. They were evidently desirous of giving us an exhibition of their hunter-prowess, and we were ready to witness it. We had noticed them busied with a pair of large wolf-skins, which they had taken off the animals entire, with the heads, ears, tails, etcetera, remaining upon the skins. The purpose of these was to enable the hunters to disguise themselves as wolves, and thus crawl within shooting distance of the buffalo herd.

Strange to say this is quite possible. Although no creature is a greater enemy to the buffalo than the wolf, the former, as already stated, permits the latter to approach quite close to him without making any attempt to chase him off, or without exhibiting the slightest symptoms of fear on his own account. The buffalo cannot prevent the wolf from prowling close about him, as the latter is sufficiently active, and can easily get out of the way when pursued by the bulls—on the other hand, the buffaloes, unless when separated from the herd, or in some way disabled, have no fear of the wolf. Under ordinary circumstances they seem wholly to disregard his presence. The consequence is, that a wolf-skin is a favourite disguise of the Indians for approaching the buffalo, and our trappers, Ike and Redwood, had often practised this *ruse*. We were likely then to see sport.

Both were soon equipped in their white wolf-skins, their heads being enveloped with the skins of the wolves' heads, and the remainder tied with thongs, so as to cover their backs and sides. At best the skins formed but a scanty covering to the bodies of the trappers; but, as we have already remarked, the buffalo has not a very keen sense of sight, and so long as the decoys kept to leeward, they would not be closely scrutinised.

When fairly in their new dress, the hunters parted from the company, leaving their horses at the camp. The rest of us sat in our saddles, ready to gallop forward, in case the *ruse* did not succeed, and make that kind of a hunt called "running." Of course the trappers went as far as was safe, walking in an upright attitude; but long before they had got within shot, we saw both of them stoop down and scramble along in a crouching way, and then at length they knelt upon the ground, and proceeded upon their hands and knees.

It required a good long time to enable them to get near enough; and we on horseback, although watching every manoeuvre with interest, were beginning to get impatient. The buffalo, however, quietly browsing along the sward, seemed to be utterly unconscious of the dangerous foe that was approaching them, and at intervals one or another would fling itself to the earth in play, and after kicking and wallowing a few seconds, start to its feet again. They were all cows, with one exception—a bull—who seemed to be the guardian and leader. Even at a mile's distance, we could recognise the shape and size of the latter, as completely differing from all the rest. The bull seemed to be more active than any, moving around the flock, and apparently watching over their safety.

As the decoys approached, we thought that the bull seemed to take notice of them. He had moved out to that side of the herd, and seemed for a moment to scrutinise them as they drew near. But for a moment, however, for he turned apparently satisfied, and was soon close in to the gang.

Ike and Redwood had at length got so close, that we were expecting every moment to see the flash of their pieces. They were not so close, however, as we in the distance fancied them to be.

Just at this moment we perceived another buffalo—a large bull—running up behind them. He had just made his appearance over a ridge, and was now on his way to join the herd. The decoys were directly in his way, and these did not appear to see him until he had run almost between them, so intent were they on watching the others. His intrusion, however, evidently disconcerted them, spoiling their plans, while in the very act of being carried into execution. They were, no doubt, a little startled by the apparition of such a huge shaggy animal coming so suddenly on them, for both started to their feet as if alarmed. Their pieces blazed at the same time, and the intruder was seen rolling over upon the plain.

But the *ruse* was over. The bull that guarded the herd was witness to this odd encounter, and bellowing a loud alarm to his companions, set off at a lumbering gallop. All the rest followed as fast as their legs would carry them.

Fortunately they ran, not directly from us, but in a line that inclined to our left. By taking a diagonal course we might yet head them, and without another word our whole party put to the spur, and sprang off over the prairie.

It cost us a five-mile gallop before any of us came within shooting distance; and only four of us did get so near—the naturalist, Besançon, the Kentuckian, and myself. Our horses were well blown, but after a good deal of encouragement we got them side by side with the flying game.

Each one chose his own, and then delivered his shot at his best convenience. The consequence was, that four of the cows were strewed out along the path, and rewarded us for our hard gallop. The rest, on account of saving our horses, were suffered to make their escape.

As we had now plenty of excellent meat, it was resolved to encamp again, and remain for some time on that spot, until we had rested our horses after their long journey, when we should make a fresh search for the buffalo, and have another "run" or two out of them.

Chapter Thirty Five
Unexpected Guests

We found Ike and Redwood bitterly angry at the bull they had slain. They alleged that he had made a rush at them in coming up, and that was why they had risen to their feet and fired upon him. We thought such had been the case, as we had noticed a strange manoeuvre on the part of the bull. But for that, our guides believed they would have succeeded to their hearts' content; as they intended first to have shot the other bull, and then the cows would have remained until all had fallen.

A place was now selected for our night-camp, and the meat from the cows brought in and dressed. Over a fire of cotton-wood logs we soon cooked the most splendid supper we had eaten for a long time.

The beef of the wild buffalo-cow is far superior to that of domestic cattle, but the "tit-bits" of the same animal are luxuries never to be forgotten. Whether it be that a prairie appetite lends something to the relish is a question. This I will not venture to deny; but certainly the "baron of beef" in merry old England has no souvenirs to me so sweet as a roast rib of "fat cow," cooked over a cotton-wood fire, and eaten in the open air, under the pure sky of the prairies.

The place where we had pitched our camp was upon the banks of a very small spring-stream, or creek, that, rising near at hand, meandered through the prairie to a not distant branch of the Arkansas River. Where we were, this creek was embanked very slightly; but, at about two hundred yards' distance, on each side, there was a range of bluffs that followed the direction of the stream. These bluffs were not very high, but sufficiently so to prevent any one down in the creek bottom from having a view of the prairie level. As the bottom itself was covered with very coarse herbage, and as a better grass—the buffalo—grew on the prairie above, we there picketed our horses, intending to bring them closer to the camp when night set in, or before going to sleep. The camp itself—that is the two tents, with Jake's waggon—were on the very edge of the stream; but Jake's mules were up on the plain, along with the rest of the *cavallada*.

It was still two hours before sunset. We had made our dinner, and, satisfied with the day's sport, were enjoying ourselves with a little brandy, that still held out in our good-sized keg, and a smoke. We had reviewed the incidents of the day, and were laying out our plans for the morrow. We were admonished by the coldness of the evening that winter was not far off, and we all agreed that another week was as long as we could safely remain upon the prairies. We had started late in the season, but our not finding the buffalo farther to the east had made a great inroad upon our time, and spoiled all our calculations. Now that we had found them, a week was as much as we could allow for their hunt. Already frost appeared in the night hours, and made us uncomfortable enough, and we knew that in the prairie region the transition from autumn to winter is often sudden and unexpected.

The oldest and wisest of the party were of the opinion that we should not delay our return longer than a week, and the others assented to it. The guides gave the same advice, although these cared little about wintering on the prairie, and were willing to remain as long as we pleased. We knew, however, that the hardships to which we should be subjected would not be relished by several of the party, and it would be better for all to get back to the settlements before the setting in of severe weather.

I have said we were all in high spirits. A week's hunting, with something to do at it every day, would satisfy us. We should do immense slaughter on the buffalo, by approaching, running, and surrounding them. We should collect a quantity of the best meat, jerk and dry it over the fire, load our waggon with that, and with a large number of robes and horns as trophies, should go back in triumph to the settlements. Such were our pleasant anticipations.

I am sorry to say that these anticipations were never realised—not one of them. When we reached the nearest settlement, which happened, about six weeks after, our party presented an appearance that differed as much from a triumphal procession as could well be imagined. One and all of us were afoot. One and all of us—even to the fat little doctor—were emaciated, ragged, foot-sore, frost-bitten, and little better than half alive. We had a number of buffalo-skins with us it is true, but these hung about our shoulders, and were for use, and not show. They had served us for weeks for beds and blankets by night, and for great coats under the fierce winter rains. But I anticipate. Let us return to our camp on the little creek.

I have said that we sat around the blazing fire discussing our future plans, and enjoying the future by anticipation. The hours passed rapidly on, and while thus engaged night came down upon us.

At this time some one advised that we should bring up the horses, but another said it would be as well to let them browse a while longer, as the grass where they were was good, and they had been for some days on short commons. "They will be safe enough," said this speaker. "We have seen no Indian sign, or if any of you think there is danger, let some one go up to the bluff, but by all means let the poor brutes have a good meal of it."

This proposal was accepted. Lanty was despatched to stand guard over the horses, while the rest of us remained by the fire conversing as before.

The Irishman could scarcely have had time to get among the animals, when our ears were saluted by a medley of sounds that sent the blood to our hearts, and caused us to leap simultaneously from the fire.

The yells of Indians were easily understood, even by the "greenest" of our party, and these, mingled with the neighing of horses, the prancing of hoofs, and the shouts of our guard, were the sounds that readied us.

"Injuns, by God!" cried Ike, springing up, and clutching his long rifle.

This wild exclamation was echoed by more than one, as each leaped back from the fire and ran to his gun.

In a few seconds we had cleared the brushwood that thickly covered the bottom, and climbed out on the bluff. Here we were met by the terrified guard, who was running back at the top of his speed, and bellowing at the top of his voice.

"Och, murther!" cried he, "the savage bastes—there's a thousand ov thim! They've carried off the cattle—every leg—mules an' all, by Jaysus!"

Rough as was this announcement, we soon became satisfied that it was but too true. On reaching the place where the *cavallada* had been picketed, we found not the semblance of a horse. Even the pins were drawn, and the *lazoes* taken along. Far off on the prairie we could discern dimly a dark mass of mounted men, and we could plainly hear their triumphant shouts and laughter, as they disappeared in the distance!

We never saw either them or our horses again.

They were a party of Pawnees, as we afterwards learned, and no doubt had they attacked us, we should have suffered severely; but there were only a few of them, and they were satisfied with plundering us of our horses. It is just possible that after securing them they might have returned to attack us, had not Lanty surprised them at their work. After the alarm they knew we would be on the look-out for them, and therefore were contented to carry off our animals.

It is difficult to explain the change that thus so suddenly occurred in our feelings and circumstances. The prospect before us—thus set afoot upon the prairie at such a distance from the settlements, and at such a season—was perfectly appalling. We should have to walk every inch of the way—carry our food, and everything else, upon our backs. Perhaps we might not be too much burdened with food. That depended upon very precarious circumstances—upon our hunting luck. Our "stock" in the waggon was reduced to only a few days' rations, and of course would go but a few days with us, while we had many to provide for.

These thoughts were after-reflections—thoughts of the next morning. During that night we thought only of the Indians, for of course we did not as yet believe they had left us for good. We did not return to sleep by the fire—that would have been very foolishness. Some went back to get their arms in order, and then returning we all lay along the edge of the bluff, where the path led into the bottom, and watched the prairie until the morning. We lay in silence, or only muttering our thoughts to one another.

I have said until the morning. That is not strictly true, for before the morning that succeeded that *noche triste* broke upon us, another cruel misfortune befel us, which still farther narrowed the circumstances that surrounded us. I have already stated that the herbage of the creek bottom was coarse. It consisted of long grass, interspersed with briars and bunches of wild pea vines, with here and there a growth of scrubby wood. It was difficult to get through it, except by paths made by the buffalo and other animals. At this season of the year the thick growth of annuals was now a mass of withered stems, parched by the hot suns of autumn until they were as dry as tinder.

While engaged in our anxious vigil upon the plain above, we had not given a thought either to our camp or the large fire we had left there.

All at once our attention was directed to the latter by a loud crackling noise that sounded in our ears. We sprang to our feet, and looked into the valley behind us. The camp was on fire!

The brush was kindled all around it, and blazed to the height of several feet. We could see the blaze reflected from the white canvas both of waggon and tents, and in a few seconds these were licked into the hot flames, and disappeared from our view.

Of course we made no effort to save them. That would have been an idle and foolish attempt. We could not have approached the spot, without the almost certain danger of death. Already while we gazed, the fire spread over the whole creek bottom, and passed rapidly both up and down the banks of the stream.

For ourselves there was no danger. We were up on the open prairie covered only with short grass. Had this caught also, we knew how to save ourselves; but the upper level, separated by a steep bluff, was not reached by the conflagration that raged so fiercely below.

We stood watching the flames for a long while, until daylight broke. The bottom, near where we were, had ceased to burn, and now lay beneath us, smoking, smouldering, and black. We descended, and picked our steps to where our camp had stood. The tents were like black cerements. The iron work of the waggon alone remained, our extra clothing and provisions were all consumed. Even the produce of our yesterday's hunt lay among the ashes a charred and ruined mass!

Chapter Thirty Six
A Supper of Wolf-Mutton

Our condition was now lamentable indeed. We even hungered for our breakfast, and had nothing to eat. The fire had consumed everything. A party went to look for the remains of the buffalo-bull killed by the guides, but returned without a morsel of meat. The wolves had cleaned the carcass to a skeleton. The marrow bones, however, still remained, and these were brought in—afterwards, the same parts of the four cows; and we made our breakfast on marrow—eating it raw—not but that we had fire enough, but it is less palatable when cooked.

What was next to be done? We held a consultation, and of course came to the resolve to strike for the nearest settlement—that was the frontier town of Independence on the Missouri River. It was nearly three hundred miles off, and we calculated in reaching it in about twenty days. We only reckoned the miles we should have to traverse. We allowed nothing for the numerous delays, caused by marshes and the fording of flooded streams. It afterwards proved that our calculation was incorrect. It was nearly twice twenty days before we arrived at Independence.

We never thought of following the trail of the Indians to recover our horses. We knew they were gone far beyond pursuit, but even could we have come up with them, it would only have been to imperil our lives in an unequal strife. We gave up our horses as lost, and only deliberated on how we were to undertake the journey afoot.

Here a serious question arose. Should we at once turn our faces to the settlement, how were we to subsist on the way? By heading for Independence we should at once get clear of the buffalo-range, and what other game was to be depended on? A stray deer, rabbit, or prairie grouse might suffice to sustain a single traveller for a long time, but there were ten of us. How was this number to be fed on the way? Even with our horses to carry us in pursuit of game, we had not been able on our outward journey to procure enough for all. How much less our opportunity now that we were afoot!

To head directly homeward therefore was not to be thought of. We should assuredly perish by the way.

After much discussion it was agreed that we should remain for some days within the buffalo-range, until we had succeeded in obtaining a supply of meat, and then each carrying his share we should begin our journey homeward. In fact, this was not a disputed point. All knew there remained no other way of saving our lives. The only difference of opinion was as to the direction we should ramble in search of the buffalo; for although we knew that we were on the outskirts of a great herd, we were not certain as to its whereabouts, and by taking a false direction we might get out of its range altogether.

It so happened, however, that fortune lately so adverse, now took a turn in our favour, and the great buffalo drove was found without much trouble on our part. Indeed almost without any exertion, farther than that of loading and firing our guns, we came into possession of beef enough to have victualled an army. We had, moreover, the excitement of a grand hunt, although we no longer hunted for the sport of the thing.

During that day we scattered in various directions over the prairie, agreeing to meet again at night. The object of our thus separating was to enable us to cover a greater extent of ground, and afford a better chance of game. To our mutual chagrin we met at the appointed rendezvous all of us empty-handed. The only game brought in was a couple of marmots (prairie dogs), that would not have been sufficient for the supper of a cat. They were not enough to give each of the party a taste, so we were compelled to go without supper. Having had but a meagre breakfast and no dinner, it will not be wondered at that we were by this time as hungry as wolves; and we began to dread that death by starvation was nearer than we thought of. Buffaloes—several small gangs of them—had been seen during the day, but so shy that none of them could be approached. Another day's failure would place our lives in a perilous situation indeed; and as these thoughts passed through our minds, we gazed on each other with looks that betokened apprehension and alarm. The bright blaze of the camp-fire—for the cold had compelled us to kindle one—no longer lit up a round of joyful faces. It shone upon checks haggard with hunger and pallid with fear. There was no story for the delighted listener—no adventure to be related. We were no longer the historians, but the real actors in a drama—a drama whose *dénouement* might be a fearful one.

As we sat gazing at each other, in hopes of giving or receiving some morsel of comfort and encouragement, we noticed old Ike silently glide from his place by the fire, and after a whisper to us to remain silent, crawl off on his hands and knees. He had seen something doubtless, and hence his singular conduct. In a few minutes his prostrate form was lost in the darkness, and for some time we saw or heard no more of him. At length we were startled by the whip-like crack of the guide's rifle, and fancying it might be Indians, each sprang up in some alarm and seized his gun. We were soon reassured, however, by seeing the upright form of the trapper as he walked deliberately back towards the camp-fire, and the blaze revealed to us a large whitish object dangling by his side and partly dragging along the ground.

"Hurrah!" cried one, "Ike has killed game."

"A deer—an antelope," suggested several.

"No-o," drawled Redwood. "'Taint eyther, but I guess we won't quarrel with the meat. I could eat a raw jackass jest about now."

Ike came up at this moment, and we saw that his game was no other than a prairie-wolf. Better that than hunger, thought all of us; and in a brace of seconds the wolf was suspended over the fire, and roasting in the hide.

We were now more cheerful, and the anticipation of such an odd viand for supper, drew jokes from several of the party. To the trappers such a dish was nothing new, although they were the only persons of the party who had partaken of it. But there was not one fastidious palate present, and when the "wolf-mutton" was broiled, each cleaned his joint or his rib with as much *goût* as if he had been picking the bones of a pheasant.

Before the supper was ended the wolf-killer made a second *coup*, killing another wolf precisely as he had done the former; and we had the gratification of knowing that our breakfast was now provided for. These creatures, that all along our journey had received nothing from us but anathemas, were now likely to come in for a share of our blessings, and we could not help feeling a species of gratitude towards them, although at the same time we thus killed and ate them.

The supper of roast wolf produced an agreeable change in our feelings, and we even listened with interest to our guides, who, appropriate to the occasion, related some curious incidents of the many narrow escapes they had had from starvation.

One in particular fixed our attention, as it afforded an illustration of trapper life under peculiar circumstances.

Chapter Thirty Seven
Hare Hunting and Cricket Driving

The two trappers, in company with two others of the same calling, were on a trapping expedition to one of the tributaries of the Great Bear River, west of the Rocky Mountains, when they were attacked by a band of hostile Utahs, and robbed not only of the produce of their hunt, but their horses and pack-mules were taken from them, and even their arms and ammunition. The Indians could have taken their lives as well, but from the interference of one of the chiefs, who knew old Ike, they were allowed to go free, although in the midst of the desert region where they were, that was no great favour. They were as likely as not to perish from hunger before they could reach any settlement—as at that time there was none nearer than Fort Hall upon the Snake River, a distance of full three hundred miles. Our four trappers, however, were not the men to yield themselves up to despair, even in the midst of a desert; and they at once set about making the most of their circumstances.

There were deer upon the stream where they had been trapping, and bear also, as well as other game, but what did that signify now that they had no arms? Of course the deer or antelopes sprang out of the shrubbery or scoured across the plain only to tantalise them.

Near where they had been left by the Indians was a "sage prairie," that is, a plain covered with a growth of the *artemisia* plant—the leaves and berries of which—bitter as they are—form the food of a species of hare, known among the trappers as the "sage rabbit." This creature is as swift as most of its tribe, but although our trappers had neither dog nor gun, they found a way of capturing the sage rabbits. Not by snaring neither, for they were even without materials to make snares out of. Their mode of securing the game was as follows.

They had the patience to construct a circular fence, by wattling the sage plants together, and then leaving one side open, they made a "surround" upon the plain, beating the bushes as they went, until a number of rabbits were driven within the inclosure. The remaining part of the fence was then completed, and the rabbit hunters going inside chased the game about until they had caught all that were inside. Although the fence was but about three feet in height, the rabbits never attempted to leap over, but rushed head foremost against the wattles, and were either caught or knocked over with sticks.

This piece of ingenuity was not original with the trappers, as Ike and Redwood admitted. It is the mode of rabbit-hunting practised by some tribes of western Indians, as the poor Shoshonees and miserable "diggers," whose whole lives are spent in a constant struggle to procure food enough to sustain them. These Indians capture the small animals that inhabit their barren country by ways that more resemble the instinct of beasts of prey than any reasoning process. In fact there are bands of these Indians who can hardly be said to have yet reached the hunter state. Some of them carry as their sole armour a long stick with a hooked end, the object of which is to drag the *agama* and the lizard out of its cave or cleft among the rocks; and this species of game is transferred from the end of the stick to the stomach of the captor with the same despatch as a hungry mastiff would devour a mouse.

Impounding the sage hare is one of the master strokes of their hunter-craft, and forms a source of employment to them for a considerable portion of the year.

Our four trappers, then, remembering the Indian mode of capturing these creatures put it in execution to some advantage, and were soon able to satisfy their hunger. After two or three days spent in this pursuit they had caught more than twenty hares, but the stock ran out, and no more could be found in that neighbourhood.

Of course only a few were required for present use, and the rest were dried over a sage fire until they were in a condition to keep for some days.

Packing them on their backs, the trappers set out, heading for the Snake River. Before they could reach Fort Hall their rabbit meat was exhausted, and they were as badly off as before. The country in which they now found themselves was if possible more of a desert than that they had just quitted. Even rabbits could not dwell in it, or the few that were started could not be caught. The *artemisia* was not in sufficient plenty to make an inclosure with, and it would have been hopeless to have attempted such a thing; as they might have spent days without trapping a single hare. Now and again they were tantalised by seeing the great sage cock, or, as naturalists call it, "cock of the plains" (*Tetrao urophasianus*), but they could only hear the loud "burr" of its wings, and watch it sail off to some distant point of the desert plain. This bird is the largest of the grouse kind, though it is neither a bird of handsome plumage, nor yet is it delicate in its flesh. On the contrary, the flesh, from the nature of its food, which is the berry of the wild wormwood, is both unsavoury and bitter. It would not have deterred the appetites of our four trappers, could they have laid their hands upon the bird, but without guns such a thing was out of the question. For several days they sustained themselves on roots and berries. Fortunately it was the season when these are ripe, and they found here and there the prairie turnip (*Psoralea esculenta*), and in a marsh which they had to cross they obtained a quantity of the celebrated Kamas roots.

All these supplies, however, did not prove sufficient. They had still four or five days' farther journey, and were beginning to fear they would not get through it, for the country to be passed was a perfect barren waste. At this crisis, however, a new source of subsistence appeared to them, and in sufficient plenty to enable them to continue their journey without fear of want. As if by magic, the plain upon which they were travelling all at once become covered with large crawling insects of a dark brown colour. These were the insects known among the trappers as "prairie crickets," but from the description given of them by the trappers the hunter-naturalist pronounced them to be "locusts." They were of that species known in America as the "seventeen years' locust" (*Cicada septemdecem*), so called because there is a popular belief that they only appear in great swarms every seventeen years. It is probable, however, that this periodical appearance is an error, and that their coming at longer or shorter intervals depends upon the heat of the climate, and many other circumstances.

They have been known to arrive in a great city, coming not from afar, but out of the ground from between the bricks of the pavement and out of crevices in the walls, suddenly covering the streets with their multitudes. But this species does not destroy vegetation, as is the case with others of the locust tribe. They themselves form the favourite food of many birds, as well as quadrupeds. Hogs eagerly feed upon and destroy vast numbers of them; and even the squirrels devour them with as great a relish as they do nuts. These facts were furnished by the hunter-naturalist, but our trappers had an equally interesting tale to tell.

As soon as they set eyes upon the locusts and saw that they were crawling thickly upon the plain, they felt that they were safe. They knew that these insects were a staple article of food among the same tribes of Indians—who hunt the sage hare. They knew, moreover, their mode of capturing them, and they at once set about making a large collection.

This was done by hollowing out a circular pit in the sandy earth, and then the four separating some distance from each other, drove the crickets towards a common centre—the pit. After some manoeuvring, a large quantity was brought together, and these being pressed upon all sides, crawled up to the edge of the pit, and were precipitated into its bottom. Of course the hole had been made deep enough to prevent them getting out until they were secured by the hunters.

At each drive nearly half a bushel was obtained, and then a fresh pit was made in another part of the plain, and more driven in, until our four trappers had as many as they wanted.

The crickets were next killed, and slightly parched upon hot stones, until they were dry enough to keep and carry. The Indians usually pound them, and mixing them with the seeds of a species of gramma grass, which grows abundantly in that country, form them into a sort of bread, known among the trappers as "cricket-cake." These seeds, however, our trappers could not procure, so they were compelled to eat the parched crickets "pure and unmixed;" but this, in the condition in which they then were, was found to be no hardship.

In fine, having made a bundle for each, they once more took the route, and after many hardships, and suffering much from thirst, they reached the remote settlement of Fort Hall, where, being known, they were of course relieved, and fitted out for a fresh trapping expedition.

Ike and Redwood both declared that they afterwards had their revenge upon the Utahs, for the scurvy treatment they had suffered, but what was the precise character of that revenge they declined stating. Both loudly swore that the Pawnees had better look out for the future, for they were not the men to be "set afoot on the parairy for nuthin."

After listening to the relations of our guides, a night-guard was appointed, and the rest of us, huddling around the camp-fire, were soon as sound asleep as though we were reposing under damask curtains, on beds of down.

Chapter Thirty Eight
A Grand Battue

The spot we had chosen for our camp was near the edge of a small rivulet with low banks. In fact, the surface of the water was nearly on a level with that of the prairie. There was no wood, with the exception of a few straggling cotton-woods, and some of the long-leafed willows peculiar to the prairie streams.

Out of the cotton-woods we had made our camp-fire, and this was some twenty or thirty paces back from the water, not in a conspicuous position, but in the bottom of a bowl-shaped depression in the prairie; a curious formation, for which none of us could account. It looked as if fashioned by art, as its form was circular, and its sides sloped regularly downward to the centre, like the crater of a volcano. But for its size, we might have taken it for a buffalo wallow, but it was of vastly larger diameter than one of these, and altogether deeper and more funnel-shaped.

We had noticed several other basins of the same sort near the place, and had our circumstances been different, we should have been interested in endeavouring to account for their existence. As it was, we did not trouble ourselves much about the geology of the neighbourhood we were in. We were only too anxious to get out of it; but seeing that this singular hole would be a safe place for our camp-fire—for our thoughts still dwelt upon the rascally Pawnees—we had kindled it there. Reclined against the sloping sides of the basin, with our feet resting upon its bottom, our party disposed themselves, and in this position went to sleep.

One was to be awake all night as guard; though, of course, all took turns, each awaking the sentinel whose watch was to follow his.

To the doctor was assigned the first two hours, and as we went to sleep, we could perceive his plump rounded form seated upon the outer rim of the circular bank above us. None of us had any great faith in the doctor as a guard, but his watch was during the least dangerous time of night, so far as Indians are concerned. These never make their attack until the hours after midnight, as they know well that these are the hours of soundest sleep. The horse-drive of the previous night was an exception, but that had happened because they had drawn near and seen no horse-guard. It was a very unusual case. They knew that we were now on the alert; and if they had meditated farther mischief, would have attempted it only after midnight hour. We had no apprehensions therefore, and one and all of us being very much fatigued with the day's hunting afoot, slept soundly. The bank against which we rested was dry and comfortable; the fire warmed us well, and redoubled our desire for repose.

It appears that the doctor fell asleep on his post, or else we might all of us have been better prepared for the invasion that we suffered during that night.

I was awakened by loud shouts—the guides were uttering them. I sprang to my feet in the full belief that we were attacked by Indians, and at first thought caught hold of my gun. All my companions were roused about the same time, and, labouring under a similar hallucination, went through a like series of manoeuvres.

But when we looked up, and beheld the doctor stretched along the ridge, and still snoring soundly, we scarce knew what to make of it.

Ike and Redwood, however, accustomed to sleep with one eye open, had waked first, and had already climbed the ridge; and the double report of their guns confirmed our suspicions that we were attacked by Indians. What else could they be firing at?

"This way all of you!" cried Redwood, making signs for us to come up where he and his companion already were, waving their guns around their heads, and acting in a very singular manner, "this way, bring your guns, pistols, and all—quick with you!"

We all dashed up the steep, just at the moment that the doctor suddenly awaking ran terrified down. As we pressed up, we could hear a mingling of noises, the tramp of horsemen as we thought, and a loud bellowing, as if from a hundred bulls. The last sounds could not well have been more like the bellowing of bulls, for in reality it was such. The night was a bright moonlight, and the moment we raised our heads above the scarp of the ridge we saw at once the cause of our alarm. The plain around us was black with buffaloes! Tens of thousands must have been in the drove which was passing us to a great depth on both sides. They were running at a fast trot—some of them even galloping, and in some places they were so thickly packed together, that one would be seen mounting upon the hind-quarters of the other, while some were thrown down, and trampled over by their companions.

"Hyur, hyur, all of ye!" cried Ike, "stand by hyur, or they'll git into the hole, and tramp us to shucks!"

We saw at a glance the meaning of these instructions. The excited animals were rushing headlong, and nothing seemed to stay their course. We could see them dashing into and across the little streamlet without making any account of it. Should they pour into the circle in which we stood, others would follow, and we might get mingled with the drove. There was not a spot on the prairie where we could have been safe. The impetuous mass was impelled from behind, and could neither halt nor change its course. Already a pair of bulls had fallen before the rifles of our guides, and to some extent prevented the others from breaking over the ring, but they would certainly have done so had it not been for the shouts and gestures of the trappers. We rushed to the side indicated, and each of us prepared to fire, but some of the more prudent held their loads for a while, others pulled trigger, and a succession of shots from rifles, double-barrels, and revolvers soon raised a pile of dead buffaloes that blocked up the passage of the rest, as though it had been a barrier built on purpose.

A breathing space was now allowed us, and each loaded his piece as fast as he was able. There was no time lost in firing, for the stream of living creatures swept on continuously, and a mark was found in a single glance of the eye.

I think we must have continued the loading and firing for nearly a quarter of an hour. Then the great herd began to grow thinner and thinner, until the last buffalo had passed.

We now looked around us to contemplate the result. The ground on every side of the circle was covered with dark hirsute forms, but upon that where we stood a perfect mass of them lay together. These forms were in every attitude, some stretched on their sides, others upon their knees, and still a number upon their feet, but evidently wounded.

Some of us were about to rush out of our charmed circle to complete the work, but were held back by the warning voices of the guides.

"For yur lives don't go," cried Redwood, "don't stir from hyur till we've knocked 'em all over. Thur's some o' them with life enough left to do for a ween o' ye yet."

So saying, the trapper raised his long piece, selected one of the bulls that were seen on their feet, and sent him rolling over.

Another and another was disposed of in the same way, and then those that were in a kneeling position were reconnoitred to see if they were still alive, and when found to be so were speedily disposed of by a bullet.

When all were laid out we emerged from our hole, and counted the game. There were no less than twenty-five dead immediately around the circle, besides several wounded that we could see straggling off over the plain.

We did not think of going to rest again until each of us had eaten about two pounds of fresh buffalo-beef, and what with the excitement of this odd adventure, and the jokes that followed—not a few of them levelled at our *quondam* guard—it was near morning before we closed our eyes again in sleep.

Chapter Thirty Nine
The Route Home

We awoke more confident of our future. We had now provision enough and thousands of pounds to spare. It only remained for us to make it portable, and preserve it by drying; and this would occupy us about three full days. Our guides understood well how to cure meat without salt, and as soon as we had breakfasted all of us set to work. We had to pick and choose amidst such mountains of meat. Of course the fat cows only were "butchered." The bulls were left where they had fallen, to become the food of wolves, scores of which were now seen skulking around the spot.

A large fire was kindled, and near this was erected a framework of branches, on which was laid or suspended the meat, cut into thin slices and strips. These were placed at such a distance from the fire that it acted upon them only to dry up the juices, and in less than forty-eight hours the strips became hard and stiff, so that they would keep for months without danger of spoiling. Meanwhile some employed themselves in dressing buffalo-skins, so as to render them light and portable, in other words to make robes of them that would serve us for sleeping in.

At the end of the third day we had arranged every thing, and were ready to set forth on our homeward journey. Each was to carry his own rations of the jerked meat, as well as his arms, robes, and equipments. Of course, loaded in this manner, we did not expect to make a long daily journey, but, supplied as we were with provisions for thirty days, we had no fear but that before the end of that time we would reach Independence. We were in high spirits as we set out, although, before we had walked far, the pressure of our packs somewhat moderated the exuberance of our feelings; and before we had been fifty hours upon the road, an incident occurred that once more reduced us to a new state of despondency, and placed us once more in peril of our lives. Many an accident of flood and field, many a "hair-breadth 'scape" are to be encountered in a journey through prairie-land, and the most confident calculations of the traveller are often rendered worthless in a single moment. So we found to our consternation.

The accident which befel us was one of a deplorable character. We had reached the banks of a small stream, not over fifty yards in width, but very deep. After going down it for several miles no place could be found that was fordable, and at length we made up our minds to swim across, rather than spend more time in searching for a ford. This was easy enough, as we were all swimmers, and in a few minutes most of the party were safely landed on the other side.

But it remained to get our provisions and other matters over, and for this purpose a small raft had been constructed, upon which the packs of meat, robes, as well as our arms and ammunition, were laid. A cord was attached to the raft, and one of the party swam over with the cord, and then several taking hold commenced dragging over the raft with its load.

Although the stream was narrow, the current was strong and rapid, and just as the raft had got near the middle the towing line snapped, and away went the whole baggage down stream.

We all followed along the banks, in hopes of securing the raft when it should float near, and at first we had little apprehension about the matter. But to our mortification we now perceived a rapid just below, and there would be no chance of preventing the frail structure from going over it. The packs, robes, and guns had been laid upon the raft, not even fastened to it, for in our careless security, we never anticipated such a result.

It was too late to leap into the stream and endeavour to stop the raft. No one thought of such a thing. All saw that it was impossible, and we stood with anxious hearts watching the floating mass as it swept down and danced over the foaming waters. Then a shock was heard—the raft heeled round—and poised upon a sharp rock, stood for a moment in mid stream, and then once more washed free it glided on into the still water below.

We rushed down the banks, after an effort secured the raft, and drew it ashore; but to our consternation most of the provisions, with the guns and ammunition, were gone!

They had been tossed off in the very middle of the rapids, and of course were lost for ever. Only three packs of the meat, with a number of robes, remained upon the raft.

We were now in a more serious condition than ever. The provision saved from the wreck would not last us a week, and when that was consumed how were we to procure more? Our means of killing game was taken from us. We had no arms but pistols and knives. What chance of killing a deer, or any other creature, with these?

The prospect was gloomy enough. Some even advised that we should go back to where we had left the buffalo carcasses. But by this time the wolves had cleaned them of their flesh. It would have been madness to go back. There was no other course but to head once more towards the settlements, and travel as fast as we could.

On half rations we continued on, making our daily journeys as long as possible. It was fortunate we had saved some of the robes, for it was now winter, and the cold had set in with extreme bitterness. Some nights we were obliged to encamp without wood to make a fire with, but we were in hopes of soon reaching the forest region, where we should not want for that, and where, moreover, we would be more likely to meet with some game that we could capture.

On the third day after leaving the stream that had been so fatal to us, it began snowing, and continued to snow all night. Next morning the whole country was covered with a white mantle, and we journeyed on, at each step sinking in the snow. This rendered our travelling very difficult, but as the snow was only a foot or so in depth we were able to make way through it. We saw many tracks of deer, but heeded them not, as we knew there was no chance of capturing the animals. Our guides said if it would only thaw a little, and then freeze again, they could kill the deer without their rifles. It did thaw during the day, and at night froze so hard, that in the morning there was a thick crust of ice upon the surface of the snow.

This gave us some hope, and next morning a deer hunt was proposed. We scattered in different directions in parties of two and three, and commenced tracking the deer.

On re-assembling at our night-camp, our different parties came back wearied and empty-handed.

The guides, Ike and Redwood, had gone by themselves, and were the last to reach the rendezvous. We watched anxiously for their return. They came at length, and to our joy each of them carried the half of a deer upon his shoulders. They had discovered the animal by his trail in the snow, and pursued it for miles, until its ankles and hoofs became so lacerated by the crust that it allowed them to approach near enough for the range of their pistols. Fortunately it proved to be a good-sized buck, and would add a couple of days to our stock of provisions.

With fresh venison to our breakfast, we started forth next morning in better spirits. This day we intended to make a long journey, in hopes of getting into heavy timber, where we might find deer more plentiful, and might capture some before the snow thawed away. But before the end of the day's journey we were so stocked with provision, that we no longer cared about deer or any other game. Our commissariat was once more replenished by the buffalo, and in a most unexpected manner. We were tramping along upon the frozen snow, when upon ascending the crest of a ridge, we saw five huge forms directly in front of us. We had no expectation of meeting with buffalo so far to the eastward, and were somewhat in doubt as to whether they were buffaloes. Their bodies, against the white hill side, appeared of immense size, and as they were covered all over with hoar frost, and icicles depending from their long shaggy tufts of hair, they presented a singular aspect, that for awhile puzzled us. We took them for pine-trees!

We soon saw, however, that they were in motion, moving along the hill, and they could be no other than buffaloes, as no other animals could have presented such an appearance. Of course they were at a long distance, and this prevented us from at once recognising them.

This was an important discovery, and brought our party to a halt and a consultation. What course was to be adopted? How were we to capture one or all of them? Had the snow been of sufficient depth the thing would have been easy; but although as it was, it might impede their running, they could get through it much faster than we. The only chance was to "approach" them by stealth; but then we must creep within pistol range, and that upon the plain white surface would be absolutely impossible. The foot of the hunter crunching through the frozen snow, would warn them of their danger long before he could get near. In fact, when every circumstance had been weighed and discussed, we every one despaired of success. At that moment what would we not have given for a horse and a gun.

As we talked without coming to any determination, the five huge forms disappeared over the sharp ridge, that can transversely to our course. As this ridge would shelter us from view, we hurried forward in order to see what advantages there were in the ground on its other side. We were in hopes of seeing timber that might enable us to get closer to the game, and we made for a small clump that grew on the top of the ridge. We reached it at length, and to our great chagrin, saw the five great brutes galloping off on the opposite side.

Our hearts fell, and we were turning to each other with disappointed looks, when a tumultuous shout of triumph broke from Redwood and the wolf-killer, and both calling out to us to follow them, dashed off in the direction of the buffalo!

We looked to ascertain the cause of this strange conduct. A singular sight met our eyes. The buffalo were sprawling and kicking on the plain below; now rushing forward a short distance, then spreading their limbs, and halting, while some of them came heavily down upon their sides, and lay flinging their legs about them, as if they had been wounded!

All these manoeuvres would have been mysterious enough, but the guides rushing forward had already given the key to them, by exclaiming that *the buffalo were upon the ice*!

It was true. The snow-covered plain was a frozen lake, and the animals in their haste had galloped upon the ice, where they were now floundering.

It cost us but a few minutes' time to come up with them, and in a few minutes more—a few minutes of fierce deadly strife—in which pistols cracked and knife-blades gleamed, five great carcasses lay motionless upon the blood-stained snow.

This lucky capture, for we could only attribute it to good fortune, was perhaps the means of saving the lives of our party. The meat furnished by the five bulls—for bulls they were—formed an ample stock, which enabled us to reach the settlements in safety. It is true we had many a hard trial to undergo and many a weary hour's walking, before we slept under a roof; but although in wretched plight, as far as looks went, we all got back in excellent health.

At Independence we were enabled to "rig" ourselves out, so as to make an appearance at Saint Louis—where we arrived a few days after—and where, seated around the well-filled table of the Planters' Hotel, we soon forgot the hardships, and remembered only the pleasures, of our wild hunter-life.